Lodestar

BY

Jackson Peoples-Rosenblatt

ISBN: 0615818994
ISBN 13: 9780615818993
Library of Congress Control Number: 2013946458
ESC Press, San Diego, CA

For Heather Cline Rosberg, in loving memory

. . .It is an ever-fixed mark
That looks on tempests and is never shaken;
It is the star to every wandering bark,
Whose worth's unknown, although his height be taken.

William Shakespeare

Prologue

Approaching True North

San Francisco: 1971

I arrived in San Francisco for the first time on a deceptively sunny June afternoon. Stepping off the Greyhound, I was assaulted by near artic cold. It was a disorienting slap in the face after the tropical misery I'd left behind in New York. My t-shirt and jeans were as ineffective against the frigid breeze as they would have been on Everest. I had always taken Mark Twain's quote about summer in the City by the Bay as ironic, but it suddenly seemed arrestingly literal. I stood pondering this while my fellow passengers crowded to retrieve their baggage. They were impatient with that glassy eyed, nearly inert antsiness that comes at the end of a seemingly endless journey, relieved to be free of their confinement but at the same time almost incapable of movement. They had destinations beyond the bus terminal. They had intentions. My duffel was the last object to come out of the cargo compartment. I didn't rush to claim it.

I had come to San Francisco to start a new life. Since the summer of my sixteenth year I had attempted this repeatedly, in a variety of locales. So far I had tried good works, love, politics, and war as my tactics. I had fought for civil rights in Mississippi, demonstrated for peace on dozens of campuses across New England and the Midwest, and saved lives as a combat medic in Viet Nam. Recently there had even been a brief flirtation with domesticity. The best that could be said about any of these experiments was that they had proven inconclusive. The results resembled farce or tragedy, occasionally both, and I had turned my back on them all. Now it seemed there was nothing left to try but a sort of blind reliance on destiny. I had been given some assurances on that score but didn't know whether I should credit them or how much. The speaker's sanity had been as questionable as her motivations had been unclear. And what did it mean? How did you proceed when being overtaken by destiny was your objective? Did you go off in search of it, or did you wait for it to find you?

I didn't come close to solving the riddle that day but I did find the Y. You're never homeless in a city that has a Y, and you're no lonelier there than you choose to be. But those verities, though eternal, are nonetheless temporary in their practical effects.

Of course when you're waiting for destiny, everything is.

The next morning, armed with the previous Sunday's newspaper, I set off in search of an apartment. It was warmer than the day before but still not at all like America in summer, and in every direction the vistas reinforced the impression that I'd left everything familiar behind. My quest didn't take long. The first apartment I looked at suited me as if I'd ordered it from some great cosmic catalogue. Perhaps there was something in what the oracle had told me to expect from my future. The ad had attracted me with its old fashioned diction and quaintly formal syntax. It might have been composed decades earlier and left running in the newpaper unaltered as generations of tenants took up residence and later departed. Unprepossessing as it was, the building was nevertheless evocative of generations past. The landlady, when she appeared in response to my ring, was similarly out of step with the times. I reckoned that her hairstyle and clothing had been the height of fashion about the time the ad debuted. The building itself would already have appeared antique then.

"Good morning," she said, giving me a sunny but strangely out of focus smile. "My name is Mrs. Wilkins. I'm the proprietor."

"Tristan Bentley. I've come about a flat."

"I knew of some Bentleys who lived outside Shaker Heights."

"Not our tribe," I told her, letting my accent underline it.

"No matter."

I moved in that afternoon, if you can actually call what I did moving in. I unpacked my duffel into the chest of drawers and tiny closet of the spotless but nevertheless shabby room. That's how light I was traveling. Then I went off in search of the minimal household items that would be required by the spartan existence I anticipated.

I was not destitute but I lived like I was. The building had been thrown up quickly and as cheaply as possible in the aftermath of the great quake, and despite its pretentions had never been anything grander than a working men's residence. Despite that extravagant façade, it was no St. Petersburg or Budapest mansion abandoned by or expropriated from aristocratic owners in the wake of economic upheaval or revolution and subsequently broken up into tiny apartments or even cells. There was no "former glory" it had declined from. It simply was as it was despite its architectural aspirations. It was flanked by nearly identical structures, and its front windows looked out onto a streetscape that only the most charitable or deranged observer could have described as quaint or picturesque, which was populated almost exclusively by winos in daylight. They were joined by prostitutes at night. Only the steep incline of the street and the distant clang of cable car bells hinted at the romantic locales mere blocks away. Presumably Mrs. Wilkins factored the immediate surroundings into the rates she charged, but it might as easily have been that she was sufficiently gaga as to be ignorant of what the current market would bear. I almost felt guilty handing her the envelope each month. She preferred that rent be paid in cash and I suspected she'd have liked gold even more. She had lost all her money, she once told me, in the bank closures of 'twenty nine.

Down at the heel as its exterior might be, inside the building everything was peace, order, and morality as far as Mrs. Wilkins could enforce those conditions. And she tried mightily, though her exertions were restricted to the first floor due to unspecified ailments. The rental agreement I signed prohibited me from consuming alcohol on the premises or entertaining female guests in my room and required me to attend Methodist worship services weekly. I had no disagreement with the first two of these provisions and violated the third with impunity for the entire period I lived there. I shared a kitchen at the rear of the ground floor with the other residents, most of whom never set foot there. There were bathrooms on each floor of the building, each one serving four rooms. My memories of army life were fresh enough that none of this struck me as objectionable.

Uncle Gunnar had invested my army pay, and I had saved most of what I earned during my brief stint selling Volvos for him back in Chattanooga after my discharge. I was by no means wealthy, but I could easily have afforded to buy a used car and rent an apartment in a somewhat better neighborhood for a few months while I shopped for a career and began my new life. But I had no such aspirations. I was marking time. If I didn't spend the money right away, I'd have it later. Meanwhile, my unencumbered state indicated a freedom I wished reflected my inward condition.

If I was prepared to work for minimum wage, jobs were plentiful around the city. During those first few months in San Francisco my only periods of unemployment were voluntary and brief. At my jobs I was punctual, industrious, pleasant and reliable. I gave my employers excellent value. And I quit each job the moment anyone showed anything more than cursory interest in me. I couldn't see that anyone needed to know anything about Tristan Bentley. This, I told myself, was how espionage agents behaved in the field. Their cover had to be maintained at all costs. My situation wasn't at all like theirs, but somehow I considered their psychology a relevant example to follow.

I subsisted on eggs, pasta, rice, beans, canned tuna, and fresh fruit. On paydays I would go to North Beach for pizza. Every other week I got my hair trimmed by a barber in Chinatown who enquired gravely as to the welfare of my family as I took my seat in his chair. I gave him the impression that I saw them daily and all was well. That was half true, and the other half hardly constituted enough of an evasion to trouble me. My off hours I spent at the public library, and I never missed a day working out at the Y. When I wasn't otherwise engaged, I explored the city in the best way any city worth exploring can be. On foot. I took in all the local attractions, no matter how obscure. I soaked up the lore of the place, avid as an immigrant newly discovering America.

I visited one additional site, significant only to me. I stood across the street from it on my first afternoon in the city and said to myself "that can't be the place" though I knew I hadn't mistaken the address. The Tudor cottage had ivy growing up the walls, a flagstone walk meandering through a thicket of rose bushes on its way to the front door, and a red brick and black wrought iron fence defending it from passersby. It couldn't have been more pleasant or projected a more respectable, bourgeois impression. And this was unbearable and false. It was totally inadequate to the case. I had expected something far more operatic.

I knew what I was supposed to do. Or at least I knew what I had been instructed to do. But I couldn't bring myself to approach that front door. I told myself it was because I wasn't sure I could trust the source of the advice. Not because I had sensed any possible malicious intent, but because I wasn't certain of her, well, capabilities. She had seemed cryptic. Oracular, even. I hadn't believed my ears. Literally—what my ears heard, my mind refused to credit. She couldn't possibly have meant what she seemed to be saying. She had lacked some crucial degree of comprehension of the matter at hand. A traditional, old world Italian auntie of the most stereotypical sort wouldn't know about that kind of thing. No. It simply wasn't possible. She had been confused. At the very least, she hadn't expressed herself clearly.

I told myself all that as I trudged back down the curving street toward the bus stop. And as I said it I knew that once again I was making excuses. The real reason I couldn't walk up to that front door was as plain as could be. I was convinced I wasn't worthy of such a calling as she had proposed. I had failed everyone who ever mattered to me, and I saw no hope that this instance would be any different.

Really, I should never have come.

But you have to be somewhere. And something had brought me to San Francisco, some force as invisible and inescapable as gravity. I felt it every day, very nearly every waking hour. I was there because I could be nowhere else. That was the only thing I was certain of. I observed my routines with military precision. That kept me from having to think. I ate, slept, worked out, made my living, and studied. It seemed crucial to fill my head with other people's thoughts.

And I waited.

Part One

"Freedom Summer"

New Jerusalem, Mississippi: 1964

I

That summer I ran before daylight every morning. Waking up in the dark, I slipped on my jockstrap and shorts, gym socks and sneakers. I moved silently from my room to the landing and tiptoed down the stairs on feet that from long experience avoided each and every creaky tread. Then I slipped out onto the front porch. People didn't lock their doors at night in New Jerusalem. On summer nights we left them standing wide open to capture passing breezes. We believed we were safe sleeping behind the flimsy hook and eye latches of those rickety old screen doors.

I did my stretching exercises on the front porch. Just when I was good and loosened up and began running in place for a few seconds prior to takeoff, I'd catch sight of Miss Althea Chandler's Old Shep sitting at the curb waiting for me, his prick ears twitching one at a time since at his age he could no longer raise them to attention simultaneously and his grizzled snout scanning the breeze like radar. We started off slow, and long before I ever worked up a sweat my bare skin would be streaming with dew that hadn't quite found its way to the ground during the night. Daddy always asserted, regarding the local climate, that New Jerusalem natives were all born with gills and new arrivals had to sprout some right fast or perish. I never located mine but I felt the need of them every morning on those long runs we took through the damp, clinging cotton wool of not quite sunrise.

We ran down Oak Street, not toward Jackson Street and downtown but in the opposite direction toward the outskirts, where it joined up with Portman Trace and climbed the gentle slope of Mockingbird Hill past the gates of the old Davidson Place before shanking off abruptly to run straight as a die between broad fields of cotton to the junction with County Road 18. That's where Shep and I turned around. Out there and back was exactly twelve miles measured by the odometer in Miss Althea Chandler's 1947 Chevrolet. On good days it felt like ten miles, or increasingly that summer, nine and a quarter. On bad days it felt like fourteen miles, or sixteen, or a thousand.

Old Shep was an aging canine of indeterminate breed who had arrived on our street out of nowhere and adopted Miss Althea Chandler the week her husband Ollie passed away. Looking at him you were left with the impression that his forebears included, in addition to hounds of innumerable varieties and herding dogs of all imaginable types, the timber wolf and the brown bear. Terrified neighborhood children would have included the crocodile and the Tasmanian devil in his lineage. Neighborhood mothers, my own included, he rendered speechless with a glance of his glowing, malevolent eyes, leaving them to purse their lips and shake their heads with the profound disapproval distinctive to southern womanhood when he stalked by their houses on his infrequent but much dreaded forays off Miss Althea's front porch. I alone was his partner and confidant. Our collaboration had been cemented on a far off afternoon when he yanked me by the seat of my new Sears Roebuck jeans off the heaving chest of Bobby Davidson, whose nose I had just bloodied over some insult only a kindergartener could have taken as an occasion for violence, and dragged me kicking and screaming all the way home.

I never once got into a fight that Old Shep allowed me to finish, so despite his reputation around town I will maintain to my dying day that he was essentially a Dog of Peace. And that summer he never missed a day running with me. Though he was an ancient dog you couldn't tell it to watch him. He seemed ageless. Still, he was closer to the end than anybody realized. And a superannuated dog, unkempt and mangy in the fashion of generations of barely domesticated southern *canis familiaris*, was, whether my fellow citizens and I recognized it or not, our essential and collective metaphor.

That morning, the last morning of peace, I bade Old Shep farewell at the curb when we ended our run and watched as he checked both ways for traffic—I swear by Almighty God he did, every single time—before crossing back to his own yard. I trudged up the front walk, slick as a porpoise, panting like the victim of a near suffocation. I sat on the porch steps while my pulse slowed and my breathing came back to normal. Inside the house I could hear the first noises of Daddy stirring from bed. The toilet flushing was my signal to go upstairs and shower. With Mama and my sisters in Chattanooga for the summer, I could take as long as I liked.

"Good morning, young sir," Daddy greeted me, brandishing his spatula like a symphony orchestra conductor waving a baton during one of those loud, dramatic passages in, for instance, Mahler's Eighth. "Scramble them for you?"

"Yes, Daddy," I said, tumbling into my chair at the kitchen table. He knew that I never ate eggs any other way if I had a say in the matter but invariably asked nevertheless. "Thanks."

"Don't let the biscuits and gravy get cold," he admonished, not that there was ever any danger I'd let food sit undisturbed long enough for that to happen. We were Baptists but our breakfast ritual was as liturgical as could be.

He had set his usual breakfast table. A plate of biscuits smothered in fragrant gravy steaming at my place. A platter of thick sliced tomatoes, yellow as sunshine. A dish of apples he had baked the night before, the chilled pyrex sweating onto the tablecloth. Spicy patties of bulk pork sausage fried in his cast iron skillet to a blackened crust. A plate heaped with additional biscuits, which was surrounded by jars of preserves the colors of the precious stones you could imagine the Queen of Sheba wearing to impress King Solomon, peach, plum, blackberry, muscatine grape, crabapple, and my favorite watermelon rind.

Save for the contents of the salt and pepper shakers, ingredients of the biscuits and gravy, and the coffee he poured for himself and drank black, nothing on that table had ever seen the inside of a grocery store. Small town southern preachers in those days ate like kings, and much of what they consumed was free. They and their families were nourished by the produce of a hundred kitchen gardens, chicken coops, orchards, berry patches, pigpens, smokehouses, and milking barns. Mama never shopped for groceries on Saturdays like the other women of the town. She shopped on Monday morning after she'd had an opportunity to inventory Sunday's take, which in summer was often too voluminous to store properly or use before it spoiled and had to be shared with neighbors sworn to secrecy.

Unlike some others in this enviable position, Mama and Daddy always took great pains not to let it appear that they expected any of that bounty. These were gifts, pure and simple, not something they considered themselves entitled to. Each bag was a surprise and a delight, a once in a lifetime, never to be seen again phenomenon, remarkable as Halley's Comet. "Look," Daddy would say, reverently surveying a skillet of okra he'd just fried up or a bunch of sweet corn he expected me to shuck for dinner. "Would you look at what comes of being beloved by the People of God? Can you imagine such selfless generosity?" That summer he had set me to reading about Martin Luther. When I got to the part concerning his objections to the sale of indulgences by the Roman Church, I began to question, though silently, the motives behind the largesse of certain of the parishioners. It's an extremely rare pastor's son who hasn't become a cynic well before he has his license to drive, and I was no exception. The case seemed clear. But though there is obviously such a thing as an ulterior motive, I never saw the least sign that Daddy was suspicious of any of that produce.

Hamilton's Shell Station opened six mornings a week at seven sharp, so I arrived on Miss Althea Chandler's doorstep at precisely a quarter to that day, resplendent in my uniform. I was in no doubt that I was dashing. Nearly everyone I encountered while in uniform commented on it. I swaggered in those threads like an admiral reviewing the fleet.

"Morning, Miss Althea."

She had appeared in the doorway wearing a forty year old housedress and slippers whose fuzz had finished molting a generation earlier.

"Why, good morning, Tristan," she smiled, squinting up at me through bifocals long overdue for replacement. "How in the world are you this lovely morning?"

"Fine, ma'am, and your good self?"

"I'd be fit as a fiddle except for this bursitis. Not worth complaining about, though. Just leave it at the feet of Jesus."

"Yes'm. Thought I'd stop by for the Chevrolet."

"Why, yes," she said as if only that moment recalling the solemn promise she'd extracted from me the evening before to take it in for an oil change and chassis lube. "Just let me get you the keys. Have you had breakfast?"

"Yes'm."

"Well, I reckon you won't say no to one of my special sticky buns. You never have before."

"No'm," I assured her. Miss Althea's huge, puffy sticky buns, dripping with thick caramel and encrusted with chopped pecans, were a neighborhood legend. I had woken up dreaming of them on more occasions than I could count.

I waited at the screen door while she went for the keys. Old Shep dozed at my feet, deliberately ignoring me. Except for heralding with astonishing ferocity the arrival of the mailman later that morning, he would hibernate until nightfall.

"Here you are, Tristan," Miss Althea said, returning to the front door with a triumphant little smile. She was not always able to locate her keys with such dispatch. She handed them out to me along with a much used brown paper sack. "I've put three buns in there for you. One for now and two for later. Now you watch how you pull the Chevrolet out of the garage, you hear? That old door is so narrow."

"Yes'm. And thank you kindly for the buns."

"Have a nice day, Tristan. Try not to let this awful heat melt you away to nothing."

"Yes'm."

"Drink lots of lemonade. That's what you must do. Nothing better in this weather. And whatever you do, stay away from that cokecola. I know an ice cold cokecola tastes good to a thirsty young man on a hot afternoon, but it'll ruin your bowel. Just ruin it. Liked to killed my Ollie, it did. That's what Dr. Montgomery said after the surgery. They put that acid in it, you know."

Miss Althea's car was a 1947 Chevrolet Fleetline sedan. Her husband had bought it new a few months before he died. That made it slightly older than I was, but its splendor persisted due to the ministrations of a succession of New Jerusalem's young men who kept its paint and chromium gleaming and Chief Hamilton, who made sure it always ran right smart. I had been driving it over to Hamilton's Shell for regular service ever since starting to work there, a good two years before I got my license. Miss Althea never once expressed misgivings over his arrangement. So the legend that she held no license and didn't believe in such bureaucratic fol-de-rol may have been true. Accurate gossip was unusual but not entirely unheard of in New Jerusalem. Chief Hamilton complained constantly about her refusal to buy a new car, but I knew he secretly got a kick out of maintaining it for her. He admired eccentricity in others above all things and diligently cultivated it in himself. This was one of those time honored southern traditions which set us apart from the lower species, not to mention the yankees.

The Chief's real name was Hiram, but I never heard anyone address him that way, not even the kin he employed. I was the only outsider he had offered a job to since his nephews came home from World War II. He was simply the Chief, and his wife, who really ran things, was Miss Charlotte Marie. They were Baptists and members of our church though they never attended Sunday services, restricting their formal religious observances to weddings and funerals. Their absence in no way lessened their fervor, however. Rather, it seemed to compound it. They regarded me with profound suspicion, believing, as I think most Baptists do, that a preacher's son's sole purpose in life is to be an embarrassment to his father, a heartbreak to his mother, and a constant source of consternation and gossip for the congregation. That I was none of these things filled Miss Charlotte Marie with a thinly disguised fury which raged unabated year in and year out. The Chief simply refused to credit the tales he heard of my honesty, responsibility, and industriousness. In his eyes I was a spectacularly successful charlatan, and he lived for the day of my unmasking. His imagination stewed with lurid scenarios. Some underage girl—he seemed not to be concerned that I was underage myself—turned up carrying my twin babies. I was caught robbing the graves of the recently departed whose funerals Daddy had conducted, plundering the corpses of their jewelry and gold teeth. I ran off in the dead of a Sunday night with a gunny sack filled with the tithes and offerings from that day's services. He recounted elaborate narratives of my purported atrocities to me during slack times at the station. These were frequent enough to tax even his powers of invention. Indeed, I believe to this day that the only reason he offered me work in the first place was in order to reserve a front row seat for my inevitable downfall.

That Saturday morning he was perched on a stool behind the cash register like a tobacco chewing, scripture misquoting Buddha when I arrived in Miss Althea's Chevrolet, while Miss Charlotte Marie stalked around the tiny office looking for something that needed doing and somebody to order to do it.

"Morning, Tristan," he grunted.

"Morning, Chief. Brought in Miss Althea's Chevrolet."

"Huh," he grunted.

"There's our boy," Miss Charlotte Marie chimed in a tone pitched indeterminately between a sigh and a sneer. "Just look at yaw'll, sonny, with yer cornsilk hair and big blue eyes. Purty as a china doll, I'll swan."

"Morning, Miss Charlotte Marie."

"Hellfire and damnation, woman," Chief growled. "Open yaw'll's goldurn eyes, will yaw'll? Fer oncet in yaw'll's life? That ain't no china doll. That there's five feet ten inches and two hunnert pounds of Grade A Prime Heart a' Dixie beef. Show 'er, son. Make a muscle."

I pretended to believe he was joking. I always pretended that at this point of our ritual.

"That there young man," he continued, "dammit, son, I said make a muscle."

I flexed my left biceps.

"Is what's agonta lead the Panthers to the state football championship this season. C'mere, son, give us a feel of it 'fore yaw'll put it back away. Hard's a rock. Now that, woman, is what's going ta win the goldurn state wrestling championships in the one ninety-eights this year, yaw'll hear? And that is what's going t' have half the universities in the south knocking on Brother Daniel's door totin' valises full of scholarship money. So don't go on callin' him no goldurn china doll and makin' such fuss a them big baby blues of his and that hair he's always got combed so fine, 'cause everbody can tell that he's all boy and turnin' into a man's man right in fronta yaw'll's eyes."

"I still say he's the spit and image of his mama," Miss Charlotte Marie said, stomping into the workroom to verbally assault the first person she happened to see, who in this case was her youngest son, Eugene, toiling away underneath Deacon Benton Crowell's Mercury Montclair.

"Don't yaw'll pay her no mind, son," Chief said.

"Where do you want me this morning, Chief? Inside on the grease rack or out front?"

"Let's put yaw'll out front fer a spell. Some a yaw'll's little girlies might take it inta their purty heads ta stop in for a fillup."

"Yes, sir."

Chief Hamilton overstated my size that morning. I was an inch shorter and eight pounds lighter than he gave me credit for, though from the ever tighter fit of my clothing I sensed that I'd soon grow into his exaggeration. But he didn't exaggerate about anything else. His prognostications would have been echoed by most of the male residents of the county. I had been elected team captain back in the spring, and Coach Renfro had already announced that I would be the starting quarterback come fall. The Fighting Panthers had won the state football championship in our class two years running, and with most of last season's starters returning had to be considered serious prospects at the very least to score the hat trick. And in wrestling I had lost the state championship in my weight class the year before by a single fall in the finals to a graduating senior from Jackson who'd had to puke his guts out to make weight while I'd been gorging on bananas and milkshakes with the same end in mind. And I'd grown since then. I wasn't as optimistic about my prospects as everyone told me I ought to be, but even so there seemed to be a reasonable chance.

People in New Jerusalem took my athletic prowess as a given. Mama's three younger brothers had achieved notoriety throughout the south as college football heroes. Uncle Gunnar had gone on to the pros, and the television commercials in which he smilingly used a popular hair dressing to keep his blond locks shining, perfectly in place, and alluringly fragrant were running on all three networks. After graduation, my other two uncles, Lars and Tor, turned up their noses at the results of the NFL draft and instead hit the regional professional wrestling circuit as a tag team. You could catch their televised matches every Saturday afternoon on local stations across the south. They were perennial good guys, boy next door types as famous for their always perfect hair, which they made a production of combing and checking in hand mirrors in the ring before their matches began, as for their awesome strength and brilliant tactics. Even though pure blooded Swedes were about as exotic in those parts as Armenians, they stalwartly upheld honesty, courage, motherhood, fried catfish, blackberry cobbler with home cranked ice cream, and all other traditional southern virtues against the mortal threats posed by such despicable heels as Admiral Hamamoto and his sidekick Chang, inscrutable weirdos Silver Flash and the Dragon, and those disreputable British aristocrats Lord Charles Darkraven and Sir Bertram Wilde.

All my life, if I or anyone else wanted a preview of my future appearance, we had only to look at any one of my uncles, for since the day of my birth there'd never been any question that my last name might be Bentley but most of my genes were Ingebrittsen ones. The three of them gave the impression of being a cross between Viking princes and Eagle Scouts. All three came in just under six feet tall, and bulked up for their respective careers weighed in somewhere between two forty and two fifty. So the town fully expected similar size and accomplishments from me, and the question I fielded most frequently at church on Sundays was what colleges I expected to be offered scholarships by.

I was just giving Miss Earline Richardson's windshield a final polishing when Suzanne Morgan's lilac colored Buick Electra convertible swished up to the island, its radio blaring out some Beatles tune I wasn't familiar with though I knew I was supposed to be. I thought it was awfully convenient that Mary Louise's mom had a car big enough to transport the entire New Jerusalem High School varsity cheerleading squad, though it did mean that the back seat was pretty packed.

"Hey, Tristan," Mary Louise called from the driver's seat as Amy Sue Bradley and Patsy Smithers stood up in the back and started ransacking Ellie Campbell's purse for change to use in the soda machine.

"Hey there, Mary Louise," I said, feeling no little trepidation. Conversations with her were as risky as tightrope walking without a safety net.

"Fill 'er up with high test," she drawled, smiling with what always seemed like sixty or seventy gleaming teeth.

"Check under the hood?"

"Don't bother," she said. "Bobby looked under there yesterday. Everything's fine."

"It's no trouble," I insisted, feeling Miss Charlotte Marie's eyes on me from inside the office.

"Really, there's no need."

"Looks like she's just been washed, too," I said, unscrewing the gas cap.

"Daddy said I had to or he'd ground me," she explained. "I told the girls I wouldn't drive them to the pool this afternoon if they didn't help."

"Car this size is a chore to wash."

"Sure enough," she agreed. "So how yaw'll been?"

"O.K., I guess."

"Wish yawll'd ask Becky Travis out on a date," she suggested. "Then yaw'll could double with Bobby and me."

"That'll be two dollars and seventy-eight cents," I told her.

"What do you think, girls?" Mary Louise asked. "Wouldn't little Becky and Tristan be perfect together?"

"But she's just a tenth grader," Jenny Garrison pointed out, "and she hasn't made varsity yet."

"Yeah, Mary Louise," Debbie Lynn Brown said. "Starting quarterback can't date a JV cheerleader. Wouldn't be right."

"She'll be an eleventh grader this fall," Sarah Bates said.

"Besides, who knows what might happen to a sweet girl like Becky?" Mary Louise mused. "So pretty and all. I mean, if she had the right boyfriend?"

"Busy this morning," Chief observed. "Them wimmen been runnin' yaw'll ragged, son."

"I like it when it's busy."

"Makes the time go quicker, don't it?" Chief nodded. "What my mama always said."

"Right." I didn't tell him the real reason for my preference. When things slowed down Miss Charlotte Marie had a bad habit of finding odd jobs for me to do around the place. I didn't mind working for my pay, but cleaning out the women's restroom took all the glamour out of the job somehow.

"Yaw'll should sneak off for a break," Chief said. "Been a coupla hours since I saw yaw'll finish off those sticky buns. Yaw'll're probly wantin' one a yaw'll's daddy's sandwiches. What he give yaw'll today?"

"Roast beef on whole wheat bread."

"Whole wheat?" Chief asked. "Yaw'll mean that brown bread?"

"Right."

"Miss Elizabeth buys that stuff?"

"This is home made."

"Aw, right," he said, nodding. "That'll be Martha Anne Talbot."

"Guess so."

"Crazy woman. She shouldn't ought to do that to people. It ain't decent."

"Hello, Miss Augusta," I greeted the tiny, wraithlike figure behind the wheel of the pink and gray Packard. She was perched on top of a couple of sofa pillows so as to be able to see out over the dashboard. I had no idea how her feet reached the pedals.

"Why, hello there, Tristan," she smiled. "My, haven't you grown?"

"Yes'm," I agreed, though she'd been in to buy gas just two days before. "What can I get for you today, ma'am? Fill up?"

"Well, just let me think for a minute. Now what grade are you in these days over at the school?"

"I'll be graduating next spring."

"Oh, you always were a kidder," she giggled. "Graduatin' high school, my Great Aunt Fannie."

"Yes'm. You want high test today?"

"Are you sure that's what I'm supposed to use in this Packard?"

"Yes'm."

"It's frightfully expensive, isn't it?"

"Yes'm, it does cost a little more. But an engine job would be even more expensive."

"That's what that greedy Hiram Hamilton told you to say, isn't it?"

"He just doesn't want you having car trouble, Miss Augusta."

"God sends all liars to hell, Tristan," she said. "You know that, don't you?"

"Yes'm. How much can I get you today?"

"Oh, well, I guess about three and a half gallons ought to do it."

I was just finishing up cleaning Miss Roberta Nelson's battery terminals when Miss Charlotte Marie's foghorn of a voice rang out across the drive.

"Come and get it, Tristan, 'fore it's all ate up."

"That woman needs to learn some manners," Miss Roberta grumbled. I knew they had been sworn enemies since before grade school and that Miss Charlotte Marie wouldn't have summoned me that imperiously if I'd been helping any other customer.

"She should start up just fine now," I said.

"Oh, I know," Miss Roberta grinned. "Won't say a word against her, will yaw'll? That's 'cause your mama and daddy raised yaw'll right. Not like that one in there did with her younguns. It's a blue miracle they're not all in the county jail waitin' their turns for th 'lectric chair. Well, yaw'll'd best take off 'fore she gobbles up yaw'll's share herself. Greedy ol' thing that she is."

"Yes'm. Have a nice afternoon."

"That I will. See yaw'll in church."

Along about three o'clock, Bobby Davidson drove up in his Sting Ray convertible. He was on lunch break from his job as lifeguard at the country club. He had the tan of a movie star. That afternoon he was wearing sunglasses to match. He lolled behind the wheel like he was shooting a scene in the latest Annette Funicello/Frankie Avalon film and flashed me that smile of his. Unlike me, Bobby didn't lift weights. All the exercise he got was from swimming, but it apparently was enough. He looked like Michelangelo's David with Ricky Nelson's head.

"Thought you might be hungry," he said, handing me a paper bag.

"I am right peckish."

"It's your usual."

My usual was a double meat double cheese burger from Mina's Blue Miracle Diner down on the courthouse square. From the heft of the bag, I thought I could sense the presence of a triple order of fries.

"Oh, and here's your T. B. Special," Bobby said, handing me the tall, perversely named drink. A T. B. Special was the milkshake Mina had invented and named just for me, a chocolate malted with a shot of strong coffee added and a whole banana sliced into it.

"Thanks. I'll pay you when I get my check cashed."

"No sweat. Got plans tonight?"

"Curl up with a good book."

"That all?"

"You work sixty hours a week and see what you feel up to on Saturday night."

"You should ask somebody out."

"Heard this sermon once already today."

"Yeah?"

"Mary Louise was in."

"Oh."

"Easy, boy," I laughed. "Had the whole cheerleading squad with her in case you need witnesses. I was a perfect gentleman."

"'Course you were," he grinned, pretending a little less than successfully that his suspicion had been a joke.

"She was after me about some little sophomore girl I don't even know."

"Becky Travis," he nodded. "You'd best get busy on that. The squad already took a vote."

"It's none of their business."

"You know better than that."

I shrugged.

"I know guys like you and me don't appreciate bein' bossed around by those girls," he said, "but you should do it anyway. We could double."

When I got home there was a note on the refrigerator from Daddy. Miss Lula Sutherland was having emergency surgery and he had no idea when he'd get home. This was par for the course. Small southern towns were full of aging widows in precarious states of health, and it was a rare week when there was no crisis for Daddy to attend to. A whole month without a funeral was all but unheard of. Inside the refrigerator, the note instructed, I'd find a plate of fried chicken, a bowl of potato salad, some of the ubiquitous sliced tomatoes, and the fixings for strawberry shortcake. My mouth watered and my stomach growled. But my work was not yet done. My uncles had set up a complete weightlifting outfit for me in the basement and shown me the ropes, and after changing out of my now reeking Shell uniform I headed down there to, as they called it, pay my dues.

When Daddy finally got back from the hospital, he found me dozing in the hammock in the back yard, a copy of *Mrs. Dalloway* face down in my lap and the last movement of Brahms' Fourth Symphony playing on his reel to reel tape deck. He roused me just enough to get me upstairs. I was practically asleep again by the time he pulled the sheet up over me.

II

Sundays were marathons at our house. A day of rest for nearly everyone else in the town, it was Daddy's busiest twenty-four hours of the week. He and Mama rose early, he to go over his sermon one last time, she to go over my sisters' clothing yet again for pretty much the same reason. It was not just Daddy who was on display. We all were, representing the ideal southern family, unflinchingly patriotic but profoundly and implacably suspicious of any and all yankees, fun loving but exemplary in word and deed, deeply and serenely God fearing. My sisters' dresses had to be spotless and crisp and their patent leather shoes as shiny as mirrors. Their raven curls had to be lustrous and tangle free, garnished with bows coordinated with their outfits. My neat blond cut, trimmed for free at Frankie's Barber Shop every other Saturday until I went to work for Chief Hamilton and had to fit it into my schedule after school and start paying for it out of my wages, had to be pomaded into immobility with the product Uncle Gunnar hawked on television, which he shipped me by the case. When I graduated from wearing a bow tie to a regular one, it had to hang perfectly straight at just the right length and the knot had to be as compact and tight as human hands could make it. When I graduated from short pants to trousers their creases had to be sharp enough to carve roast beef.

In the absence of the Bentley womenfolk that summer, the house seemed more deserted on Sunday mornings than at any other time. There was too much room to move, too much quiet to listen to, too much air to breathe. Most of all there was too little backstage confusion. It disoriented both of us but Daddy far more than me. Watching him wander through the downstairs rooms in the unaccustomed calm of those seven-thirty a.m.'s, I wasn't sure he knew up from down.

Thank heaven he had no objections to my breaking the Sabbath for an early morning run. I knew certain parishoners would disapprove, however, and made sure to be up and out and back again before the town was stirring. I relished Sunday morning runs above all others. The exertion kept me from going crazy. I had no sermon to polish, no children to perfect. I had only myself to get ready and the prospect of being scrutinized by hundreds of church ladies and their dour menfolk to comtemplate.

After my shower it was my job to get breakfast, Daddy being incapable of any practical task from five a.m. until midnight on that one day of the week. He was almost completely uninterested in food until after evening worship was over and he was back home again, at which time he wolfed down whatever was put in front of him like a wild eyed prophet who had just spent forty days fasting in the wilderness. It didn't matter what I fixed him for breakfast because he wouldn't eat it and rather than waste it I'd eat it myself, my reaction to nerves being the exact opposite of his. Television evangelists may not suffer from stage fright. Indeed, I'd be surprised to learn that they possess any human qualities whatever, but Daddy's Sunday morning jitters were monumental.

For as long as I could remember, Mama had gone straight home from church on Sunday mornings. She lingered not a moment longer than was required to placate the church ladies and then she was off without a backward glance. She took my sisters with her. She changed into comfortable clothing, put the finishing touches on Sunday dinner, and waited for Daddy and me. Usually she waited a long time. Because it was a rare Sunday on which Daddy didn't take me on to services over at Ebenezer Baptist Church after our own. This routine started before I could walk. There was always some Deaconess or ranking member of the Sisterhood there who was delighted to hold the napping baby Tristan while Reverend Daniel Bentley sat on the platform as an honored guest. The Bentley baby was actually very pretty for a white infant. Those saintly women never missed an opportunity to tell me that when I encountered them later on, in boyhood and adolescence. I can't count the kisses on the cheek I received from those big hearted black women or the businesslike caresses of their workworn hands as they smoothed my cowlick down or straightened my clothing or conducted me up the aisle to their pews in the musty old sanctuary. There was not one of them that ever made me feel afraid to be led away from my father.

To the parishoners at First Baptist this was the wildest eccentricity on Daddy's part. They didn't like it one bit that he regularly worshipped with the Negroes, and taking his young son along instead of leaving him safe at home with his mother just compounded the error. It's a measure of the enormous respect they had for Daddy that they permitted it. Even so, it was an uneasy truce at best. Their remonstrances were more or less perpetual. If Daddy had ever once come back to services at our church talking of his experiences in that place where no white man should have gone there would have been hell to pay. If he had ever let slip the gentlest implication that he considered all was not right with the way the races coexisted in New Jerusalem he'd have been out of a job no questions asked. If he had ever taken one of my sisters along, even once, though they clamored for it constantly and complained bitterly about being left out, there might well have been bloodshed. A son might manage not to be hopelessly twisted by such exposure to his black skinned inferiors. Young white men, well brought up, are more or less indestructible or so goes the mythology. But a daughter's life would inevitably be ruined.

Some people would say that this story really begins on that Sunday and that it starts in the sanctuary of Ebenezer Baptist Church, though I will forever maintain that it began several hundred years before that and perhaps not even on this continent. It was a cool day for July and Daddy had left the Volkswagen at home, so after the service ended we walked over there. Their services started at the same time ours did, but an hour and a half later when Daddy and I arrived they'd usually still be laboring through the preliminaries. In the foyer we were greeted by various ushers and members of the Sisterhood. When Deacons of sufficient number and eminence had assembled they escorted Daddy down the center aisle of the sanctuary and stood by straightbacked as pharaohs while he took his place of honor next to their pastor, the Reverend Isaiah Washington. Meanwhile, I made my way to the back of the sanctuary.

The order of worship was interrupted just long enough for Rev. Washington to welcome the congregation's great good friends, the Very Reverend Daniel

Wentworth Bentley, Bachelor of Arts and Master of Theology, Senior Pastor (there wasn't a junior one, but Rev. Washington's effusiveness made it sound as if there must be dozens of underlings at Daddy's beck and call) of the First Baptist Church of New Jerusalem, and that Fine Young Christian Gentleman, his son Tristan.

There was then a solo by Ebenezer Baptist's first string soprano, Zuleika Jefferson, a woman who, had she been born white, would long since have made her Metropolitan Opera debut but who instead was Miss Marilyn Roberts' day girl, three houses down from us, coming and going from work in her simple black dress and starched white apron and cap. During her rendition of "His Eye Is on the Sparrow", the collection plates were passed. From the first quarter I had ever received from my parents as a weekly allowance, every cent of my tithes and offerings had been dropped into these plates and that day was no exception. The white folks at First Baptist could well afford to do without my contributions, and I delighted in imagining Chief Hamilton's fury had he known that even one cent of the money he paid me was going into the coffers of the black church.

The offering finished, it was time for the main event. In full cry in his own pulpit, Rev. Isaiah Washington, with all of a fourth grade education, gave up nothing to Dr. Martin Luther King, Jr. He could match that great man for eloquence as well as fervor, and sitting there listening to him thunder away in his big bass voice, long strings of parallel constructions flowing off his tongue like molasses soaking through hot cornbread, you could close your eyes and imagine you were listening to God Almighty Himself. Daddy's sermons were meticulously researched and prepared, excruciatingly sincere, and as forceful as the congregation at First Baptist would stand for. For all practical purposes they paid Daddy to be insipid, and whenever he pushed them too hard they pushed right back. Rev. Washington's sermons were the voice of prophecy, pure and simple. Daddy idolized him and basked in the warm sweetness of his gentle solicitude. But that day as the accustomed hush fell over the congregation he spoke words that changed the lives of everyone there forever.

"Bretheren and sisters," he began, his voice soft, its pitch as carefully modulated as the pipes of a cathedral organ, "before I begin breaking the bread this fine Lord's Day I have an announcement to make. It is of a momentous nature, and I ask every one in the sound of my voice to attend prayerfully to it. As all of you know, teams of volunteers from all over the length and breadth of this great nation have converged on Mississippi this summer to help us in our struggle. They are teaching our people to read in order that more and more of us may register to vote. They are standing witness as our brothers and sisters take the literacy tests. They are observing the procedures of the county registrars of voters to ensure that not the slightest irregularity takes place, either by accident or design."

There was a murmuring across the sanctuary at this, hushed but fervent.

"They are sacrificing their time and giving of their energies to help the black people of this state take their rightful places as members in full standing of the electorate. Many are college students who could have chosen to spend their summer vacations traveling in Europe or visiting pleasant far off seashores. I do not have to tell you any of this. These are things you already know.

"The news of their labors has come to us in a hundred different ways. And thus, these volunteers and their holy efforts have been in our prayers for many, many weeks already. Though they are strangers, nevertheless they are as close to our hearts as a newborn infant is to its mother's. The news I have to share with you today concerns them. And it concerns all of us as well, from the Chairman of our Deacons to the tiniest child slumbering in the cradle room and from the Madame Chairwoman of the Sisterhood to the humblest little grandmother mopping in our sanctuary on Saturday night after her long week's labors to put a crust of bread on her table. For now we must each and every one of us redouble our prayers and petitions on behalf of this great endeavor.

"But the time has also come when we must prepare ourselves to put feet to our prayers. I have just this morning been informed that a group of these volunteers will be arriving in New Jerusalem on Saturday next. They will be guests of this congregation Saturday night for a prayer rally and dinner on the grounds. And my dear bretheren and sisters, here is what I have to tell you. They will not just be passing through our fair town. The most earnest prayers of our hearts have been answered. They are to be our guests here for as long as their great work causes them to remain among us. All of them are white, few of them Baptist, some are not Christian at all. Yet the Lord has chosen to use them to bring His justice to fruition in our midst. Most of them are from the cities of the north. They know little of us and even less of our ways. But our Lord Jesus has laid it on their hearts to join us in our great journey toward the promised land and travel awhile our long, bitter path alongside us. And each and every one of us will welcome them as members of our own family, even as we would our fondest loved ones."

Daddy was silent on our way home. There was nothing unusual in this. He was exhausted from preaching his morning sermon. He was dazed from his hour in Rev. Washington's presence. He was hungry for lunch, though he did not know it and would have to be coaxed to eat a single bite. Most of all, he was anxious. Because there were committee meetings to attend in the late afternoon and another service to conduct in the evening, another sermon to deliver. And if anything was to go wrong at First Baptist Church, it would go wrong after the sun went down. This was when deacons exerted themselves in ungodly ways. This was when leaders of women's missionary circles came to Daddy with their endless complaints and lamentations. This was when gossip flew like dark winged bats above shadowy rooftops, when intrigue and hypocrisy clotted the air like plagues of locusts, when backs were stabbed and coups plotted, when faction vied with faction for Daddy's support or at least his tacit approval, and he hated and feared Sunday evening above all other days and times.

But I sensed more in his preoccupation that afternoon as I served up the one Sunday dinner in my limited culinary repertoire. I do not know who it was who first hit on the sublime notion of dousing pork chops with cokecola and baking them in a slow oven until the sugar in the soft drink caramelizes and the meat comes off the bone with the slightest touch of a fork. Back when I believed in God, I thought He must have granted His people this recipe in an instance of divine inspiration. A little something extra sent down the mountain with Moses, though in that case the chops would have been lamb, I suppose. Along with the pork chops I had prepared escalloped potatoes, another dish that could be left almost indefinitely in a slow oven with ambrosial results.

I knew all too well what had Daddy in such a funk. I could hardly bear to contemplate it myself. It was long past time somebody did something. It was inexcusable the way things still were. But why did something have to be done about it right here in our own backyard? And why did it have to be done right now? After clearing up the lunch things I went up to my room and tried to take my regular Sunday afternoon nap. This was usually one of the special treats of my week; several hours when I didn't have to go anywhere, do anything, or meet anyone's expectations. But it's hard to enjoy anything so simple as that when you have a sneaking suspicion you're staring the end of the world in the face.

Mercer Swinford was the organist at our church. The unanticipated only child of two only children who married in late middle age, he was sent away to private school in Vicksburg while still in short pants and returned to New Jerusalem after graduating from Vanderbilt to care for his by then elderly, widowed mother. Doctors from Memphis to Mobile all agreed she had but a few months to live. Contrary to all expectations she hung on for another twelve years, and to this day I believe she did it just to spite her son. Everything I ever heard about her cried out that she was capable of it

For his part, Mercer was the very model of a dutiful son. He came home from Nashville the minute his mother summoned him and got a job in the county attorney's office. This lasted only a few weeks before it became impossible for him to perform his duties as expected by his superiors and still attend to his mother to her satisfaction. After he left that job, they lived on a small income left by Mercer's father, which they supplemented from time to time by selling off parcels of land and the occasional family heirloom. Twelve years always at his mother's tyrannical beck and call, yet no one in New Jerusalem ever heard a word of complaint pass Mercer's lips. During those twelve years he only left the house on family errands or to attend church services and choir rehearsals.

He never married. His mother never would have stood for sharing him with another woman, and it was difficult to imagine the sort of young woman who would agree to play second fiddle for so long to such a thoroughly disagreeable woman as Myrtle Anderson Swinford was. This, of course, was the explanation for Mercer's bachelor existence considered fit for public consumption. And in most instances it would have been completely sufficient. There had been enough previous examples of the phenomenon to make it almost commonplace. But Mercer was Mercer, and you only had to look at him—one glance was enough, honest to God—to know that his case was different. The real reason he remained single, the one people whispered about behind his back and professed they were horrified by, was that he was not the marrying kind.

The kind he was was tall and lanky and languid. Not a single, fine textured, light brown hair of his head was ever observed to be out of place. It glistened from applications of brylcreem that barely escaped being excessive by even the questionable standards of that time and place. His immaculately trimmed pencil line mustache belonged on the face of a nineteen thirties matinee idol. Since that was just the sort of face he had it fit there perfectly even though it didn't remotely harmonize with his surroundings. His light gray eyes were deep set and serious, and I couldn't recall ever seeing him smile. He traveled in a cloud of Yardley for Men dense enough to mask the rankness of a locker room full of New Jerusalem High School varsity athletes just off the football field at the end of a long, sweaty practice.

In summer he wore suits of seersucker or white linen and was usually to be seen carrying a rakish straw hat that lent a faintly tropical air to his ensemble, as if he were off to catch the Pan American Clipper to Honolulu. Between Labor Day and New Year's he wore flannel suits of gradually darkening hue and carried hats to match, a progression which reversed itself between New Year's and Palm Sunday. On Easter, regardless of the actual weather, the summer wardrobe was once again on display. He'd never been seen outside the house without a necktie in all those years. He was a walking, talking fashion plate, circa 1938. A generation before that, he'd have been the Arrow Shirt man. In Hollywood, in any decade, somebody would have tried to make him a star. And would have had a reasonable chance of success. The soap operas were full of his type, and those actors had to come from someplace.

This peacock's plumage was all the evidence the town needed to cast him into outer darkness, unmistakable corroboration of suspicions which had troubled the citizenry since his visits home on school vacations. So that, a year earlier, his mother finally dead and his finances on the razor's edge of disaster, when he hung out his shingle as a teacher of piano, young ladies of all ages, some quite advanced and my four sisters included, flocked to his parlor to commence their studies but not a single young man of the town darkened his door. It would have been as unthinkable as flying to the moon on a broomstick.

That Sunday evening in the church parking lot his dreamy cinematic beauty took on a somewhat vampirish cast as he leaned against the door of his cream colored 1939 Packard roadster. He was speaking quietly but with visible animation to Daddy, who surprised me a moment after I emerged from the shadows behind the sanctuary by motioning me over to them. I couldn't remember having been within twenty feet of Mercer Swinford in my entire life. In fairness, I have to say that whatever avoidance impulse was responsible for this was on his part, not mine. I had heard all the jokes about him and as much of the gossip as was ever allowed to reach teenaged ears but had never feared him in the least. Does anyone ever truly fear his own reflection in a mirror? There's always something that holds you there staring into the glass whatever contrary impulse may be telling you to run like hell. I sauntered across the dew sodden grass intrigued by the tete-a-tete I was being summoned to join.

"Evening, Mr. Swinford," I said, as if we'd been on speaking terms for decades and nothing the least bit remarkable was taking place. This was not schoolboy aplomb so much as good southern manners.

"Good evening, Tristan," he said, very nearly smiling, though neither of us made a move to shake hands.

"Young sir," Daddy said. "Mr. Swinford will be joining us for a little refreshment back at the house. Will you please ride over with him and get things started? I'm likely to be a short while yet."

"Certainly," I said. Preachers' sons learn by the time they're in grade school to mask any and all astonishment, not to mention resolutely swallow curiosity, but this occasion was one of the most challenging I'd ever experienced. Whatever was Daddy up to?

"I'll see you at home, then." He turned and strode purposefully toward the sanctuary, whose stained glass windows still blazed with light. I stared as he crossed in front of the one in which Jesus was walking across the wavy surface of the Sea of Galilee.

"It was stupid of me to leave the top down during services," Mercer Swinford said, staring, like me, after Daddy. "I can't imagine what I was thinking. I'm afraid the car seat will be rather damp."

"It doesn't matter," I said, crossing behind the car to get in on the passenger side. "As humid as it is, my clothes can hardly get any soggier."

"You're probably right, at that," he mused, climbing in behind the wheel.

"You know the way to our house?" I asked, as he hit the starter button and the old straight eight engine thrummed to life.

"I believe so, yes."

I was speechless with gratitude for this opportunity to observe him more closely. It was not the morbid curiosity of the townspeople bent on finding yet more reasons for suspicion and censure. My upbringing would never have allowed it to be as base as that. But it so far transcended the good manners my parents had so carefully inculcated in me since birth as to make them irrelevant. For it had occurred to me as I sat down on the red leather upholstery of that old Packard that I was about to get some hint of what kind of man I might turn out to be. I hoped during those few moments of close observation to discover something in that hitherto unimaginable future identity that I could admire and respect. Mr. Swinford must have been aware of my intense interest. Sixteen year old boys are as transparent as thin air. But I don't believe he recognized its basis. He was accustomed to being stared at and must have assumed that my scrutiny of him was no more than what he had to bear daily. Once the car began to move he appeared to pay me no more attention until we pulled up in front of the house. But though I took whatever pains possible to conceal it, I never once took my eyes off of him. His aristocratic profile, lit by the inevitably romantic glow from the instrument panel, was more glamorous than I had ever seen it, and he handled the gearshift and steering wheel with a masculine forthrightness quite at odds with what the gossip led me to expect.

"What can I get you to drink?" I asked, bustling around the kitchen out of my head with anxiety and mortified by what he must think of it. "Iced tea? Cokecola? Water? I'll be glad to make a pitcher of fresh lemonade if you'd like. Though if you want coffee I'm afraid you'll have to wait for Daddy. Mine hospitalizes people."

"Iced tea would be delightful," he said, nearly smiling once again from where he leaned elegantly in the kitchen doorway. He was in his shirtsleeves now, his trousers held up by picturesque suspenders.

"What about this weather we've been having?" I asked, frantic to sound mature and matter of fact.

"You know, in all the years since I came home to take care of Miss Myrtle, Brother Daniel and Miss Elizabeth are the only people ever to speak to me about anything other than the weather and the state of my mother's health. Your parents are remarkable."

The squeaking screen door hinges interrupted our conversation about some of the more bizarre incidents in New Jerusalem history. Mercer was a treasure house of arcane local lore, and he seemed to enjoy having an appreciative audience. Daddy entered the kitchen to see Mercer smiling and me punctuating the end of a sentence by waving a half eaten chicken drumstick in the air.

"Thank heaven you're here," I greeted him. "I'm afraid your idiot son has been boring our poor guest to distraction. He's far too polite to complain."

"I knew I could depend on you, young sir," Daddy chuckled. "I see he's at least fed you, Mercer."

"That he has, Brother Daniel."

I had done my best. I had made a platter of deviled eggs that afternoon. There was left over fried chicken from the night before and some cold ham from earlier in the week. There were assorted pickles—all homemade, of course—and the perennial plate of sliced tomatoes. And reigning over the center of the table like a potentate was a blackberry cobbler Miss Althea Chandler had brought over that afternoon in gratitude for my "kind help and consideration" in taking care of her beloved Chevrolet. Not a bad spread for late Sunday evening. Mercer had actually picked at a thing or two.

But I knew Daddy's arrival was my cue to head upstairs. Over the years Mercer had spent hundreds, perhaps thousands, of hours unburdening himself in Daddy's study. Tonight's visit must herald another installment of his tale of woe. I had just helped myself to seconds on everything except the cobbler, which hadn't yet been cut. I stood and picked up my heavily laden plate.

"Don't go, Tristan," Mercer said. "There's nothing I have to say to Brother Daniel tonight that you can't hear as well."

"If you're certain," I stammered.

"Mr. Swinford asked you to stay," Daddy said.

I sat. Mercer waited until Daddy had served his plate before he said anything else. And when he did speak, it was with the apparent lack of concern or obvious relevance which marks all high drama in the south, at least in the first act.

"I was out to the county home this afternoon," he said in a voice no more portentous to the untrained ear than that of the state agricultural agent who read the daily crop forecast on New Jerusalem's lone radio station. But I knew what this was really about by the time he'd finished that first sentence. I knew a little local lore myself, and I'd always been good at playing connect the dots. "You know I visit our Rita Bel every week."

"How's she keeping?" Daddy asked, punctilious as a United Nations delegate though I knew his heart had to be racing as wildly as mine was.

"Well, Brother Daniel, she's just a pistol, that girl," Mercer said. "Always was, and she hasn't slowed down. Not one teeninecy bit. Sharp a tongue as Miss Myrtle herself, and don't you know when those two got going at each other it liked to peel the paint off the walls. Sometimes I'm not sure why my house doesn't collapse from sheer silence with neither of them around any more."

"She's a character, all right," Daddy said.

I was ready to scream at them both.

"Took her an African violet," Mercer said. "Always did like African violets. Had a golden touch with them. 'Course Miss Myrtle claimed she raised all the prize ones for the county fair herself, but I say it was Rita Bel should have taken those ribbons home. Miss Myrtle'da killed 'em sure if Rita Bel hadn't snuck around behind her back and given 'em proper care. Those were the days."

"Miss Myrtle gave Elizabeth one once," Daddy recalled, "and a couple of days later Rita Bel stopped by on her way home from visiting Zuleika Jefferson down the street at Miss Marilyn Roberts'. Stood out on the back stoop and spent twenty minutes telling Elizabeth just exactly how to take care of it. Wouldn't even step foot in the kitchen. And you know we've always welcomed anyone at our front door."

"That's right, Brother Daniel, you always have. Everybody around here knows that. It's just like I was telling Maisie this afternoon. She was there, too, you know. Just come in from church as I was fixing to leave. She's her mother's daughter, and no mistake."

"Handsome young woman," Daddy smiled. "An amazon."

"Yes, indeed," Mercer agreed. "And you know what she told me? Said the yankees are coming to town. Going to teach reading classes in the basement there at Ebenezer Baptist. Like to burst, she was, so excited and all. Can't wait to register to vote, she said. Missed out on votin' for Jack Kennedy last time, but thinks ol' LBJ'll do right by her if he gets a chance."

"Lots of people excited, Mercer."

"So it's true?"

Daddy nodded.

"Thought it must be. Those Jackson women never went telling tales. Well, how do you like that? So they're coming here to New Jerusalem."

"Big doings," Daddy said.

"About time, if you ask me." Mercer glanced at me to see what kind of reaction he had elicited with that remark. I stared back at him, astonished. I hadn't imagined a single white person outside our household would welcome the outlander volunteers.

"Think so?" Daddy raised an eyebrow.

"Thought you knew me better than to have to ask a thing like that."

"I suppose I do, Mercer," Daddy mused. "It's just that you go around thinking you know folks and like as not it turns out you don't. Expect there'll be a lot of unpleasant surprises the next few weeks. May not be a real nice thing to face up to. We'll just have to see."

"Well, now," Mercer said, "I believe I know what you mean there. But now what I want to know is this. Exactly where are those folks going to put up? Can't expect them to stay in the basement at Ebenezer Baptist. They'll need facilities. And Rev. Washington's people can't keep 'em. Most of them barely have roofs over their heads themselves, without taking in strangers."

"I raised that question with Rev. Washington this morning," Daddy nodded.

"What'd he say?"

"He's trusting the Good Lord to provide."

"Uh huh," Mercer nodded. "He'd have to say something like that, wouldn't he?"

Daddy shrugged.

"Well, Brother Daniel, I don't know what he'd think of the Lord providing accommodations in my house for all those folks. Might not think a thing like that would be decent."

He blushed slightly, and Daddy nodded.

"But if you and he didn't have any objections, I'd be right proud to have as many of 'em as are willing to accept my hospitality. I can feed 'em, too. I'm a right smart cook, if I do say so. Watchin' Rita Bel in the kitchen all those years. And there's those eight empty bedrooms just sitting doing nobody any good. Three bathrooms, too. I figure with a little doubling up I could take care of about twenty. More for meals, of course."

"God bless you, Mercer," Daddy said.

"Now I don't want to make any trouble. And if you or Rev. Washington'd rather me butt out I will, and not another word said."

"You know you won't have a friend left in this town," Daddy said.

"How many you figure I have now, Brother Daniel?"

"Well, I hope you know you always have Elizabeth and me, if no one else."

"I know."

"Make that three friends," I said, finally finding my tongue.

III

The next morning, Daddy was more preoccupied than I had ever seen him. He was unshaven and uncombed, an almost unheard of condition except immediately after he had risen, which he ordinarily did so early that no one, not even Mama, witnessed it. His eyes were puffy and had the deep bruises beneath them that I recognized as a sign he hadn't slept. But I hadn't heard the phone in the night so I knew this wasn't from being summoned by an emergency call. It's a rare preacher's son who can sleep through the ringing of a telephone at two a.m. and the ensuing drama of whispers in his parents' bedroom and a hurried departure from the house. I'd have had to be drugged to miss such goings on. But I'd been wide awake. So something other than a trip to the hospital, the mortuary, or the county jail had kept him awake, and no points scored for guessing what it was. The same thing had me tossing and turning all night, too. I was stifling a yawn when I first glimpsed him. He barely managed a greeting as I entered the kitchen, though the breakfast he served me was as sumptuous as ever. Silly of me, I realized staring without apetite at my heaping plate, to have thought that life would go on as if nothing out of the ordinary were about to take place. Silly to have expected any calm before the storm. We had long since used all that up.

"What's your impression of Mercer Swinford?" Daddy asked. The question surprised me. I was primed to discuss the imminent invasion of our sleepy town by Godless Yankees bent on blasting Our Way of Life to smithereens and the all too predictable reaction of the locals to this unspeakable threat. All this involved Mercer Swinford, of course, but only peripherally. I had known for years that Daddy and I would ultimately have a discussion on this general topic but I hadn't anticipated it that morning or even that year. It was obvious that Daddy was sympathetic to Mercer Swinford, but I took little comfort in that. A parishioner is one thing. A son is another. Then too, sympathy is fine and good in its place, but I'd be hoping for more than that when the time came. I'd want to be told that he and mama loved me regardless—nothing less. I took a deep breath but couldn't see a way to begin.

"It's all right, son," Daddy said. "I really want you to be honest with me."

"He's probably the loneliest person in New Jerusalem," I stammered.

"That's a fair assessment," Daddy nodded.

"I can't imagine why he stays here now that Miss Myrtle is gone. You'd think he'd be off to the big city as fast as that old Packard would take him."

"Yes, yes," Daddy said, obviously impatient with my temporizing, "but what's your opinion of him?"

There I was, backed into a corner. Could Daddy possibly know that he'd just posed the crucial question of my existence? No, he'd never be so oblique about it if he suspected anything. That wasn't his style. He'd ask me straight out.

"Well, I've heard plenty of gossip," I said. "I'd have had to be stone deaf all these years not to. And I'd have to be a fool to believe even half of it. But supposing it was all true, every last gruesome detail."

"Yes?"

"Well, I think I read the same Bible as everyone else. It says we're to love our neighbors as ourselves and treat others as we would want them to treat us. And I don't recall any exceptions being mentioned. No escape clauses, right? So from where I'm sitting, it looks like a lot of good Christian folks around here have a lot to answer for on the subject of Mr. Swinford. Not that they don't have plenty of other things to repent of."

"But you find him gruesome?" Daddy asked, and I saw his back stiffen. Just a bit. Someone who didn't know him as well as I did might have missed it.

"I didn't say that."

"You used the word gruesome."

"I meant the gossip."

"Just the gossip?"

"That's right."

"Because he disgusts most folks around here."

"I thought I sent them all to hell in a basket already."

"Including your friends?"

"I have about as many real friends as he does," I said. I'd always known this, but admitting it aloud hurt more than I would have expected. "Oh, everybody's ready to be pals with the star football player. Or date him. But that's not really me. Or at least it's only partly me. Maybe not even a very important part when you really think about it. But it seems like it's the only part anybody around here is interested in."

"Even Bobby Davidson?"

The name made me blush in spite of myself.

"I don't know," I said. "Maybe Bobby's different from the others."

Which I was pretty sure was wishful thinking.

"You'll be off to college soon enough," Daddy said. "It won't matter so much there."

"Unless it does," I said, "but back to the point. . ."

"Mercer Swinford."

I realized I'd been slow on the uptake. I'd completely fallen for Daddy's gambit. What I thought of Mercer Swinford didn't signify. Asking me about it was simply Daddy's way of raising the subject so he could tell me what his opinion was. I thanked my lucky stars that I'd come to my senses before saying anything more revealing than I already had.

"You know, son," Daddy said, and his use of that word was the signal I needed of how serious he was, "I can't begin to understand the feelings Mercer has described to me. I truly can't. I'm sure you can't, either."

I could no more have replied to this last remark than I could have said "abracadabra" and made the stove disappear, but he didn't wait for me to respond.

"He's tortured by those impulses, but how else is he to feel about it? Given what he's spent his entire life being told about himself, that is. I'm no expert on such matters. I've read some books on the subject but I can't honestly say that they explained much. What I have done, though, is honestly try to put myself in his position. Which hasn't been easy."

This was Daddy's trusty answer to any and all moral conundrums. Putting himself in the other person's place. There was no question that this was a scripturally based response, but, it had to be acknowledged, a highly subjective one as well.

"All right," I said.

"After much thought and prayer, I have to say I've come to believe that his feelings are probably as natural to him as mine are when I think of your mother. I don't know if that makes any sense to you or not."

I shrugged, unwilling to commit myself.

"It took me a long time to figure that out," he said. "A lot of prayer and hard study went into it. A lot of struggle. At first I felt the same way about him as everybody else around here does. I regret that now, but I simply wasn't equipped to consider the subject objectively when he first showed up back home. He's been very patient with me. And of course you're right about how he ought to be treated as well as whatever conclusions you've drawn from the fact that he's not. But now, how about this plan of his to help with the voter registration drive?"

Yes, how about that? At least it was an easier question to respond to. I knew exactly what I was supposed to say. So I did. And I pretty much even meant it.

"It's as plain as the nose on your face that we can't go on forever like this. The blacks are folks just like we are. And waiting around another century or two for public opinion to ratify it won't do. Anybody who doesn't see that is a fool. And anybody who doesn't help out is part of the problem. As for Mercer Swinford, you remember that sermon of yours about the time Jesus was preaching and some men brought a friend of theirs to be healed but couldn't get close to Him because of the crowds? So they went up on the roof of the house where he was preaching and tore a hole in the roof and let their friend's cot down through it? In that sermon, you said that most people miss the point. All they get out of the story is that Jesus performed a miracle and the man was healed, but what's really important is that somebody ended up having to pay for the damage to that roof. Somebody always has to pay a price or the Lord's work doesn't get done. Well, after last night I guess we know who it's going to be this time."

"Just so."

"This is why you sent Mama and the girls to Chattanooga, isn't it?"

"They visit your grandparents up there every summer."

"Not for the whole summer. And not with the station wagon loaded up like a Conestoga heading for the Oregon territory. The girls' bedrooms are practically stripped to the four walls. I swear I don't know now Mama got that car out of the driveway packed that heavy. Should have ripped the floorpan clean out going over the curb. Should have blown out the tires before she ever got to the county highway."

"I didn't know this was going to happen."

"You knew it might."

"I wanted to be prepared for it," he said, "just in case."

"Prepared for what? Does this really have anything to do with us? Here in this house?"

He knew I was playing devil's advocate, and he didn't flinch.

"Son, you and I both know this town won't be fit to live in if things don't change soon. That's assuming it is now or ever has been. The blacks need their fair shake, and they can't be expected to wait forever for it. Even if their patience was infinite, the whites here need the experience of doing the right thing. They need that every bit as bad as the blacks deserve justice. It's about simple human decency."

"Not to mention the Constitution of the United States."

"But it's much more even than that," he insisted. "It's about things that can only happen in the hearts of people when they've done the right thing even though it hurts. I want our people to experience that particular kind of grace. I want that so badly for them."

"I know," I said. Daddy's theology had never been about saving people from hell but from themselves. That's why what was about to happen was inevitable. "So it's not just Mercer Swinford we're talking about here. You're going to help with the voter registration drive, too."

"I won't be able to look myself in the face again if I don't. I won't be the father you and your sisters deserve."

I nodded.

"You're not angry?"

"Why would I be angry? What else were you going to do? I know you better than to think you'd sit on the sidelines."

"But you know what it means."

"At least as well as Mercer Swinford does."

"I don't mind for me," he said slowly. "I may never preach again after the good folks of this town get through with me. I've made my peace with that. I'm as prepared as a man can be to see his life's work end before its proper time. I've seen it coming for years, you know. I'm told I'm idealistic to a fault, and I suppose it's true. But I'm not blind. Change has got to come, but it won't come easy. And every preacher knows that some time in his ministry a thing like this is going to come along and he won't be able to tiptoe around it pretending it's not there. He's going to have to walk right through the fire."

"Not every preacher," I said.

"Well, no, maybe not," he smiled, "but you know I'd rather sell tractors than be that other kind of preacher. Your mother can get a teaching job easily enough. We'll never starve. She's been wanting to go to work for years, Lord knows. I'm sure I'll figure out what to do with myself eventually. Now, I don't mind so much for your sisters. They're young enough they won't have much trouble adapting. In six months they'll hardly remember this place. No, it's you that's going to bear the brunt of this, son."

"Don't worry about me."

"How can I help it? How can I ask you to give up everything you care about? You won't play football with Bobby and Travis and Bucky and your other buddies this fall. Wherever we end up, it's not very likely you'll get to be starting quarterback in your new school. You might have an easier time of it on the wrestling team, but you may never see any of those college scholarships you've been working so hard for all these years. And I know what all that means to you. I wish I could promise you your mother and I will send you to school anywhere you want to go, but you know I can't. We'll do everything in our power, but there's no guarantee it will be good enough. And my stars, you won't even get to graduate with your friends next spring. I know what I have to do, but how will I ever forgive myself for what it's going to do to you?"

"It's not your fault."

"But I'm your father."

"That's right. You're my father. Not God. Not even the President of the United States. It's not you that's going to run us out of town for doing the right thing. It's not you screwing up my senior year of high school. And anyway, what's all that stuff compared to what the black folks in this county have had to put up with all this time? I'm not a baby. I'm not going to start whining about how unfair everything is the minute I have to give up something I care about. So just do what you have to do, and I'll chip in with Mr. Swinford on that roof."

But despite my kitchen table bravado, I wasn't as noble as all that. I was Daddy's son so I could make a pretty speech, but I was pretty sure I couldn't live up to it. It was a crushing disappointment, and even though I'd been halfway expecting it since the afternoon before, now that he'd come out with it I was devastated. It was all I could do not to burst into tears right there over my breakfast. And though I had insisted otherwise, I did blame him for bringing down the roof and walls around us. At least partially. Him and his principles. Him and his interpretations of scripture that anyone else in town would have insisted were rank heresy. Him and his bizarre, pigheaded insistence on not leaving all that "love thy neighbor" stuff safely locked up in the church building when services ended like everyone else in town seemed able to do with little or no effort, but on actually living by all week long. So the minute I left the house that morning, instead of heading straight to work I ran for the one place in the universe where I could fall apart in peace.

When Miss Althea Chandler's husband died and his unrelenting battle against the undergrowth ceased, their orchard rapidly turned into a jungle, impenetrable to everyone but Old Shep and me. At the extreme bottom of it stood the ruins of an ancient well house, and over the years since I had first discovered it its cool old stones had been my refuge of last resort. Crashing headlong through brush that tore at the fabric of my uniform and the bare skin of my arms, I cursed the fate that had decreed my father would not be like other men, wishing instead that he had been a farmer, insurance agent, salesman of tractors, broker of cotton, or banker. Anything else would have done, really, as long as his career allowed his conscience to be less demanding and his moral sensibility less highly developed. I wished he had been someone who could just have gone along and gotten along and taught me to do the same and not worry about it. Someone who didn't perpetually bear on his shoulders the heavy load of being his brother's keeper while being brother to the wide world.

By that telepathy of his, Old Shep met me there that morning, and as I sat with my back propped against the mossy stones of the one remaining wall of the well house, he laid his mangy old head on my knee while I sobbed. Come what may, his grave old eyes said to my tear blurred ones, I would always have one true and faithful friend in this God forsaken town.

It wasn't for disappointment only that I wept that day. I read the newspapers same as everybody else. I listened to the news reports that issued from the old Zenith Chief Hamilton kept playing in the office all day every day. I knew as well as anyone the terrible things that were happening across Mississippi that summer. They were the stuff of nightmares, and they could happen in New Jerusalem, too. I had no illusions about that. Mama and the girls were safe, but what about Daddy? What about me? There was terror as well as fury in the noxious cocktail racing uncontrollably through my veins. I wasn't such a fool as not to realize that my career as a high school athlete was far from the most important thing I had to lose.

In all my years of working at Hamilton's Shell Service, I had never once been late. That day I slunk onto the drive well after nine, expecting to feel something very like the wrath of God directed at me. My reprieve was as unexpected as Moses' burning bush. Inexplicably, Miss Charlotte Marie hadn't been in all morning. It was Chief Hamilton who saw me first. He had just finished pumping gas for Miss Leora Bradley, and one look at me set him to chuckling.

"Well, looka here," he panted as the Bradley's aging Lincoln pulled away onto Main Street. He wiped a shiny film of sweat off his forehead with a handkerchief I knew had started the morning white though now it was a rainbow of grime. "What a mangy critter yaw'll are this afternoon. Or is it still morning?"

"Must have overslept," I told him. "It won't happen again, I promise."

"All that tomcatting around yaw'll do, sonny boy, ain't surprised yaw'll couldn't roll out of bed of a Monday. Not t'mention burnin' yaw'll's candle at both ends mornin', noon and night. Bound ta catch up with yaw'll sooner or later. I only wonder it ain't happened long 'fore now. It 'us that full moon last night musta done it, sure as yaw'll's livin' and breathin'. Makes everbody extra frisky. Them little gals a yaw'll's ain't about ta let yaw'll alone on a night like that."

I shrugged.

"Nawsir. They all gotta have their turns. That's womenfolk. Share and share alike. Well hell, boy, go on, get to work," he grinned. "I oughta dock yaw'll, but devil take it I ain't agoin' ta. It's worth it just ta see yaw'll caught red handed like this 'steada some pretty boy what just stepped offa magazine cover. And if I see yaw'll leanin' 'ginst them pumps today I'll know yaw'll's just catnapping, but if her majesty catches yaw'll at it, yaw'll best look out."

IV

Of course Daddy couldn't proceed with his plans and let the congregation figure out what he was up to on their own and decide at their leisure how to respond. He had to do the gentlemanly thing. I heard him on the telephone Monday night asking Howell Rutherford, the Chairman of the Board of Deacons, to call a special meeting of that group. It would convene after Wednesday night prayer meeting. He had called Mama in Chattanooga just before that, and I figured all this meant he'd be without a job before sunrise Thursday. I couldn't imagine the meeting ending in anything but his firing or resignation. I knew he wouldn't give in no matter what they said to him, and it was just as certain that the deacons wouldn't stand by and let him get away with what he was proposing to do. They'd see him in hell first. Or at least in the state home for the mentally disturbed. They'd be looking for a new preacher by the time their wives served them their Thursday breakfasts. The whole county would be talking about it over lunch.

Daddy and I weren't the only ones on edge. The coming of the outlanders was all you heard anyone talking about. Callers to Chet McMurtry's radio show were unanimously livid about the invasion and suggested hair raising manners of repulsing it. I overheard our neighbors chewing over the news, contributing their outrage to the general sum. The *Clarion* published an editorial decrying the interference of outsiders in what were clearly our private concerns. Nearly everyone I pumped gas for voiced similar sentiments or worse and seemed to take for granted my agreement. Indeed, if any of the town's white population held contrary opinions they kept their mouths shut.

Even more troubling, people weren't just talking. They were preparing to defend themselves and their homes against rampaging yankee hordes. And they made sure their preparations didn't go unnoticed. Confederate flags were flying all over town, a colorful but poisonous display. I saw them hanging on people's front porches up and down the streets I walked on my way to work. They flapped from the radio antennas of passing cars, including police cruisers. I saw them on fire engines and farm tractors—even on the town ambulance and at least one hearse.

More frightening than this array, across the street from Hamilton's Shell Service, Wainwright's Sporting Goods was doing a roaring trade. And it wasn't fishing tackle and tennis racquets people were stocking up on. Customers weren't bothering to have those brightly colored ammunition boxes bagged. They were proud to bursting to be seen carrying them out of the store, and over the coming days the noise of target practice became almost continuous throughout the town. It was a miracle that no one was killed accidentally with all that hot lead flying around. The few blacks I saw on the streets were obviously terrified, and I didn't blame them. I couldn't imagine how they slept at night.

"They's just a dirty no good bunch a comm'nist agitators," Chief Hamilton proclaimed the minute I showed up Wednesday morning. "That's all. They ain't real Americans nohow. Real Americans keep ther noses outa other folks' business. Real Americans know not to go whur they ain't welcome. Real Americans understand that the Nigras have ther place just like you and me. See, they ain't us is the thing. They live the way they live fer a reason. And they shouldn't be allowed ta vote 'cause they ain't capable of it. Ther simple people 'cause that's how the good Lord made 'em. So who're we to question it? These bunch a yankees just aim to come in here an' stir up the Nigras and fill ther heads full a' I don't know what all kinda nonsense until decent folks ain't safe in ther own beds at night and no white woman can walk the streets 'thout a gun in her handbag. You'd best believe Miss Charlotte Marie's packin' heat and so's all the daughters-in-law."

I gritted my teeth and pretended to be preoccupied sorting credit card charge slips.

"I hear tell that bunch're bringin' a jew boy or two with 'em," he continued. "Ain't never heard the like of it. Hell, ain't no hooknose jew boy college smartie gonna tell me how to live my life. No way, no how. Let 'em all go back where they come from 's what I say about it."

"You mean New York," I snapped, feeling the reins slipping out of my grasp.

"I mean Poland or that Yugoslovakia or wherever in Sam Hill it was. Hell, they got ther own damn country these days. Let 'em go there and mind ther own damn business. Too many of 'em here, that's fer damn sure. Shouldn't ever 'a let 'em inta the country in the first place. They's just like the Nigras pretty much. Only they's white. Almost white, that is."

* * *

"Go on home now, young sir," Daddy commanded as he walked past the end of my pew and the prayer meeting crowd broke up around us and the choir began to assemble for rehearsal. "I'll be along home later."

"No sir," I said. "I'm staying. I'll be waiting for you right outside."

He stopped in his tracks.

"What did you just say?"

"I'm not going home and leaving you here by yourself. I'll meet you out front after the deacons' meeting."

"Ssh," he hissed, looking over his shoulder. "Not so loud, please. I'd just as soon the whole county didn't hear this conversation. Now get on home. I won't be by myself."

"You'd be safer if you were," I said. "Who do you think you are? Daniel about to go into the lion's den? Shadrach, Meshach, and Abednigo rolled up into one? Don't you know what they're going to do to you in that meeting?"

"Tristan," he shook his head.

"Daddy?"

"If you stay here and wait for me, that'll just be one more thing I have to worry about. Understand?"

"But. . ."

"Go on home, son," he said, his eyes sadder than I'd ever seen them. "I know you only mean to help, but this isn't helping. Please, son. Go."

In New Jerusalem communication was more or less instantaneous. News of even the most trivial incident was disseminated effortlessly. More important matters became common knowledge with the speed of thought. Thus it was no surprise that by the time I got to work Thursday morning, Chief Hamilton had already heard about Daddy's shenanigans. His reaction was completely predictable. I had given him the benefit of the doubt by even showing up. He took a less charitable view than that of my appearance on the drive that cloudless morning, my uniform spiffier than it had ever been and my smile just as bright as I could make it. He seemed to consider all this a provocation, and as he waddled out of the office to intercept me I could clearly see that he was struggling to master his fury.

"Tristan," he grunted from a distance of ten paces, "go on. Yaw'll git outta here."

"But Chief."

"Yaw'll heard me," he said. "Now I ain't got no kinda beef with yaw'll personally. Yaw'll ain't responsible fer Brother Daniel's lunacy. I know that. But yaw'll know good'n well I cain't have yaw'll round here no more. Not with things the way they is. Customers won't stand fer it, and I cain't afford to lose the business. So go on home. I'll see that Miss Charlotte Marie mails yaw'll whatever's owin', and yaw'll can drop them uniforms by whenever yaw'll got the time. Now go on. Git."

I got. I trudged home through the sweltering morning, shoulders drooping, shod with leaden boots. There was no swagger left in me. It was less and less possible to view our predicament as hypothetical. Events were demonstrating more clearly each day that the optimism I'd been indulging in was a daydream. I was tallying up losses more quickly than I'd allowed myself to admit was possible. And others loomed ever nearer. I could no longer think of the end of my athletic career as a worst case scenario. Even if the Bentleys somehow managed to hang on in New Jerusalem, I knew now that the coaches at school would give me the same reception that Chief Hamilton just had. And in the unlikely event they didn't, there would be booing from the stands when I appeared on the field or in the wrestling ring. And no use fantasizing about my teammates rallying around to defend me. With me out of the picture, every one of my teammates moved up one notch. Especially Bobby.

He was the bitterest loss of all. I couldn't imagine any kind of future without him in it. Every time I thought about it my chest hurt and I got a lump in my throat and I wanted to die. And this heartbreak was all the worse for having to be suffered in secret. I had told Daddy I didn't understand why Mercer Swinford stayed in New Jerusalem after his mother died. But that had been my biggest lie in that harrowing discussion. I understood all too well. I had spent the last several years imagining myself in his place. He hadn't left because he couldn't. His heart wouldn't let him. I couldn't begin to guess who the man was that kept Mercer Swinford from leaving town, but I knew he was out there somewhere. And pondering this I had become more determined by the day that as long as Bobby Davidson was in New Jerusalem there was nothing anyone or anything could to do tear me away.

Oh, sure, for college. I thought I might endure it for that long. Bobby would go away to college, too. If I got very lucky, we might go away to college together. But he would come back afterward. His family's business interests were in New Jerusalem, and he was the only son of an only son. I wasn't stupid enough to believe he'd ever feel the same way about me as I did about him. Hell, I'd do everything in my power to keep him from ever knowing how I truly felt about him. That was the price I was willing to pay to come back home and be near him. I could be best man at his wedding. I could watch his children grow up. I would always be there, the best friend, the faithful sidekick. Southern men spent no more time than necessary with their wives and children, preferring instead the company of their fishing and hunting buddies. Bobby would be no exception. He exemplified the species. I knew he would have plenty of time for me. And if that was the way my love had to be expressed, so be it. Secret as it was, I would always know what I was doing and why I was doing it. Somehow that would have to be enough. That and growing old alongside him. That's what I had learned from observing Mercer Swinford.

Now that plan was on the junkheap. Now I knew that there would be no coming back to New Jerusalem. Even if Bobby would have anything to do with me, nobody else would. His wife wouldn't let me in their house or anywhere near their children and his other friends would make him feel like a traitor. The dream was over. I was past the point of denying it. Everything Daddy thought I was going to lose out on was just window dressing. It was this loss that meant the end of my world.

"Didn't waste any time, did he?" Daddy asked as I walked into the kitchen not quite ten minutes after leaving Hamilton's Shell Service.

"No sir, he didn't."

"I'm sorry," he said, burying his head in the *Clarion*. "I hope you know how terribly sorry I am."

"If you're going to apologize every time somebody does me wrong around here it's going to be an awfully long summer," I observed, struggling to master my emotions. "And more than likely you won't get another thing done."

"I was hoping he'd let you finish up the week," he said, "since the official announcement isn't until services this Sunday. Really, that's the least he could have done. It's not like you've done anything wrong."

"Well," I said, "that was a little too much to hope for."

"Where will it all end?"

"I'd just as soon you didn't ask questions like that when I'm in the room."

"Oh, sonny."

"I'm going upstairs and change," I said. "Can't hardly go looking for a new job in this Shell uniform. Probably have to shower, too. I bet I picked up enough gasoline smell to be unemployable even though these things just came back from the cleaner."

"I have a better idea," Daddy said.

"What's that?"

"Come over to the study and help me pack up my books. I'd like to be all moved out of there before Sunday, and there's no way I can get it done by then on my own."

"Did the deacons say you had to have everything out of there that soon?"

"They told me to take as long as I need."

"An ultimatum if I ever heard one."

"Sonny," he said, shaking his head sadly. "I can about handle this if I can have some hope it won't turn you into a cynic."

"What are you going to do for boxes? Shall I drop you at the church and then head downtown to pick some up?"

"Way ahead of you, young sir. I spent all day Tuesday and yesterday begging them all over town. You should have seen people biting their tongues. You could tell they were fit to bust with curiosity. 'What's Brother Daniel want with all these boxes?' 'Course they'd have died rather than ask me straight out. It was enough to make a cat laugh."

"All right," I said. "I'll go change. Are we bringing them back here? To the basement?"

"I thought we could set them up on bricks down there. In case there's damp."

My father's library was enormous. Floor to ceiling shelves lined his study, making it seem cavelike, and then there was the small room next door even more crammed. There were row on row of volumes of collected sermons by giants of the faith who'd been long dead even in my great-grandparents' time. There were impenetrable volumes of theology as heavy as small children. There were hundreds of biographies of missionaries who had preached heroically, healed selflessly, and in many cases died prayerfully in the snake infested jungles of Africa, the leprosy infested villages of India, and on dozens of cannibal inhabited tropical isles; among the farmers of China, the llama herders of Peru, and the subsistence fishermen of a thousand coastlines. There were multivolume collections of Bible commentaries that dwarfed the *Encyclopedia Britannica,* of which Daddy also had sets of varying vintages. There were dictionaries and grammars in Hebrew, Aramaic, and both Classical and New Testament period Greek, as well as copies of scriptures in all those languages. There were Latin grammars, German grammars, French grammars, and dictionaries to match them. Finally, there were more English translations of the Bible than even well informed lay persons would probably have realized existed. And that was just for starters. He'd been an English major in college, so there was all of that, from *Beowulf* to the moderns.

Except for the sheer number of books, this much of Daddy's library differed in no respect from those of his colleagues and peers throughout the south. Pastors weren't called "men of the book" for nothing. They considered themselves men of culture as much as men of faith. But Daddy had always maintained, though in no more than a faint whisper outside our own home, that Baptists had no monopoly on the truth and that to be a minister one had to understand the whole world of religious thought, so his library included way more Jewish, Catholic, and Anglican material—hellfire, even Methodists were suspect and there were lots of them lining the shelves, too—than a truly sound Baptist preacher would have dared read much less own copies of, but even this was not the worst of it.

That amounted to shelf after shelf of Darwin, Freud, Marx, Engels, Lenin, Trotsky, and even Stalin. And as if Ibsen, Chekov, and Shaw weren't depraved enough, alongside them on the shelves you'd find works by Brecht, Beckett, and Gorky. The complete works of Dr. Benjamin Spock might not have raised an eyebrow, though in a town like ours even that was far from certain, but the works of Dr. Alfred Kinsey most definitely would have. And as for modern fiction, there was lots of that, too, and not of the kind most church ladies would have found uplifting. There was a whole shelf of Faulkner's novels, for instance. And another of Joyce. And Daddy's copies of *Lady Chatterly's Lover* and *Lolita* were probably the only ones in the county. So if the deacons had ever bothered looking closely at his shelves, they'd undoubtedly have demanded his resignation years earlier.

We spent all day Thursday and again Friday moving those books. I filled the back of the Volkswagen with boxes I don't know how many times, driving load after load of those heavy old tomes back to our house and then lugging them down to the basement and stacking them neatly along the walls. Rank on rank they rose toward the basement ceiling, the boxes strangely like the blocks of stone medieval barons used to construct their fortresses. Could books form a bulwark? Daddy apparently believed they could. I understood more clearly than ever that he had lived his whole life trusting that the pen was indeed mightier than the sword and behaving accordingly. But as I pondered them resting there in the stacks I had erected, they seemed as flimsy as the paper they were made of. How could something as evanescent as thought provide shelter and protection?

V

Saturday morning after breakfast I put on my second best pair of trousers and a white shirt. I put on the Sunday shoes I had spit shined the night before and a tie everyone said went with my eyes. I had shaved so close I almost gave myself razor burn. The last time I had paid this much attention to my appearance was the night of that notorious prom Bobby Davidson asked Mary Louise Morgan to before she got a chance to make her friends make me invite her to. I ended up going with Mollie Jean Maddux as a favor to her great aunt, Miss Althea Chandler. Mollie Jean, the senior class tomboy, tried extra hard to be a girl that night on account of how Miss Althea had told her it was a favor to me (not the other way around, as had been explained to me) and we ended up having a rip roaring time and agreeing it was a shame we'd never gotten to know each other until the week before she graduated and went off to join the army and see the world.

After making sure one last time that my hair was perfect, I headed downtown. I started at the south end of Main Street and I went up the east side. I entered every place of business I came to. My plan was to ask every single owner, proprietor, and manager in town to give me work until someone did. I didn't care what the job was. I would even mop out a beauty parlor if it came down to it. I couldn't afford to be particular.

I only halfway expected to be successful in this quest, though I was certainly prepared for a miracle if one occurred; prepared to be suitably grateful, start immediately, and work my tail off under whatever conditions obtained for whatever wages were offered. I was desperate for a job. Two days of unemployment had almost driven me around the bend. I had been busy enough, God knows, moving Daddy's books, but I had generated no income.

And this rankled. I was not greedy by nature. I did not worship money for its own sake. There were things I would have liked to have, of course. But there were other boys in New Jerusalem who didn't have cars either so there was no dishonor in hitching rides, and there was nowhere to wear any better clothing than I already had in my closet. I wouldn't have watched a portable television even if I'd had one in my bedroom because television and boredom were synonyms in my vocabulary, and my clock radio was good enough to pick up the rock and roll station in Oklahoma City that all my classmates listened to. I was used to doing without more than I already had and it didn't particularly bother me, though I will admit to an occasional pang as I saw, or even just heard, Bobby blasting through town in his Sting Ray. Midnight blue, the perfect color for a car like that if there ever was one. But that was too much even to dream of, and besides, it was almost enough that he had let me drive it once or twice.

In other words, I didn't need work for any of the usual teenage reasons. I needed work because very soon I might have to start contributing more than good spirits, obedience, and cooperation to my parents' efforts to keep our family going. I needed work because with my athletic scholarships set to go up in smoke college had just gotten disastrously more expensive than I'd been anticipating. And I lacked even one tenth of Daddy's faith. He might be able to serenely contemplate how the lilies of the field neither toiled nor spun, but I worried about money. And more than actual cash money was at stake. The free lunches, too, were about to run out. Come Monday we couldn't expect we'd have those bags of free produce to inventory and store away.

But even more than that, I wanted those people to have to look me in the eye and tell me no. I didn't want them to have the comfort of ignoring what was happening to me or blaming it on someone else. I wanted them to understand exactly how responsible they were. If Daddy was right about the world all they needed was for someone to give them the opportunity to do the right thing and all would be well. It wasn't as if each and every one of them had to respond. God had spared whole cities for the sake of one righteous individual. And after all, I only needed one job or at most two.

So I labored up one side of Main Street and back down the other several hours later and though you wouldn't have thought one measly job was too much to ask for, no one hired me. No one even promised to consider it or to be on the lookout for something for me. They all but slammed their doors in my face. And it wasn't just the people I actually spoke to in the shops and offices who disappointed me all the livelong day. The ones I met on the sidewalks seemed nervous as I greeted them, many by name. I forced myself to keep smiling and wish them good day as if nothing was wrong, and I forced myself not to listen to their whispers hissing in my wake. I stood erect and kept my tie tightly knotted and hanging straight and I stopped every now and then to make sure the creases in my trousers were holding up. The day grew hotter and sweat ran in sticky rivulets inside my clothing and my collar chafed at my carefully shaven neck, and I ignored the hunger pangs ravaging my ordinarily well satisfied stomach, and I listened to people tell me no over and over again like voices on a broken record. I listened patiently as they brazenly gave me an astonishing variety of transparent excuses for telling me no, and I resolutely kept my smile in place as I marveled at their willingness to lie so blatantly and shamelessly and elaborately. Eventually I began to wonder why they even bothered trying to keep up the illusion of civility.

Pretty soon I realized that I was accomplishing nothing. I was no Old Testament prophet who could pull such a stunt and bring the people to their knees in repentance or find even one righteous man or woman. I might as well have gone home after my first half dozen stops. But I walked on through the heat, humidity, and frustration. Businesses in New Jerusalem closed at five p.m. sharp on Saturday and I supposed I would persist in my efforts until there simply were no more unlocked doors.

I was coming out of Anderson's Grocery when I ran into Miss Althea Chandler. She was pushing a grocery cart in through the front doors and I remember thinking she'd best get a move on because the store would be closing in about twenty minutes. She very nearly ran into me with that grocery cart before noticing me there.

"Why, Tristan," she yelped in alarm. "I'm sorry. I didn't realize it was you. I like to mowed you down."

"Afternoon, Miss Althea."

"Why aren't you at work, young man?" she peered at me through grimy lensed glasses. "Chief Hamilton let you off early for good behavior, did he?"

"Not exactly, ma'am."

"No?"

"I'm not working there anymore."

"You're not? Well, what on earth?"

"I reckon you know what on earth, ma'am."

"He didn't," she shook her head with great certainty. "I've known Hiram Hamilton all my life. I graduated with his big sister Nettie. I helped her torture him when he was a little boy. He wouldn't have."

"I'm afraid he did."

"Well, I'm sure you won't have any trouble finding another job. Everybody knows how hard you work and how dependable you are. Did you try in here? They're always short handed in this place. Last week I had to bag my own groceries. Can you imagine? The very idea. Mamie Anderson was just complaining at missionary circle on Tuesday night that they couldn't find enough help."

"I just asked them," I said. "They told me they couldn't use me."

"You must not have heard them right."

"I'm afraid I did. They said they didn't need anyone right now."

"Well where else have you tried?"

I rattled off a list of businesses.

"All those places?"

"Yes, ma'am."

"And they all turned you down?"

I nodded.

"But that's just not possible, Tristan. It just can't be."

"Listen," I said, "the store's about to close, and you haven't even started your shopping."

"Oh, bother my shopping. I can shop on Monday. I don't know why I don't. It's always impossible in here on Saturday afternoon. And if your mama can shop on Mondays I certainly can. But this, why, we have to do something about this. You want to work."

"Miss Althea, please," I said. "I'm embarrassed enough already. Please don't go making a fuss over this. It won't change anything."

"I can't believe what's happening around here," she said, her voice all quavery and her hands shaking on the handle of her grocery cart. "First those darn fool deacons go and do that to Brother Daniel, and now nobody will give you work. I thought I knew these people better."

"Oh, now, Miss Althea, you're all upset. I didn't mean to get you all upset."

"Bother upset," she snorted. "This is serious. Now I don't mean to poke my nose in your business. I'm not a busybody like some people we both know, but just how much was that tightwad Hiram paying you down at the Shell Station?"

"Two dollars an hour."

"Two dollars an hour? That seems fair enough."

"Oh, yes'm. He was always real good about that kind of thing."

"All right," she nodded. "Now you know my orchard is just been let go to rack and ruin since Mr. Chandler died. We used to have such good fruit off those old trees. And so much of it. I'd can and can and still we had to give most of it away. Just makes my mouth water thinking about it. Those cobblers I made. I was thinking just the other day how wonderful it would be to have all that fruit again. So you just get yourself over to my place first thing Monday morning. All the tools you'll need are in my garage, and I'll pay you that same two dollars an hour to clear the place."

"Miss Althea, that's awfully nice of you, but you don't have to do it."

"Not another word, young man. Tristan Bentley wants work and Tristan Bentley shall have work."

The big prayer rally and dinner on the grounds to welcome the volunteers was that evening, and I was just leaving the house to walk over to Ebenezer Baptist when Bobby Davidson pulled up to the curb in his Sting Ray. His hair was sun streaked from his job as lifeguard at the country club pool and as perfect as brylcreem could make it. He smelled like the world's handsomest boy done up for Saturday night. Breathless as I was looking at him, it was almost a relief not to be spending the evening in his company.

"Where you off to all slicked up?" he asked over the V-8 rumble. "Hah, don't tell me, boy. It's that Nelda Whitfield, I bet. Been nosing around asking questions about you all week. That's one hot mama."

"Do tell."

"Just ask Rance Cutler, if you want the real low down," he chortled. "And low down is where she goes, if you get my drift."

"I'll bear that in mind," I told him.

"You best do more than that, boy," he laughed, racing his engine. "I'd offer you a ride over there but I'm already late picking up Mary Louise."

"It's all right," I assured him. "I can use the exercise."

"Well, don't wear yourself out too much 'cause that Nelda, she'll give you a workout."

"Yes sir."

"Say, T., you're not still sore about that stuff last spring, are you?"

"What do you mean?"

"Me and Mary Louise."

"I told you before, Bobby. I never was sore."

"Sure," he said. "You always were too much of a gentleman for your own good."

"As if you'd know anything about gentlemen," I laughed. "Honest, boy, I don't care. You and Mary Louise or you and whoever, that's your affair. I wasn't going steady with her or anything like that. Heck, we never even dated. Not really. Just talked in the school library a couple of times."

"Yeah," Bobby nodded. "What she said, too. Couldn't help wondering, though. I mean a guy can't never be too sure, what with the way those still waters 'a yours always runnin' so deep 'n all."

"Cut that out."

"What it said in the yearbook," he grinned. "Must be true. And you're getting big enough lately I sure wouldn't want to tangle with you."

"Don't worry about me, man."

"All right, T. See ya around."

He floored the accelerator and screeched up the street. I stood there sniffing exhaust fumes and burning rubber until I saw his headlights disappear around the corner two blocks up. My white shirt lit up like a torch in the glow of the streetlights and I didn't want him glancing in his rear view mirror and seeing me head off in the opposite direction from Nelda Whitfield's house. I hadn't actually told him that's where I was going, so maybe it didn't count as a lie.

I took a roundabout route as Daddy had instructed and was late getting to the church. Because that night's festivities were a joint gathering of Ebenezer Baptist and Mount Calvary African Methodist Episcopal Zion Church, the sanctuary was more than packed. There were well over a hundred people standing outside the building listening in through the open windows and I'd have been perfectly happy to join them but wasn't allowed to remain there. A couple of superannuated deacons saw me and before I knew it I'd been shoved through that mass of humanity into the sanctuary and plonked down in a pew. I could see Daddy sitting in his usual place on the platform. I could also see, in the front two pews, a double row of white people's heads. Reverend Isaiah Washington was in his accustomed black robe. Beside him at the pulpit and a head and a half taller, Reverend Maurice St. Jacques Lincoln was as colorful as a peacock in a robe of white festooned with satin stoles in all the colors of the rainbow.

"And now, brothers and sisters," he intoned, "on behalf of our gracious host my dear brother Reverend Isaiah Washington and the joined congregations of Ebenezer Baptist and Mount Calvary African Methodist Episcopal Zion here assembled, it's my honor, privilege, and delight to invite our great good friend and brother in this holiest of struggles, the most Reverend Daniel Wentworth Bentley, to take his place with us here as we welcome our honored guests."

Daddy rose from his seat. In his plain navy suit, he looked like a duck among swans. He seemed a little overwhelmed as he moved toward the pulpit, like he didn't quite understand what he was doing there. If Rev. Lincoln hadn't grasped Daddy firmly by the elbow and maneuvered him into place between himself and Rev. Washington, I'm not sure he would have found his way to the spot. Even from the rear of the sanctuary I could tell how ill at ease he was. All he truly wanted was to be allowed to sit back down.

"Brothers and sisters," Rev. Washington intoned, his honey smooth voice dramatically hushed, "it is my proud honor at this time to ask our most highly esteemed friend and my heart's true brother, Rev. Daniel Wentworth Bentley, to grace us all with a few words."

"My dear brothers and sisters," Daddy began, "and when I call you my brothers and sisters, I mean it from the very bottom of my heart. For surely the Lord God in His wisdom and kindness has made us brothers and sisters, every one. I am profoundly humbled and deeply honored to stand before you tonight in the company of these two great men of faith and add my voice to theirs in beseeching the Lord God's blessings on this gathering. Thank you for letting me share with you here this evening."

"Amen and amen," Reverend Lincoln said.

"God bless you and keep you, Brother Daniel," Reverend Washington said.

"And now on behalf of our two congregations," Reverend Lincoln continued, "I ask our honored guests to rise from their seats and stand with us here to receive our welcome."

The volunteers stood up and filed somewhat awkwardly onto the platform. As the single line of neatly dressed young white men and women took their places facing the thronged pews, Zuleika Jefferson rose from her seat in the choir loft and began to sing. She started off soft, almost tentative, but before she'd finished the second phrase her voice had turned into pure molten steel, and when she got to the part where His Truth Was Marching On, we were all on our feet, all singing along and believing every word, and many were dancing in the aisles.

The tables set out under the huge oaks and beeches in the church yard were laden with such an array and sheer volume of lovingly prepared food it was a wonder they didn't collapse under the weight of it all. Dozens of different recipes for fried chicken vied for the favor of the crowds. Roasting pans heaped with crunchy nuggets of fried catfish took up one entire table. Cold hams glazed with brown sugar and decorated with pineapple slices and maraschino cherries were picked to the bone in mere minutes. Steaming casseroles of pork chops baked in cokecola and others of pork chops baked in Campbell's cream of mushroom soup and still others of pork chops baked in canned fruit cocktail stood in a row like a county fair display. And the heady, insistent tang of barbecue livened the evening air.

Huge bowls of potato salad sat chilling in tubs of ice alongside even huger bowls of cole slaw. Pyrex dishes of escalloped potatoes sat alongside pyrex dishes of baked apples and pyrex dishes of candied sweet potatoes. Pots of baked beans, green beans of a dozen different species, butter beans, black eyed peas, crowder peas, field peas, all of them seasoned with slabs of fatback or salt pork, shared a table with rank on rank of pots of mustard greens, collard greens, turnip greens, and my favorite swiss chard. There was a table just for pickles and relishes. Imagine the colors and the spices. There was fried corn, corn pudding, boiled corn, and creamed corn, all these in both yellow and white types. All the known varieties of squash were represented, prepared in every imaginable fashion. There were platters stacked with slices cut from tomatoes the size of grapefruit, tomatoes twenty or more different shades running from the deepest reds through the brightest oranges and sunniest yellows.

There were enough pies, cakes, breads, and pastries to overflow a state fair exhibition hall, and each and every one of them worthy of a red ribbon at least. There were enough fudge brownies to satiate even the most desperate addicts. There were a full three dozen freezers of freshly turned ice cream in vanilla, chocolate, strawberry, peach, and praline, and an equal number of watermelon which had been in the fields no more than hours earlier. King Solomon in all his glory never feasted more lavishly than we did that night.

I was on my fourth plate of food when I first met Laddie. That evening, anxiety had added a second hollow leg to my perennial single one. I had found myself a spot a little removed from the crowds and was methodically attacking a heap of okra fried just the way I liked it best, sliced into small rounds, mixed with cornmeal and egg, and shaped into flat patties, when he just up and started talking to me. No southerner would ever have made conversation with a complete stranger that way, and it alarmed me at first.

I'm sure my parents would have been horrified had they known of it, but despite their diligent efforts the most odious of stereotypes invariably fixed themselves in my consciousness the minute I heard Jews mentioned. The Jew was scrawny as a banty rooster, thickly bespectacled, crook nosed, kinky haired, and spoke loudly and unceasingly in a distinctive honking whine. He was neurotic, cowardly, argumentative, given to hysteria, and a tightwad. He was intellectually brilliant but lacked practical skills. He was not athletically inclined. And so on. If either of my parents had known I was laboring under such a misapprehension, they would have washed not my mouth but my brain out with soap.

I knew good and well, of course, that none of the traditional myths about blacks stood up to even the slightest scrutiny. I had spent my life learning this first hand. I had ample opportunities every day for observation. And if those same opportunities and observations failed to dissuade my friends and neighbors from their long held beliefs and superstitions, it was their lookout. But honest to God, I had never laid eyes on a Jew before. At least not to know it.

So when Laddie sauntered up I simply wasn't equipped in any way, shape, or form to apprehend his reality. At least that was the excuse I gave myself for my tremendous unease, though of course I soon enough recognized it for what it truly was. Which was even more disconcerting. Though all handsome men were scary, Laddy got to me in a way nobody but Bobby ever had. I don't know how long I stared at him. Long enough to get a good eye full, that's for sure, not to mention send a pretty clear signal, even it if was inadvertent. Laddie was several inches taller than I was and even broader in the shoulders. His jet black hair was wavy and only partially tamed with Vitalis. His cheekbones were confrontational and he had a cleft chin. His eyes, large and twinkling and dark enough to be called indigo, were nothing short of terrifying.

"Mind if I join you?" he asked.

"It's God's own grass," I said, way too alarmed at the prospect to smile and at the same time afraid he'd suddenly disappear if I didn't say the magic word.

"I'm Vladimir," he said, sitting down crosslegged facing me. "Vladimir Zitronblatt."

"Welcome to New Jerusalem."

"And you, unless I'm very much mistaken, must be Tristan Bentley."

“That’s what they tell me,” I said, wondering what he’d heard about me.

“Tristan,” he mused, studying my face in a manner I found hideously disquieting, “the sad but valiant knight.”

“My mother had a very vivid imagination post partum. Not to mention both my parents read way too many books.”

“Really?”

“Honest to Pete.”

“I would have said it suits you.”

“Think whatever you like,” I told him, bluffing furiously, “just as long as you’re not expecting me to die for love. And if you don’t believe me about Mama, just ask anybody about my sisters’ names.”

“Which are?”

“Ondine. Portia. Hyacinth. And Zoe.”

“I see what you mean.”

“So I wouldn’t waste much time pondering the significance of the mythological and legendary allusions,” I jabbered, more anxious with each breath I took. “We’re just ordinary kids despite our outlandish names. You’d only be barking up the wrong tree if you convinced yourself otherwise.”

“Oh,” he said cryptically, “I rather think I’d very much enjoy doing exactly that.”

VI

I wasn't surprised when Vladimir came home with us at the end of the evening's festivities. While he and I had been gorging on ice cream, I witnessed a conversation between Mercer Swinford and Daddy which was punctuated by meaningful glances in our direction and instinctively knew what it was about. If Mercer Swinford found Vladimir even half as attractive as I did, I could well imagine him not wanting such a temptation under his roof. Renaissance Italian princes might have been just fine in fifteenth century Florence, but I imagined that in your own kitchen that sort of manifestation might prove more of a distraction than you'd want to face day in and day out. I wondered just how I was going to cope.

But there was no way out, not with our house so empty. And I couldn't dream of raising an objection because how in the world could I explain it? Poor Daddy would think I had lost my mind. I was more or less trapped. Of course Daddy would be around to chaperone. And Vladimir probably wouldn't do anything more in our house than sleep there, what with his friends all at the Swinford place. Not to mention that he would be busy night and day. I'd hardly know he was there. And on further reflection I decided that even though he was the first man ever to distract me, even momentarily, from Bobby, there was still no reason to believe that my usual routine of working myself more or less into a stupor every day, dependable as it had been since seventh grade, could no longer be relied upon to keep things in check.

I skipped Sunday School the next morning, threatening as it did to become a purgatory of awkward emotions. I visualized myself in the church basement, sitting in a circle with two dozen or so kids I'd known all my life and who by all rights should have been my closest friends, every last one of us unwilling or unable to talk about what was uppermost in our minds. I couldn't face the curiosity, the whispers, the stares, the phony veneer of normality we would all feel forced to maintain. Whatever we had been together was a thing of the past. It would have ended in another year when I graduated and left town anyhow, so what was happening was just a little ahead of schedule.

I timed my arrival at morning worship for just after the opening hymn had begun and had to find a seat way down front. The crowd was the biggest there had been at a service since Easter. Indeed, I wasn't sure it didn't dwarf even that turnout. I thought of the old Roman regimen of bread and circuses and Christians being fed to the lions, which seemed apropos. But if this crowd had come to see fireworks they were bound to be disappointed. If they'd come expecting any kind of spectacle at all they just didn't know Daddy. They probably never had.

Still, there was a tension in the air as if everyone present could hear the ticking that warned a bomb was about to explode but nobody was willing to be the first to head for an exit. And as we moved through a perfectly ordinary order of worship, this sensation grew. Was this what these people would do when the world ended? Simply try to ignore it? Knowing them as I did, it seemed pretty likely. Finally the offertory rolled around, followed by the choir singing the morning anthem. The substitute organist muffed the accompaniment disastrously, and I thought it served these people right having to listen and be reminded of Mercer Swinford, who wouldn't be coming back either and who had never in all his years been responsible for such a fiasco at the keyboard. Then at last it was the time we'd all been waiting for. The main event on the card. Daddy rose from his seat and settled himself at the pulpit. If there was a nerve in his body you couldn't have told it to look at him. I was sweating bullets myself and about to jump out of my skin.

"Dear friends," he began. "As you may or may not already have heard, in a specially called deacons' meeting last Wednesday night, I communicated to that body my intention to resign from the pastorate of this congregation effective at the end of this service. The deacons graciously accepted my resignation on behalf of this congregation. In lieu of a sermon, I will therefore make only a few remarks. Before I leave this pulpit for the last time, my deep love for you all compels me to take a brief moment to thank each and every one of you for eighteen wonderful years as your pastor. My family and I will never forget your many kindnesses and you and this church will be forever in our thoughts and prayers. And so in this time of parting, my prayer is that the Lord bless you and keep you; that the Lord shine his countenance upon you; that he give you peace; and that he be gracious to you forever and ever. Amen."

He picked up his Bible as if he had finished delivering just another sermon, turned from the pulpit, walked down the short flight of steps from the podium, and strode up the center aisle. I had to rush to catch up with him almost like when I was a little boy, but once I did we walked side by side. Like Daddy, I stood tall and straight. I kept my head up and my eyes focused into the distance ahead of us. We walked like that, wordless, past row on row of the familiar faces of strangers and through the swinging doors into the foyer. Daddy had observed just a few weeks earlier that I had finally grown as tall as he was, but I never felt it until that moment. We walked out of the building and down the broad steps to the sidewalk. We walked side by side down the street and neither of us looked back.

Daddy shut himself up in his bedroom after only a halfhearted attempt to eat lunch, but not before making sure the telephone was still off the hook. God only knew what demons he was wrestling with. I would have done anything in the world for him right then, but when I knocked on his door he didn't answer. I didn't bother him again.

There was nothing on television but baseball and golf, so the set stayed silent for the afternoon. I would even have risked being alone with Vladimir for the sake of the conversation, but he had left the house while I was dressing for church and hadn't returned. Ordinarily I found Sunday's enforced inactivity soothing. It was the one time during the week when I could do nothing without feeling guilty. But that afternoon was oppressive and endless. I went upstairs feeling out of sorts. I tried reading but couldn't concentrate and eventually fell asleep.

When I woke, night was falling and the day's heat had begun to abate. On the refrigerator I found a note from Daddy. He had gone to Mt. Calvary African Methodist Epsicopal Zion Church for evening services. There was no sign of Vladimir, and I fought off the temptation to go up to Ondine and Portia's room and snoop through this things only by making myself a chocolate milkshake.

It was the first time except for a few occasions when I'd been sick that I'd ever stayed home from church on a Sunday night. I had missed years and years of Sunday evening television programming, and I should have been ecstatic at the chance to watch to my heart's content. But the sudden freedom to indulge made the prospect merely annoying. Things are never as much fun when you have permission to do them, and preachers' sons are particularly susceptible to this quirk of human nature. I wandered around the house aimlessly, further breaking the Sabbath by doing some light dusting and a load or two of laundry.

Unable to stand it any longer, I fled to the refuge of the back yard.

Which was where Vladimir found me several hours later, lounging in the hammock and reading by the light of a bug lamp I hung in the branches overhead every spring.

"So here you are," he said, grinning enigmatically. "Listening to the Shostakovich Fifth, of all things, and reading—what?"

I showed him.

"Virginia Woolf?" he laughed. "So the rumors about Tristan Bentley are true."

"What rumors?" I demanded, blushing furiously. "What are you talking about?"

"You should come inside," he said, ignoring my question. "Your father thinks we're starving to death."

I sat up and pulled on my t-shirt. I grabbed my books and rolled out of the hammock. I followed Vladimir into the house. Daddy was in the kitchen whistling a Souza march and ransacking the refrigerator.

"Nice evening, young sir?" he asked, smiling a remarkably carefree smile.

"You know how I thrive on inactivity."

"This is great, isn't it?" he enthused. "The three of us really didn't have a chance to get to know each other last night. Now there's cold fried chicken. And we can make sandwiches out of this ham."

As he handed things out of the refrigerator, I took them from him and set them on the table. Pretty soon there was more spread out there than we could have eaten in three meals. We sat down and started helping ourselves.

"Now Vladimir," Daddy said, "I'm afraid you've caught us unprepared. Is there anything here you can eat? Anything at all?"

"My tribe are secular Jews, Daniel," he laughed. "We never encountered a dietary law we didn't immediately break. I'm inordinately fond of pork products. And shellfish."

"I'm shocked," Daddy laughed. "Better pass him that plate of ham, young sir."

"There you go."

"Thanks, T."

"What did you just call me?"

"I honestly didn't tell him," Daddy insisted.

"What's the matter?" Vladimir asked. "Did I do something wrong?"

"You used the nickname his buddies gave him back before kindergarten."

I could remember that afternoon when Bobby had first spoken it like it was yesterday. A chill ran down my spine.

"Really," Vladimir said. "That's funny. It just came to me, you know. I won't do it again."

"I don't mind," I told him, desperate to make light of it. "Call me anything you like as long as you don't call me late for dinner. You surprised me, that's all."

"In that case," he grinned, "maybe you'll call me Laddie. All my rugby buddies do."

"It does sound more American," I observed. "But not much."

"Now did someone in your group tell me you grew up Israel?" Daddy asked.

"A kibbutz outside Haifa," he nodded. "We emigrated when I was in grade school."

"Zionists," Daddy said.

"Hardly," Vladimir snorted. "Back in St. Petersburg before the Soviet revolution, my father's family considered themselves completely assimilated. My father and uncles weren't even Bar Mitzvahed. My brothers and I only were because my mother insisted on it. And the fact is we didn't go to Israel voluntarily."

"What do you mean?" I asked, mystified.

"My grandfather was a Menshevik," he explained. "Do you know what that is?"

"Sure," I said. "They were Marxists who weren't followers of Lenin."

"So he's not just a pretty face," Vladimir grinned at Daddy.

"Heavens, no," Daddy laughed. "He has many practical uses and even a modicum of intelligence. You'll see if you're around here long enough."

"Amazing," Vladimir marveled.

"Cut it out, you two," I snapped. I could tell I was blushing again, and I didn't like it. "I believe we were talking about the Mensheviks."

"Well you know all about them coming out second best after the Revolution," Vladimir explained. "Lenin pretended to make room for them in the new government at first. At least those of them he'd never tangled with personally. But Grandpa saw the writing on the wall, so he and Grandma and my father and uncles came to America. That was in 1919. If they had left it much longer, getting out would have become impossible and they'd undoubtedly have died in the Stalinist purges sooner or later. But just because they came to America didn't mean they stopped being communists."

"Of course not," Daddy nodded. "Those were great years for the Communist Party in the United States."

"Right," Vladimir said. "Grandpa had the time of his life. He was able to agitate to his heart's content without ever once going to jail. Needless to say, my father and uncles were raised in the faith. Their whole neighborhood in Brooklyn was practically a communist ghetto. They were raised speaking Russian, too, in case things changed and they could all go back. Until the day he died, Grandpa still had plans to go back to St. Petersburg. Then when World War II started, being able to speak Russian made my father and my uncle Sergei particularly valuable to the U.S. military. They were both sent to Moscow and worked as translators at the U.S. Embassy."

"I think I see where this is going," Daddy said.

"It's a common enough story," Vladimir nodded.

"What is?" I asked.

"When the Cold War began, men like them became immediately suspect. They had the wrong political associations, and worse than that they'd spent time in Moscow working directly with the Soviets. They were under suspicion. For a while it wasn't too bad, but then the McCarthy business made life pretty much impossible. They were afraid they'd end up in jail. That's when we went to Israel. Ironic, isn't it? Because my grandfather detested Zionists. He thought world revolution along Marxist lines was the only real answer for Jews and anything else was just bourgeois sentimentality. But Israel was the only place they could go to feel safe."

"You must have been in the army over there," Daddy observed.

"I did my hitch," Vladimir nodded. "Then I came to the States to go to university. My Uncle Yevgeny had stayed behind. In New York. He had gone into business instead of academics, so it was easier for him. I got my B.A. at N.Y.U. Now I'm in a doctoral program at Columbia."

"What are you studying?" Daddy asked.

"What else would a good Marxist study?" Vladimir's eyes twinkled.

"History?" I suggested.

"Exactly," he laughed.

When I went downstairs the next morning, he was sitting on the front porch glider.

"Your father told me you jog every morning," he explained. "I wondered if you might like some company."

I tried very hard not to notice that he was dressed just like me, shirtless and in gym shorts. He couldn't have looked less like a historian.

"It's not entirely up to me," I stammered. It was one thing knowing he was in the house, but being expected to spend time alone with him, especially looking like that, rattled my cage but good.

"No?"

"We'll have to ask him," I said, nodding toward Old Shep, who was waiting at the curb.

"I didn't know you had a dog."

"I don't. He has me."

"Ah, well," he chuckled, "I'm sure he'll approve."

"Not so fast," I warned, following him down the front walk. "He'd just as soon chew your arm off as look at you. The only safe thing to do is not to get too close and wait for him to approach you."

But Laddie wasn't listening. I watched in mounting terror as he crouched down beside Old Shep. I could practically hear the screams of terror and the crunching of bones. Then Old Shep did the most astonishing thing I had ever witnessed, something no one in the whole town would have credited even if I'd sworn to it on a stack of Bibles. He licked Vladimir's face.

"Thought you could scare me with some schoolboy tall tale," he accused, laughing. "Fat chance, mister."

VII

"You really have a gift, Tristan," Laddie said. "The way you work with those people. The way they respond to you is amazing. You have them eating out of the palm of your hand."

It was Friday night, and we were walking home from the class we taught.

"It's no gift," I snorted. "I'm the white boy, that's all. They know how they're expected to act around us whether we're being nice or torturing them, and it's got nothing to do with me personally. It's centuries of social conditioning. If I wasn't trying to teach them to read I could just as easily be making them scrub my floors or pick my cotton."

"No, it's more than that," he insisted. "I've been down here long enough to tell the difference. It's not just that they're accustomed to taking orders from any and all white people they encounter. Something else is going on in the way they interact with you. Something very special."

"Maybe it's because they've known me since before I could crawl. They helped raise me. We know the same stories. They know I know how it all works."

"And they can't make the same assumptions about us," Laddie nodded. "I get that. But still, I was watching you and Altarella Brown tonight and you were so patient with her. Gentle, actually. After Monday night I didn't think she'd ever come back to class she was so discouraged. You could see she didn't think she had any business being there. But just as she was leaving I heard you say, 'good work, Altarella', and I saw her stand up a little straighter. She hasn't missed class all week. Say what you like, but it's obvious that she's trying her heart out because she knows you really believe she can do it. She came back the next night because she didn't want to disappoint you. But now she's coming to class because she's starting to believe it herself. You can see it in her eyes. It's like somebody turned on a switch. Nobody's ever made her believe in herself before. Perhaps nobody bothered to try. I'm not sure anybody but you even could."

"She was there when I took my first step. I've heard the story about a million times. Mama and Daddy were visiting somebody in the hospital and she was taking care of me because my regular babysitter wasn't available. They came home and there I was, walking. She was afraid they'd be upset with her, letting me take my first steps without them there."

"Not your parents."

"No, they were thrilled. They've never let her forget that that moment she became part of our family. I guess that makes it possible for her to accept my help. But it's nothing I ever did."

"I bet she's known other people just as well and doesn't believe she can trust them like she does you."

Our walks home after class had gotten progressively longer all week. I varied our course nightly. I contrived detours. I led us far out of our way. I knew Laddie noticed, though he didn't remark on it to me. I wondered if he mentioned it to Daddy, however. As nonchalantly and apparently aimlessly as I conducted us through the streets, alleys, fields, and orchards, I knew it all must seem monstrously calculated. But I couldn't stop myself. I could talk to him like I'd never been able to talk to anyone before, and the sensation was both intoxicating and addictive. I lived for those conversations like a deep sea diver lives for the surface of the water. Tonight I had led us far afield, our route a good four times longer than necessary to get us from point A, Zuleika Jefferson's small, tidy cottage where we held classes in the black quarter of town, to point B, the Bentley residence. I knew what I would say if either Daddy or Laddie said anything about our walks. I'd claim our meanderings were a security precaution. We'd all been told to be careful. But I doubted very much I could make that claim at all convincingly, so painfully aware I was of my unholy motivation.

"What are your plans, anyway?" Laddie asked.

"Get out of these clothes and make a thick sandwich out of left over roast beef. Top it off with some of that peach cobbler, if Daddy didn't hog it all. Peach cobbler is his favorite."

"I'm not talking about when we get back to the house," Laddie laughed.

"When I grow up, you mean?"

"You already did that. From the looks of you."

"Well, college of course," I said. "Mama and Daddy wouldn't hear of me not going. They'd sooner have me become an axe murderer than not get a degree."

"Where will you go?"

"Haven't thought that much about it."

"You must have," he insisted. "You've already finished your junior year. A smart guy like you should have it all figured out by now."

"Well until quite recently," I said, hoping I wasn't about to say something that would sound hopelessly arrogant, or worse, like I was feeling sorry for myself, "we all pretty much assumed that I'd go wherever the best offer came from. There was a widespread belief that college coaches would descend from far and wide carrying scholarship letters, swooping down on the four winds with their pens at the ready."

"I see," Laddie said.

"That may not actually materialize. Probably won't, since there's a pretty good chance I won't even play this fall. So you're right, I'd better start thinking about my options. As for careers, I believe Mama would like me to become a doctor. She's never come right out and said it, but the look on her face when she talks about what an admirable profession it is would be pretty hard to misinterpret."

"Do I detect a slight lack of enthusiasm?"

"I don't think I'd look very good in a lab coat."

"Seriously."

"I seriously hope one of my sisters will take the hint. It's just not for me. Grandpa and Grandma Bentley would like me to come back to Bagwell and farm the old place. I don't have but a couple of boy cousins on Daddy's side, and I guess so far nobody thinks they look like they'll amount to much as farmers. Grandpa hates to think of the place without any of his kin working it. But somehow I can't see myself doing that. Daddy won't say anything because he's determined not to run his children's lives. But I know he leans more toward the idea of me being an attorney. Especially since Mama made him read *To Kill a Mockingbird*."

"Not a minister?"

"Heavens, no," I guffawed. "He knows me too well to have any illusions about that. Not to mention he seems a trifle disenchanted with the pastorate of late. That would be the church ladies who think I'm supposed to go down that road. At least they used to. By now I'm sure they all think I've got horns and a tail."

"You don't believe they'd take their disapproval of your father out on you?"

"Baptists are pretty funny about preachers' kids. You'd hardly credit some of the things I could tell you. I wouldn't be a bit surprised if you told me some people around here think the whole mess is an escapade I thought up and inveigled him into."

"Perhaps," he said, but I could tell he was dubious. Which was typical, I thought. No matter how profoundly outsiders might decry our customs and folkways, when they came face to face with our foibles, they were inevitably shocked at their perversity.

"But what do you want to do with your life?"

"Well, so far I've got it narrowed down to fireman, cowboy, pilot, and railroad engineer."

"Come on," he protested.

"I honestly have no idea," I said. "My uncles on Mama's side say if I gain another twenty pounds they'll get me on the professional wrestling circuit with them."

"You're joking."

"Oh, no. Family acts go over real big."

"You wouldn't do that."

"I might. They make it look like bags of fun. Then there's the fame, of course. And the money's surprisingly good. Have to change my name, though. Tristan's too theatrical even for that. I'm considering Spike. Spike Bentley. What do you think?"

"I think I'd like to be able to have a serious conversation with you that lasted more than three minutes."

"I'm a sixteen year old white boy," I said. "I've been playing football since I could walk and been concussed countless times. Consequently I'm shallow and have a short attention span."

"So says the guy who listens to Shostakovich when he's not listening to Rachmaninoff and reads Virginia Woolf and W.H. Auden. Sorry, but I'm not buying it. You're not the lunkhead athlete you pretend."

"Guilty as charged," I said. "I'm a chameleon. And look how much intellect they have."

This sort of banter had been going on all week. I didn't want Laddie getting too close. I didn't want him knowing things about me and I absolutely didn't want him trying to make me into someone I wasn't. People had been doing that to me all my life. But at the same time, I found his attention highly seductive. Sixteen year old boys adore being taken seriously by young adults and I tried my best to explain it to myself that way, but I knew that was far from being the whole story. I had always wanted a hero to worshp. And if he turned out to be handsome, athletic, and exotic, so much the better.

"I love watching you and Daniel together," he said. "You're almost not like father and son. I kind of get the feeling that you think of yourself as his older brother and he goes along with it, if that makes sense."

"I guess that is how I think of myself," I said, "and he'd better go along with it because it's his own fault. I don't remember a time when he didn't treat me like a little adult. Anyway, don't all boys want to be pals with their fathers? All my friends do."

"Sure," Laddie said. "But what's between the two of you, I don't know, it just seems very unusual. There's a closeness you don't often see between father and son. You obviously love him very much."

"Love really isn't the point," I said. "I mean, of course I love him. But that's not what he needs from me."

"I don't understand."

"Everybody loves him. The whole county, really. For instance, the people at church. Even after what's happened they still truly believe they love him, and when he comes to his senses they'll take him back in a flash. He's got more love than he knows what to do with. Respect, too, though you'd probably have a hard time getting people to admit to that right now. What he doesn't have is people who understand him. And more than anything else, he's the kind of man who needs to be understood. It's what's so special between him and Mama. She understands him."

"And you do, too."

"Maybe," I admitted. "At least I come closer than just about anybody else. And the reason I could never do what he does is I don't have the right kind of faith. I'm not talking about whether I believe God or not. It's Daddy's faith in people I can't live up to. He still believes that if he just keeps reminding them to love their neighbors all this will eventually clear itself up."

"And you don't think so?"

"Laddie, I look at those people every Sunday morning, sitting in their pews and singing and praying. They've been hearing what God expects of them all their lives. It's been preached to them more or less constantly. It's in the Bibles they tote around. The women stitch it up on needlepoint samplers that they hang in their dining rooms. They know it as well as it's possible to know anything. And they just keep on living the way they've always lived and doing the things they've always done. They simply won't make the connection. That's why I could never be a minister. I couldn't stand to watch people ignore everything I'm trying to teach them and go on about their business like nothing's wrong. I'd go out of my mind. I'd never say anything like that to Daddy because he'd think it meant I believe he's wasted his life."

"Don't you?"

"It's not that simple."

"Oh?"

"It really isn't," I insisted. "See there's a certain kind of person who's so sure what he's doing is right that it's just not possible people won't eventually come around. If he lives to be a hundred and things around here still haven't changed, on his deathbed Daddy won't say 'it never happened. I must have been wrong'. He'll say something like 'it hasn't happened yet, and boy I wish I could be around to see it when it does.'"

"You know," Laddie mused, "what you're describing sounds so much like the relationship my father had with my grandfather. I don't know if that makes any sense."

"Why wouldn't it? Marxists, Christians, aren't they really after the same thing?"

"What do you mean?"

"Think about it. Is there anything more revolutionary than true Christianity? Or true Judaism? They both ask us to go against human nature and be genuinely good people. Ultimately they're both concerned with justice as they define it. At least that's how Daddy sees it. If he can just get people to love their neighbors like they're supposed to, there'll be justice. No need for laws and debates. It will automatically follow. Because if you really love another person, you can't treat him unjustly. Daddy honestly believes that. And I bet your grandfather thinks that if people can ever be convinced to live by the right economic rules, justice will result. Isn't that how it's meant to work?"

"Are you sure you're only sixteen?"

"Come on," I said. "Don't tell me you didn't have all that figured out when you were my age."

"Maybe I did."

"Damn and blast," I muttered, catching sight of Bobby's car parked in front of our house. "Shit, shit, shit."

"Such language," Laddie sighed.

"I'm a football player." I told him. "Last I heard, I was supposed to be starting quarterback this fall, although there may have been further developments lately. But once a football player, always a football player and don't you forget it. We all have potty mouths. Besides, I wrestle, too. And don't even get me started on that."

"O.K." Laddie laughed. "I get the picture. But what's up?"

"See that car?"

"The Corvette?"

"That'll be Bobby Davidson. He's my best friend."

"Shouldn't you be happy to see him?"

"Not looking like this. No, sir. He doesn't know what I've been up to all week. Dressed up like this on Friday night can only mean two things. And it won't take him long to figure out I wasn't on a date."

"Should it matter?" Laddie asked. "If he's really your best friend?"

That wasn't a question I was in any mood to ponder.

"You know it matters," I said. "Where do you think you are?"

"Sorry."

"When you walk in, you'll most likely find Daddy feeding him sandwiches in the kitchen. You know Daddy wasn't crazy about me helping you out at class because of what might happen if people around town find out, so he will have been pretty vague with Bobby about my whereabouts this evening. That's O.K. because Bobby thinks Daddy is too dotty to live, so he won't be suspicious. What I'd like you to tell them is that you just ran into me on Main Street and I told you I was on my way to get a burger. That way Daddy will know I'm all right and Bobby will know where to find me."

"I don't know. . ."

"I know," I grimaced, pulling off my necktie and unbuttoning my shirt. Once I'd stripped to my t-shirt, Bobby just might overlook the dress pants and shiny shoes. "The preacher's son asking you to lie."

"It's not that," he said.

"What is it?"

It was a long six count before he spoke.

"Never mind."

"Please, Laddie," I begged.

"All right."

"Toss these things into a corner on the front porch before you go inside. I know it's just about all over with me and Bobby. Any day now all hell's going to break loose and he'll never speak to me again. I know it's going to happen. I only want a little more time to be friends with him, O.K?"

I was just tucking into my hamburger when Bobby walked into Mina's Blue Miracle Diner. I had caused a minor sensation in the kitchen by ordering my burger without fries because of the potential threat Laddie claimed eating them posed to his abdominal muscles, which truth to tell were well worth preserving. I was drinking iced tea with it instead of my usual chocolate shake because Laddie said that if you were going to ingest fats you shouldn't add insult to injury with sugar. You should ingest them in a form which provided additional protein. So I'd ordered double meat on the burger. I knew it was risky having Bobby witness me doing something so out of the ordinary. I expected he'd be full of questions and suspicions.

"Your daddy," he said, sliding into the booth across from me. "I was just over there waiting for you to come in. Talk about your southern eccentrics."

"So what else is new?"

His dark brown hair was shinier than I could remember ever seeing it, and his tan was deeper and richer. His hazel eyes were bright. A little too bright, I thought, wondering what it was that had him so excited.

"Shouldn't you be out with Mary Louise?"

"I was. She got a headache." He grabbed my glass and took a swig of tea. "God, what's wrong with this stuff?"

"I'm drinking it without any sugar."

"Why the hell would you do that?"

I shrugged.

"That Mary Louise has been getting a lot of headaches lately. Figured I'd better call her bluff before she gets the idea she's in charge, you know?"

"Women."

"Damn right," he nodded, "so I took her home early instead of being Mr. Nice Guy and driving her over to Sissy Powell's place so they could sit in the living room and play Beatles records while I listened to them gossip. I just don't get the Beatles, do you?"

"Give 'em time, boy, give 'em time. They'll grow on you."

"You mean you like them?"

"Don't rightly know. Haven't grown on me yet, I guess."

"And they're not going to," Bobby said. "Know why? They're damned sissies is why. English guys are worse sissies than yankees, I swear. Anyhow, that's the way the girl cures her headaches. Listening to Beatles records with Sissy Powell. Damndest medical treatment I ever heard of. Definitely not my idea of a hot date."

"No," I said. Not with him looking and smelling like that, it wouldn't be. Mary Louise had best be careful because there were plenty of girls around who'd happily cooperate if she remained obstinate.

By nearly unanimous agreement, Bobby was the best looking boy in our school. Much was made of his resemblance to Ricky Nelson of the celebrated television family, and though for the most part I practiced strict atheism when comparisons between our schoolmates and world famous actors and athletes were made, in this one case I had to admit that the young women of New Jerusalem were right on target. Whether he'd have been quite as wildly attractive to them if his family hadn't been old money rich wasn't a question much worth pondering in a town as status conscious as ours, though I'd have considered him stunning even if he lived in a backwoods shanty with an outhouse, a plank floor, and no electricity, and came to school shaggy haired, grimy necked, barefoot, and wearing bib overalls. His being a star athlete didn't hurt, either. Nor did his obvious self confidence, his gregariousness or his boisterous albeit dead conventional sense of humor. But spectacular as he was, I suspected there was a boy like him in every high school in America. Not that this made me any less in love with him. All I really wanted was to be ordinary in exactly the same way he was.

"What?" he asked, noticing my stare.

"Nothing," I muttered. "Just, you know."

"Yeah," he nodded. "Been thinking about it myself. What's going to happen? I mean your daddy is just doing this to get attention, isn't he?"

"Is that what people are saying?"

"Brother Daniel's trying to prove a point," he said. "They think once he blows off some steam he'll get back to normal and ask for his job back. They're not even talking about looking for a new preacher. My daddy says they already decided to wait him out. Sure hope they're right. Don't want to think about you having to leave town or anything like that. Not right before senior year."

"Me either."

"Say, you got a dime? I ought to call Mary Louise. I promised I would. And if I make it too late her mom won't let her come to the phone."

I fished two nickels out of my pocket and slid them across the table.

"Thanks," he said. "I'll be right back."

"Want me to order you anything?"

"Your daddy stuffed me to the gills. When you finish, let's go for a drive."

"Where to?"

"What do you mean, where to?" he laughed. "Since when does that matter? It's Friday night, and I've got the top down on the Sting Ray."

VIII

When I woke the next morning, Daddy was sitting on the edge of my bed. This was something he'd often done when I was little, and I recalled how much I had always loved for him to be there when I first opened my eyes. I had never felt safer than at those times. He wasn't the kind of man to tell people he loved them. Instead, he showed us his feelings through a multitude of simple deeds, and this was a special, unmistakable way he had of showing me. As I'd gotten older and my sisters were born, there were fewer and fewer occasions to enjoy this private ritual, but I never stopped missing it. I didn't take much time to ponder all this, however, because his expression banished any possibility of comfort.

"What is it?" I grunted, sitting up. "Did something happen to Mama or the girls?"

"No," he said. "I just spoke to your mother. They're all fine up there. But I'm sure glad now that I sent them away for the summer."

So despite his fervent optimism it had gone beyond those Confederate flags flying all over the place and semi-hysterical discussions among neighbors.

"Who is it?"

"Mercer Swinford."

"Oh, no," I croaked. "Dead?"

"Jack Murchison and Benton Willis were out at daybreak with their coon hounds and found him in the river a little downstream of Veteran's Bridge. His car was parked just this side of the bridge itself."

For as long as there had been a bridge there the spot had been a favorite of suicide jumpers, enough so for the place to have become a local cliché. Even as I fought not to believe what Daddy had just told me, my brain rattled off the names of previous victims.

"He wouldn't have."

"Sonny, we don't know that," Daddy shook head slowly. "It's something you can never be absolutely certain of about anyone. His life here hasn't been easy. And lately, with Miss Myrtle gone, he's been on his own. She was certainly a difficult woman, but at least he wasn't alone in the world."

"I know all that. But he didn't," I insisted. "He's been like a kid with a new toy, feeding and cleaning up after all that company in his house. You've seen him lately. He's never looked less suicidal."

"I know," Daddy admitted.

"It's just a plausible story. It gives everyone an excuse not to ask questions. It lets them off the hook. The guys who did it, I mean."

"That's what I believe myself," Daddy agreed, "but you'd best prepare yourself to be in the minority, holding an opinion like that."

"What makes you think I'm not used to it?"

"Anyway," Daddy continued, "I'm on my way to see Sheriff Ellsworth. But before I go I want you to promise me one thing."

"What's that?"

"Don't go out jogging this morning, please?"

"Daddy, nothing's going to happen to me. Whoever did this wouldn't dare try anything else so soon. They'd never get away with it."

"What makes you so sure? Because you're you and Mercer was who he was?"

"Not that. They can't go after anyone else right now. You know how people around here hate coincidences. Besides, Laddie will come along with me. I'll be perfectly safe."

"No," Daddy said, and I could tell that arguing further was futile. "No, no, and no. You're assuming the people who did this think the same way you and I do. You're assuming they're smart like you are. You could end up dead making assumptions like that. Please. This is no time to be pigheaded. I need you to do what I say."

"All right," I told him. "I won't go jogging. But you can't expect me to just lie around the house at a time like this. I'm coming with you."

"Son, please."

"It's one or the other. You decide."

"All right."

"Just give me ten minutes."

I splashed cold water on my face, but it didn't help. I stared at myself in the bathroom mirror. I couldn't say I was surprised that they had gone after somebody. I'd been expecting it. Hell, the whole town had. We'd been holding one great collective breath. But Mercer Swinford? He might have been giving aid and comfort to Laddie and company but I hadn't thought they'd go after him for it. Any more than they'd have gone after Daddy or me. And the reason I'd thought that didn't do me any credit. I'd thought we were all safe because we were white. I'd been taking comfort in that, thanking my lucky stars I hadn't been born black. I'd been thinking all along that they'd go after some poor black man or woman just like they'd always done before. I realized I'd been hoping that when it happened it would happen just like that, as if the death of a black were somehow less tragic.

Oh, sure, Mercer Swinford had been a homosexual and pretty much everybody in town had known it. But while they went after blacks with horrifying regularity, I'd never known them to go after a white man. It was the one taboo they recognized. But now they'd broken it. No wonder they'd been so tentative about it, making it look like suicide. They'd been rash enough to break a cardinal rule of our community but observant enough of the local sensibilities to be nervous about it. They simply wouldn't risk doing such a thing again. Twice, regardless of what Daddy had said, would be too much. New Jerusalem wouldn't abide it.

Besides, they had obviously done it to send the rest of us a message. They woudn't go after anyone else until they'd given that message time to soak in. They would wait to see what we all did next. At least until Mercer Swinford was buried, nothing else was going to happen. So in my mind I was sure I was safe, but in my guts it was another matter. I looked at my hands. They were trembling.

I splashed more water on my face, and it still didn't help. It didn't calm me down any and it didn't make me feel clean. If they'd killed Mercer Swinford for being homosexual then I was only alive because I was too chicken to own up to it and too careful to let anybody figure me out. Over the years, Daddy had exhorted me to be brave far more often than to be good, but I wasn't brave enough for that. I was letting Mercer Swinford down with every breath I took, and I hated the face that stared back at me out of that mirror, that face of a coward.

I dunked my head in the basin and attacked my hair with a comb, working the overnight tangles out of it, wrestling it into some kind of reasonable shape. Except for when I went running, I didn't like leaving the house in any condition less than pristine, but there was no help for it. I could feel Daddy's impatience from clear downstairs, so I toweled off quickly and pulled on my shirt.

Peaceful and law abiding as New Jerusalem liked to think it was, no place on earth is without at least some sort of criminal element. It doesn't take big city professional hoodlums to vandalize property, steal the occasional car or pickup, or once every decade or so torch someone's barn. Our ne'er-do-wells also demonstrated a notable aptitude for aggravated assault, which they generally committed on each other, and rape, which most often involved young black women and thus went unreported. I knew who they were. Everybody in town did. It wouldn't have occurred to them to try keeping their activities or identities secret. They apparently took it as given that sooner or later they'd be caught and incarcerated for something or other, so what was the point?

I suppose our familiarity with them made them seem less dangerous than they actually were. Then again, it could have been their much commented upon ineptitude that made them seem comical rather than scary. Maybe it was because they accepted clear limits on their misdeeds, a self imposed code that kept most of us perfectly safe. In any case, ninety year old widows encountering them on the streets were far more likely to razz them about their latest misadventures than cower in fear. When they got out of jail they didn't find themselves ostracized. As long as they kept their noses clean, their neighbors were willing to let bygones be bygones. And their infinitely patient families always took them back in. I had witnessed these tearful reunions myself. They generally did stay out of trouble just as long as their temperaments would allow, though for the most part this merely meant destroying their own property instead of other people's and beating their wives and children instead of their drinking buddies. This last fell into the category of a man's prerogative. Domestic violence as a phenomenon in which the law might take an interest was unheard of, and as long as nobody ended up dead was believed to concern no one but those directly involved.

But although they'd never gone as far as killing a white man before, except by accident, it seemed likely that any one of several dozen good old local boys was capable of having ended the life of Mercer Swinford. Especially some hothead who got tanked up and was then egged on by his associates. As I mentally checked off the rollcall, I suddenly realized I could all too easily imagine such a thing. Hell, it was probably long overdue. I'd be more shocked to learn that the crime had been committed by a stranger. It was just a question of which of the usual suspects had done it and how it had happened, and I knew Daddy was thinking pretty much the same thing as I drove us over to the sheriff's office. We could have passed the time comparing our lists. This was no idle speculation about the guilt of this individual or that one, either. Every last one of the possible culprits had family in town that would be drawn involuntarily into the tragedy. It couldn't help but get messy, and unlike me Daddy must be regretting that. I was more in a mood to blame them all for not straightening out their wayward sons and brothers and savor whatever consequences they suffered.

I couldn't put the whole town on trial for murder. But I didn't need to worry about that. The guilty parties themselves would be sufficient. And the sheriff didn't need any help from me rounding them up. As meek as Mercer Swinford had been, he was a large man and undoubtedly a strong one. He would have understood the threat and would have struggled accordingly. That, and the natural cowardliness of everyone I could think of who might have been involved led to the inevitable conclusion that there must have been several assailants. Perhaps as many as half a dozen. And that many of them couldn't keep a secret for long. Certainly not the way they all drank and carried on. Somebody would blurt it out sooner or later. Possibly under interrogation, because the sheriff was undoubtedly already checking out the alibis of every one of them. By the time he got a confession out of somebody a trial would have become unnecessary.

I figured taking time out to discuss it all with Daddy would probably hold up Sheriff Ellsworth's investigation for all of fifteen minutes.

* * *

"So unless Dr. Fenwick finds something suspicious, which my money says he won't," Sheriff Ellsworth drawled, "there's no reason to think it was foul play, Brother Daniel."

"Are you saying you aren't going to investigate?" Daddy was thunderstruck.

"I told you. We did investigate," Ellsworth insisted, gnawing on his already slimy unlit cigar. "There wasn't a mark on him except what you'd expect to find on somebody who jumped off a bridge that high. That didn't leave him looking as pretty as usual, but it don't mean anybody killed him."

"The fall and the impact could have covered up other marks, couldn't they?" Daddy asked.

"'Could have' don't put nobody in prison," Ellsworth grunted. "You know that as well as I do. And besides that, there was no evidence of robbery. His car was right where he'd have left it if he was fixing to jump, and there wasn't a mark on it either. His keys were in the ignition, and his wallet was in the glove compartment. Over two hundred dollars that nobody took, you hear? C'n yaw'll really imagine somebody killin' him and leavin' that much money alone?"

"It's exactly what somebody would do who wanted to make the death look like suicide," Daddy pointed out. "Did that occur to you?"

"I ain't stupid, Brother Daniel," Ellsworth snapped. "And I don't remember ever askin' yaw'll a similar question regardin' yaw'll's line of work."

"What about tire tracks or footprints in the area?" Daddy demanded, undeterred.

"Who are yaw'll," Ellsworth growled, "Perry Mason? Sherlock Holmes? Tarnation, Brother Daniel, you shouldn't ought to watch so much television."

"Well?"

"We didn't find nothin' suspicious. It's a free country. People can walk around or drive pretty much wherever they please. They can even pull their cars off the road for a look at the river. It don't mean they were there at the time. It don't make them murderers."

"Did he leave a note?"

"We ain't found one yet. But lots of times we don't. Ain't had time to look everywhere. Besides, who'd he leave one for? His mama's dead and they ain't nobody else. I'm on my way back over to the Swinford place right now and we'll keep looking. Anyway, reckon it's high time to roust those squatters out of there."

"They're not squatters," Daddy said. "They're Mr. Swinford's guests, and you will not attempt to evict them from the property."

"I won't?"

"I have a copy of Mercer Swinford's will right here," Daddy said, opening the manila envelope he hadn't answered my earlier questions about. "You'll notice that I'm listed as executor. And as executor I'm telling you this, so listen carefully. Except for whatever you have to do to investigate this matter, you have no jurisdiction over any of Mr. Swinford's property."

"Don't I just? Now listen here, yaw'll may be my preacher, but don't think yaw'll can come in here and give me orders. I'm warnin' yaw'll, hear?"

"No," Daddy snapped, "I'm warning you. If you want this to be a nice, neat case of suicide then you just stay off that property unless I'm there to observe you, and leave those people alone. If you decide there's a murder that needs to be investigated, I'll be glad to cooperate in any way I can."

"Will yaw'll get off your high horse for one minute and listen to me?"

"Not if all you're going to do is waste time making excuses for not doing your job and generally talking nonsense."

"Brother Daniel, I don't like to discuss this in front of Tristan here."

"I'll worry about him, thank you," Daddy said. "I don't tell you how to raise your kids."

"Well," Sheriff Ellsworth said, looking slightly nauseated, "we both know what Mercer Swinford was."

"So?"

"There ain't a jury in this state who'd convict anybody for killing a man like that. Yaw'll know it and I know it. So even if I had reason to think there was foul play, which I ain't sayin' I do, I'd just be wasting my time trying to find out who did it. And I'm not paid to waste my time. I'm paid to protect the folks of this county, and as far as I'm concerned, ever last one of 'em is safer with that man dead."

"You're going to regret saying that someday," Daddy said. "You're going to regret it deeply."

"I doubt it," Ellsworth snorted.

"So you're not going to do anything more about this? You're actually going to sit by and let murderers walk the streets of this town?"

"Yaw'll'd best not speak to me like that again."

"Truth make you uncomfortable, does it?"

"Brother Daniel."

"If that's really how it is, then you won't be expecting me to allow you access to the property without a warrant. Understand?"

"All right," Ellsworth relented, "but if yaw'll or any of those agitators find a suicide note, I expect to hear about it."

"If anything like that turns up, I'll let you know," Daddy said, "but don't hold your breath. Come on, Tristan. We have things to do."

We stopped at Mina's Blue Miracle Diner for a late breakfast. It suddenly seemed like months rather than hours since I'd been there. Saturday morning was perhaps Mina's busiest time all week. The dining room was full of farmers, businessmen, and off duty sheriff's deputies. Deacons Waverly and Ratchford sat in the booth Bobby and I had shared the night before. Conversation and tobacco smoke hung in the air like fog over a winter beach. And though some of that conversation concerned us, it didn't trail off into embarrased silence as we entered the way you'd normally expect but continued unabated, and at a volume which made ignoring it pretty near impossible. I felt my fists clench. Daddy led the way through a maze of tables, and we took the last available booth, right beside the pay phone. We might as well have been invisible. No one looked up from their morning paper or plate of fried grits. No one turned from his companions to spare us even the briefest of glances. No one said so much as good morning. Except for Judy our waitress not a soul spoke to us at all, though I knew Daddy must have known every soul in the place by their first names. I couldn't begin to imagine what he was feeling, though he was as poker faced as ever.

Adding to the peculiarity of the scene was the fact that though I was a regular myself, I couldn't recall the last time I'd set foot there in daylight. After dark it was a place for my classmates and other young people of the town who hadn't yet taken on the responsibilities of adulthood. Six nights a week this was our undisputed territory, but that morning there was no one there within twenty years of my age except the busboy, and the breakfast menu might as well have been written in Sanskrit for all my familiarity with it. I finally ordered what Daddy would most likely have fixed for my breakfast had we eaten at home. Biscuits and gravy with a double order of bacon.

I was bursting to discuss our confrontation with Sheriff Ellsworth but knew it wasn't the time or place. So while we waited for our orders and Daddy pretended to read the front page of the Jackson paper, I took the sports section and pretended to read the baseball scores.

When we got to the Swinford place, Laddie had all the volunteers gathered in the dining room. Some of them looked miserable and some of them looked angry, but most of them just looked scared. I didn't know if Laddie had taken charge of this meeting because he had some official status among them, because he was staying with us and had been the first to hear of Mercer Swinford's death, or simply through the force of his personality, but everyone there seemed to take it for granted.

"Until we know what happened to Mr. Swinford, nobody goes out alone," Laddie was saying as we walked in. "Understood?"

There were whispers and muttering.

"Anything you'd like to add, Brother Daniel?"

"Tristan and I have just come from talking with Sheriff Ellsworth. At this point he's treating the matter as a possible suicide. He's expecting an official finding from the coroner by the end of the day. If any of you saw or heard anything over the last few days that might be important, I'd appreciate it if you would share it with me before you talk to the sheriff or any of the deputies. But nobody here heard me say that. Sheriff Ellsworth is annoyed enough with me already, as Tristan here can attest."

There was some uneasy laughter at this.

"Meanwhile, if anyone approaches you and tries to get you to leave the property, please refer them to me. I now have legal responsibility for Mr. Swinford's affairs and as far as I'm concerned you can all stay here until doomsday, but some busybodies may try to make you think they know better. Just ignore them, but let me know about it immediately. As soon as the coroner releases the remains we'll be able to make funeral plans. You're all welcome to participate in any way you feel led to.

"Finally, please take this tragedy as a warning. It may be what the authorities insist it is but it may not. Given the circumstances, I think we'd be naïve to accept their explanation. The only safe thing is to view it as an attack on what you're doing here in New Jerusalem. A message that certain people want you stopped and a warning of the lengths they're willing to go to. So whatever you do, don't go out alone. I wouldn't go anywhere in a group of less than four or five. And even then you must be careful. Stay in populated areas. Stay inside at night if at all possible. And when you do go out, let somebody know where you're going and how long you expect to be gone. I'm afraid nobody's going to protect you but yourselves."

"I'll second that," Laddie nodded. "I know we're all pledged to follow Dr. King's philosophy of non-violence. But that doesn't mean we have to go out of our way to make ourselves targets. The best course of action is not to get into a situation where having to defend ourselves would even be an issue. Everybody understand?"

"I didn't go to class last night," Marytza O'Connor told us, tapping cigarette ash into an empty coffee cup. Daddy, Laddie, and I sat around the kitchen table with her. I studied her carefully, unwilling to admit even to myself the reason for my intense interest. While her accent was pure Boston, her appearance was pure Stockholm. Not used to thinking of the Irish as Scandinavians, I assumed she, like I, most closely resembled her relatives on her mother's side, whoever they might be. "I stayed here at the house. My grandfather had a serious stroke Thursday night, and I was waiting for a call from my mother. I might have to go back home at any time. I spoke to Mercer—Mr. Swinford, that is. . ."

"It's all right," Daddy said. "I'm sure he would appreciate being spoken of by his first name."

"O.K. Well, he knew I was expecting that call," she continued. "When we first got here, he told all of us to feel free to give out this number to our families and friends back home and to pick up the phone whenever it rang. He said he hardly ever got any calls so any that came in would probably be for one of us anyway. I guess it must have been about ten-thirty. I can't believe I didn't check. I'm usually such a clock watcher. But I was wrapped up in my book. Trying not to think about Grandpa, you know? The phone rang and I answered it. It was a man asking for Mercer. So I went to find him. He was in his room reading. After I fetched him I didn't go back downstairs. I didn't want him worrying that I might be eavesdropping. A few minutes later I heard him leave the house and drive off."

"He didn't speak to you before he left?" Daddy asked.

"No," she shook her head. "I didn't see him again after he went downstairs to take that call."

"What did the man on the phone say?" Laddie asked.

"He just asked to speak to Mr. Swinford," she said. "He didn't say anything else. And I don't know that I'd actually call him a man. No offense, Tristan, but he sounded more like someone your age. Of course, I could be wrong about that."

"Regardless of his age, it's the call itself that's significant," Laddie said. "Don't you agree, Daniel?"

"They had to get him there somehow," Daddy nodded.

"Of course," I said, finally getting the point. Realizing that there was a good chance someone I knew had lured Mercer Swinford to his death made my stomach churn. "They couldn't just kidnap him off the street."

"What is Daniel not telling me about this business?" Laddie asked, spotting me on my bench presses late that afternoon. Ever since moving in with us he had been working out with me in my basement gym. Taller and less heavily muscled than I, he was nevertheless markedly stronger, handling heavier weights than I could and doing more reps besides. Whether this was because his lifting technique was better than mine or was a result of his military training or that he was simply more determined, I hadn't been able to figure out.

"What do you mean?" I grunted, knocking out one last bench press just in case he was keeping count.

"Don't play games with me," he said. "You know what I'm talking about. I heard him take that call from Sheriff Ellsworth just before we came downstairs. The coroner says no foul play, but your father isn't buying it. And under the circumstances there's no reason he should. But why isn't he raising more hell about it? I don't think I'm just being dense. Does your father think the sheriff and the coroner are in on it? Is that why he isn't pushing them any harder?"

"I don't think Daddy believes they're involved," I said. "At least he doesn't think they're corrupt enough to cover up a murder to protect the killers. Isn't that what you're asking?"

"I guess."

"Anyway, Daddy pushed Ellsworth pretty hard this morning. I've never seen him talk to anyone that way. And it didn't get us anywhere."

"Well there must be some reason Ellsworth isn't going after the bad guys."

"Oh, there is."

"You know that? Or are you just speculating?"

"I was there," I told him. "Remember, I heard him with my own ears."

"So what is it?"

Suddenly I thought I knew how a cornered animal feels. I didn't see how I could possibly explain without revealing something about myself.

"Let's just say Daddy and I both understand that Ellsworth isn't going to budge," I said, getting off the bench and starting my upright rows. "Especially since the coroner has given him cover."

"He's not the only law in Mississippi," Laddie fumed. "Hell, there are federal marshals. There's the FBI. Daniel should get them involved."

"And they won't get anywhere fast without Ellsworth's cooperation," I said. "They'll have nothing that will stand up against the report Dr. Fenwick will issue. How long do you think they'll stay on the case once they realize that? There's nothing we can do but let it rest."

"Right," Laddie snorted. "A man is dead and you and your father want to let it rest."

"Listen to me, Laddie. I knew Mercer Swinford all my life. I cared about him. I wish I'd been a better friend to him but things didn't work out that way. Daddy's not the vindictive type. I'm sure you've noticed that by now. But I'd like to see the bastards who threw Mercer Swinford off that bridge rot in prison for the rest of their lives. Hell, send them to the electric chair and I'll throw the switch myself. But that's not ever going to happen, and there's nothing you or I can do about it. So believe me, it's harder for me to say 'let it rest' than it is for you to hear it."

"God, I'm sorry. I didn't mean to suggest that you and Daniel don't care."

"It's all right," I choked.

"No, it's not," he said. "Please don't cry."

I sniffed a couple of times. I wiped my eyes with the back of my hand. I couldn't look at him. What I really wanted to do was run and hide.

"I just don't understand," he said, almost inaudibly. "Why won't you explain it to me?"

"You won't leave it alone, will you?" I asked, struggling to master the quaver in my voice.

"Tristan."

"All right. Here it is. But if you breathe a word to anybody, if you say I told you this, I'll swear on a stack of Bibles I didn't. And I will never forgive you as long as I live. You got that?"

"I understand."

"I hope so," I grumbled. "'Cause I absolutely mean it. O.K. The thing is Mercer Swinford was a homosexual. He was never in trouble with the law for it or anything like that. At least not that Daddy or I know of. But the whole town knew he was that way. Don't ask me how people know a thing like that if a man tries his best to keep it a secret. They just knew it, is all. And as you'd expect, people had as little to do with him as possible. I have no idea how Daddy managed to keep him on as church organist all these years. Anyway, as far as Sheriff Ellsworth is concerned killing a homosexual is not a prosecutable offense in the state of Mississippi. I'm sure Dr. Fenwick agrees with him. It's not because they're corrupt. It's because they've lived here all their lives and they know how everything works. They don't see that any good whatever can come of calling it what it is because in the long run whoever did it will walk away scot free anyhow. That's how Ellsworth put it to Daddy this morning, and that's why even though he disagrees with it he's going to go along. It's pretty near killing him."

IX

Daddy shocked Frank Stephens the mortician speechless by insisting on an open casket viewing for Mercer Swinford and compounded the outrage by ordering five hours of visitation to be held on Sunday afternoon. Not that he, or I, expected anyone to actually show up at the funeral home during that time. Saturday evening the relations in South Carolina had expressed their total lack of interest in anything other than what they stood to inherit, adding to Daddy's silent fury. We didn't anticipate any better from Mercer's neighbors or fellow church members, but after a cold lunch we walked over to the Stephens and Murray Funeral Home still in our church clothes just in case anyone surprised us. Even if nobody came to view the body we'd at least be comfortable, since the air conditioning made it the coolest place in town.

By the time Daddy finished putting the fear of God into Frank Stephens, he did his level best. But a corpse was a corpse. This one, though not noticeably disfigured, didn't resemble the departed so much as it did a zombie from a horror movie or a vampire snoozing away the hours until sundown. Which wasn't at all how I wanted Mercer Swinford to appear in death. Until I looked into the casket, I guess I must have been hoping that it had all been a terrible mistake and that the dead man wasn't Mercer Swinford at all. This unwelcome confrontation with reality made me wobbly, and failing to convince myself it was merely because I'd had very little sleep and hadn't eaten more than a few bites since the morning before, I sank into the nearest chair like an antebellum virgin suffering the vapors. I didn't move until Laddie and a contingent of the volunteers arrived for a short, subdued visit.

"It's horrible, isn't it?" Marytza O'Connor sobbed, enveloping me in cigarette breath as we hugged. "Poor Mercer. Nobody deserves to die that way."

* * *

I was on the point of dozing off when Rev. Isaiah Washington and his wife Savannah came in, accompanied by Rev. Maurice St. Jacques Lincoln. I couldn't think of anyplace in the whole town more segregated than this funeral home, and the audacity of their arrival left me wide eyed and open mouthed. I lurched to my feet and steadied myself with a hand on the coffin as Daddy welcomed them.

"You look so tired, Tristan," Savannah Washington said, laying a gentle hand on my shoulder.

"I've spent all afternoon trying to send him home," Daddy said, "but he won't listen. And that's not the worst of it. He proposes to sit with Mr. Swinford all night. I wish you'd talk some sense into him."

"It's hardly possible with young men his age," Mrs. Washington smiled. "If he's even half as stubborn as our boys, I wouldn't waste my breath trying."

"I know," Daddy said, "but I shudder to think what his mother would say if she found out I let him."

"You've got a point there. We mothers can be right fierce."

"Brother Daniel," Rev. Washington said, staring hard into the coffin, "I've been authorized by the deacons of our congregation to invite you to move Mr. Swinford's funeral to our church sanctuary. As he died in our struggle, they don't feel it's appropriate for him to have to be buried from a funeral parlor."

"I bring a similar invitation from my people," Rev. Lincoln said.

"But surely they must know about. . ." Daddy stammered. "Surely they must all have heard what people said about Mr. Swinford."

"It was mentioned in the deacons' discussion of the matter," Rev. Lincoln admitted.

"In our deliberations as well," Rev. Washington nodded.

"We are all sinners in the eyes of God," Rev. Lincoln said. "We all fall short in many ways. And it's not the place of any one of us to sit in judgement. The holy scriptures are crystal clear on that point. 'Judge not, that ye be not judged.' We are commanded to love our neighbors as ourselves. The second great commandment of our Lord Jesus. It's not merely a suggestion."

"'Let him who is blameless cast the first stone'," Rev. Washington quoted. "'Do unto others as you would have them do unto you.' 'For as much as ye did it to the least of these. . .' There's plenty of teachings in the Good Book to give us guidance. Even in a situation such as this."

"Mr. Swinford is one of our people now," Rev. Lincoln asserted. "Our congregations know that. We musn't let his courage and generority be forgotten. The Lord Jesus won't turn him away at the gates of Paradise. We need look no further than the parable of the Good Samaritan to understand that. We won't turn him away from our door."

"This is so tretnemdously generous of both your congregations," Daddy told them, and in his voice was the sound of tears.

"He didn't shrink from his Christian duty, Brother Daniel," Savannah Washington said. "Neither do we."

"But do you truly think this is a good idea?" Daddy asked. "With things so tense around town? People are stirred up enough already. There's no telling what might happen if someone decides we're trying to make a cause of this."

"That's very true," Rev. Lincoln said, looking infinitely grateful that Daddy had had the good sense to voice a reasonable objection to their proposals. "We might be seen as trying to antagonize the authorities."

"More than they already are," Daddy nodded.

"Indeed," Rev. Washington said, looking nearly as relieved himself. "We wouldn't want to do anything to make matters worse. And if you think it best that the funeral service be held here as originally planned, we wouldn't presume to disagree with you."

"Not for a moment," Rev. Lincoln said.

"But the Lord did lay it on our hearts to extend this invitation," Rev. Washington said, "and you must understand that we extend it sincerely."

"Of course you do."

"So we'll abide by your decision, and the Lord will take care of the rest."

"And God love you for it," Daddy smiled. "God love you and God bless you."

I didn't keep Mercer Swinford's remains company that night. It wasn't Daddy's remonstrances, or Laddie's either, or even what Mama would say when she heard. Nor was it from fear of what might happen to me alone there in the empty mortuary. I simply wasn't man enough to stay. My intentions were noble but I couldn't live up to them. My loss of resolve mortified me but by the end of the scheduled hours for visitation I was starving. Daddy's observation that it would do Mercer Swinford no good and offer no lesson to anyone if I were found snoring and drooling beside the casket the next morning was all the excuse I needed to chicken out. It was uncanny the way I kept finding opportunities to disappoint myself. When Daddy left I went with him, and a few silent minutes later we were sitting at the kitchen table staring gloomily at a supper of cold leftovers. I yawned uncontrollably and chewed on some watermelon pickle while Daddy took what seemed an in ordinate amount of time to assemble a chicken salad sandwich.

"Son," he finally said, looking down at his food with an expression of profound discouragement, "the day you were born, I promised myself I'd do everything in my power not ever to become a disappointment to you."

"I'm not disappointed in you," I said. "Have I done anything to make you think I am?"

"No," he said, "but I don't see how you can help but be."

"Why?"

"The murderers will probably never be brought to justice."

"The murderers have their own consciences and God Himself to answer to," I snapped. "So do Sheriff Ellsworth and Dr. Fenwick. I don't see how anybody white in this whole town sleeps at night, as far as that goes."

"I'm not asking you to go easy on me," Daddy complained. "That only makes me feel worse."

"Last I knew you were a Baptist preacher. I don't remember anybody making you chief of police around here, or nominating you to replace J. Edgar Hoover. So eat your sandwich and stop talking nonsense."

"I wanted to be the best father any boy ever had," he said, hanging his head.

"Who said you're not? Now will you stop moping and pass me that ham?"

When the telephone rang, I nearly jumped out of my skin. For all their insistence that no one go out alone and especially not after dark, my father and our houseguest were apparently incapable of taking their own advice. They were absent, they hadn't told me where they were headed, and they hadn't said how long they would be gone. Three strikes and you're out at the old ball game. 'Physician, heal thyself' and assorted other clichés. I knew exactly what kind of hell I'd have caught from both of them if I had pulled such a stunt.

Sunday night, and once again I had the house to myself. I had the doors locked and only the upstairs windows were open. I told myself it wasn't because I was frightened but that I didn't want the repercussions of either of them finding my precautions wanting.

"Hello."

"Tristan."

"Mama."

"How are you, son?"

That familiar voice was almost enough to bring me to tears. I felt like a three year old who's just been found after getting lost in the woods. I gulped back the lump in my throat before speaking again.

"All right. How are things there? Are you and the girls O.K?"

"We're fine. They miss you. I haven't said anything to them about what's going on. They don't need to have that worry."

"Daddy's not here. He must have gone to church somewhere."

"I know. That's why I'm calling now. I know better than to expect any honest answers out of you if he's listening."

I didn't argue. Daddy had always been the soft touch at our house.

"How bad is he?"

"Worse than I've ever seen him."

"That's what I was afraid of."

"He sits alone in your bedroom for hours on end. He fixes food and then doesn't eat it."

"What else?"

"He believes he's failed," I blurted. "He believes he's letting everyone down. Sometimes I just want to shake him until his teeth rattle. I don't know what to do, Mama. I don't know how to help him."

"I know, son." Her voice was calm. "If it's any consolation, I don't know either. He made me promise not to come home when we talked last night, and I don't know what alternative that leaves me."

"I heard him," I said.

"Are you frightened? It's all right if you are. Anyone with a lick of sense would be."

"Yes," I choked.

"Is it bad?"

"Uh huh."

"Do you want to come up here?"

"I'm more afraid of leaving him alone than of being here myself."

"Is that the truth?"

"I'm afraid he'll just collapse."

"He won't, Tristan. He's stronger than you and I give him credit for. He always has been. We see another side of him because we're the only ones he can allow to see it. But he'll be all right."

"I hope so."

"You can't stay there just for his sake."

"I'm not," I insisted. "Not really. I just feel I belong here right now."

"It's all right if you change your mind," she said. "He'll never hold it against you if you decide you have to leave."

"I know."

"Don't leave it too late. Promise?"

"I promise."

"Don't tell him I called, all right?"

I waited until the house was completely silent before getting out of bed. I pulled on my clothes and sneaked downstairs as if walking on eggs. Thanks to Mama's sense of order, I found everything I was looking for within seconds of reaching the basement and I was outside in the dark rose garden not long after that.

I had considered bringing a flashlight along but feared it would only slow me down. I knew from memory which bushes bore the yellow roses and I located the best blooms by touch. The thorns made cutting the stems tricky, but my fingertips soon educated themselves and after that it went fairly quickly. I stopped when I had filled two buckets and went back inside. I worked in the glow of the bare light bulb hanging over Mama's potting bench. I stripped off excess leaves and trimmed the ends of the stems with sharp diagonal cuts like I'd seen Mama do probably a thousand times. I saved the most perfect of all the buds to wear in my lapel. I would wear it like Mercer Swinford had always worn that single yellow rosebud on Sunday mornings. I had no idea what its significance might have been for him all those years, but sitting beside his casket that afternoon I had become obsessed with the necessity of offering nothing less than this as my personal tribute.

X

"Where did you get those gorgeous roses?" Marytza O'Connor asked as I emerged from the kitchen. "Why, there must be at least four dozen of them there. I ransacked the florist downtown for something nice yesterday afternoon but I never saw anything like those."

"Mama raises the best roses in town," I mumbled, feeling my deep blush rise instantaneously.

"I heard her roses were the best in the county," Laddie corrected me.

"It figures," Marytza nodded. "From what I hear, there's nothing she can't do."

"I'm afraid I haven't been taking good enough care of the bushes lately."

"Are you joking?" Marytza gasped. "They're astonishing. And the fragrance."

"Maybe you'd better drive," I said, handing the Volkswagen keys to Laddie. "I'm a little shaky."

"Fine," he smiled.

"You should always wear blue," Marytza mused, fingering the sleeve of my navy suit. "It's the perfect color for you. Don't you think so, Laddie?"

"Absolutely," Laddie agreed.

Marytza's beauty unnerved me. She could easily have been a fashion model or actress. Indeed, she bore more than a passing resemblance to Grace Kelly. Yet she gave the impression that she was completely oblivious to her looks. She certainly didn't go out of her way to call attention to her appearance, unlike most of the girls and women I knew. This paradox made her all the more stunning. Though there was nothing unfeminine about her, there was at the same time a swaggering aggressiveness to the way she carried herself that was completely unlike any of the familiar types of southern womanhood that constituted my entire, though obviously limited, experience. Combined with a quick intelligence she did nothing whatever to disguise, it said emphatically that as far as she was concerned a woman's place was wherever she wanted it to be, and that any man who thought of her as fragile or weak or likely to find herself in need of rescue was in for a rude awakening. She could bring home her own bacon, and heroes on white horses belonged between the covers of novels she'd never dream of wasting her time reading. I could visualize her piloting experimental aircraft, scuba diving for sunken treasure off the Yucutan, or scaling Himalayan peaks. These images came far more readily to mind than scenes of her gossiping with the girls down at the beauty parlor or whipping up angel food cakes or bringing her husband his pipe and slippers when he came in from a long day at the office. I knew that my sisters would adore her and aspire to similar levels of intrepidness when they grew into women. I imagined Mama and her playing Scrabble to a draw.

It was even easier to see her as the ideal woman for a man like Laddie. Such a pairing seemed inevitable. They would read each other's minds, complete each other's sentences, and produce scandalously attractive children who would win Olympic medals and Nobel Prizes. My certainty that the two of them were a couple grew every time I saw them together, though there was nothing overt in their behavior to suggest this. But what did I know of the courtship rituals and mating habits of yankees? Even normally inclined locals were all but incomprehensible to freaks of nature like me.

Overpowering as Marytza was, I didn't find her at all attractive in the conventional sense, though as a partner in crime I reckoned she'd be terrific, indefatigably loyal, dependable in a tight spot, and not given to panic, rather like the quintessential Eagle Scout except with the difference of her anatomy. And, indeed, she had given every indication she'd enjoy having me as a friend. But pal or co-conspirator are not the roles small town boys are expected to cast such glamorous women in, and that was a problem. I knew I should have been exhibiting unmistakable signs of a raging crush. The degree to which Marytza left me unstirred seemed as if it must be painfully obvious to anyone who observed me in her company, Laddie of course being the main focus of my anxiety. As her boyfriend, he couldn't help but be extremely sensitive to her attentiveness to me, and my failure to respond like a red blooded American male had to stick out like a sore thumb. How could he fail to connect the dots? How could anyone? I felt like a laboratory specimen on display.

I stood beside the grave with my armload of roses and painfully few fellow mourners filed past. Daddy's graveside remarks had been even briefer than usual. He was exhausted, of course. In addition, I knew he felt truly defeated for perhaps the first time in his life. And what could he say to this group of people who had barely known Mercer Swinford and were only present out of an admittedly commendable sense of duty? I knew the apparent futility of a funeral without any true mourners weighed heavily on him. He needed huddled relatives to comfort in their loss and affirm in their faith, not these minimally involved strangers who wanted for nothing he was prepared to offer. He longed for something more than the sterile emptiness of that sweltering afternoon. As a Baptist, he recognized nothing sacramental in the ritual, no benefit which might accrue to the departed from the prayers and scripture readings. That wasn't what justified his supreme efforts.

Of course there was a mourner present. Not that I had any standing to claim such a status for myself. But over the hours since first hearing the news of Mercer Swinford's death, I had come to sense more and more clearly that his passing marked a turning point in my life. I seemed to see myself standing with Adam and Eve as we stared back at the gates of Eden obstructed by flaming swords. For the first time in my life I saw myself set absolutely apart from others, from my friends and classmates and the uncomplicated lives they would lead, perhaps even from Mama, Daddy, and my sisters. I saw doors slamming shut and bridges burning behind me. I sensed all this, but for the life of me I couldn't visualize what sort of future might lie ahead of me. I felt as if I were standing alone at the edge of an abyss.

"It's all right if you don't feel up to helping out with class tonight," Laddie told me, breaking the gloomy silence of the supper table several hours later.

"What are you talking about?"

"I just thought you could stand to stay in and rest tonight."

"The hell I will," I said. Daddy was locked in his room upstairs, but even if he'd heard this profanity I suspected he was beyond protesting it. "I heard what Barry Cochran told you at the funeral. About how they got six people registered to vote over at the courthouse this morning."

"I know it doesn't sound like a lot," Laddie said.

"I live here, and I'm in a better position to judge," I told him. "Six black people registered to vote is practically a miracle. Even if you're determined to be tyrannized by arithmetic, it's still six more than there were this time last Friday. And now that they've seen it happen, all kinds of folks are going to crawl out of the woodwork. Classes are going to be jam packed after this. So it's no time for anybody to be taking the night off because they're a little tired and don't feel up to it."

"Tristan, you're not just a little tired. You've had a horrible shock. You're exhausted. Anybody can see that. You've been working way too hard at acting brave. Nobody's going to think any less of you if this one time you're something less than perfect. So go easy on yourself."

"Is that what they told you in the Israeli Defense Force? Go easy on yourself?"

"No."

"What would you have done if they had?"

"Laughed in their faces, probably," Laddie admitted. "Either that or fallen down in a dead faint. But it's hardly the same situation."

"You don't think so?"

"Israel has never been at peace in its whole history. A decade and a half now since independence and we still have to fight constantly. No one in the whole country is ever safe. Our enemies are everywhere and they never give us a moment's rest."

"And there's peace around here? People are safe in their houses? They go about their business as they see fit and nobody minds? Mercer Swinford's not really dead, and six hundred more black people will register to vote tomorrow morning without incident and I can afford to take the night off? Who the hell are you kidding? There's more to do now than there ever was. And what happens at the end of the summer when you all go back north to school? Who'll be left here to keep fighting then?"

* * *

Zuleika Jefferson's front porch light was out when we arrived that evening. The front door was closed, and only the dimmest of glows could be seen in the living room windows. We climbed out of the car and walked silently onto the porch, where Laddie rapped tentatively on the frame of the screen door. After a long moment, the front door opened no more than an inch, letting out only a sliver of light.

"Who is it?" Zuleika Jefferson asked in a hoarse whisper. "What you want?"

"It's us," Laddie said. "Vladimir Zitronblatt and Tristan Bentley. We're here to start class."

"Class? Ain' no class tonight," she snorted. "Ain' you gen'men heard? They killed that there Mercer Swinford. It all over now."

"No, it isn't, Zuleika," I told her. "Not as long as you or any of your family or friends still want to register to vote."

"You'll see, Mr. Tristan," she hissed. "All them yankee college boys and girls, they go home now. They go 'way 'fore somebody else get killed."

"I don't know anything about that. But I'm not going anywhere. I'm not like them. I don't have anywhere to go any more than you do. Got no job, either. So I might as well go on helping you all learn to read. What do you say?"

"Don' know. Nobody done come tonight. They all think you too scairt now. They all think it ain' no point goin' on wid it."

"Do they still want to learn to read?" I asked her. "Do they still want to be able to vote someday?"

"You know they does."

"Have they given up?"

"'Course not."

"Well, I haven't, either."

"'Spose not, or you wouldn' be here."

"Then why are we wasting time?"

"You best come on in, I reckon," she said, swinging wide the door and unlatching the screen. "I'll send my Viola 'roun and tell 'em all you's here."

I waited for more than an hour after I heard Laddie go to bed, listening for any movement in the house. Then I got up. Moving as silently as I could in the darkness of my room, I pulled on the clothing I had laid out earlier, a black, long sleeved turtleneck that seemed to have shrunk several sizes since I'd worn it last, my darkest pair of trousers, my quietest pair of shoes. I pulled a maroon baseball cap as low over my face as it would go. I put on navy blue mittens I couldn't for the life of me remember the origins of and tucked them inside the tight cuffs of my shirt.

I stood listening at my door for a long time before stepping out into the hall. I would only ever have one opportunity to leave the house undetected. If either Daddy or Laddie caught me, no explanation would suffice. I'd be under house arrest more or less until the end of time. So I crept down the hall holding my breath, and my descent of the stairs felt like it took a good five minutes. In the basement, I retrieved the remaining two dozen yellow roses from the refrigerator and carefully wrapped them in the length of dark gray burlap I had found in Miss Althea Chandler's garage.

I slipped out the back door as silent as a ghost. I had plotted my route carefully, all six miles of it. I had laid out a different route for my return. I believed I had anticipated every single danger spot along my route. I knew the exact location of each place of concealment where I might hole up at the first sign of trouble. I had rehearsed the journey over and over in my mind's eye until I honestly believed I could make it blindfolded.

I sweated profusely inside my clothing and silently thanked God for the thick clouds which had gathered during the afternoon and still hung over the town, obliterating the moon and stars. Determined as I was, I wasn't certain I could have made this pilgrimage in moonlight, and the gloom the clouds provided was small enough price to pay. I evaded each and every loose and squeaky plank on the back porch and a few strides past Mama's rose garden, I entered the deep shadows behind the garage. The darkness welcomed me, and I prayed for continued invisibility.

Past the edge of the thicket, I could just make out the two lanes of blacktop and the bridge beyond. Here I would be at my most exposed. And here, if I hadn't been careful enough, if I'd been followed through the alleys, the orchards, the fields, and the gulleys, I might encounter the danger I'd done everything in my power to elude.

Would I be luckier than Mercer Swinford had been? Would I be able to hang onto consciousness as I hit the dark water? Would I be able to swim to safety in this clothing so tight it almost cut off my circulation? Would I be able to escape my attackers somewhere downstream and make my way home to see another dawn? I had already chosen the bend in the river beyond which I hoped I might crawl unobserved into the overhanging brush. I crouched in the bushes for a last moment and untied my shoes so I'd be able to kick them off at a moment's notice.

Then I rose slowly to my full height, relishing a good stretch after six miles covered bent over to aid my concealment. Crouching like that would do me no more good. I stepped out of the thicket into darkness only fractionally less impenetrable. I reached the pavement and felt its unaccustomed hardness under my feet. Then I was on the bridge itself, walking along the left rail. I could feel the extra dampness in the air. I could hear the faint whisper of the water moving past the banks and bridge piers far below. I had no idea where exactly Mercer Swinford had been flung into eternity, so I made the middle of the river my objective.

There wasn't a breath of wind and there was no sound. I had traveled slowly and I reckoned I must have been gone from the house for the best part of three hours. I probably had no more than two hours of darkness to cover my return journey, so I didn't dare linger. But I couldn't rush this, either. So when I reached the place I'd selected in my mind over twenty-four hours earlier, I took my time. I crouched down and laid my bundle on the blacktop, which was still warm from the day's sunshine. I carefully unwrapped the roses. Grasping them in my mittened hands, I leaned on the railing and buried my face in their fragrance for a last time. If I had dared to speak, it would have been to promise Mercer Swinford I would never forget him and that I would live whatever life remained to me in a manner worthy of that memory. Then I flung the bundle into the blackness before me, ears straining for the splash as they reached the water, eyes straining downward for any glimpse I might have of their ghostly brightness in the abyss.

I heard no splash above the sound of the river, though I waited for far longer than gravity could possibly have taken to do its work. I saw no shadowy glimmer below me, though I stared until tears obscured my sight.

XI

There was light drizzle that morning. The uneven blacktop we ran along between fields dark with row on row of cotton plants was shiny, wet enough to be treacherous underfoot. That's exactly what I thought had happened when, in the proverbial blink of an eye, I found myself face down in the ditch that ran alongside Weston Granville's south forty. Laddie must have lost his footing and in crashing to the ground had taken me down with him.

"Ow. What the hell are you doing?"

But in no more time than it took me to grunt that out, he had flipped me over onto my back and spread himself lengthwise on top of me, covering my mouth with a large, bony hand. That's when I finally heard the rifle fire, but even that wasn't enough to command my full attention. What did was the look in Laddie's eyes as he stared deeper into me than anyone ever had.

"Don't move," he whispered. As if I needed to be told. As if it were obligatory that someone provide an impregnably innocuous excuse for our position and he couldn't wait any longer for me to do it. And I didn't move. Unless you count breathing. By then he had removed his hand from my mouth. But I didn't say anything, and he didn't stop staring at me. I didn't stop staring back. I had no idea what he thought his eyes were saying, but I knew what mine were. As mortifying as that was, I couldn't help myself. It would have taken more than a high powered hunting rifle to force me to look away before he did, or think about baseball, or inaudibly repeat the multiplication tables. Miraculously, my body retained control of itself.

We lay like that for a long time in the wet grass at the bottom of the ditch. We lay there even though the firing had stopped just a few moments after we took cover.

All that time Laddie's eyes blazed into mine. I could have sworn he was counting my heartbeats. I was ready to lie there with Laddie on top of me for the rest of my life, his chest slick and hairy against mine and his breathing in rhythm with my own.

Then I heard a car engine fire up perhaps a quarter mile away. The V-8 rumble was unmistakable, but I didn't want to admit that to myself any more than I wanted to admit all the other things I was thinking and feeling. I listened to the rise and fall of revs as the driver shifted up through the gears—racing shifts, a four speed transmission. I listened as the sound moved away in the direction of town. Next thing I knew Laddie had rolled off me and straightened up to where he could see above the level of the weeds. And only then did Bobby Davidson begin to exist again, but I knew as sure as the tide rises and falls that I'd never be the same. My feelings had been pretty hypothetical up to then. Now I had proof.

"I think the coast is clear," Laddie said.

I really doubted that, much as I wanted to believe it. But we probably weren't thinking about the same thing.

"Oh, my God," he muttered.

"What?"

"They got Old Shep."

"You won't tell Daddy about this," I insisted as we trudged back home through what had turned into a driving rain.

"The hell I won't."

"You can't. You know what he'll do."

"What he should have done three weeks ago," Laddie said. "Send you to Chattanooga the minute Mercer Swinford was buried. I shouldn't have let you talk him out of it. I've been kicking myself ever since."

"I'll just come back," I threatened. "Cross my heart, I will. Put me on a bus and I'll get off at the first stop and hitchhike back."

"God," he shook his head. "Just how stubborn are you?"

"You don't want to find out."

"Tristan, don't you see how dangerous it is for you around here?"

"Didn't you say not ten minutes ago that those were only warning shots? That anybody who could have shot Old Shep at that range could easily have gotten either or both of us if they'd been a mind to?"

"Yes, I said that. But that's the whole point. We've been varying our schedule and our route every morning since Mercer Swinford died, and they're sending a message that that's not good enough. They want us to know that they can get us any time they want to."

"And that's news?"

"Isn't it?"

"To you, maybe. I've known it all along," I said.

"Then why won't you listen to reason?"

"If anybody approaches me with any, I'll give it due consideration. Until then, here's the thing. My father needs me. Worse than he knows. If I leave now and something happens to him I'll never be able to forgive myself. Never. I'll spend the rest of my life wondering if I could have saved him by staying around. The rest of my life, you hear? You can't make me risk something like that. Nobody can."

"What if Daniel makes you?" he asked.

"He won't if he never hears what happened."

"You're not serious."

"Try me."

"Even if I don't tell him, who's to say he won't find out some other way?" he asked.

"What other way is there?"

"Old Shep is dead."

"Old Shep was already old when God was a little boy. Nobody's going to think twice about it when we say he collapsed and died while we were out running this morning. Nobody's going to fly any flags at half mast, either."

"When *we* tell them?"

"Please, Laddie."

"You really won't go to Chattanooga?"

"No."

"Even if Daniel and I both beg you?"

"Even then."

"All right. I'll keep my mouth shut about this on one condition."

"What's that?"

"No more morning runs. It's too big a risk."

"But."

"But nothing," he said, in a tone that told me I'd get no further arguing with him. "We'll do longer workouts in the basement to make up for it. I'll show you some conditioning drills we used to do in the IDF when we were confined to fortified positions. You either agree to that or I tell Daniel everything, which is probably what I should do anyway. At least then I won't have your blood on my hands. You don't want him on your conscience, but I don't want you on mine."

Telling Miss Althea Chandler that Old Shep had died was harder than I had expected and not merely because I was concealing the real cause of death from a woman who'd been my Sunday School teacher during some of my tenderest years and my constant benefactor ever since. I knew perhaps better than any of her friends and relatives that despite her perpetual complaints and lamentations about his temperament, smell, mangy coat, woefully unreliable house training and absolute refusal to submit to even the most minimal degree of domestication, she was genuinely and deeply fond of him. To all intents and purposes he was the ghost of her long dead husband, and I had heard enough gossip about Ollie Chandler over the years to suspect that Old Shep spent his days suffering for that man's sins.

Miss Althea received the news with visible but carefully modulated distress in the time honored manner of southern womanhood. I recognized the slight quiver of the chin, the eyes brimming with tears which would be dabbed away with a hankie before they could actually be shed, and the fatalistic tone of voice in which she uttered a few simple platitudes about the tenuous and transitory existence of all living, breathing creatures before sending me off to the orchard to resume my labors as the profoundest expressions of grief she was capable of. I ached for her but knew better than to hang about and make a nuisance of myself offering comfort. She'd want solitude more than anything else. In a region with a higher proportion of teetotalers in the population than any other in North America, solitude was the drug of choice for grieving womanhood, and I knew she'd only feel better if I left her alone to have her fix.

I knew she was on the mend when she called me back to the house at lunchtime and served me her special deviled ham sandwiches and brought out the pickled watermelon rind for good measure. These delicacies had never been known to last more than five minutes on any pot luck table no matter how high she heaped the platter or how many jars she set out. I knew more than one of her missionary circle friends had spent long hours in the kitchen attempting to duplicate the recipes, and I had prayed more than once that her gratitude to Daddy for his years of selfless pastoral care and her often expressed approval of the way Mama ran her household and raised her children would sooner or later result in these secrets' being divulged.

No luminary was ever honored with a finer memorial feast. Each bite of those sandwiches and each sip of that fresh made lemonade spoke volumes of Miss Althea's recognition of me as Old Shep's only other mourner in the whole town and her profound appreciation that I was present to share her grief. She sat on the back porch with me as I ate, and we bade our farewells to him by way of reminiscences concerning his more or less constant enormities, many of which predated any conscious memories of him I could summon. The tenor of Miss Althea's running commentary was that he had been blessed with a rich, full life. She had provided him with as safe and comfortable a home as ever such a ne'er-do-well canine had enjoyed. As for me, every dog should have his very own boy, and Miss Althea seemed to consider that he had been more than fortunate in that regard as well.

Laddie was preoccupied nearly to the point of catatonia when we met in the basement that afternoon to work out. After what had happened that morning, I'd have walked on nails before I'd have mentioned it to him. Because I understood it all too well. He knew the truth about me, and every moment spent in my company now was much more duty than pleasure. He knew about me, and our close physical proximity down there in our makeshift gym was little short of unbearable. I was sure it was no coincidence that this was the first time he'd ever worked out in a t-shirt and sweat pants instead of his usual uniform consisting of skimpy gym shorts. He must have been miserable in all that clothing but apparently thought it beat the alternative of giving me the opportunity to stare at so much of him. It was as if I'd suddenly grown horns and a tail and been issued a pitchfork, though I wasn't sure that particular figure had any significance in either Israeli or Marxist mythology.

My heart was hardly in our workout that afternoon. Forcing myself to greater efforts than ever before failed either to elicit his notice, much less approval, or pull my thoughts away from my own mortification, and the more distant Laddie seemed the more heartsick I felt.

XII

Within a couple more days Marytza O'Connor had all but moved in with us. She still slept over at the Swinford house but her spare time was spent under our roof, most but by no means all of it in Laddie's company. She was with us at breakfast time receiving instruction in southern cookery from the master chef. When she wasn't over at the courthouse keeping the registrars honest you might well find her in our basement browsing through the refugee library. Her hijinks enlivened dinner time and her erudite conversation was welcome at any hour. After dessert each evening Laddie and I would drop her off at the evening class she taught. Afterward, we'd pick her up on our way home. Laddie would drop me at our house and drive her on over to the Swinford place. Hours later, barricaded in my bedroom, I'd hear Laddie return in the Volkswagen.

Daddy welcomed her with open arms. He missed a feminine presence around the house terribly. But it was more than just the absence of Mama and my sisters that contributed to the funk Marytza helped relieve. He was accustomed to the more or less constant adoration of generations of church ladies, and going cold turkey had taken a serious toll. The attention Marytza paid him was the best medicine anyone could have prescribed short of a full scale reunion with the Bentley womenfolk. I don't mean to suggest that anything improper was ever in prospect. If ever a man was incapable of violating his marriage vows, that man was Daddy. And at the same time it was as obvious as a sunrise that Marytza only had eyes for Laddie. So what she and Daddy offered each other was the kind of companionship between man and woman that's always been the rarest of commodities, friendship and mutual appreciation uncomplicated by sexual undercurrents. You could wander into the kitchen or living room at odd times during the day and find them so intent on their discussion of the Progressive Movement, the poetry of William Cullen Bryant, or the theological implications of Einsteinian physics that the world could have ended without either of them noticing it. In addition, they shared a juvenile sense of humor that left Laddie and me rolling our eyes and quickly exiting rooms. She was the precocious tomboy kid sister Daddy had never had or one of his own daughters in fifteen years time. I didn't in the least regret the passing of the spectacle of him wandering around the house like Hamlet's ghost in search of an audience.

Marytza's presence sweetened Laddie's mood, too. His sulks vanished overnight. He no longer held his tongue around me or shoved his nose into a book he obviously wasn't reading when I entered a room. As long as she was present he was himself again. We went back to spending hours on end together without him evidencing the profound discomfort that so distressed me. Marytza apparently made it safe for him to be, or at least act like, my friend. I recognized this as no more than a temporary solution. Things between us would never be the way they had been before he found me out. And our fragile pretense of friendship would never survive her absence if she were called to her grandfather's bedside back in Boston. But it would all be over soon anyway. The summer was drawing on, and whether their business was finished or not Laddie and Marytza and their co-workers would return north like so many migrating birds. By then I'd be God only knew where myself and I didn't expect I'd see or hear from them again.

I had known from the start that the task of clearing Miss Althea's orchard ranked with the Labors of Hercules and since I didn't even remotely qualify as a mythical hero I knew better than to expect to finish it. Miss Althea must have sensed this as clearly as I did but she never complained about my slow progress. Her memories of the Civilian Conservation Corps, in which two of her cousins had served for several years during the Great Depression, seemed ample justification for our arrangement. It wasn't that I didn't put forth my noblest effort. Every day I pruned and chopped and trimmed until I could hardly stand. But it quickly became apparent the job was simply too large for one man. At least a man not blessed with mechanized equipment. The neglect had been allowed to go on for far too long. An additional factor in the equation was the local climate, in which vegetation grew visibly over night. It was great for the farmers. It made kitchen gardens flourish almost beyond usefulness. But that unbridled fertility made Miss Althea's project very much a three steps forward, two steps back proposition. I doubted she would live to see the day when her orchard's former glory was restored.

I'd have cut out my tongue before I'd have complained about either the difficulty or futility of the work. I was grateful beyond words to be kept busy with taxing physical activity—particularly once Laddie went haywire—doubly grateful for the two dollars an hour Daddy had pronounced excessive but which I deposited faithfully in my savings account every week, and most grateful of all that Miss Althea's cooking continued sublime. Every noontime brought a feast fit for the gods on Mount Olympus.

One day not long after Old Shep's death I was eating salmon salad served in a pair of hollowed out beefsteak tomatoes that had been picked just that morning when a chance remark of Miss Althea's reminded me of something I had all but forgotten.

"Mamie Ellsworth was telling me on the phone this morning that Junior's Ellie May has her litter of pups just about weaned. Said I should come by and pick one out on account of Old Shep being gone now. Beagles aren't that big, of course, but they're right yappy and that makes them good watch dogs. Said she was sure Junior'll give me a good price on one and maybe even a special deal if I take two. That woman knows a thing or two about being a grannie."

"Junior's in town?" I gaped. Miss Althea must have gotten the story garbled. "Didn't he go into the Marines?"

"He came home weeks ago," she said, peering quizzically at me. "Hadn't you heard?"

"No, ma'am."

"Strange Bobby Davidson didn't mention it to you," she mused.

I shrugged. I wasn't surprised by that part of the story. It wasn't the kind of thing Bobby would have bothered to tell me. It didn't have anything to do with either of us. But perhaps I'd been mistaken in thinking so.

"Just between you and me," Miss Althea lowered her voice as if we were smack in the middle of a women's missionary circle tea and might be overheard, "I think

Junior must have gotten into some kind of trouble in boot camp. I don't believe for a minute he's on special leave like Mamie said. I think he's home for good."

"You're sure about that?" I asked. "Miss Mamie didn't get him mixed up with one of her three dozen other grandchildren?"

"Why Tristan, I'll swan if you don't look like you just saw a ghost."

It wasn't what I'd seen. It was what I'd heard. Junior's Pontiac GTO, his graduation present from his father, Sheriff Ellsworth, was the first one sold in the county. With its three two barrel carburetors and dual exhausts, it made a sound like no other car around. Lying in Weston Granville's ditch, I simply hadn't believed my ears.

Eugene Ellsworth, Junior, was my long-time nemesis for reasons I had never fully understood. I was in good company. Nobody else in New Jerusalem understood either. Once, after a particularly dramatic incident at a Sunday School picnic when he'd fallen out of a tree I'd escaped his bullying by climbing farther up than he could follow, his mortified mother had begged Daddy to pray that Jesus would help the two of us get along. Divine intervention didn't take, though his broken leg did heal in record time. His obvious jealousy of my friendship with Bobby Davidson had never made sense, either, given that he was a full two years older than we were and shouldn't have wanted to have anything to do with either of us. He had failed second grade, which hadn't done anything for his disposition, but I didn't see how that could have had anything to do with me. Even after being held back he was one grade ahead of us and he'd always had plenty of friends his own age. Bucky Duncan, for one, and he was nobody to sneeze at, having been starting quarterback three years running.

But there hadn't been any mistaking his animosity. Old Shep had taken a hunk out of his backside when he'd tried to beat me up on the way home from school one afternoon, but I doubted Junior had even recognized him as the same animal who had accompanied Laddie and me the morning of his death. Besides, Junior lacked the attention span to have held a grudge for that long, except the one against me. This was all assuming it had actually been Junior taking those shots. He might just have been the driver of the getaway car. It was exactly the kind of thing a bully like him would do, and I figured he considered he had plenty of reason after all the times last fall when Coach Ussery had benched him and sent me in at quarterback.

That didn't make him a killer, however, and the more certain I became that he'd indeed been the one pulling the trigger out there in the Granville's cotton field the less real danger I reckoned I was in. It was just Junior blowing off steam as usual and hoping to give me a good scare. As always, it had the opposite effect.

The next morning I didn't ask anyone's permission and I didn't invite anyone to come along for protection. I left the house as if I hadn't a care, as if there was nothing in the world to be afraid of, as if things were exactly as they had always been in New Jerusalem. I ran along streets I knew like the back of my hand and past houses as familiar as my mother's smile. I stretched my cooped up legs in longer and longer strides and I breathed in gulp after gulp of cool, damp air that smelled like no other air on earth. The pounding of my heart was not from fear and scarcely even from exertion. It was a rhythm that said I was alive.

I ran and I didn't think about Mercer Swinford plummeting from a bridge or Old Shep's body buried in the depths of Miss Althea's orchard. I didn't think about shadowy figures lurking in the underbrush or lone gunmen escaping in conspicuously loud Pontiacs. I didn't think about Daddy's fears for my safety or Laddie's sudden coolness. I didn't think about not lusting after Mary Louise Morgan or Nelda Whitfield or Marytza O'Connor or what people would make of it if they knew I didn't. I didn't think about losing my job, losing my friends, or having my dreams vanish like morning fog under an August sun.

The last thing I had been expecting as I sneaked up the front walk was that I'd find Marytza sitting on the porch swing reading Emily Dickinson. But there she was big as life and glamorous as a movie star, looking as if she were on the point of saying she was nobody and asking me if was too. Which meant I'd be stammering out excuses to one or the other of my jailers any minute and long before I had them prepared. I was sweating buckets and felt all but naked.

"Looks like somebody's been playing hookie," Marytza chuckled. "Have a seat."

"I stink."

"And I haven't shaved my legs since Monday so I'd say we're even."

I didn't join her on the swing. I perched on the top porch step.

"Where's Laddie?" I asked, wondering if my absence had already been noticed and search parties sent out.

"Still asleep, I hope. I haven't heard anything going on inside."

"You didn't walk over here." The audacity of it astonished me.

"Well, I sure as hell didn't fly," she laughed. "I won't tell if you don't."

"They'll figure it out. But you're grown up. You won't get in trouble. They'll crucify me."

"Not if we go in right now and you get into the shower so they don't know you've been running. I'll say we planned it ahead of time. You came to pick me up in the car because I wanted to surprise everyone with a traditional Boston Irish breakfast."

"They would have heard the car."

"When you left, you pushed it halfway up the street before you started it. You're a big enough boy you could have done it easy. When we came back, you coasted the last block in neutral with the engine turned off. I notice the street has a gentle slope in that direction."

"Who are you? James Bond?"

"Who are you, Sherlock Holmes?"

"Shouldn't you at least have a bag of groceries with you?" I demanded, determined to get the better of her.

"Curses, foiled again," she laughed. "Daniel couldn't possibly have eggs, bacon, bread, jam, butter, and a few potatoes lying around the kitchen, could he?"

"Is that what Boston Irishmen eat for breakfast?"

"Do you think either Laddie or Daniel knows the difference?"

"Daddy certainly won't," I admitted, "but I can't speak for Laddie."

"I can. Besides, I'm half Polish."

"That explains a great deal," I said.

"That's not funny."

"Who was joking?"

"You'll pay for that," she said.

"We'll see. What would you have done if I hadn't shown up right about now?"

"Thought of another excuse. But I'd never have come over here in the first place if I hadn't seen you run past the Swinford house forty minutes ago."

"What if I'd beaten you back here?"

"You were going in the opposite direction. And Laddie showed me a short cut. I've been here for twenty-five minutes, and unlike you I didn't even break a sweat. Not that it isn't attractive on you."

XIII

"'The quality of mercy is not strained'," Marytza quoted. "'It droppeth. . .'"

"Too easy," I shouted. "*The Merchant of Venice*. Portia. 'If like a crab you could go backward'."

"Simple," she said, wrinkling her nose. "Hamlet to Polonius in one of those scenes where he's pretending to be mad. 'I shall see thee at Philippi'."

"Trick question," I snapped. "It could either be Brutus to the Ghost of Julius Caesar or the Ghost to Brutus. It's the eve of the final battle."

I was pretty sure Marytza was going easy on me, choosing her quotations carefully so we'd play to a draw. So far I hadn't even broken a sweat, and I knew my English 10 teacher, Miss Eileen LeDoux, would have been proud of me though she'd have gone to any length necessary to conceal it. Marytza had only introduced me to this game recently, and I sensed that her choice of recreation had as much to with figuring out who I was as it did with arcane forms of amusement or some quest on her part for intellectual stimulation. Had she been there, Mama would have proven a competitor of far more serious mettle. Still, if Marytza was inclined to waste her time matching wits with a lunkhead like me I had no objection. It was a pleasant enough diversion while we waited for Daddy to ring the dinner bell, though as we played I kept my ears pealed for the rattling roar signifying Laddie's return in the Volkswagen. His disappearance that afternoon right around the time we should have been starting our workout troubled me, and not even Shakespeare was enough to take my mind off my suspicions.

"'Full fathom five, my father lies,'" I began, knowing she'd get it immediately.

Just then, Miss Althea Chandler's Chevrolet rolled into view in all its white side walled glory. She gave a couple of long blasts on her horn and before she had actually come to a halt in her driveway she was gesticulating exuberantly out the window. Our duel to the death halted in midsyllable, Marytza and I rose in unison from the porch swing and headed across the street.

Through streaked and smudged windows I'd left immaculate that morning after giving the car a wash, the back seat appeared full of leaping, yowling puppies. It took a moment to discern that there were only two of them.

"Help me herd these girls inside," Miss Althea grinned.

With Marytza backing me up, I opened the rear door and grabbed one. The puppies' yelping verified their breed better than any pedigree document ever could have. I felt needle sharp teeth nipping at my fingers.

"Just picked them up from Junior Ellsworth."

"They're adorable," Marytza laughed, as I handed her the first wriggling bundle and scooped the second out of the back seat.

"Their names are Daisy and Petunia," Miss Althea said, climbing out of the driver's seat. "But please don't ask me which one is which. They haven't told me yet."

"Boy, Miss Althea," I said, rubbing the round little belly of the beagle squirming in my arms, "you sure do have your hands full here."

"Don't I know it," she giggled, a little breathless. "Got to get over to the library first thing tomorrow and find me a book about puppy training."

"I'd be glad to help you with them," Marytza suggested.

"Oh, well, I don't know," Miss Althea stammered, and I finally remembered my manners.

"This is Marytza O'Connor, Miss Althea. She's down here from Boston. You know. . ."

"How do you do," Marytza smiled.

"Well, I'm right pleased," Miss Althea smiled back. "Know about these critters, do you?"

"My mother breeds and shows whippets," Marytza explained. "I've been raising puppies all my life."

"And you're sure you wouldn't mind lending a hand?"

"I'd love to help. I've been missing my babies back home."

"You vouch for this young woman, Tristan?"

"Why, of course, Miss Althea, she's a Classics major, and she. . ."

Then Miss Althea's face cracked into a grin and I knew she'd snookered me again.

"Better get 'em inside, then," she cackled. "Come on."

When I emerged sweaty and caked with filth from Miss Althea's orchard the next day at lunchtime, Marytza had just left. Miss Althea told me proudly that the puppies now knew their names and were learning to come when called. Behind the thick lenses of her glasses I sighted a wild glint in her eyes and wondered if it was excitement over Daisy and Petunia or titillation at consorting with a glamorous communist agitator with an exotic accent.

"It's funny," she said, watching me tuck into a plate of her cold beef vinaigrette. "If I hadn't known him since the day he was born, I'd swear that Junior wasn't the same young man when I went over yesterday to pick out the puppies."

"What do you mean?"

"Well," she said, "you know how sullen he's always been. You can hardly get a civil word out of him. But yesterday for some reason he was polite and pleasant and smiling. It was all 'yes, ma'am, Miss Althea,' and 'no, ma'am, Miss Althea'. Wouldn't let me pay a cent for the puppies. Said Ellie May had had a right big litter and with his Bonnie Sue due any day now he was might tickled to make me a gift of them. I can't imagine what could have happened to him in the Marines to sweeten him up like that. Wouldn't have thought they were in the business of teaching deportment. Too busy storming the Halls of Montezuma."

Guilt at killing Miss Althea's previous dog was the explanation that came to mind, but I didn't consider voicing that opinion. If Miss Althea was happy, that was all that counted. The minute I expressed the faintest suspicion of Junior the whole thing might come gushing out of me and there I'd be, looking and sounding like a lunatic. Or worse, she might believe me and insist on doing something about it. No good could come of that.

"Perhaps he just needed to get away from home for a spell before he could truly appreciate it," I mused.

"As if you mean a word of that," she snorted. "Whole town knows there's no love lost between you boys. I'm not pointing any fingers, mind."

I shrugged.

"Lord knows that youngun was trouble from day one. Liked to drove his mama to an early grave."

"I'm sure he was just misunderstood."

"Misunderstood, my Aunt Fannie. And as for you, young man. . ."

She'd gone from zero to dead serious in nothing flat.

"What about me?"

"You know I despise folks who spend all their time minding other people's business. But that Marytza gal—you'd best watch out."

"What are you talking about?"

"You know what I'm talking about. Now, I know she's beautiful and charming. Smart as a whip, too. But she's a good deal older than you, and she's a big city girl. So you just be careful."

"But Miss Althea, I hardly know her," I stammered, astonished. "Anyway, she's going with one of the guys in the group."

"Doesn't matter who she's going with," she insisted, peering through her glasses at me. "I'm not talking about that. Been right tough for you lately. Easy to get your feelings hurt when you're smack in the middle of hard times. Girl like that'll break your heart without even knowing she's doing it. Hate to see anything like that happen."

"Isn't this nice?" Daddy observed, grabbing a drumstick. "A pitcher of tea, a piece of chicken, and thou amid the however it goes."

"I believe the speaker was addressing his girlfriend," I said, spooning cole slaw onto my plate. "I'm sure if you looked it up, you'd verify that."

"That's the wonder of it," Daddy nodded. "Truly great poetry can be adapted to any situation."

"Tell it to Omar Khayyam."

He ignored me and spread butter on a slice of cornbread, particular as an Amsterdam diamond cutter, while I fished around in the pickle jar.

"Marytza and Vladimir are charming young people, to be sure," Daddy said, "yankees though they be. I enjoy their company at least as much as you seem to, but I've been missing our times together."

"Me too."

"Been a lot to think about lately."

"I'll say."

"You know, sonny," he said, setting down his drumstick, which he still hadn't actually taken a bite of, "I'm afraid I've neglected my children."

"You haven't," I said. Over the previous weeks, disagreeing with him the second he began to express such self criticisms had become almost a reflex.

"All those years stuck in meetings three and four nights a week. Always at somebody else's bedside or sitting in somebody else's living room listing to some sad story or other I already knew by heart. I pretty much left your mother to raise the five of you single handed."

"Have you ever heard any of us complain?"

"Oh, son, you were always such a brave little soldier. It breaks my heart when I recall some of the times I lit out of here on my way somewhere I believed was more important than my own home. That time on your fourth birthday when I didn't even wait for you to blow out the candles on your cake because they thought Ida Scott's appendix had burst. It's not like I was her doctor. He was already there anyhow. I could have given you another five minutes. When I think about doing things like that, I despise myself."

"I understood."

"No," he said. "You were four years old. You only pretended to understand. You even kissed my cheek before I left. It would have broken my heart if I hadn't let myself be so preoccupied. You were always like that when I was running off somewhere. Smiling and pretending it didn't matter. And I took for granted that you really meant it. I'd never been a Daddy before, but lack of experience was no excuse. I should have known better. In the back of my mind I'm sure I did. No matter how you acted, you were hurt just like any four year old would have been hurt if his

Daddy walked out at a time like that. You had a perfect right to be hurt. I know now that wanting to serve God and help others is no excuse for treating your own child like that. I did a better job with your sisters. I know I did. But I can't help wondering what that did to you."

"It didn't do anything to me," I insisted, staring a hole in my plate. "I'm just fine."

"If you are, it's no thanks to me," he said. "If you're still pretending not to mind and all it taught you was to be angry with me, I guess that's what I deserve. But if I managed to turn you against the Lord, I don't know how I'll be able to face it."

"Don't talk rubbish."

"Is it rubbish, sonny?"

"I just said it was," I told him, wanting to scream.

"I promise you it's not going to be like that any more. When this is all over, I'm going to get some kind of job that will let me devote my time to my wife and children. I know it's a little late for that to make much difference to you. But maybe there's enough time to make it up to your sisters."

"I'm sorry," I told him, getting up from the table. "I can't talk about this right now."

XIV

"That's perfect, Altarella," I said, closing the book and smiling at her.

She stared at me like I'd suddenly started speaking Serbo-Croat. All around us you could hear the murmur of her classmates practicing their reading.

"Now, Tristan," she protested, "ain' nothin' perfect. You know that."

"I mean it," I said, watching her squirm with pleasure at the compliment. "Letter perfect. Not a single word wrong. And you didn't stumble once. Lots of college educated people don't read any better than you just did. I told you you could learn how."

"Wa'nt as hard as I always thought," she admitted, smiling tentatively. "Shoulda learned long time ago."

"Yes, you should," I agreed, "but that's no never mind. You can make up for lost time by being the readingest great-grandma in the county."

"See if I don'."

Now came the tough part. We'd seen it over and over again during the last weeks. We could teach people to read but we couldn't teach them not to be afraid of white authority. It was like pulling teeth, getting our students to agree to go to the courthouse and try to register to vote.

"So what do you say?" I asked, keeping my tone as level as I could. "Ready to go to the courthouse?"

"Oh, I don' know," she said, fear suddenly flashing in her black eyes. "They not like you down there. They make me all nervous like an' give me somethin' I cain' read. Better not go right yet."

I knew exactly how stubborn she could be so I didn't argue head on.

"How about this?" I suggested. "How about if I give you something really hard to try right now. Marytza O'Connor keeps a list of the things they're making people read over at the courthouse for the tests, and I know this is every bit as difficult as anything they might throw at you. If you can read it you go with me to the courthouse tomorrow. If you can't, we'll practice for a few more days."

"Ain' it enough I can read now? Do I really got to go through wid the res' of it?"

"I can't answer that for you."

"'Spect not."

"You trust me, don't you?"

"Shucks, boy."

"You know I wouldn't send you to the courthouse if I didn't think you could do it."

She didn't answer.

"Come on, now."

"I'm right scairt. Guess you know."

"Of course you are," I said, "but I'm not because I know you can do it and I know you really want to do it. And the whole town knows how you are when you really, really want something. Why, you're practically legendary that way."

"You got me," she chuckled.

"Just being able to read stories to your little ones won't ever be enough. You want to vote."

"Yes sir, Tristan, I do."

"That's settled, then. You can be scared for both of us, and I'll come along so you won't be by yourself. Everything will be fine."

"All right," she laughed. "Brang it on."

"Just give me a minute to find something you can't possibly read."

"I'se ready."

"Believe me, I know."

At breakfast the next morning Daddy was preoccupied, Marytza subdued, and Laddie, as was more and more often the case, absent. We made a grim little trio.

Daddy had fried some fresh trout, made sausage biscuits, and warmed some of Miss Althea's sticky buns. But even those sumptuous aromas failed to arouse us. It was as if we were sleepwalkers. I made no mention of my plans for the day and didn't ask about theirs. I had lied to Altarella Brown the night before. I had looked her in the eye and said I wasn't scared. I was terrified that it would all go wrong and I would have let her down. I'd as soon gargle with razor blades as let Daddy and Marytza in on what was I was feeling. Discussing it would only make things worse.

I had sworn off the local papers weeks earlier but had to tear my eyes away from the front page Daddy lurked behind. Marytza was reading *Between the Acts,* Mama's all time favorite Virginia Woolf novel, and once again I was struck by the notion that somehow they were one and the same person. I wondered if they would ever meet and tried to imagine the conversation when they did. Would their opposing accents and life histories hold sway, or would they connect as surely and completely as they were already connected in my mind? Marytza was exactly the kind of woman Mama must dream of when she thought about my future.

She looked up from the book and gave me a tired little smile. I knew there still hadn't been any good news about her grandfather after all these weeks, and though for the most part she was able to keep from dwelling on it, from time to time she felt it keenly. I returned her smile, grateful that she was older than me and Catholic and a yankee. Grateful for all those disqualifying characteristics, so that I'd never have to explain myself to anyone.

My best suit had grown so snug as to be uncomfortable. It would soon be unwearable. My chest and shoulders wanted to bust right out of the jacket. My thighs strained the dark blue fabric of the trousers till it was shiny. I'd have to watch how I moved or there'd be an accident, and I'd best go shopping for something new as soon as I got the chance. My hair was several weeks past needing a trim because I'd been too chicken to face the crowd at the barber shop lately, so I glopped more pomade into it than usual and wrestled its shagginess into submission. I had spit shined my shoes the night before. I knew Altarella would be in her Sunday finest and I couldn't let her down.

She was waiting on her front porch when I arrived, tiny and frail as a rag doll. She looked about a hundred years old. She teetered on high heels in a size I wouldn't have thought they made if I hadn't seen her in them dozens of times at Ebenezer Baptist. The shiny wooden cherries on her jaunty little hat quivered as she walked down her front steps. Her black eyes glittered out from behind her net veil like chips of obsidian.

"Bet you thought I'd chicken out, didn' ya?" she greeted me.

"Thought never crossed my mind," I said, offering her my arm.

"You a liar," she cackled, "but just this once I'll let it pass."

"Much obliged."

It was over almost before we knew it. Ray Sue Ellis gave Altarella the test without ever once looking at me even though she'd babysat me when she was in high school. I might have been a fly buzzing around the ineffectual ceiling fan for all the attention she paid. The only proof of my presence was that she didn't try to pull anything, just went about her job with a frosty efficiency that belied both the climate and her fury. Altarella didn't falter once, and she walked out of that lion's den a fully credentialed member of the electorate. She'd be voting come November and every election after that as long as she drew breath. Here was a woman whose mother and father had both been born slaves, whose first husband had been lynched, whose daughters had been raped by white men, and who had suffered untold other terrors during her nearly fourscore years just because of the color of her skin, and she finally had her rights. She was a living, breathing monument to persistence. I couldn't take any credit for what had just occurred. It had been inevitable all along. She'd just been biding her time, waiting for the right opportunity. Her astonishing faith had helped her survive. Her granite determination had brought her to that searing morning ready to stare down the last obstacle between herself and full citizenship. I'd never felt so humble in my entire life as I did when we stepped back out into the shadowy, silent corridor outside the registrar's office. Judging from Altarella's posture, she might have been an empress rather than a housemaid. She didn't teeter on her heels or grasp my proffered elbow as we walked toward the main doors of the courthouse. She needed nothing from anyone in that moment and owed nothing either. I only hoped someday I would be that strong myself, but it didn't seem possible without the intervention of supernatural forces. I couldn't imagine what she must be feeling. Whatever it was, we both knew better than to celebrate inside the building.

In the deep shade of the portico, we paused. Only then did I allow myself to consider how terrified I had been since leaving home that morning.

"You did it," I told her, a lump rising insistently in my throat.

"Lord 'a mercy, didn' I jus'?" she panted, finally recognizable as the tiny old black lady from my earliest memories.

"I knew you could do it. Didn't I tell you you could?"

"Yes, sir, Mr. Tristan," she said, clutching my hand in a vise grip. "You mos' surely did, Lord bless you. I cain' never thank you enough for evathing you done. And when I go in that votin' booth next fall, I'm a goin' to stop a moment 'fore I marks my ballot and say a prayer to Jesus for you, boy. Lord hep me, I will."

"I didn't do it," I told her. "You did. But thank you for your prayers."

"Won' never forget this long as I live."

"Me either."

"Jesus save us," she muttered, looking past me. "What that ol' woman doin' here?"

I turned to see Eula Simmons storming up the walk toward us. About a hundred years old, she'd been my first Sunday School teacher. Altarella had been her domestic since about the time the Archduke Franz Ferdinand was assassinated.

"What in blue blazes do you two think you're up to?" she shrieked at us from the foot of the courthouse steps.

"Why, Miss Eula, Mr. Tristan here just heped me get registered to vote."

"Did he now? Did he indeed?"

"Yes, ma'am, Miss Eula," I said. "Not that Altarella needed much help."

"Is this really the best thing you can think of to do on a Tuesday morning when you ought to be beating my rugs?" Miss Eula demanded, scaling the steps as if they were a traverse on the Matterhorn.

"It my day off, Miss Eula. You know that."

"I never heard the like of it. I do not give you Tuesdays off so you can get up to comm'nist sabotage like this. I most certainly do not."

"Now, Miss Eula," I protested.

The blow took me completely by surprise. She may not have weighed more than eighty-nine pounds dripping wet, but those ancient southern women can pack a right smart wallop. It felt like being kicked by a mule. I tasted blood in my mouth almost before I realized she had slapped me.

"Now, Miss Eula, he didn' do nothin' wrong."

"He didn't, my Great Aunt Fannie," Miss Eula stormed. "He should be ashamed of himself, encouraging indecent goings on like this. He should hang his fool head for the shame of it. I don't know what the world is coming to. I swear and vow I don't. I thought I'd never live to see the day when a well brought up, Christian young man would turn his back on all that's good and holy and spit in the face of the whole town that fed and clothed and helped raise him. It makes me want to cry. His daddy may have taken leave of his senses but poor Miss Elizabeth must be hearbroken to think what all he's gotten up to since she's been gone. And as for you, Altarella, well, there's no need for you to come to work tomorrow. I'm sure I'll be able to find another girl."

"Yes'm."

"But Miss Eula, you can't fire her. Not for wanting to vote."

"Not that it's any concern of yours, young man, but I most certainly can. And I just have. And I'll thank you to stop interfering in my business. Good day."

We stood silent as she stomped away, muttering and fuming.

"She shouldn'a done that," Altarella murmured. "Slappin' you that way."

"I don't care about that. She can't hurt me. But what about your job?"

"Oh, now, don' go worryin' 'bout my job."

"How will you live?"

"Plenty white women ready to hire me."

"How can you be sure of that? Sometimes I think every white person in town has gone crazy."

"You think they white ladies really a mind to clean they own toilets? Miss Eula an' all they others?" Altarella laughed, "er scrub they own kitchen floors?"

"Don't expect so," I grinned, imagining any number of Baptist women of my acquaintance on their knees wielding brushes. It seemed as unlikely as science fiction.

"Anyways, she done fired me before. Plenty times. Always aks me back. That how it is and that how it always gone be."

"I hope you're right."

"So I'll have me a nice little vacation for a few days. Sleep late in the mornin' and not wait on nobody. And when she come 'roun' to aks me back, I'll make her give me a nice little raise."

"She won't do it."

"She always do," Altarella chuckled. "I could use me a nice new pair of shoes. And a purse to match. Had my eyes on some things down at the mercantile. Now boy, you'd best get on home and soak that lip. Look like you done been in a street fight. You want to wrap some ice cubes up in a washrag, you hear?"

"I'll walk you to your place first."

"No need. I be fine. You go on home now."

We parted at the curb. As I leaned down to let her kiss my cheek I heard Bobby Davidson's Sting Ray rumble through the square. When I looked up I saw that he was staring at me. He waved, but I couldn't see his expression behind his sunglasses. He didn't slow down.

So Bobby had seen me. He had seen me dressed in my best suit, being kissed by a tiny black woman in front of the courthouse in broad daylight. He was no Einstein, but he wouldn't have to be to know what it meant. Before that moment he might have suspected that I'd been helping out with the registration drive, but even so I believed he would give me the benefit of the doubt. Now he couldn't any more. There wasn't much question what his opinion would be.

What he might do about it was another matter. I hoped that for old time's sake he would pretend not to know. I thought he was just about decent enough to do that. He had never cared about me the same way I did about him, obviously, but nothing had happened yet to cause me to doubt that he did have some genuine affection for me. Whatever he thought about the current events in New Jerusalem he was no monster. As long as Junior Ellsworth or Bucky Duncan or any of our other teammates didn't find out and he wasn't forced to admit that he knew, he'd have just enough cover to let it pass.

That's what I believed, slouching home through the hottest day of the summer so far, soaking inside my soon to be discarded suit and suddenly exhausted as if I, not Altarella Brown, had just run the gauntlet. I believed that because I didn't want to live in a world where it wasn't true. I recognized clearly that Bobby hadn't truly been the love of my life, that regardless of how it had felt at the time it had been no more than a schoolboy crush. But he had to have been worthy of my feelings in some way. I couldn't have just thrown them away on nothing. And as shrunken and withered as they seemed now there was still something about him that I couldn't get free of. A feeling I didn't imagine I'd ever completely forget. It was more than just an appreciation of his physical beauty, and it was deeper than mere boyhood friendship. I could only really define it in terms of what it wasn't. But it was no less real for all that. I felt it in my bones that day and I couldn't imagine not feeling it, whatever it was. It had little or nothing to do with my feelings about Laddie. It had no power to make me any less head over heels in love with my new friend. Still, it was there, insubstantial but nonetheless unmistakable, like the shadow cast on a sidewalk not by sunshine but by a full moon.

Laddie had seen me with Altarella, too. He'd been sitting on a bench in an alcove off the corridor outside the county recorder's office. He had watched Altarella and me go in and come back out. I had felt his eyes on me the whole time. But he hadn't waved, hadn't spoken a single word. I wasn't sure anyone had ever worked as hard at ignoring the presence of another person in the history of civilization. It would have been comical if he had been anyone else. It hurt like having a limb amputated.

Instead he had hidden behind his book. He had known exactly what was happening and how important it was to me. He had known how terrified Altarella and I both were going into that office, and he must have seen how exhultant we were coming back out. He had to have known how much something as apparently insignificant as a nod could have meant. But I was disgusting. A pariah. I deserved no such consideration, not even at a moment of flagging courage which threatened to leave me in a state of true terror. Not even with so much at stake. Altarella Brown might be black but I was what I was, unspeakable.

Laddie wasn't Bobby. I had no history with him that made ignoring unpleasant facts not only possible but practically obligatory. Laddy had no reason to give me the benefit of the doubt. There were no old times for whose sake he might be inclined to believe I was the boy I'd seemed to be. Or perhaps yankees simply didn't have it in them. Maybe the easy hypocrisy that lubricated our interactions in New Jerusalem had been bred out of them, leaving them with a kind of steely implacability in the face of things they disapproved of.

But like that ghostly whatever it was I still felt about Bobby now that the flaming swords barred my path back through the gates of Eden, I knew I would never forget Laddie's vacant stare over the edge of his book, as if he had barely noticed a young stranger pass in the distance.

XV

"Here comes the young hero now," Daddy exclaimed as I entered the kitchen the next morning. He seemed almost like himself, presiding over the range top with the panache of a chef at the White House.

"He does look like he just returned from some epic or other," Marytza observed. She, too, was more chipper than I remembered seeing her in a week or more. I wondered what was responsible for their high spirits. In any case, I made up for both of them. I was anything but cheerful and I couldn't have felt less heroic. More like a bedraggled tomcat slinking home after losing a fight.

"Everyone's talking about you and Altarella Brown at the courthouse yesterday," Daddy said. "I keep hearing that I should be bursting with pride."

"Everybody? Aren't you exaggerating?"

"A little," he said, turning away to flip some pancakes and stir the scrambled eggs.

"Well, I wouldn't go as far as bursting."

"I'll be the judge of that," Daddy said. "Why didn't you tell me you were going?"

"So you could talk me out of it because I was running the risk of being abducted off the street? I can hardly step out onto the front porch these days without you unleashing the guard dogs."

"I'd have come along," he said, smiling past my sarcasm. "I could have basked in your reflected glory."

"Altarella was nervous as a cat as it was," I said. "It was hard enough just getting her to go. I didn't want anyone spooking her."

"How could Daniel spook anyone?" Marytza asked.

"No, Tristan's right," Daddy told her. "It would only have put more pressure on her. Which would have been the last thing she needed. He was right to keep it quiet and low key. Good job, son. That was a very brave thing you did."

"Oh, hell," I said, "it wasn't anything to what everybody else has been doing around here."

"But still," Daddy insisted, "there aren't many sixteen year olds who'd have done it. I mean, look around. Do you see any of your friends fighting the good fight? What I don't understand is why you didn't say anything about it last night at dinner. We could have had a real celebration."

I shrugged. I couldn't have begun to explain that a celebration without Laddie would have felt worse than no celebration at all. I had awakened with the realization that as much as any desire on my part to help Altarella out I'd been hoping to prove myself to him once and for all. There didn't seem any end to finding reasons to despise myself.

"Laddie told me he saw the two of you there," Marytza said.

"What did he say?" I blurted, immediately mortified at my eagerness.

"Just that he saw you," Marytza said.

I felt the roller coaster hit bottom again. I'd be in tears there at the breakfast table if either one of them said the wrong thing.

"What's wrong, son? Didn't you sleep well?"

"Not really," I grunted.

"Something on your mind?"

"Nothing in particular," I lied, feeling like a five year old caught with a stolen Hershey bar. "Just cabin fever."

"And this weather won't help," Daddy said. "Looks like you'll be indoors all day."

The summer had been unusually dry. That morning's downpour was some of the first real rain there had been in weeks. The near drought conditions had only been partially relieved that drizzly morning when Laddie had found me out, and there hadn't been a drop since then. I was probably the only person in New Jerusalem who wasn't happy that the heavens had opened up. All I could think of as I absent mindedly swallowed my breakfast was Miss Althea Chandler's orchard, where I wouldn't be working out my frustrations with pruning shears and machete.

* * *

In naming me, Mama had been as inaccurate as she had been imaginative. I had never aspired to die for love like the Tristan of song and legend. Instead, the knight I had taken as my exemplar in early childhood was the cowardly and morally confused but ultimately honorable Gawain. There was a knight a boy could truly identify with. He would never leave you feeling inadequate, yet you could admire how he turned out. He screwed up but after much agonizing redeemed himself. Even as a little tyke I had found his fallibility comforting. I had often wondered why he wasn't considered the patron saint of preachers' sons. I grabbed my copy of the poem whenever I was particularly out of sorts. I was reading of the Green Knight's arrival in Arthur's great hall when Marytza stepped out onto the porch.

"Mind if I sit down?"

I had stationed myself on the porch swing like a sentinel on a watchtower. Laddie wouldn't be able to slip inside without my knowing it, and I was spoiling for a confrontation. I wasn't particularly looking forward to Marytza's company, but it occurred to me that he could hardly weasel out of talking to me with her there.

"Be my guest."

She sat, and we stared out into the rain.

"Your father is worried about you."

"He's got more important things to worry about."

"More important than his own son? You don't really think that."

"Don't I?"

"My God. I guess you do."

"It's very bad for him to worry about me right now," I insisted. "Talk to him for me. Tell him to stop."

"Fathers worry. Nobody can make them stop."

"You can. Daddy listens to you. Tell him you talked to me and I'm fine. That's all he needs to hear."

"Tristan, no."

"Then I'll tell him myself," I said, scrambling to my feet. "I'll go in right now."

"Sit down and save your breath," she said. "He won't believe you."

"Why shouldn't he?"

"Because you're not fine. Anybody can see that. If your mother were here she'd have a stroke."

"What are you talking about? I'm just a little tired."

"Don't bullshit me."

"Who's bullshitting?"

She stared me down.

"I get the message," I told her. "I'll try to stop moping."

"That's not what I meant."

"Oh."

"I just wanted to remind you that he cares about you," she said, running fingers through her wheat colored hair. "He's sick over what you're going through."

"I know he is. That's part of the problem. I wouldn't feel so bad if he wasn't so worried about me. Talk about your vicious cycles."

"It's O.K. to have people worry about you, you know. It's not a sign of weakness. If that's what you think, you just need to get over it. Your life won't be worth living otherwise."

"I swear I don't know what you're talking about."

That stare again. I couldn't meet it.

"I care, too, you know," she said, taking my hand and absentmindedly tracing my lifeline. "I care about you more than you realize. I never had a little brother. I always thought I'd make a great big sister, though."

"You would have," I said, gulping ineffectually at the lump in my throat.

"I'd have been one of those fiercely protective types, you know? Wanting to fight all his battles for him?"

"Half the time he'd have wanted you to and the rest of the time he'd have told you to butt out."

"Exactly."

"That's the only thing the two of you would ever have fought about."

"You do know, don't you?"

"Know what?"

"Don't play dumb. The first time I heard Laddie mention you, I knew exactly who he was describing. The brother I never had."

"Well, sorry," I said, "but I've got more sisters than I know what to do with."

"My imaginary little brother was a wiseass, too."

The rain didn't let up, and there was no sign of Laddie. Time stood still, and Gawain's predicament offered no guidance, or too much of it. For the first time in my life the tale failed to enthrall me. It seemed stale, like everything lately. It was just a story, and a very old one at that. People didn't act like that in the modern world, if they ever actually had. I had been stupid to make so much of it, just like I had been stupid about so many other things. I set the book on the piano bench inside and headed off to brave the elements. They were a whole lot less daunting than human nature.

Eventually, being soaked to the skin didn't feel good any more. Being out in the rain felt worse than being cooped up inside. Once I knew for certain I was all cried out, I crept home like a drowned rat. I stripped to my underwear on the back porch and went upstairs to shower. The house was as quiet as a mortuary on a day when nobody was being buried.

He was sitting on my bed when I came in from my shower, and he looked up from the book he was reading like a safecracker caught in the act.

"I hope you don't mind," he said.

I minded a lot, but I didn't say so.

"I found this downstairs," he explained. "I came up here looking for you."

"I went for a walk."

"In this weather?"

"A little rain never hurt anyone."

"It's practically a hurricane."

I shrugged.

"You could be struck by lightning."

"I wasn't."

"You could catch pneumonia."

"You're joking, right? It's the middle of the summer."

I willed him to get up and leave, but he didn't move. I willed myself to disappear, but that didn't happen either. I was mortified, standing there in a towel.

"This book's been through a lot."

"Mama had it in high school. Then my uncles. They're very hard on books."

"And you've never read it?"

"Only about forty dozen times."

"Oh," he said, "so you know how it ends."

"Uh huh," I nodded. "Everybody thinks he's handsome and brave and wonderful. But really he's nothing but a big old coward. Finally he makes up for it and salvages some of his honor."

He'd been staring, but now he looked away. I was desperate to pull on clothes, but loath to drop my towel.

"I've been an awful coward," he finally said, looking up from the book. His eyes were bloodshot.

"Yes, you have," I said. Looking into those eyes I wanted to offer him absolution, but even if I could have that seemed backwards somehow.

"I'm sorry," he said, shaking his head slowly. "I'm so very sorry. I never meant to hurt you. I know it was wrong to shut you out like I did, but I couldn't help myself. I've never been so terrified. I've been ready to come up here and talk to you dozens of times. And every time my fear talked me out of it. Then yesterday at the courthouse. It was a revelation, that's all. I was so proud of you. You were my hero. I wanted to jump up and hug you on the spot. You had been so brave. I decided I could be, too. For a few moments I knew I could do what I had to. It was almost enough. Sometimes I think that's the ugliest word in the English language. Almost."

"You could at least have said something," I said, "or waved. You didn't have to sit there pretending you didn't even see me."

"You don't know what it's like," he shook his head sadly. "You have no idea."

"Is that the best you can do?" I snorted.

"Tristan, this is hard."

"How dare you," I shouted. "How dare you try to turn it around so that you're the one who's got it bad? Is that what you learned on the kibbutz?"

"No. I wouldn't claim for a minute that you've got it better than I do. I know you're losing almost everything you care about. But this other thing. . ."

"So you know about me," I choked. "So you figured it out that morning in the rain. O.K. I admit it. It's not worth the effort trying to hide it any more. But you couldn't even be civil after that? You couldn't pretend you didn't know about me and go on like before? What did you think I was going to do? Attack you?"

"What are you talking about?" he asked, a befuddled look on his face.

"Don't," I snarled. "Don't play innocent. You were afraid, weren't you? Admit it, Laddie, you were a big coward."

"I already admitted it."

"You thought I was going to try something. You thought I wouldn't be able to keep my hands to myself. As if you weren't strong enough to defend yourself. Oh, God, how icky. Tristan wants to kiss me. Whatever will I do?"

"What the hell?"

"That's right. You figured out I'm just like Mercer Swinford and you couldn't handle it. All your talk about equality for everyone and guaranteeing the dignity of the individual at any cost. I guess it doesn't go as far as someone like me. I suppose I can understand that. I guess that's how any normal guy would react. But somehow I thought you were better than that. That you were stronger and truer than all the other guys I've known. That I could depend on you. I thought maybe we could still be friends. Not like before. I know that. But some kind of friends anyway. And I would never have done anything, Laddie, you have to believe it. I would never. . ."

"I don't believe this," he said, chuckling mirthlessly.

"Well, you'd better believe it."

"Hush," he said.

Something in his eyes stopped me dead in my tracks. Once I had lost my momentum, there was only one thing left to do.

"Don't cry," he said, getting up from the bed. "You've been just as confused as I have, but that's over now."

"What are you talking about?" I sobbed.

He was at the door then, but he wasn't leaving. He locked it.

"What are you doing?"

"Something I've been wanting to do since I first met you. Tristan, after that morning, I wasn't afraid of what you might do. You were completely wrong about that. But I see now why you thought what you did. You really didn't know about me. I thought you had it figured it out, and that's why I couldn't be around you. I was afraid of what I might do."

"I don't know what you're talking about," I said. "You shut me out, sure, but you would never have actually done anything to hurt me."

"I'd have done this," he said. And then he kissed me.

XVI

I woke cold and dew soaked, which would teach me to fall asleep in the hammock. There was a glimmer of light filtering through the fog, just enough to indicate that dawn was imminent though the owl residing in Miss Althea's most venerable oak tree hadn't yet closed up shop. It was impossible to tell what kind of day it would be, whether the fog would burn off or whether this was the underside of a thick cloud bank that would persist all day and perhaps bring rain. All mornings in New Jerusalem were damp and this time of year most were gloomy no matter what was to follow, so the humidity was no guide. You'd do as well to examine the entrails of a goat. I wondered if this rule of the climate was a strictly local phenomenon or would also hold true wherever the Bentleys ended up. I knew for instance that Chattanooga could be this inscrutable, but my visits there had never been extended ones so I had no idea whether that was typical or anomalous.

Beside me, sprawled in a chaise lounge, Laddie snored like a sawmill. His face was poignantly relaxed and his touseled hair cried out for someone to smooth it. Looking at him this way it would be easy to convince yourself that no uncertainties or ambiguities troubled his sleep, but I knew better. The last couple of weeks had unscrewed the lid and revealed his complexities and depths. Not all of them, I was sure, but enough to make it apparent that he wasn't the man I'd thought when I'd fallen in love with him. He was not less, however, but far more than a schoolboy's fond dream. He was no less mythical but simultaneously far more actual, and thus even more intimidating than I'd previously reckoned.

During the night someone had thrown blankets over both of us, and no points for guessing who. Over the last couple of weeks Laddie and I had sat up talking later and later each night and I knew that couldn't have gone unnoticed, though I constantly insisted to myself that Daddy had no inkling what it signified. Laddie and I were nothing if not careful on that score, and as far as I knew Daddy was no psychic. But it was more than that. It was our secret because it simply had to be.

I swung out of the hammock, stretching like an old dog fixing to light out after the postman. I yawned like I'd been asleep for twenty years. My muscles and joints craved a long run through the silent streets of the town like an alcoholic craves a drink, but Laddie constituted my best reason so far for avoiding risks, so I went inside to shower.

"Scramble them for you this morning, young sir?" Daddy asked as I entered the kitchen.

"Thanks."

"Now don't let the biscuits and gravy get cold." His tone was admonitory as always, and I wished to the soles of my feet that inattentiveness to lovingly prepared food was at the top of the ever lengthening list of my shortcomings. Then maybe I'd actually be the son he thought he had. Every day my dread of his inevitable disappointment loomed larger. I could hardly look him in the eye any more. What had he and Mama done to deserve me?

I tucked into the steaming plate, marveling at the dazzling bounty weighing down the tabletop. My fears of earlier that summer, that without regular employment we would starve, had so far proved groundless. The lilies of the field toiled not and neither had we, except in the most rudimentary fashion. Yet here we were no worse off than before. In spite of that, I was skeptical that we might continue so for much longer. Summer ends, winter comes. Orchards, berry patches, corn fields, and kitchen gardens wither and sleep. Scarcity looms and hunger finally gnaws. It seemed well past time for somebody to make definite plans, but just as surely it wasn't my place.

Still, the food on that table inspired a kind of wonder. Arrayed around me, it formed a bulwark that seemed impregnable. Ironic, I thought, how you couldn't tell by looking at any of it that it had been planted, nurtured, harvested, and delivered by black rather than white hands. Perhaps the true irony was that only in a town like New Jerusalem would this question of origins arise.

"I don't see how you two slept out there without freezing," Daddy said, refilling my glass of orange juice.

"Perhaps it was because a forest elf or somesuch came to our rescue."

"Perhaps," he said, eyes twinkling. "I don't want to spoil your breakfast, but there's something I have to tell you that can't really be put off."

"What is it?"

"Indeed," he nodded, looking like a young boy caught with his hand in the cookie jar, "the movers are coming Tuesday. Bright and early."

"So you finally made up your mind."

"Not guilty, your honor," he shook his head. "Though by all rights I guess I ought to be. Your mother put her foot down is what did it. I was all for giving things another couple weeks just to see what might chance to occur. Ten days or so more, you understand? In case? When you've been praying so long for a miracle, you don't like to give up hope prematurely. You stare at that mountain waiting for it to move, and when it doesn't you start to sense your lack of faith pretty keenly."

"Oh."

"Lots for a young man your age to do in a city the size of Chattanooga," he mused. "Maybe you won't hate it too bad there."

"Daddy, please."

"Movie theaters and a public library like you've never seen. I know it's a shock, all of a sudden like this."

"I don't know what makes you say that," I scoffed. "Volunteers are all set to leave town first thing Monday. Big victory celebration at Ebenezer Baptist tomorrow. Not to mention it's been as plain as the nose on your face we'd be leaving eventually."

"Eventually," he nodded, smoothing back his hair, in which I noticed for the very first time a few silvery strands. "Eventually can postpone itself for a long time. Some people even manage to outlive it."

"Maybe that's why they have a special word for it."

"Sometimes you remind me so much of your mother I can scarcely credit it."

"Really."

"Honestly," he said. "And you know there's no higher praise I could give."

His compliment slashed me like a dagger. I scrambled to change the subject.

"One thousand five hundred and sixty-three. That right? The grand total?"

"Yes," he smiled. "That's how many we got registered. Don't know that it's enough to swing any elections in the county, but it's a start. Maybe it'll at least give people around here something to think about. Besides, the precedent is set now. The gates are open and they'll never keep the people out again."

"Laddie not around?"

"Left while you were in the shower," Daddy said. "Took off without any breakfast. Couldn't so much as give him coffee. Looked as if he had things to attend to."

I nodded. With him and the other volunteers set to leave town on Monday morning, it just got harder for us to be around each other. There was too much to say, and we couldn't trust ourselves to keep our mouths sufficiently closed.

"You'll miss him right smart," Daddy said. "I will, too, of course. Seems like you two have been awfully close of late."

There wasn't a ghost of insinuation in his tone. He couldn't possibly know what had been going on. I was as sure of that as I had ever been about anything, but I still couldn't meet his gaze.

"Laddie and I had a talk about you," Daddy said, turning back to the stove top.

"Oh?"

"Must have been day before yesterday," he nodded. "Seems he's convinced that you need to go to New York for college."

"We've discussed it."

"Not a bad idea," he said. "Great schools there. Columbia. NYU."

"Yes."

"Your mother will be thrilled. She's been concerned you might end up at Auburn or somesuch institution."

"I'm thinking my gridiron days are probably a memory."

"She'll be doubly happy."

"That's certainly a reason."

"Seriously, son, if New York is what you decide on, your mother and I will do everything we can to make it happen."

"Thanks."

"You know, what with the movers coming in on Tuesday I thought you might want to go through your things. See what all you want to bring and what you might be ready to throw out."

Going through my things served only to depress me further. I couldn't imagine getting rid of anything, but I couldn't imagine taking everything along, either. I knew Daddy would say I shouldn't leave anything behind unless I was certain I'd never want it again, but how can you be sure of something like that? It seemed a hopelessly mundane matter considering all we were embroiled in. And pondering it hardly took my mind off anything. It was a relief when I heard the first whoops drift in through the open window.

I joined Miss Althea, Marytza, and the two beagles in Miss Althea's front yard. Daisy and Violet were growing like weeds. Obviously, Miss Althea was as diligent about keeping them fed as she'd always been with Old Shep. She seemed a good ten years younger, as though the puppies had shared some of their youth with her. Her giggle pealed out more clearly and more highly pitched than I could ever remember it, and the color in her cheeks was rosy as any schoolgirl's.

"Daisy, sit," Marytza commanded, whereupon both puppies immediately plonked their rears in the damp grass, their eyes on her like compass needles aiming at the pole.

"It's perfect," Miss Althea laughed, breathless. "Whatever you tell one to do, they both do. I won't ever have to remember who I'm talking to. Lordy, Tristan, this young woman is a miracle worker."

"Now you try it, Miss Althea," Marytza suggested, winking at me as though we were co-conspirators. "After tomorrow, I won't be just a couple of blocks away if these two get recalcitrant. Show them who's boss."

Miss Althea did, and we all stood there laughing fit to kill.

In the basement as I worked out that afternoon, the boxes of Daddy's refugee library loomed taller than ever before. Where could we possibly go that there would be room for all those books? I knew they had to be rescued from their exile, because how was Daddy to live if he had to be separated from them? I couldn't conceive of him coping if they had to go to a warehouse somewhere. If he wasn't going to have an office, he needed them under the same roof with him. I had caught him visiting them more than once. It wasn't for something to read, I knew. He needed a kind of reassurance he apparently could only find by actually holding one of them in his hands and running his fingertips over its binding. I would see him open a book only to sniff at its mustiness and then replace it in the box with the others. Some people have family albums. Others keep scrapbooks. Still others dust their heirlooms daily. These were Daddy's mementos. I knew that if I asked him what he had been reading in the hospital waiting room when I was born, he could not only tell me the title and the author's name but discuss the contents of the volume in detail and point out the exact box where that volume was stored. I knew somewhere in that pile was the book he'd been reading the afternoon he met Mama at college; that somewhere else was the book he'd been snoozing over when the news came that my Uncle William had died on Omaha Beach. Every one of those books not only contained a story within its covers but also represented an event from Daddy's life. Cut Daddy off from his books and I didn't see how he'd remember anything important that had ever happened to him.

It wasn't the rows and stacks of boxes that filled the room that afternoon nor even the books themselves. It was the words in them, the ideas they expressed and the messages they conveyed, that seemed to expand and fill every inch of available space, squeezing out even the air so that I struggled for breath as I exercised. Would any of this be happening if not for those books? Would it ever have occurred to Daddy to swim against the tide without their influence? Would he ever have mustered the courage to be the man he was without those generations of wise men and women cheering him on? I thought of my classmates and their parents crammed into the grandstands as I fell back to throw a touchdown pass. That's what all this literature represented to Daddy, that solid wall of understanding, encouragement, and good wishes. It was as hard to imagine as catfish walking across a parking lot.

Without centuries worth of concepts, narratives, and reflections swirling around him like that morning's fog, who would he even be?

Not that I blamed all those prophets and sages for our predicament. They had spoken as they must and their words had been vigorous seeds sown in the fertile ground of his intellect. You might as well blame the clear sky when it rains, the sun for darkness after nightfall. You might as well pretend the whole history of humankind had never taken place.

When I heard footsteps coming downstairs, I almost called out. But it wasn't Laddie who appeared in the basement a moment later. It was Bobby Davidson, and I was glad I had held my tongue.

"Your daddy told me you were down here,"

"You sure look serious."

"Just heard you're leaving," he frowned. "You should have said something."

"Daddy only told me this morning."

"I never thought it would turn out like this," he said. "I was sure it would all work out somehow."

I had no answer for that. I had thought I was over him, but seeing him sulking like that I suddenly wasn't sure.

"T.," he said, staring hard at me.

"What?"

"I don't know," he shrugged. "Just. . ."

XVII

Some time not long before the turn of the century, Bobby Davidson's great grandfather, General Archibald Abernathy Duncan, hero of the Battle of Chickamauga and legend of the Confederate Army, built his infant daughter a playhouse. General Duncan had an even dozen grown sons by three different wives but had despaired of his young fourth wife ever presenting him with an heir. Indeed, he had grandchildren already grown by the time this long anticipated event occurred. Bobby's grandmother was that belated child, the only offspring of his last marriage. Gen. Duncan died while she was still a toddler but not before he had lavished on her everything that a man of his generation and station in life could think to give an only daughter.

While the family never referred to the structure as anything other than a playhouse, that term gave a completely inadequate impression of it. It might have reminded a casual onlooker of a storybook cottage, but it was more than merely quaint. It had electric light, hot and cold running water, and a full bathroom. This in a time when most folks in the county did their business in outhouses and bathed in tubs of water heated on their kitchen stoves. When a telephone was installed in the main house, the playhouse got one too. Though ostensibly built for one lone child, it was more than large enough to host adult parties if they were fairly intimate. It was equipped with serious, grown up furnishings, including an imported crystal chandelier in the dining room, persian carpets, and a grand piano in the parlor. Should Bobby's grandmother wish to spend the night under its roof, and she often did, she wouldn't be the only one sleeping comfortably. There were two additional small but sumptuously appointed bedrooms and separate accommodations for her governess. Indeed, few were the families in the county who lived in comparable style, space, and luxury, but the Duncan family's position was so unassailable that such ostentation occasioned no criticism.

General Duncan willed his extensive agricultural properties to his sons, who were of that generation of southern men so preoccupied with what had been lost due to Yankee interference that they frittered away what they had left through inattention and indolence. Not that after being split twelve ways there was that much property for any of them to manage in the first place. If you think that this should have been ample incentive for them to be good stewards, you're not a southerner. Wisely, Gen. Duncan left the family home and all the capital to his young widow, who had a better head for business than was generally considered appropriate, or even possible, for a woman. She invested wisely and prospered, much to the fury of her stepsons and their families. She never remarried despite being beset by suitors nearly as numerous and persistent as Penelope's. It was the only way, she explained to those few who were bold enough to inquire, to ensure that everything would eventually go to her daughter. When Regina Divina Duncan grew up and married Osbert Davidson and he and his widowed mother moved into her house, it became known as the Davidson place, the rest of the Duncans being by then deeply in eclipse. Bobby's grandmother never fell out of love with the little house, and knowing which side of their bread the butter was on, the help on the property worked harder keeping it shipshape than they did on the big house.

A generation later, when Bobby's father and uncles came of age and found that they needed a place of assignation, they had to look no further than their own back yard. Particularly once hedges were planted screening it from the big house and the swimming pool was built just past the veranda. They earned the gratitude of their many friends by graciously granting free access to its splendors, and it attained an unquestioned notoriety. As early as sixth grade, Bobby would occasionally look around among our classmates pretending to judge which of them might have been conceived there. And the tradition exceeded itself when Bobby and all his friends hit puberty. A pool table replaced the grand piano, the fanciest Wurlitzer jukebox in the county was restocked with the latest hits, a huge new refrigerator was shoehorned into the kitchenette, and Bobby's rumpus room was inaugurated on his fifteenth birthday. Not long after that, extra keys to the playhouse were cached in various local hidey holes, signals were arranged, and a new generation of virgins began to be sacrificed.

"Why don't we go for a swim?" Bobby suggested the minute we got there.

"Sounds good to me."

"Go on out," he said, pulling a comb from his back pocket to repair the damage resulting from driving the Sting Ray with the top down. I remembered when I used to love watching him comb his hair. "I'll get us drinks. What'll you have?"

"Cokecola."

"Come on, boy," he complained, "you're not in training. And you're not the preacher's kid any more."

"Just cokecola."

"Suit yourself."

I left him in the kitchen and wandered out onto the veranda. I slipped off my clothes and dove into the water. I backstroked out into the middle and floated there trying not to think about anything. It wasn't yet dark enough to see any stars.

Bobby had seemed awfully strange in the car. He talked about how much he had missed hanging out with me lately and how he was looking forward to our evening together. He made it sound like a very big deal, but with Bobby nothing was a big deal. It had been like listening to a stranger, like somebody I had never met had taken over his body. I couldn't believe the news of our leaving town could have had such a profound effect on him. Maybe falling in love with Laddie had made me paranoid. I'd better relax or Bobby would think there was a stranger inhabiting Tristan Bentley. Come to think of it, wasn't there?

"Here you go," Bobby said coming out the back door naked as God made him and carrying a bottle of Lone Star and a tall tumbler of cola. "Cheers."

I paddled over to the deck and hauled myself out. He handed me the drink.

"Damn," I sputtered. "What the hell did you put in this?"

"Nothing," he said, looking baffled. "Mom bought some new brand of soda I never heard of. Is it awful?"

"Foul."

"Don't have anything else in the house," he said. "'Less you want to join me in a beer."

"I think I can just about choke this down," I said, "if you're sure you're not trying to poison me."

"That's the spirit," he chuckled, watching me drink.

"That'll be Mary Louise," he said when the phone rang. "Won't be more'n five minutes. Don't go anywhere."

"Where would I go? Didn't I hear some rumor about steaks?"

"Soon's I get off the phone."

He climbed out of the pool and shook himself like a dog. I watched his white butt as he walked away. I didn't move until I heard the back door close. I climbed out of the pool making as little noise as possible and padded along the deck into the shadows at the side of the playhouse. I didn't believe for a moment he thought it was Mary Louise on the phone. Not with that look on his face. He had always been hopeless at poker. I couldn't think of any reason for him to be lying about it, but I had known him a long time and could always tell when he was lying. He should have remembered that. He shouldn't have said anything about who it was. He should just have gone to answer the phone. I could just about have ignored his expression in that case, and I wouldn't have had to sneak after him and listen in through the kitchen window.

"Yeah, he's here," he said. "We got here about an hour ago. What do you mean, how long's he going to be here? I told you when we planned this, Junior. I'm going to keep him here all night. He won't be anywhere near the place. What? I slipped him some of Mom's sleeping pills, is how. Crunched two of them up in a cokecola. I'm fixing him another one right now, and I'll put more in his potato salad. I'm not going to stop shovin' 'em down him until he's out cold, so don't worry. Just go on 'bout your business."

Three strides and I had my clothes gathered up. Another two and I was at the poolhouse door. I went inside, locking it behind me. I turned on the shower full blast. With any luck, he'd hear it going and wouldn't come inside looking for me for a while. When he finally did get anxious he'd have to go back to the playhouse for the key, so I should have plenty of time if I could just keep from making too much noise. I had pulled on my clothes and was out the side window before I heard the back door open.

"Brought you a refill, T."

By then I was through the hedges and out around the far side of the big house. I heard him knock on the poolhouse door.

"T.," he yelled, "don't stay in there forever. I'm fixing to put the steaks on."

Once clear of the house, I nearly lost my train of thought. Damn that Bobby and the drug he had slipped me. Damn and double damn his insomniac mother. I knew I was supposed to be in a hurry and I thought I knew where I was supposed to be headed, but I couldn't seem to remember why and I couldn't manage to move very fast. It was like in those dreams where you're running for your life but at the same time you can't seem to move. You see the train coming but you can't make those last few feet to the other side of the crossing. I slapped myself in the face a couple of good ones, but my head still felt like someone had stuffed a pillow into it through my eye sockets.

Next thing I knew I was leaning against a tree. I could see the lights of the Davidson place off to my right. I listened but I didn't hear anything. Bobby hadn't started after me yet. I knew he would use the car. He didn't like being out in the bushes on foot even in the daytime on account of snakes. I took some deep breaths and tried to clear my head. How much time did I have? Should I try to find a telephone and warn Daddy that trouble was on its way or should I just haul ass? Where was the nearest phone, anyway? I decided I'd better start running while I tried to figure that one out. I didn't dare waste time standing still.

Next thing I knew, I was on the ground. Bobby must have followed me on foot after all. He had never tackled me that hard before. I was seeing stars and gasping for breath. In another moment I knew there was no Bobby. I had tripped and gone down hard. And it didn't feel so bad stretched out in the cool, soft grass. Just what I needed, a little rest. But no, there was no time for that. No, no time. I had to get up, get moving. I gasped in a few pitifully shallow breaths before trying to get back to my feet. I had just about made it when I heard the explosion. That cleared my head right up.

In the sanctuary, choir practice had been going on. In the basement, the youth group had been rehearsing a pageant that was to be the centerpiece of the next morning's victory celebration. The ladies of the sisterhood had been all over the building, hanging banners, arranging flowers, polishing pews, making the sanctuary resplendent for the festivities. Rev. Isaiah Washington had been in his study going over his notes for the morning sermon as was his habit on Saturday evenings. There were way too many people at Ebenezer Baptist Church that night when the bomb went off. I heard the screaming and the cries for help from a long way off. It was a sound out of your worst nightmare. Dopey as I was, I had never run faster in my life.

When I got there, stumbling and out of breath, people from all over the negro quarter of the town had gathered and were pulling the injured from the rubble. I saw Shadrach Washington climb out of the basement and ran over to help him. A gash on his forehead was bleeding like hog killing time. I ripped a sleeve off my shirt for a compress.

"Anybody else down there?" I asked.

"Lots, T., lots," he grunted.

"I'm going down," I said. "I'll help them up. You get somebody over here to work the top side."

"Careful, boy. It's might jumbled down there. And real dark. Theys broken glass and nails and such all over. Might even be some live wires."

"Don't worry about me. Keep that cloth on your cut. And find help."

I let myself over the side of the foundation, feeling gingerly below me for a foothold. It was as black as pitch. I would be very lucky not to break my neck. But there was no time to worry about that.

"Anybody down here?" I yelled.

"Over here," a girl sobbed.

"Anybody else?"

"Me too," came another girl's voice. "Me 'n sissy. I think she's hurt real bad."

"Try and stay calm," I said, as much for my own benefit as for theirs. "It won't help anything if you panic. We're going to get all of you out of here."

"Who that?" a boy asked.

"That Tristan Bentley, you dummy," another girl's voice said. "Don't you recognize his voice? Now you watch yourself, Tristan. Don't hurt yourself, hear?"

"What Tristan Bentley be doin' here?"

"What you think, boy? He gone hep get us'n out of here. So do what he say, hear now?"

"O.K." I said, making it up as I went along. "We need to get the injured ones out first. Except anybody who's hurt too bad to be moved."

"How the devil we spose to know that? None of us here ain'doctors."

I moved no more than a couple of inches at a time, testing my footing before resting my whole weight in a new spot, my hands groping in front of me. I had been an idiot not to wait for a flashlight.

"All of you keep talking, you hear?" I yelled into the darkness. "That way I'll be able to find you."

* * *

"How many more down there?" a gruff voice called some time later.

"That you, Sheriff Ellsworth?"

"Tristan? What you doin' here?"

"I was out walking and heard the explosion. I ran over here to help out."

"You weren't here when it went off?"

"No sir. Thank God. It's just Celeste Johnson and me left down here, but she's hurt pretty bad. I'm afraid to try and move her."

"I'll send a couple boys from the fire department. Now you come up outa there. Reckon you done enough. Besides, the whole place could cave in any minute."

"Not till the firemen come," I said. "I promised Celeste I wouldn't leave her."

"She that bad off?"

"She's hurt and she's scared. You wouldn't want to be left alone down here, either."

"Oh, hell. Well, won't be two shakes. At least I hope not."

"You hear that, Celeste?" I murmured to the young girl lying half conscious beside me. I checked the tourniquet I had made out of what was left of my shirt. I hoped to God she'd hang on. "It won't be long."

I followed the firemen through the rubble as they took Celeste out on a stretcher. They told me I had saved her life, and I hoped they were right. I had done everything I could think of, and if that hadn't been enough I didn't know how I would ever face myself. In the light of the firemen's torches, the devastation of the church basement was astonishing. It was a scene out of a bombed out European city of a generation earlier, not sleepy little New Jerusalem, Mississippi. It simply couldn't have happened. I could hardly believe anyone down there had survived, much less that I had found my way to them in the darkness. The others couldn't possibly have gotten out without the shine of thirteen year old Rayburn Lincoln's cigarette lighter, and I hoped his mama wouldn't be too hard on him for having one. Everybody knew Lizabeth Lincoln for a right strict woman with her kids.

"Tristan, thank God," Marytza gasped as I emerged into the nightmarish glow of headlights and torches that made her pale as a vampire queen. "We've all been worried sick."

"I'm fine," I said. "Just tired and a little scratched up."

"Where's your shirt?"

"We needed bandages down there. And a tourniquet."

"Your forehead is all clammy," she said. "I bet you're about to go into shock."

"Really, I'm O.K."

'We need a blanket over here," she shouted. "We need it now."

"Is Laddie around?"

"Under that tree over there. He's been doing first aid since we got here. It's that training he got in the Israeli Army. He's practically as good as a doctor."

"Is he O.K?"

"He's fine. Except for being half out of his mind worrying about you, that is. He was nowhere near here when it happened."

"Why who's this here?" Zuleika Jefferson asked, tossing a quilt across my shoulders. "Lord have mercy, Tristan Bentley, that you?"

"Don't use your good quilt, Miss Zuleika," I protested. "I'm a mess. You'll get it all bloody."

"This here ole rag been through worse than anything what you can do to it. Practically come offa the ark with Mrs. Noah, it did. Hear tell you some kinda hero or somethin', hepin' the young folks out down in that basement. But even big strong heroes ain' made of stone. You hush now and come with me. You need some good hot tea. And Miss Mamie Samples just brought over some of her special cheese toast. Lord, that woman do use the Tabasco. It'll warm you up good."

"I know that hurts," Sarah Anne Ellsworth said, suturing up the gash on my left shoulder. "You don't have to play brave soldier with me."

"It's not so bad."

"It is so," she smiled. "I watched Junior getting stitches once. He liked to fainted and fell right out of the chair. Never let him forget it."

"You couldn't have been the one working on him."

"Naw," she said. "It was old Doc Forster just before he retired. That man was pretty rough, all right. I'd have driven clear to Bagwell not to have him put stitches in me. Hell, I'd have gone to a vet first, but don't tell anybody I said so. But Junior's a big old chicken and everybody knows it. He must have been in ninth grade at the time. I had just graduated and come back here to work. In nursing school I hadn't done much more than practice giving injections to navel oranges. And stitches? Well, Granny Huckaby had taught me to truss up a turkey right smart, but that's the closest I ever got to it before coming to work here. Reckon that good for nothing brother of mine been in this emergency room more than anybody else in the whole county. There. Now let's have a look at the other one."

I showed her my right forearm.

"And you wanted to go home to bed," she clucked. "Thank heaven that smarty pants college girl wouldn't listen to you. This one's worse than the other one. Must hurt right bad."

She chattered on while sewing me up. Like all the Ellsworth women clear back to the War of Northern Aggression, Sarah Anne had never needed any help keeping a conversation going, and I let my eyes close. Except for the discomfort of the stitches going in, I'd have fallen asleep. Pretty soon she finished, and I did just that.

"You looking for Tristan Bentley? Why, he's right in here, Papa," Sarah Anne said a while later.

"Need to speak to him," Sheriff Ellsworth said, pulling back a corner of the curtain and peering into the cubicle like he wasn't sure she was telling him the truth.

"Oh, I don't know about that, Papa. Not until Dr. Meadows says it's all right."

"It's mighty important, Missy."

"I'm sure it is, Papa. But this is a hospital. You're not in charge here, even if you think you are."

"I know it's a hospital, dammit."

"Don't use that kind of language in front of my patient," she admonished. "I don't care if you're J. Edgar Hoover himself."

"Sarah Anne, I'm fine," I said. "I don't mind talking to Sheriff Ellsworth."

"Well now, I'm not sure it's a good idea," she shook her head. "Dr. Meadows ordered that you're to be kept as quiet as possible. There's still a chance you could go into shock. And we've got enough seriously injured people around here as it is."

"I'm not fixing to have him dig fence rows or muck out a barn, girl," Sheriff Ellsworth growled. "Just need a few minutes of his time."

"All right," she said, "but I'm going to get Dr. Meadows right now, and if I find out you've been upsetting my patient I'm going to get you thrown out of here. You see if I don't."

"Yes, ma'am," Sheriff Ellsworth said, watching her bustle out of the cubicle. I could tell how proud of her he was. "Takes after her ma, that one."

"She's a good nurse."

"'Course she is. And she's right to be lookin' out for yaw'll, Tristan. It's just, well, there ain't no help for it."

"What's wrong?"

"Son," he said, hanging his head, "I'd give anything not to have to be telling yaw'll this. Anything in the whole wide world."

"It's Daddy."

"Yep," he said. "'Fraid so. They just found him. Over there to the church. Just pulled him out of a pile of. . .well, yaw'll was there, yaw'll saw what it's like."

"Is he hurt bad?"

"He didn't make it, son."

"Where did they find him?"

"Looks like he musta been in the study with Rev. Isaiah. Best as we can tell, anyhow. Tristan, his neck was broken. Yaw'll know what that means?"

"I think so."

"It musta been real fast. He probably didn't feel much of anything."

"Oh."

"Now Brother Daniel and I didn't see eye to eye on a whole lotta things, but don't mean nothin'. He was one of the finest men I ever knew, yaw'll hear me?"

"Yes, sir."

"One of the finest. I will always be proud to call myself his friend. I don't care what anybody says. And I'll miss him. Not like yaw'll will, of course. But I will. He buried my daddy. And he was so good to my mama when she had that cancer. Won't never forget how good he was to her. Came to see her nearly ever day, and always with a joke or a story to tell her. Helped her make her peace with it, he did. She said she wasn't ever afraid of what was gonna happen because Brother Daniel give her the courage she needed. Said we wasn't to fret none over her,'cause Brother Daniel give her the faith to face her troubles and just leave it all at the feet a' Jesus. She never was a church goer, but that didn't stop him from takin' an interest. That's some kinda man, can help a sick old lady smile in spite of her pain and everthing. Help her live out her days like he done. Wasn't just that, either. Nearly everbody in this town got something like that to remember about him, so no matter what's done happened, yaw'll just remember that they all loved him in their way and won't none of us forget him. Never, no way."

"Thank you."

"Now I know Miss Elizabeth is up to Chattanooga with the girls. Be glad to call her for yaw'll. Boy your age shouldn't have to make that kinda telephone call."

"That's all right," I said. "I'll call her. Just as soon as Dr. Meadows lets me out of here and I can get a ride back to the house."

"Right," Sheriff Ellsworth said. "Well, see, there's one more thing."

"What is it?"

"Well, yaw'll know we pretty much had our hands full there at the church, what with all them people hurt and all. I guess the boys didn't respond to the alarm as fast as they might have. And it all happened pretty fast. Anyways, what I'm tryin' to say is, there ain't no more house, Tristan. Burned clean to the ground."

"What?"

"Miss Althea Chandler says she heard a car. Come up the street kinda slow, like the driver was lookin' for somethin', and then speeded up all of a sudden. Next thing she knew, your house was just goin' up like a torch. All I can think of, they musta thrown some a them Molotov cocktails or somethin' like that."

"What kind of car was it?"

"Miss Althea couldn' tell nothin'. Had its lights off and all. Tristan, I'm sure sorry about all this."

XVIII

I spent that night in Mercer Swinford's bed. It was a huge, ornate structure far too grand for merely sleeping in unless one was rather grand oneself. You had to climb two steps to get into it, and I felt like nothing so much as a pauper perched there in a grimy, sweaty heap. It had been an old bed by the time Mercer was born, and I wondered who all the earlier occupants had been. Were the two of us the only ones who had lain sleepless with those four heavily carved posters for sentinels, or had those earlier occupants also found themselves tragically beset? I knew that heartbreak visits every generation, but pondering the misfortunes of others was beyond my capabilities that night. The old house was silent through the endless hours as if intent on hearing some omen or portent outside its walls. I did not strain my ears along with it, believing that nothing good or comforting lurked in the darkness. Instead I prayed. I prayed as if God actually existed, as if He cared what happened to His people, though I was beginning to doubt. I prayed for all I was worth that none of it had really happened and in the morning I would awaken in my own bed in my own house. I prayed through the night but stopped when the first glimmering of dawn shone through the open window. No miracle had occurred, and sooner or later I heard signs of life in the old house. Eventually Laddie came in to check on me and I had to start pretending I was still alive.

I dressed in things I found in Mercer Swinford's closet and felt even more surely like a ghost. Demonstrating hitherto unsuspected domestic expertise, Marytza got the trousers hemmed up and taken in at the waist while I was in the shower. The shirt was fine except for being too long in the sleeves, so I tucked them up inside the sleeves of the jacket. I wore the most colorful necktie I could find and pair of

Mercer's quaint suspenders. Even his shoes fit me. At least they did once I had on four pairs of his socks.

There was no question of a victory celebration that morning. Not with Ebenezer Baptist Church in ruins and Meshach Washington and Daddy dead and seven others still in critical condition. Our victory, such as it was, lay in the ashes and tasted of the tears we shed. Who could think of celebration with lives still in the balance? These included Shadrach, who had gotten himself out of the basement unaided and then collapsed into a coma not long after I sent him to find help, Rev. Washington, who would never walk again, and Celeste Thompson who eventually would but on one leg and crutches.

The crowd had gathered in front of Mt. Calvary African Methodist Episcopal Zion Church, which had been heavily vandalized while we were all preoccupied on the other side of town. Obscenities had been painted across the white clapboards in sloppy black paint, and not a window was left unbroken. The big front doors to the sanctuary had been wrested from their hinges, and hymnals had been ripped to shreds and strewn across the front yard. Further enormities had apparently been committed inside. I heard my neighbors in the crowd whispering and murmuring, but I didn't want to know any more than I already did, which was almost past bearing.

It was a large gathering, subdued rather than angry, purposeful rather than dispirited. Many people in the crowd sported bandages. Several were in casts. All of them were dressed in the finest they had. There were far too many of us to have gone inside the sanctuary even if that had been our intent. Rev. Maurice St. Jacques Lincoln greeted us from the church steps. He solemnly spoke the names of the dead and reported on the condition of the injured. He read a message from Dr. King, who couldn't attend at such short notice, and then introduced Mrs. King, who had traveled all night from Atlanta to be with us. She looked both smaller and much younger than I expected. She gave the impression of being very brave. She spoke briefly, with great feeling and dignity, and closed by reading the passage from *Isaiah* where the lion and the lamb lie down in peace together. Rev. Lincoln prayed, and then the deacons of the combined congregations began to organize us for the march.

Savannah Washington was to lead the procession, but before she moved off there was a delay. Around me I heard people wondering aloud. Had there been some new threat? Was further violence expected? Perhaps right here on the spot? Would we march at all? Or would there be some closing remarks and a final prayer to send us all home?

It turned out they were looking for me. Savannah Washington refused to begin the march until I joined her. I heard my name being whispered in the crowd and resolutely ignored it. Try as I might, however, I could not become invisible. The message was officially conveyed to me by Deacons Wilson and Rush, two octogenarian gentlemen whose eyes said they had seen more than sufficient trouble long before that morning dawned but whose backs were nevertheless straight and unbowed. Would I do Mrs. Washington the honor?

"Go," Laddie hissed at me, sensing my reluctance. "You know you have to."

"I can't," I moaned. "I don't want the whole world to see me like this."

"What do you mean, 'like this'?" Marytza asked.

"You know that I mean. What if I break down? A fat lot of good that will do to honor Daddy's memory. Or Meshach's. If I'm just part of the crowd, no one will notice."

"What's wrong with you?" Laddie demanded. "You think tears are inappropriate for the occasion? What planet are you living on?"

"Take it easy, Laddie," Marytza insisted, kissing me on the cheek. "Tristan, that poor woman has had as hard a time as you have and she wants you there beside her. That's what you owe Daniel."

They had decided. The crowd around us parted, and Deacon Wilson and Deacon Rush escorted me to the head of the column.

"Good morning, Miss Savannah."

"Morning, Mr. Tristan," Miss Savannah murmured. She was regal in her black clothing. Her eyes were misty and her voice trembled but her resolve was unquestionable, and in it I found a bit of my own. "How you bearing up?"

"Oh, it's hard," I choked out, blinking back tears. "It's the hardest thing."

"Yes," she nodded. "It most certainly is."

"I was so sorry about Meshach," I said.

"And we'll all miss your daddy terribly. Lord knows what we'll do around here without him."

"Yes, ma'am."

"Have you spoken to Miss Elizabeth?"

"She'll be in Bagwell this evening. My uncles are driving her down."

"She won't be coming here?"

"No."

"I don't blame her. There's nothing good for her here any more, and she's not the kind to come around just to spite them. Best for her to stay away."

"Yes, ma'am."

"You know why we have to do this today, don't you?" she asked, taking my hand.

"For the people. All our people."

"That's right," she said. "To show that the living who can't be with us are in our prayers and that we won't forget those who have been taken from us."

"And because the struggle isn't over."

"No, sir, it isn't over. We've got two dead and a whole passel hurt and our beloved Ebenezer Baptist destroyed and Mt. Calvary desecrated, but we will keep on. Church isn't a building anyhow. It's the people. You heard Mrs. King. No death in our cause is ever in vain. Whatever happens, we aren't ever goin' back."

"But I don't know if I can go on any more," I said, sniffing. "I'm frightened."

"I'm frightened, too," she said. "But you can do it. We'll lean on each other and we'll get there. That's what God gives us each other for. So's we'll have somebody to lean on. So's we won't ever have to take up our burdens alone. That's how He blesses us with our friends and loved ones. They're not just with us for the good times, oh, no."

"Yes, ma'am."

"So I'm awfully glad you're here, Tristan. Awfully glad you're here to share my burden and awfully glad I can help you hold up yours."

"I couldn't do this with anybody else."

"Of course you could," she said, very nearly smiling. "There is nothing you can't do. You're your Daddy's son. You ready?"

"Let's go."

"All right."

We walked through New Jerusalem and the streets were lined with Federal Marshals and National Guardsmen sweating inside their uniforms. They were armed and their faces were expressionless except their eyes, which flickered with vigilance. Where had they all come from? How had they appeared so suddenly, so many of them, just overnight like that? And were they protecting us from everyone else in town or everyone else in town from us? You couldn't tell if they were even sure themselves. They were just there.

We walked through New Jerusalem and the news cameras whirred and clicked in the sunshine like swarms of insects. The only other sound was the shuffle of our hundreds of pairs of shoes on the sidewalks. We walked through New Jerusalem, and in the white neighborhoods the front doors were closed despite the heat and there wasn't a sound. The dogs weren't even barking.

We walked a long time and finally we turned a corner. We were on the street I had always thought of as home and never would again. It was deserted, almost like a ghost town. Like the day after the Russians bombed New York, Washington, and Chicago and everybody left went underground. But the street wasn't completely devoid of life. Up at midblock, directly across from the scorched scar in the earth I could hardly bear to look at, Miss Althea Chandler stood on her front porch in her Sunday best and waved a white hankie at us. When we reached the spot, she was no longer on the porch but in the middle of the street.

"Oh, Tristan," she sobbed, embracing me with arms astonishingly fragile. "Oh, you poor boy. How could these horrible things happen? How on earth? I don't understand it and I just can't stop crying."

"It's all right, Miss Althea."

"Oh, no it isn't. It can't ever be all right again. Not after this."

She released me and took a couple of deep breaths that were second cousins to sobs. She dabbed her eyes with her hankie and turned to Savannah Washington. I guessed they had never exchanged more than two words before in all their years of living in the same small town.

"I'm right sorry to hear about your son, Mrs. Washington. It's a terrible, terrible thing. You must be heartbroken."

"Thank you, Mrs. Chandler."

"And how is your Shadrach this morning?"

"Dr. Meadows says the coma is showing signs of lifting. He's very hopeful."

"Thank you, Jesus. And Reverend Washington?"

"He's out of danger."

"Amen and amen," Miss Althea said. "We need all the ministers and men of God here with us in such times. We need them to help us understand these terrible things and how we can make some good come out of them. Now you must let me know if there is ever anything I can do to help you and your family."

"Thank you, Mrs. Chandler."

"Please, you must," Miss Althea insisted. "Gonna make it my business to see to it that things are different around here. We can't go on talking about our folks and your folks like we always have before. These horrible things will just keep on happening if we do. We all have to be the same folks from now on. We just have to. So I really mean it, Mrs. Washington, please let me help out. Any way I can. Anything at all I can do."

"All right, Mrs. Chandler. Thank you."

"You won't forget now?"

"I won't forget."

We walked through New Jerusalem. And the sun beat down on us, and the sweat running off my forehead stung my already burning eyes but I didn't raise a hand to wipe them and I didn't lower my face. I held my head as high as Savannah Washington held hers, and I looked straight ahead. I didn't see where I was going, but she was my eyes and that was enough. We walked on, and walking was enough.

When we passed First Baptist Church, I could hear them singing a hymn inside. "Onward, Christian Soldiers, Marching as to War." I could almost see them all in there. The Aynseleys and the Howells and the Turners and the Morgans and the Winslows and the Davidsons and the Duncans. Hundreds of them, people I had known all my life. Over the past weeks I had come to see them as strangers and eventually as the enemy, but I hadn't reckoned on their ruthlessness or the depth of their fervor. I supposed we had all underestimated them. The organ pipes roared under the hands of someone who wasn't Mercer Swinford, and the people sang out as if they knew who was passing by. They sang of Christ leading them into battle, and I wondered who they thought His enemies were and what wars they believed He would have them wage. I wondered if they had any clear idea about Him at all. Because if they did then Daddy never understood anything, and that was what killed him.

We walked on and Savannah Washinton gripped my hand more tightly.

We walked through New Jerusalem, and the unbearable heat grew hotter, and the unbearable burden seemed to grow heavier, and the road stretching out into infinity ahead of us blurred before my eyes. We walked through the silent, sweltering streets of the town, and Confederate flags still hung on people's porches and in front of their businesses. My blood boiled and ran cold at the same time and I couldn't imagine what Savannah Washington felt when she saw that hated rag everywhere.

And then we arrived at Ebenezer Baptist Church. I had seen photos of Berlin. Of Stalingrad. Of Tokyo. This destruction, though on a far smaller scale, was as absolute. Its meaning was as profound. Humankind still hadn't learned to live in peace. Unable to go on standing I knelt in the rubble, ruining the knees of Mercer Swinford's trousers in the process, and I prayed prayers I had no hope would ever be answered and I swore vows no sixteen year old boy should ever have occasion to swear. I knelt in the rubble while the swelling crowd circled the heaps of shattered lumber and glass, the torn shingles and tattered carcasses of trees. I knelt there while Mrs. King made a final remark and Rev. Maurice St. Jacques Lincoln read a passage from *Lamentations* and led one last prayer. And Savannah Washington stood at my side and rested a hand on my shoulder.

Zuleika Jefferson sang the first stanza solo, and then we all joined in. Hundreds of voices raised the anthem of our struggle with no end. I sang along. How could I not? But deep in my heart I wasn't at all sure I believed we would ever overcome, and the sultry air of that sad morning swallowed up the sound of our voices.

XIX

That afternoon, wearing still more borrowed clothing, I went home. I didn't tell anyone where I was going for fear they would try and stop me or come along and smother me with sympathy. I walked alone through those silent streets and my heart was in my mouth the whole way. Disasters come in threes, which left one to go. And as far as I knew no culprits had been apprehended. In the chaos of the night before I had managed to forget all kinds of things. But they had come back to me during the endless hours in Mercer Swinford's bed. I knew who had done it. At least some of them. I reckoned I knew more about what had happened than anyone else in New Jerusalem other than the perpetrators themselves. And by now I figured they had a pretty good idea how much I knew. But they didn't know who I might have talked to, which might well be everybody in town before too many more hours had passed. So I had no illusions. I was a marked man walking those streets. Easy pickings. They would have a much simpler time making my death look like a suicide than they had in the previous instance.

When Sheriff Ellsworth told me our house had burned to the ground, he was not resorting to an overused figure of speech. It truly had burned clear to the ground. There was nothing standing. Even the chimney had collapsed into a pile of scorched bricks. There was nothing there but a basement full of rubble and surprisingly little of that. Aided by whatever incendiary material had been used to start it, the blaze had burned hot and long and an enormous volume of material had literally gone up in smoke. Ashes don't take up much space.

Trees and shrubbery close to the house had burned with it, while vegetation farther away still stood but was scorched almost beyond any believable possibility of recovery. Even the grass was scorched for many feet in all directions from the crumbling foundations. It seemed impossible that something so ordinary as a house fire could have been so comprehensively destructive. Obviously, nothing short of a miracle could have saved anyone who had been home at the time, though as it turned out, absence from the scene had been no guarantee of salvation.

The devastation was not quite complete, however. Across the reeking chasm that had been the basement and just outside the perimeter of destruction, my mother's rose garden blazed that afternoon in an altogether different sort of conflagration. I stared thunderstruck at the color and irrepressible vitality and mindless hopefulness.

"Tristan, what the hell are you doing?" Laddie demanded, peering over the edge of the hole.

"You first."

"Miss Althea called and said you were over here digging around," he said. "She told me you were acting strangely."

"I suppose I am."

"She was very concerned."

"Everybody's concerned. You all look at me like you're afraid I'm about to do something desperate."

"Are you?" he asked, and the look on his face finally got through to me. He was nearly frantic. I felt awful for having worried him.

"Are you crazy?"

"No," he said. "Are you?"

"I'm not having one of my best days," I said, "but I don't believe I'm crazy."

"So what are you doing down there?"

"Look," I said. "They're not all ruined."

"What?"

"Daddy's books. Most of them are buried so deep they'll never be seen again. Or they got soaked by the fire hoses and they'll be completely rotten within a week. But I came down here and poked around a little and found a few boxes here at the bottom of this pile that are completely untouched."

"You're joking."

"It's some kind of miracle."

"Which books?"

"Does it matter?"

"I don't suppose it does."

"They're all that's left. Let me pass some up to you."

"Wait right there," he said, and disappeared. A few moments later he returned with Miss Althea Chandler's extension ladder under his arm and Miss Althea herself at his heels.

"Look, Miss Althea," I shouted, waving a book at her. "Look what I found."

"Why, Lord have mercy. What have you got there?"

"The biography of Madame Curie," I said. "And this one is the collected sermons of Adoniram Judson."

"Well, I swan. It must be a sign from God. Brother Daniel surely did love his books."

"Look out below," Laddie called.

I caught the end of the ladder and steadied it in the ashes, and he climbed down.

"Hand me that carton."

I did, and he headed back up the ladder.

"You keep digging them out," he called over his shoulder, "and I'll haul them up."

When we got back to the Swinford place with the load of books, we had visitors.

"They insisted on waiting for you," Marytza explained. "I didn't know what to do, so I put them in the living room and served them iced tea."

They were two husky men in their thirties. They were wearing ill fitting dark suits. Dressed differently and less clean cut, they would have made perfect wrestling opponents for my uncles. I would have expected FBI agents to be smoother, less buffoonish. They stood when Laddie and I entered the room.

"Mr. Bentley?" the taller of the two asked.

"That's me."

"I'm agent Robinson. This is my colleague Agent Sirica. We're with the FBI."

I glanced at the identification they flashed.

"We were hoping you might be willing to answer a few questions."

XX

Grandmother Bentley had a fifth grade education. Plenty, she always insisted, for reading the Bible and *Ladies' Home Journal*. The newspaper was full of things no decent, God fearing woman should know about and she never touched it except to toss it in the trash. The newspaper came only so Grandpa Bentley could read the letters to the editor in case one had been written by someone he knew, the baseball scores, and the comics. Grannie had tried the comics once and found the material lacking either in humor or other edifying values. A straight A student, she quit school at the age of eleven to keep house for her newly widowed father, take care of the cows, hogs, and chickens, and raise her eight younger siblings. At seventeen she was a farm wife in her own right, at eighteen a mother. She bore seven sons in eleven years, two of whom died in infancy, two in World War II, and one in a farming accident. Daddy was the youngest. She was in her late sixties that summer, but her life had been anything but easy and she looked at least a decade older than that. There had been depression. There had been war. There had been drought. There had been illness. There had been lean times and even leaner times, and she had stood up to everything. So she was not so much aged as weathered, like an old barn in need of maintenance. She was a tiny, scrawny thing with a soft voice which she never raised. She looked like a stray breeze might knock her off her feet, but she possessed the determination of a charging rhino, the strength of a stevedore, and the stamina of a Sherpa. You could easily have mistaken her for one of those timid little women the south was full of, but she had the heart of a lioness.

She would never win a Nobel Prize, a Pulitzer, or an Oscar. The things she excelled at they didn't give awards and prizes for. These were the practical skills demanded of a farm wife, and she had them in an abundance that amazed her neighbors, which was all the fame she ever achieved. But all she had to show for her accomplishments was all anybody in her position ever had to show for them, the roof over her head, the continued survival of her family, and the cellar full of foodstuffs she had raised and preserved with her own hands against the coming winter. She thought of that winter even on the hottest days. If she had a nemesis, that impending winter, no matter how distant, was it. She couldn't tell you a thing about Shakespeare or Milton beyond the fact of their existence, but she could tell you to the day when you should set out your tomato plants or when you should dig your new potatoes. Her knowledge of world geography was pretty much limited to what she gleaned at meetings of the Women's Missionary Circle and she couldn't discuss affairs of state, but she could diagnose all the known ailments of all known species of livestock and successfully treat most of them. She couldn't dispute theology, but to the generations of children she taught in Sunday School her voice was nonetheless the voice of God.

Austerity was her middle name and it went way beyond material frugality. After the fashion of a certain strain of southern womanhood, she was undemonstrative as a fence post. She objected to emotional display on various grounds. It was beneath her dignity, and she set great store by what little dignity she credited herself with. In addition, it signified weakness and self indulgence, and she was determined that her small corner of the world should recognize her as neither weak nor self indulgent. Most of all, it was wasteful to the point of profligacy. The time and energy it required could be far better employed. Why snap at a surly youngster, for instance, when you could air the sheets or pull the rugs outside and give them a good beating? Why talk about your feelings when you could be darning socks or shelling peas? Why tell people you loved them when instead you could be laundering their clothing or fixing them a meal? And since hunger never took a day off neither did she, so the day we buried Daddy she was on duty from daybreak. I sat across her kitchen table from Mama and pretended to eat biscuits and gravy while Mama pretended to eat scrambled eggs. All the food did was make me miss Daddy more, and I suspected Mama felt the same.

Mama was even thinner than usual. There was a single streak of gray in her blond hair that I hadn't noticed before. Maybe it was new or maybe she had just gotten off schedule for a touch up. Her hair color had always been the subject of much speculation among the women of First Baptist Church. The majority opinion held that it couldn't possibly be natural, though as far as I knew it was or at least had been until very recently. That it matched my own hair color had always seemed all the evidence anyone could have needed. But gossip requires no reason and accepts no evidence no matter how firm, so the speculation never ended. She looked wearier than I had ever seen her, but that was no surprise given the circumstances. It showed itself not so much in the dark circles under her eyes as in the eyes themselves. I detected none of their usual sparkle. I needed desperately to see that sparkle and know that things would be all right. But it wasn't there, and I wasn't sure how I was going to manage without it.

"Tristan," she said, with an expression on her face much like that of someone who's just found a particularly beautiful mushroom growing on the forest floor and doesn't know how to determine whether it's edible or toxic, "you're the best son a mother could ever hope for."

"I am not."

"Don't interrupt."

"Sorry."

"I've always said so, though I realize I've never said it to you directly. Or in your hearing. Your father felt that one of the worst things parents could do was praise a child too highly. Or too often. So we didn't. Obviously, not very many parents agree with us. I know you've spent your whole life listening to people talk about how wonderful their children are and wondering why you never heard anything like that about yourself from your parents."

"Actually, no."

"I'm not sure I believe you," Mama said. "I know I would have wondered if it were me. Grannie and Papa Ingebrittsen were never afraid of spoiling me or the boys by bragging on us, and I think we turned out all right. But your father felt very strongly about it, and I went along because that's what you do. Anyway, I only hope you know that he was very proud of you."

"Of course I do," I said. "You don't have to be told something like that to know it."

"Don't you?"

"Well, I never did."

"If you say so. But if you've got one fault, Tristan, it's not saying what you really feel but what you think people want to hear. Don't pretend you don't do that, because I'm your mother and I know better. You've always been particularly bad about it with your father. You had that lesson learned by the time you could talk. Maybe if we had been a normal family things would have been different."

"What's that supposed to mean? We're a perfectly normal family."

"You know what I'm talking about."

"Maybe I do."

"There it is," she laughed.

"What?"

"You just backed down. The point I was trying to make is this. Everybody and his cat know how crazy a life a preacher's wife and children have and what all they have to endure, but you always brush it off. Even at a time like this you won't let down your defenses."

"Defenses? I have no defenses."

"You're awful," she said, smiling. "Anyway, this is going to sound strange coming from a woman who has just chastised you for being overly tactful, but I have to tell you that today I need to be able to depend on your tact."

"Of course."

"Not so fast, young man. Listen to me. You've been under a terrible strain. Don't say it's not true because I'm sitting here looking at you and I can tell. I ought to take you to the doctor as soon as we're finished today."

"Mama, I'm O.K."

"You're not, and we're not arguing about it. I know it's eating you up that they haven't arrested anyone yet. It's as plain as the nose on your face. I know you want that more than anything right now."

"Don't you?"

"It won't bring him back."

"I know that."

"Well?"

"They deserve to be punished for what they did," I said, only refraining from shouting by desperate effort. "They can't be allowed to go on with their lives as if nothing happened and their hands are clean."

"Vengeance is the Lord's, son."

"Well at the very least," I said, unable to meet her relentless gaze, "it'll make anyone else of the same inclination think twice before they go and kill somebody."

"I wish I could believe it's that simple," she sighed. "I truly do. But what I believe or don't believe isn't the point. You're going to be on display again today. Just like you have been for your entire life. And I'm not sure you're up to it."

"I'm not staying away from Daddy's funeral."

"I'd never suggest it. I'm simply asking you to do something I know will be especially difficult."

"Which is?"

"Make an extra effort to hold your tongue today. There's no telling who will show up. Anybody from church might take it into their heads that we'd be comforted by their presence, for instance. And people are incredibly insensitive sometimes—or rather, usually—and you may find yourself face to face with somebody who doesn't know when to keep his or her fool mouth shut. And while you might feel like there's no point any more in being nice to people around here, and you might imagine that letting yourself say exactly what you want to for once in your life will make all this hurt less—well, if you thought that you'd be wrong, that's all. Maybe it ought to work that way but it doesn't. No matter what you say, you won't change anybody's mind, because enlightenment is not what they will have come for. And you'll just give them reason to think less of you, whether you care about that or not. So you lose out both ways. And let me remind you that your father abhorred confrontations, and he'd be humiliated to know that you were involved in one at his funeral."

"Yes ma'am."

"Tomorrow's a different matter, however," she smiled, staring inscrutably into her coffee cup. "Tomorrow you can send them one and all to hell in a handbasket, and I won't utter a word of protest. But let's have one more day of silent hypocrisy."

"Is that what it is? Hypocrisy?"

"Not really," she laughed sheepishly. "Or maybe just a little. Preachers' sons aren't the only ones who have to keep their mouths shut when it might be better to just cut loose. Maybe I never really was cut out to be a preacher's wife. I certainly hated it most of the time. But I loved Daniel so much. And I wouldn't have dreamed of trying to talk him out of his calling."

Mama went upstairs to dress. I played around with my food a little more.

"Looks like you haven't got much appetite this morning," Grannie observed.

"Sorry," I said, watching her take my plate. "It was delicious, but I just can't seem to eat."

"Guess nothin' much tastes good right now."

"Guess not."

"That mama of yours, she's a saint of the Lord. You know that, don't you?"

"Yes'm."

"Best thing that ever happened to your daddy was meetin' her. No doubt about it. Pretty as a picture, she was. You always took after her that way. Pretty girls is a dime a dozen, of course. And there's a good many smart girls, too. Though I'm not sure what good bein' smart is to a young woman. Seems to get most of 'em in trouble one way or another, so it's nothin' more'n a waste, really. But a gal like your mama is rare as hen's teeth. You only meet a few of 'em like that in your whole life. And when you do you know you've got a real friend. It's ones like your mama that makes good wives and good mothers. You trust 'em and you depend on 'em. 'Cause you can. They won't never let you down. You just pray you'll have a gal like that sittin' by when it's your time.

"And as fer you, young man, you don't know it but your daddy bragged on you plenty to me. He was awful proud of his boy. And he had ever right to be, so don't you forget it."

There was to be no formal service. Mama decreed this and no one attempted to dissuade her that I heard of. Though ordinarily the funeral of a white clergyman in a town like New Jerusalem would have occasioned pomp and ceremony worthy of a senator or movie star, in this case no white church would have opened its doors to us, either there or in a neighboring town. Baptist, Presbyterian, Methodist, Episcopal, Pentecostal, it didn't matter. No black church dared welcome us for fear of being suspected by the white population of staging some bizarre or even dangerous provocation. Who would blame them for fearing the possible reaction? Mississippi was a tinderbox, and the presence of Federal Marshals and National Guardsmen was little comfort because no one knew for certain where their allegiance lay. Nor did anyone seriously believe the trouble was over. There could yet be more violence and more deaths. It was probably only a matter of time. Still, Mama refused to settle for a service in a mortuary chapel, though she had no objection to such observances in principle. Better no service at all than to have to give in like that. They could kill Daddy, she seemed to be saying, but they still hadn't won anything and weren't going to. So there was nothing to do but gather at the graveside.

Mama and I rode over there in Uncle Gunnar's Jaguar. All three of Mama's brothers had come with her from Chattanooga, and it was a tight fit with Uncle Lars, Uncle Tor and me shoehorned into the back seat. But I wouldn't have dreamed of complaining. I couldn't imagine anyone better to have in your corner than the Ingebrittsen brothers. They seemed invincible in a way I could scarcely imagine but desperately aspired to. Would any of this have happened if I had been more like them?

What little talk there was during the drive centered on my uncles' long time, fundamental distrust and disapproval of Mama's in-laws. They had idolized Daddy and made absolute pets of my sisters and me but couldn't abide his family. None of this was news to me, though I had always helped them maintain the fiction that it was knowledge reserved for adults. For once Mama didn't correct them for referring to the Bentleys as white trash in front of one of her children. She refrained from any comment.

That apparently took most of the fun out of their critique, and they continued with it only half heartedly.

The small turnout at the cemetery shouldn't have come as a surprise. Other than family, only Miss Althea Chandler and Vladimir's crew were in attendance. None of the hundreds of people whose hospital bedsides Daddy had attended, or whose sad tales he had uncomplainingly listened to for hours on end, or whose inedible cooking he had ingested and praised, or whose weddings he had performed, or whose children he had baptized, or whose parents or grandparents he had buried bothered to show up. I had expected that a few of them at least would come to pay their respects. What would that have cost them? It didn't have to mean they agreed with him or were suddenly prepared to join the cause. Only the most paranoid could possibly have thought their neighbors might disapprove of their attendance. It would merely have signified that they remembered. It wasn't like anyone was asking them for anything more than an hour or so of their time. But even that little bit was apparently too much to ask. And it wasn't just because it was a Tuesday afternoon and people had to work. Southern towns don't operate that way. They could have closed down the whole county if they had wanted to. They had done so in the past for less cause.

But they didn't.

After all he had done for them they chose to think of him as a traitor or at the very least a crackpot who should have been put away long since. He no longer existed for them, or he never had existed. Somebody else had been their friend and pastor, someone who saw the world as they did and didn't upset people with strange ideas and challenge the way things were done. Thus, they needn't spare a thought for his daughters off with their grandparents in Chattanooga. They needn't think anything at all as they drove past the barren lot where his house used to stand.

I was thunderstruck by their absence. I had believed that his death would bring them all to their senses, occasioning an orgy of remorse and repentance. You think things like that when you've been raised like I had been. You believe in the impact of dramatic events. You believe people can be shaken out of their complacency. You believe they can be touched.

Just as I was marveling over all this and thinking Mama's breakfast table pep talk had been wasted because no one who might set me off was around, I overheard Daddy's surviving brother, Uncle Niles, say that it just went to show you no good could ever come of getting involved with the nigras, and Daniel should have known better and would have known better if he hadn't forgotten his upbringing. I wanted to bash his fool brain in, but I pretended I hadn't heard.

A distant cousin of Daddy's, Rev. Arthur Braxton of Mobile, officiated. He was the archetypal small town Baptist preacher boy. Not the kind of man, in other words, who would have been the first to denounce Daddy's recent behavior from the pulpit but not the kind of man to refrain from criticism, either. I couldn't believe Mama had requested him and sensed some unwanted interference from the Bentleys. Perhaps Uncle Niles had stuck his oar in and Mama had simply been too distraught and exhausted to resist. I cringed at the thought of what he might say. I don't know how Mama managed it, because clergymen like that have minds of their own and very little regard for anyone's suggestions much less feelings, but he failed to deviate by a jot from the script she laid out. Which meant a prayer, a scripture reading, the briefest and most innocuous of remarks, a clumsy shovel full of dirt on the casket, and a benediction. We were back in the car before we knew it.

Outside the gates of the cemetery, a large crowd had gathered. I thought there must be another funeral scheduled for that afternoon and that as was customary the next group was waiting for us to leave the grounds before entering. I wondered what local luminary rated such a turnout. Then we drew closer, and I saw that all the faces were black ones.

"Gunnar, stop the car," Mama commanded.

We all got out. Mama led the way and my three uncles and I followed. She waded into that crowd in a way that could have shown a politician a thing or two. They had all just come from burying Meshach Washington. Bagwell Memorial Park was nowhere near their route home. In fact, coming there had taken them far out of their way. And it hadn't been an easy journey, I saw, noticing the Bagwell Police Department cruisers parked a little way off, their lights flashing with menace.

XXI

There is no tragedy so grave that southerners cannot incorporate a pot luck dinner into their mourning. This timeless truth is as dependable as the sunrise or the changing of the seasons. It is as if there on Mount Sinai God had handed Moses an eleventh commandment which He expected to be observed as faithfully as the other ten. When someone dies, *thou shalt prepare unto thee a casserole, salad, or dessert, place it in a vessel, cover it, and carry it with thee to the place where all are gathered together, and there thou shalt share it among all present.* Thus, when Mama, my uncles, and I finally returned from the graveyard a near multitude of Bentley relatives, friends, and neighbors had materialized, filling the rooms of my grandparents' house with the sounds of conversation and flatware clinking on dishes. The crowd spilled out into both back and front yards, a chewing, gossiping, dressed up swarm.

I recognized no more than a handful of faces from the graveyard. The rest were later arrivals, but by their demeanor and the remarks I managed to overhear I quickly understood that it wasn't the distance they had traveled which had delayed them and I mentally added them to the list of those who had let Daddy down. Many of them I hadn't seen since the last funeral in the family, when Great Aunt Ida Wentworth passed away two years previously after being bedridden since Pearl Harbor. Lots of them couldn't identify me with any certainty, though they didn't seem to have any trouble pegging Mama as the widow.

They continued arriving in a steady stream all afternoon, coming from counties I'd forgotten were on the map of Mississippi, coming from all points of the compass and as far away as Memphis. Though young couples with toddlers or kindergarten age children were the center of attention, most of those present were at least middle aged. The number of truly elderly ones, men and women who had already been middle aged when Daddy was a boy, was amazing. Their Buicks, Oldsmobiles, and DeSotos would lurch laboriously up the unpaved drive from the county road raising dust all the way. The women would check their hair and renew their lipstick with the aid of hand mirrors before stepping out of the cars and bustling into the house with their covered dishes and the men would light up their cigars or pipes and sniff the air like coon hounds scanning for a scent prior to moseying over to join the menfolk already smoking, congregated under the tall trees some ancient, barely remembered Bentley had planted there long before the War of Northern Aggression.

Some of the visitors sought me out on purpose to offer condolences or share bizarre reminiscences I couldn't be certain actually concerned my father, the late Daniel Wentworth Bentley. Hadn't I heard some of those same stories about Uncle Niles, for instance? Or Daddy's first cousin, Robert? Or even my grandfather or one or the other of his brothers? Weren't these third and fourth cousins twice removed and great aunts' sisters-in-law getting things mixed up? Or even making things up out of a fragment of a soap opera here, a case of mistaken identity there, and a final ingredient out of their own increasingly unreliable memories? Did they actually know for certain who had died?

Others of them spoke to me almost as if by afterthought, apparently realizing who I was only at the last minute as they passed me on the way to serve themselves second helpings or speak to someone else in the crowd, suddenly taken aback by my presence smack in their line of sight, reminded of the occasion and compelled by good manners to offer some dry, tasteless morsel of homespun condolence. Their eyes would well up with tears the women would shed and the men would blink back determinedly as they delivered their disastrously clichéd homilies. Their lips would tremble, their voices catch. Yet moments later I would see these same mourners off across the porch laughing with one another over some incident from thirty, forty, or even sixty years earlier. You could hardly tell that there had been a bereavement, that this was anything more than a family reunion.

I felt like screaming at them that the woods were burning and the sky was falling and the floods were raging. That the world was getting ready to end and if they couldn't turn a hand to prevent it they'd best run for their lives while there was time, and if they couldn't outrun the catastrophe they'd at least better make some plans for dealing with the aftermath. I felt like grabbing them by their shoulders and shaking them until they gave me their attention. I felt like slapping them like you slap someone who has fainted into coming back around.

Their faces and their laughter insisted that there had been no disaster far louder than I could have shouted the direst news. People died all the time. In too many ways to count. How many funerals had they attended in their time? How many sad stories had they already heard? Their long lives had taught them far more about loss and sorrow than I could imagine, and still they chose to eat, drink, and be merry. My tragedy was just that. My tragedy.

"I wish you'd eat something," Marytza said, surveying Grandma Bentley's overloaded dining table.

"I can't."

"He says he can't," she spoke past me.

"I heard him," Laddie said.

"Why don't you try a little of this?" Marytza said. "Geez, what is it anyway?"

"Fried okra," I said.

"Is that something you like?"

"He loves fried okra," Laddie said. "I've seen him eat it by the plateful. I once watched Daniel fry up a second batch just for him."

"Just one little bit?" she coaxed.

"I told you," I said. "I don't even know why I'm in this line. I can't swallow a bite. I'll just have to go out behind the barn and throw up."

"Now look here, Tristan," Uncle Gunnar said. "Nobody thinks you need a daddy."

The Ingebrittsen boys had surrounded me, unconsciously fending off attention from any quarter. Even Marytza and Laddie were shut out of this circle, and I was relieved to be momentarily free of their hovering. It was like being quarterback in the ultimate huddle. My uncles closed in tight around me, their massive shoulders an impregnable bulwark. Their neckties were immaculately knotted, their white shirts unaccountably crisp. Their blond hair glistened, still perfectly combed despite the wilting heat and humidity. Mama had been an only child until the age of twelve. Uncle Gunnar had been ten years old when I was born, and Lars and Tor even younger. And though my earliest memories of them were of what I had considered to be full grown men, I had never thought of them as members of my parents' generation. I realized with a shock that afternoon that they were closer to being contemporaries of Laddie.

"That's right," Uncle Lars nodded. "You can take care of yourself just fine."

Uncle Tor, always the silent one, nodded.

"Your sisters, however," Uncle Gunnar said.

"Are a different matter," Uncle Lars continued.

"Altogether," Uncle Gunnar completed the thought. The two of them often spoke like this, as if they shared one brain which split its utterances between two mouths. They were uncannily similar, almost like twins, though they were two years apart in age.

"They're younger, for one thing."

"And they're girls. Girls aren't independent. They need a whole lot of things from their adult male relatives that boys don't."

"That's right."

I wondered why they thought they knew this. None of them had married or had children. I had never heard of so much as a girlfriend. But I didn't raise this question. Why would you question the Ingebrittsen brothers, whose every movement reeked of supreme confidence? You'd as likely question the sky about its choice of color that day or a tree about the configuration of its branches.

"But the point is," Uncle Gunnar explained, "you don't have to worry about any of this. No matter what happens, we'll take care of everything."

"That's right," Uncle Lars agreed.

Uncle Tor nodded and looked serious.

"No matter what."

"Elizabeth, too. You don't have to worry about her, either."

"You're not coming with us to Chattanooga," Mama said. And it wasn't a question or expression of opinion but a simple statement of fact. It was that and it was at the same time a thunderbolt.

"Yes," I said, once I found my voice, tilting my head in the direction of Laddie, Marytza, and three or four of their friends. I hadn't realized it was my intention until that moment, but saying it made it a *fait accompli*. With Mama's consent, how could Laddie argue? "To Hollister. To work in the registration drive over there."

"You're not going with *them*," she said, shaking her head, so that for an instant I thought she meant to forbid it. "You're going with *him*."

She obviously meant Laddie.

"Yes'm."

She stared at me for a moment that lasted several centuries and then nodded.

"You'd best be careful with that one," she said, not quite smiling. "He's just like your father."

"What are you talking about?" I demanded. "He's nothing like Daddy."

"Do you really not see it?"

"See what?"

"You can tell from the look in his eyes," she said. "I saw it the moment you introduced him. He's on a mission like Daniel was. He's probably just as stubborn about it, too. Won't rest until he's changed the world. So just watch out."

Finally, long after the sun went down and the last of the visitors had climbed into their cars and headed back where they came from like a plague of locusts looking for another field to devour, it was time for Mama and my uncles to leave. I kissed her cheek and helped her into the back seat of the Jaguar. She smiled up at me. Neither of us spoke. I stepped away from the car, and Laddie leaned in where I had just been. I couldn't make out what they said or see her expression in the deep shadows.

Laddie's hand rested lightly on my shoulder as I stared at the receding taillights of the car. I was still staring long after they finally disappeared in the darkness.

XXII

When Laddie and I got back to the Swinford place the bus was waiting to take us all to Hollister, where the next voter registration drive was to begin in two days. The bus had stopped in Meadeville on its way and picked up a team of volunteers there. They were on their way to Buxton, thirty miles on from Hollister. There were hundreds of little towns in Mississippi where the residents were going about their business as if the great struggle was raging not in their own back yard but on the other side of the world. And in a different century. I knew nothing about Hollister but its name but at the same time I was pretty sure I knew it just as I had known New Jerusalem, both perfectly and not at all. One thing I was certain of, however. Whatever happened during our time there, nothing could surprise me. I was immune to astonishment, probably for life. As I climbed the steps of the bus, the Meadeville crew stared at me. It was as if they were contemplating an animal in a zoo seen for the first time, some strange species considered extinct or mythical until quite recently. They had heard the story, but I knew they didn't understand it, or me. No matter what had happened or what might still happen, they were visitors here for a short season, soon to be gone. Our struggle was theirs only incompletely. Our dead were not their dead.

Marytza had staked out some seats for us in the rear of the bus. I collapsed into an empty row behind her. In the aisle, Laddy peered down at me.

"Anyplace you want to see one last time?" he asked. "I can tell the driver to drive past."

"No," I said. "Let's just get out of here."

A couple of the Meadeville guys had guitars. By the time the bus pulled out of the Swinford drive and onto the county road, they were tuned up and strumming. It turned into a full blown hootenanny, just like on television. "Michael, Row the Boat Ashore," "If I Had a Hammer," "This Land is Your Land." All the signature tunes of the folkies, which, apparently, were also the anthems of our crusade. Ordinarily, I was an enthusiastic if not particularly tuneful singer, but I didn't join in. I stared out the bus windows at the darkness. It had never seemed as black or as impenetrable as it did that night. The primeval and apparently eternal darkness of my home country. Nothing ever relieved that darkness. Sunshine produced a false impression of light. The darkness never truly surrendered to it. It lurked everywhere, in the thickets, in the river bottoms, in the decaying barns, and, most of all, enshrined in the hearts of nearly every white skinned inhabitant of the region.

Gradually the crew ran out of songs and the bus quieted down and my fellow pilgrims settled in for the long, slow ride through the clammy Mississippi night. Most people stretched out on the uncomfortable seats and tried to sleep, but I had no expectations in that regard. Sleep was for another place and time. In my wakefulness I went back over everything that had happened. It was hard to get all the way back to the beginning. There had to have been a moment when matters could have taken a different course and the catastrophe might have been averted, but identifying it eluded me. My efforts carried me farther and farther into the past until, eventually, there they were, Adam and Eve staring at that confounded tree and wondering what that fruit tasted like. They knew they were supposed to leave it alone, but it was just so plump and shiny.

And I stood beside them, pondering my own special temptation. Bobby Davidson on a certain Saturday night just a few weeks earlier, his hair shining and perfectly combed and a teen idol's grin on his face. I had tried to ignore it at the time, just as I had ignored so many things for the sake of what I had insisted on calling friendship over the years of our boyhood, but I clearly recalled that his eyes that night had been as cold as a glacier and as dead as gunmetal. I recalled the husky slur of his voice as he excused himself from the table to go call Mary Louise. I remembered the sound of his pants legs rubbing together as he walked away and the soft slap of the soles of his sneakers on the worn linoleum of the diner. Each detail from those moments was as vivid as sunrise or a slap to the face. I thought of how I had sat there innocently munching on my burger, its taste unfamiliar since I'd recently foregone cheese or mayo. I sipped my iced tea and paid no particular attention while he shoved the two nickels I had given him into the slot and dialed Mercer Swinford's number instead of Mary Louise's and made an appointment he never intended to keep. Bobby hadn't needed those two nickels for the telephone. I was sure that he'd had plenty of change in his pocket. He always did, and that night of all nights he wouldn't have left it up to chance. He had borrowed two nickels from me in order to connect me forever to the event and even make me culpable in some incalculable way. And I couldn't help wondering whether it was just to share the guilt like we had always shared everything or because he knew somehow that when he helped kill Mercer Swinford he was helping to kill a part of me he could never accept in his best friend, the part that would never be tolerated in the cozy little world we thought of as home. It must have seemed a symbolic act, a baptism into death rather than life, into a brotherhood of the damned.

I recalled those few moments and I could almost taste the sweet tang of the pickles Mina's mother made in her own kitchen and brought into the diner to be served on those burgers. How many county fair blue ribbons had those pickles won? They had been legendary long before my birth. I savored those pickles like I worshipped the gleam of Bobby's hair, and I remained oblivious to almost everything significant that night. I was conscious of details only. Of surfaces, not what lay beneath them, and even less the larger reality we inhabited. I had hardly slept all summer. I had lain awake every night waiting for something to happen. But my imagination had blinded itself to certain possibilities in an inexcusable way. So as far as I was concerned, if anybody sitting in that booth had dangerous secrets, it wasn't Bobby. And if you're the one hiding something then the boy you've been in love with all your life isn't a killer and you're not his alibi on that certain sultry night, just a terrified kid sitting eating a burger. And when your buddy comes back and sits down across from you in the booth and he's so handsome he makes your heart flutter, you're too preoccupied to think of all the other hearts given to fluttering at the same sight, or one particular heart beating like that in the chest of a man who was already as good as dead the minute he put down the telephone.

I thought, too, of Bobby just a few nights since, when he drugged me to keep me at his playhouse. That night of explosions and fires. That night of blood and death. It hadn't been for the purpose of keeping me out of harm's way he had done it, though some might try to give it that interpretation. He needed me there so I could be his alibi that night, too. He was a great one for alibis. He always made sure to have one at hand, whether it was Mary Louise or some other girl he was bamboozling, or his mother, or one of our coaches, or even the principal. As if his whole life had been preparation for the last few weeks. Why did he have to pick me, of all people? Why not Mary Louise or any one of a hundred girls we knew? Why did he insist on making me part of it? The answer seemed as obvious as could be. He wanted me to be someone else. They all had. The whole town. Every day of my life they had wanted that because every day of my life I had been the wrong boy. I sat listening to the hum of the bus engine and wished he had left me alone. If he had, and if by chance as a result of it I had ended up in the wrong place at the wrong time, the outcome would have rested, as my neighbors liked to say, at the feet of Jesus.

Part Two

Letters From Stefano

South Viet Nam: 1969-1970

January 1, 1969

Dear Auntie Violetta,

Happy New Year to you! Happy, happy New Year! I hope this letter finds you well and happy. Your second parcel of cookies and treats arrived three days after Christmas. That was perfect because we had already eaten up everything anyone else had sent from home and the men were thrilled for Christmas to last a little longer. They send you thanks and salute your baking skills.

Tell Lizzie and the rest of the girls at the salon not to worry so much. It is certainly dangerous here, but it is not as bad as the television news makes it look. Most of the time our greatest dangers are boredom and running out of cigarettes. Don't worry, I haven't taken up smoking. I'm just talking about the men in general. Anyway, the rest of the time, when it is truly dangerous, I am very, very careful. I have done this before. I know what to do to be safe. So tell the girls to stop worrying, and say that I promise to dance with each one of them next New Year's Eve.

And please give Renata and Sergio big kisses for me and tell them I apologize for calling them fleabags. Tell them I made a resolution for New Year's that when I get home I will treat them like the royalty they are.

And you, *cara mia*, my precious little auntie, I give you special New Year's kisses.

Your Stefano.

* * *

January 8, 1969

Dear Auntie Violetta,

I hope this letter finds you well and happy.

No! You are not a silly old woman. You do not have a silly bone in your body, and you are not old! And if you worry it is because that is your job, just like it always has been. Thank Jesus and the angels there is one soul in the world to worry about poor Stefano! Just don't worry too much. I know what I am doing. I survived Korea as a fifteen year old, you remember. And I have survived three tours here.

I will survive this one because, I repeat, I know what to do. But mostly because my guardian angel, Auntie Violetta, goes every morning to St. Anselmo's Church to pray and light candles for me, and is always begging her friends and neighbors to do the same. So much praying. So many candles. Surely God will hear. Stefano must be safe!

Tell Bernadette and Lizzie that their cookies arrived and several of the men have offered to marry them when they get home. Though cookies are always appreciated, what we never have enough of is dry socks. If the girls use new socks as packing material to cushion the cookies next time, then they will have more admirers then they know what to do with. And some of the men are hardly ugly at all.

Our new medical corpsman reported for duty today. Corpsman Bentley. You and the girls should pray for him, too.

I send you hugs and kisses, *tesora mia*!

Your Stefano

* * *

January 17, 1969

Dear Auntie Violetta,

I hope this letter finds you well and happy. I know you hate the snow and so do Renata and Sergio, but right now I would love to step outside my tent and see everything covered with white and have to rush back inside for my coat and mittens. Yes, I would truly love a spell of cold weather. It is always too hot here. I remember it was freezing in Korea. The next war I fight I would like to be in a nice climate.

That is a joke, Auntie. No more wars for me after this one.

I know you are sad today to have that Republican moving into the White House. I did not vote for him either. Things are always better for working people when the Democrats have the power. LBJ was a southern Democrat, of course, and that was its own kind of problem. But he was better than the new man. We will just have to try our best to get by, and four years from now will be different. Courage, Auntie. No misfortune lasts forever.

Tell Father Michael that we do have a Catholic chaplain who comes and says mass and hears confession. His name is Father Patrick O'Laughlin. There is also a Baptist who comes and Rabbi Lefkowitz. But you don't have to tell Father Michael about these two it if will upset him. I know it might.

Of course nobody in the world cooks like you do, *cara*. But don't worry, we eat fine. I won't starve out here. If I don't keep up my strength they could court martial me.

That is also a joke, so don't get worried.

I send you a thousand kisses,

Your Stefano

* * *

January 26, 1969

Dear Auntie Violetta,

I hope this letter finds you well and happy. Complain about the snow all you want. You have a right to complain about anything. You got me through the first fifteen years of my life and God knows that was no picnic, so complain your head off.

We had our first chance to see Corpsman Bentley in action the other day. Every now and then, though it doesn't happen very often, a sniper will get close enough to camp to give us some trouble. This time it was MacGillivray who got hit. It wasn't a very good sniper or MacGillivray would have been dead before he hit the ground. He took a bullet to his left leg. Bentley got there before Mac really got to screaming good and shot him up with morphine, got a tourniquet onto the leg, and started a plasma drip. All of that *while the bastard sniper was still getting off shots.* It was as cool a performance as I've ever seen though you might say a bit stupid as well, not waiting until we could get Mac to cover. Still, there's no question he saved Mac's life.

The men think Bentley's pretty special after that. So do I, I guess.

We took out the sniper just about the time the chopper arrived to fly Mac to the field hospital. By that time, Bentley had him feeling so good that he was singing "Danny Boy" at the top of his lungs.

With a corpsman that gutsy attached to us, there's nothing to worry about, dear Auntie. But make sure to keep praying.

I send you hugs and kisses.

Your Stefano

* * *

February 7, 1969

Dear Auntie Violetta,

I hope this letter finds you well and happy. Yes, by the time you get this it will be Valentine's Day. Tell Bernadette and Lizzie that two of the men are Italian. Both single. Oh, and Angelotti requests some anise cookies in the next parcel. I told him about your recipe.

Yes, there are snakes galore around here, but none of them are poisonous. They are more afraid of us than we are of them. They mostly leave us alone.

So Father Michael thinks my letters sound like I'm away at Boy Scout camp? Well, let him draw his own conclusions. St. Anselmo's Parish really needs an Italian priest is what I say. At least one. The Irish and Poles are all right, I guess. But an Italian priest would know better than to say something so stupid.

Medical Corpsman Bentley is very good at his job. That time in camp with the sniper was no fluke. We have seen him in action several times now. He is originally from someplace in Mississippi but is not too bad a hick because he attended NYU and knows his way around New York. He is not one of those know it all college boys. He is very quiet and keeps to himself mostly. He reads lots of books, so you would have things to talk about if you ever met him. He doesn't seem to have a wife or a girlfriend back home. He never gets any letters at all, which I think must be very sad for him. But he never complains about it.

I send Valentine's wishes to all, and special kisses to dear Auntie!

Your Stefano

* * *

February 15, 1969

Dear Auntie Violetta,

I am sending this by way of my pal Charlie Petrucci, whose hitch is up. He will mail it from San Francisco. No APO. No snoops reading what I write.

Auntie Violetta, please, please, please do not be angry with me, but I am extending my hitch by ninety days. That means I'll be coming home next January, not in October. I have thought about this and I have said prayers, and I know it is what I have to do. I know this will be hard for you to understand. It is hard for me to explain, but I feel God has given me a special responsibility.

The officers they are sending out here now, they are good young men but they are ignorant. They have never been in war before. And in addition to this, some of them are very, very immature. The only way I can protect my men is to stay with them as along as I can because the officers can't do it.

Auntie Violetta, my men are worth saving. And I know I can. Not all of them, no. It is war. Some of them will die. But fewer will die and more will live the longer I stay out here. And in ninety more days, who knows? I may save two or three or five or six men who would die if I leave them here with a stupid lieutenant and an inexperienced sergeant who doesn't know how to protect them.

And even if it's just one man I can save, isn't that enough? Isn't it worth doing, even for that?

By then, it will be time for me to retire and come home and start my new life.

Please do not cry, Auntie. I have faith. You taught me to have faith, and I know it will be all right. I know I will save at least one of the men by staying. And just think how happy his mother will be when he comes home safe.

All my kisses I send you!

Your Stefano

February 24, 1969

Dear Auntie Violetta,

I hope this letter finds you well and happy. I know my last letter was hard for you to read. But you are the bravest person I know. We will be brave together and the extra days will pass quickly.

I am glad that Lizzie and Bernadette enjoyed the snapshot I sent. Bandini told me to be sure to let Lizzie know that when he gets back stateside he's coming to find her, so she'd better watch out!

The young man you asked about, the one standing next to me in the picture, is Bentley. Yes, as the girls noticed, he is extremely handsome. You also noticed that he has spent lots of time in the gym. You don't get built like that in six months. He's a damn fine corpsman and we're lucky to have him. I could tell you all kinds of stories about the bad medical corpsmen there are out here. Having a good one like Bentley is like having an angel around the house. Remember when I was a little boy and you always talked about having an angel around the house?

I am dry, healthy, and well fed!

I send you hugs and kisses!

Your Stefano

* * *

March 3, 1969

Dear Auntie Violetta,

I hope this letter finds you well and happy.

No! We were nowhere near the "heavy fighting" you read about in the *Post*. I know you are always anxious to know how things are here but you really must not believe everything you read in the newspapers or see on television. It just upsets you. And there is no point in being upset or frightened because you know that what will be is in God's hands. Nobody prays more than you do. You know Jesus and the Blessed Virgin hear your prayers and recognize your faithfulness.

If you don't believe me, ask Father Michael. I'm sure he'll tell you the same thing.

Be brave, my darling little Auntie! All will be well!

I send you a thousand hugs and kisses.

Your Stefano

* * *

March 12, 1969

Dear Auntie Violetta,

I hope this letter finds you well and happy.

Three more men have gone home safely. Boone, Rasmussen, and Tzolchatki. It is always a happy time when we send them on their way. But a little sad, too. I think we all wish we were the ones on our way home. It's only natural. And also because we really will miss those men. Out here we are like one big family. Which means lots of arguing, of course, but also lots of laughing and good times. When we are not fighting Charlie.

Anyway, the weather is very, very bad right now, but that's a good thing, actually, because Charlie doesn't like being out in it any more than we do, and this week nobody's shooting at anyone. Our worst problem at times like this is boredom.

And if that's all you have to complain about in the middle of a war, things aren't so bad after all!

I send you hugs and kisses.

Your Stefano

* * *

March 20, 1969

Dear Auntie Violetta,

I hope this letter finds you well and happy. Angelotti and Bandini have both finished their hitches and will probably be home by the time you get this letter. Like you said, it's a revolving door around here. Men are constantly coming and going. Yes, you're right. Hundreds and hundreds of faces. I have served with thousands of men over the years, and every one of them was different. Every one of them was an individual. But our experiences make our differences seem less important than the things we have in common. It's like when a new guy shows up, what everybody pays attention to are all the unusual things about him. But by the time he leaves what we all miss are the things that made him part of the unit.

That's why vets are such a close knit group. It doesn't matter whether they actually served together or anything like that. They understand that serving is being a member of a great big team, and they have all experienced being a member of that kind of team. So it's easy for them to become friends quickly with vets they've never met.

And if they're smart, the wives won't fight it. Because they won't win.

A hundred thousand kisses.

Your Stefano

* * *

March 29, 1969

Dear Auntie Violetta,

I hope this letter finds you well and happy. We are having surprisingly nice weather lately, which we hate because Charlie always takes advantage of good weather to make our lives miserable.

Now I've heard everything. Father Michael is a Republican? How any self respecting priest can be a member of that party. I just don't understand it. Are you sure he's a real priest? If I were you I'd speak to the bishop about it. Of course, he has a right to be anything he wants in private. But to talk about it in his sermon? To say those things about the Democratic Party being the party of the anti-christ?

This is not good, Auntie. Not good at all. I may have to go to the Vatican and bust some heads.

Really, you have no idea how upset this makes me. You're just going to have to turn him. And if your cooking can't do that, he truly is a lost soul.

I send you hugs and DEMOCRATIC kisses.

Your Stefano

* * *

April 8, 1969

Dear Auntie Violetta,

I hope this letter finds you well and happy. Please thank the girls at the salon for the parcels they sent. What a feast we had! And the socks!

A funny thing happened. Bentley, our medic, has been with us since January. But in all that time he hadn't gotten any mail. The other men were very curious about this. You can imagine. Mail call is very important here in camp. But day after day nothing came for him. Which made no sense. He had to have a family at least, even if he had no girlfriend to write to him. And what made it even stranger was that he didn't seem surprised not to get any mail. It's like he expected it to be that way. Then last week a whole bundle showed up for him. Dozens of letters. Every one of them had been opened. The whole camp was excited. The men thought they were about to have all their questions about Bentley answered. You see, the men always read their mail aloud for one another. It's like a tradition. When you first get your letters you go off by yourself and read them. But that night, or the next day, you and your buddies read your letters aloud to each other.

Don't worry, Auntie. I'm a sergeant. I don't have to share your letters with anybody.

Anyway, because Bentley had gotten *so many* letters, the men gave him several days to read them all. Finally they got impatient, and Riordan snuck into his hooch and got the letters and passed them around. Imagine everybody's surprise. No wife. No girlfriend. Just a grandmother and four sisters. Oh, and an uncle who is a quarterback in the NFL. Gunnar Ingebrittsen. You've probably heard of him. You're such a football fan. Anyway, it turned out that there was no mystery about Bentley at all. I thought Bentley was very cool about the whole thing. He didn't get bent out of shape at all and he thanked all the men as they gave him his letters back.

I send you hugs and kisses, Auntie!

Your Stefano

* * *

April 16, 1969

Dear Auntie Violetta,

I hope this letter finds you well and happy. I was so sorry to hear about your friend Adelina and her trouble. Do not worry! I am sure the advice you gave her was absolutely correct. I hope you are feeling better by now, even if you weren't able to help her.

Do you see how quickly time is passing? I told you it would. Before you know it my hitch will be over. And I will have my twenty years in and I'll be through with the army forever. Then you will have to find something else to worry about. And I will have to find something else to do. Thirty-five years and old and retired. What a joke!

That would be a good project for you, you know. Come up with some good suggestions for me for when I get out. That should keep you busy and out of trouble.

I send you hugs and kisses.

Your Stefano

* * *

April 23, 1969

Dear Auntie Violetta,

I hope this letter finds you well and happy.

The next time Father Michael talks about how much tougher they had it in World War II, please sock him in the mouth for me. Two of our men dead yesterday in a firefight and four more seriously wounded.

Not me. I got through it without a scratch. Bentley had a hell of a time, though, trying to take care of all those guys until the choppers could pull us out and get them all to the field hospital. He's tough as nails, that one. A real cool customer. Hardly broke a sweat.

The rest of the men, those of us who got back to camp unharmed—well, we're pretty thankful it wasn't us this time. And after seeing Bentley in action, we're pretty glad that no matter how bad it gets he's up to the job.

A thing like that is really good for your confidence. And you have to have confidence. If you don't, you're a goner for sure.

Pray for us, Auntie. Pray for all of us, but make a special prayer for Bentley.

I send you hugs and kisses.

Your Stefano

* * *

May 2, 1969

Dear Auntie Violetta,

Happy Birthday to you!

Happy Birthday to you!

Happy Birthday, *cara mia*!

Happy Birthday to you!

Next year we will celebrate your birthday in style. For now, extra special hugs and kisses. And when my next paycheck comes, do not put all of it into the bank account. Buy yourself a new pair of shoes. Some red ones. I know you have always wanted a pair of red shoes. So what the hell. Don't worry about what the church ladies will say, just buy them. And when I get home, I will take you out dancing in your red shoes.

Happy Birthday to you!

Happy Birthday to you!

Your Stefano
P.S. Happy Birthday to you!

* * *

May 11, 1969

Dear Auntie Violetta,

I hope this letter finds you well and happy. Thanks for the pictures of Renata and her babies. They certainly are cute. I am not surprised that all of them are spoken for already. I know you promised to save one of them for me, but honestly, Auntie, I don't think small white terriers, no matter how fierce you insist that they are, are quite my style. I hope Sergio is being a good boy around the puppies. That must be a sight, black Sergio with a flock of white puppies chasing him around.

We had a lucky escape yesterday. We had been on an operation, and it was our turn to be flown back out. But the chopper that was supposed to take us was commandeered by a colonel from the Information Office in Saigon. He was escorting a congressman, a couple of journalists, and a bunch of Hollywood types. We always hate it when "sightseers" show up. They always get in the way, and protecting them often puts us in extra danger. Lieutenant Abramson was mad enough to spit bullets when they took our chopper, but there was nothing he could do. We're supposed to bend over backward to cooperate with the Information Office. And needless to say the colonel outranked him. So anyway, the colonel and his guests loaded onto the chopper, and it took off. And it started taking machine gun fire almost immediately. It was in flames before it hit the ground. Everybody died. We had to wait for a couple more hours while somebody called in an airstrike to take out the enemy position we hadn't known was there. We were very happy when another chopper came to fly us out and not a shot was fired.

Lieutenant Abramson feels a lot better about letting those guys take that first one.

And if that's not proof that your prayers are working, I don't know what is.

Tell Father Michael this story the next time he starts talking nonsense!

I send you hugs and kisses, dear Auntie!

Your Stefano

May 20, 1969

Dear Auntie Violetta,

I hope this letter finds you well and happy. Thanks for sending the snapshot of you wearing your new shoes. The men all approved. Glienicki, our radio operator, said "red hot shoes for a red hot mama!"

Auntie Violetta, it is that time of year again. I know you hate getting this letter each year as much as I hate writing it. But I need to know that you will help me remember them. I see you now, standing on the bridge over the middle of the river, looking out toward the Statue of Liberty. I see you there and I hear your voice as you read out the names.

Xenakis. From Boston. He was a career sergeant like me. I first met him in Korea and I met him again here. Pretty wife and five pretty daughters. I know they miss him.

Reilly. A loud firefighter from Chicago. The filthiest mouth in the world but a heart of gold. Chubby little Polish wife and three cute boys. I hope his brothers will look out for them.

Ballard. Just a completely average guy. Girlfriend dumped him six months into his hitch. He didn't care about anything after that and ended up stepping on a land mine we had warned him about twice.

Horst. Big blond kid from Minnesota. Failed out of high school, which is not easy when you're that big and play football. His auntie raised him. You know that story.

Foster. Dad owns a Buick dealership in Indiana. Drunk frat boy type. Probably NOT officer material. Tried to help him out, but he wasn't a good listener. Beauty queen girlfriend committed suicide when she heard he'd been killed.

Yost. A farm boy from Wisconsin. He was allergic to cheese!

Nelson. World's best poker player. When he died, guys owed him over ten thousand in winnings he hadn't bothered to collect. We gathered it all up and sent it to his mom in Nebraska. She's a librarian and a widow.

Jaramillo. A copper miner from a small town in the mountains of Arizona. Lost out on a basketball scholarship because of an injury and had to quit college. Cute wife and two kids, a boy and a girl.

Quigley. Real smart guy and real quiet. Kind of like a ghost here in camp. Nobody really knew him, which makes me feel bad when I think about it.

Czerwicz. A Pole. The best damn baby lieutenant I ever saw, but too brave for his own good. He only lasted three weeks here. A damn shame and a horrible waste.

Meunier. Came from a family of lumberjacks in Washington State. He was planning to go to college and become a veterinarian when he got out of the army.

Zatkoff. Just out of high school. A state champion wrestler from Maine. He was a real dreamboat.

Ibarra. Parents brought him to America from Cuba after the revolution. Latin Lover type. So handsome it was ridiculous. But a short little guy. Two ex-wives. Several girlfriends. God only knows how many kids. Hardly spoke enough English to say good morning. Depended on Jaramillo to translate for him but made fun of Jaramillo's Spanish. Basically a pig, but he shouldn't have had to die like he did.

Andrews. Another one just out of high school. Threw himself on a grenade and saved six or seven guys from getting hurt or killed. There must be some kind of reward for that someplace.

Kellerman. Fast talking New York Jew. Cousins everywhere. Los Angeles, Tel Aviv, Buenos Aires, Cape Town, Sydney. Obnoxious, bossy, argumentative. Also fearless, generous, and funny. Really a great guy. He pissed everybody off, and we all loved him.

Unger. Another college boy. Used to recite the *Divina Commedia* to me from memory. His Italian sucked, but he sure loved Dante.

Pollini. Sicilian. He argued with everbody but he loved everybody like we were his brothers. His dad runs a commercial fishing boat out of Gloucester, Mass.

Dashinski. Big ugly Polish kid from Baltimore. Always clowning. Just wanted to make people laugh. I can't imagine why anybody thought it was a good idea to send him out here. He never had a chance.

O'Dwight. Just out of high school. Dad beat him and his mom. Said the happiest day of his life was the day his dad left them.

Vincent. College boy from Cincinnati. He was going to be a high school football coach when he got home. Fiancee was a Methodist preacher's daughter.

Smith. A rancher's kid from New Mexico. Hated pretty much everybody and everything. I don't think he would ever have been happy anywhere.

Edwards. Another lieutenant. Really smart. Really wanted to do well. Some of the men didn't like taking orders from a black guy. A shame he died. He'd have made a terrific captain some day.

Washington. From Mississippi. He would tell stories about playing out in the fields while his grannie and his mama picked cotton.

Galley. Nice guy from Tennessee. Always reading his Bible. Got into arguments with the Catholic chaplain, but in a nice, respectful way. Pretty sisters back home. Cheerleaders.

Help me remember them, dear Auntie!

I send you hugs and kisses.

Your Stefano

* * *

May 28, 1969

Dear Auntie Violetta,

I hope this letter finds you well and happy. I am sending it with my buddy Charlie White, who is going to Honolulu on R and R and will mail it from there.

A very strange thing happened. Two guys showed up in camp asking questions about Bentley. Army Intelligence. They talked to Lieutenant Abramson first. He didn't give them anything. He didn't have anything to give them. There's nothing to say about Bentley. And Abramson has heard enough horror stories from his officer buddies about useless medics to know that Bentley is too good to lose. I know Bentley doesn't really fit in but the guys all respect him because of the way he does his job, so I didn't think anybody would say anything those spooks shouldn't hear even if they knew something I don't.

Then they came to talk to me. And I was right. They didn't have anything on him. They were just fishing. Is there anything strange about him? We hear he reads books. What kind of books does he read? Has he ever disappeared from camp, even for just a little while? Now like I said, Bentley is too good a medic to lose, so after they left I decided I'd better get to the bottom of their visit.

"Know anything about a couple of spooks showing up here asking questions about you, Bentley?"

"Been expecting them, Sarge."

"How's that?"

"Actually thought they'd get here before this. Been reading my mail since I left the States, so it stands to reason."

"But there's nothing in your mail."

"Not in the mail they let come through. Who's to say what's in the mail they're holding onto?"

"What's that you're saying?"

"I have—I had a lot of friends in college who were communists, Sarge."

"Oh, Bentley, now—hell, my grandpa was a communist. So was my dad."

"Sure. In the twenties and thirties. Half the country was communist then."

"So?"

"Hell, Sarge, don't tell me you don't realize that things are different nowadays. And these particular communists of mine have been known to shut down the odd university here and there."

"Columbia?"

"Like that. Yes."

"You help them?"

"Some. Mostly I was too busy studying and working to pay my tuition. But I was living with them. The feds know that. They know about me. They've known about me for at least a couple of years."

"And you think your friends have been writing you and now intelligence is on your tail?"

"Probably not. If I'd been getting that kind of mail those guys would already have taken me away for questioning. But what none of them realize is the one thing they have in common with my old buddies. All of them are paranoid. Feds, radicals, all of them. The Feds probably think I'm out here to cause trouble. I must be getting my orders somehow, right? But my pals in the movement are so paranoid they'd never use the APO system to get messages to me even if they wanted to."

"Makes sense, Bentley. But wait a minute. You said even if they wanted to. What did you mean by that?"

"That's what's so ironic about this, Sarge. My so-called friends aren't trying to communicate with me because they think I'm a traitor."

"Why? What did you do?"

"I'm here, right? I let myself get drafted. When I got my notice I didn't skip to Montreal. I didn't have one of the movement's pet doctors write me up for asthma or orthopedic problems or any of that nonsense. Or get one of the shrinks to declare me psychotic. I didn't go to my physical tripping on acid. I busted my ass in basic. I was top of my class in corpsman school. And here I am saving the lives of fascists and making sure the imperialist oppressors don't run short of cannon fodder."

"Shouldn't all that. . .? I mean with that kind of record, shouldn't the Feds turn down the heat?"

"Maybe they already have. But on the other hand, why would they? Aren't they just as likely to think they got me out here too easily? That since I didn't put up a fight about being drafted I must be up to something? Slipping strychnine into people's coffee and letting wounded boys bleed to death in rice paddies?"

"You wouldn't."

"You don't know that, Sarge."

"Yes, Bentley. Yes, I do."

"Well the feds don't know that."

"I'll make sure they find out."

"You think you're big enough to take them on? Yeah, Sarge, you probably do. Well, don't go do something stupid. I'm not worth the trouble. And I don't want anybody going down with me."

"They asked about your books."

"My books? I'll show you my books. Come on."

"Just tell me about them."

"No, Sarge, I want you to see exactly what kind of subversive trash I go around with my nose stuck into."

We went into his hooch and he showed me his books. Joseph Conrad. Virginia Woolf. Walt Whitman. The complete works of Shakespeare. Honest to God, Auntie Violetta, it looked just like your bookshelf back home. Some subversive trash, huh?

So here's the thing. I've got this guy, my medic, and he's just this smart, brave, solid boy. Just really, really solid. And if he's to be believed the feds don't have anything on him but are ready to squash him like a bug because of some people he used to know who won't have anything to do with him any more either. He's too good for that. He thinks I can't help him, but I know a few tricks. I know the intelligence guys have informers in lots of units. I know how to smoke out rats. I can do more than Bentley thinks I can.

You know you can't say anything about this to anyone, Auntie!

Your Stefano

* * *

June 8, 1969

Dear Auntie Violetta,

I hope this letter finds you well and happy. Thanks for sending the snapshots of Antonietta and Rocco's wedding. You looked very beautiful that day, Auntie. I'm sure all the men there couldn't take their eyes off of you.

Yes, that Cousin Rocco is certainly a handsome devil. Way too good looking for his own good. It's very hard for a guy like that to stay out of trouble, and to be fair about it it's not his fault. Not completely. It's probably a good thing for him to be married. I hope Antonietta is as smart as you say she is. Maybe she can keep him home and out of trouble. That's his only hope, really. Short of being locked up.

By all means, give Father Michael a thousand for the renovations to the kitchen in the parish hall. But take seven hundred fifty of it out of my account. I don't want you giving him that much of your own money. And make sure you keep an eye on him so that the money goes where it's supposed to.

I send you hugs and kisses,

Your Stefano

* * *

June 19, 1969

Dear Auntie Violetta,

I hope this letter finds you well and happy. Thanks for sending me more pictures of you wearing your new shoes. *Che bella*!

Everything here is fine. Cashman left safe and sound last week, and Egerton is packing his stuff. He goes tomorrow. And Lieutenant Abramson the day after that. Bentley just showed me his newest book. E. M. Forster. *A Passage to India*. One of your favorites, isn't it?

Perhaps Father Michael is right. It sure seems like a Boy Scout camp around here.

Oh. Except one of the guys, Morrison, was badly injured. Some kind of freak accident. We're still not sure how it happened. The doctors say he'll walk again. But he's already been medevaced stateside.

I sure wish you'd stop worrying.

I send you kisses and hugs.

Your Stefano.

* * *

June 26, 1969

Dear Auntie Violetta,

I hope this letter finds you well and happy. So Renata's puppies are all gone now except for Baby Desdemona. I am not surprised that Sergio was a great big brother/uncle once he got used to the idea. I'm sure he taught those little characters lots of things that their new owners will have to train out of them. That's the kind of boy Sergio is. Full of mischief. He is just like me. That's why you love him so much.

Our new lieutenant is named Alberto. He's a very nice guy. Extremely easy going. The men are already warming up to him, and he's not afraid to ask me for advice so I think things will go well with him here. Of course you never know that for certain until you've seen how a man behaves under fire. But my gut tells me he's one of the good ones.

We had a visit from a USO troupe. Actually, we went to them. They would never come this far into the boonies. A couple of the girls took a real shine to Bentley. No surprise there. God knows he's a dreamboat. He's a very quiet guy. He doesn't show a lot of emotion. Actually, he never shows any emotion. It was funny to see how flustered he got when those girls started flirting with him. He blushed so bad I thought he might be having a stroke.

If I've seen it once I've seen it a thousand times. Those USO girls always either pick on the geeky guys or the really good looking guys who are easily embarrassed. It's show business, after all.

We had a great time, and Bentley was a real good sport about all the ribbing he took from the guys afterward.

I send you hugs and kisses.

Your Stefano

July 4, 1969

Dear Auntie Violetta,

Happy July 4th. Happy Birthday to America. We won't be celebrating the day the way you will, with parades and cookouts. But we'll celebrate, all right. You bet we will. It's a day that reminds us why we're out here with the heat and humidity and the snakes. Not to mention Charlie shooting at us day and night. I've been in this man's army long enough I don't need reminded, but some of the men, they miss their families so bad and they miss having all the comforts. The young guys especially. They get all distracted by their misery and forget what it's for. Or they read something, maybe in a letter from home, you know, about Nixon or the top brass, like it's those guys keeping us here so far from home, so uncomfortable, facing danger all the time. And they start to take it personal. And it's not personal, it's—I don't know. Bentley says it's history. I guess he's right.

Anyway, today we'll forget about all that stuff and be a bunch of proud Americans together.

I send you kisses like bombs bursting in air!

Your Stefano

* * *

July 12, 1969

Dear Auntie Violetta,

I hope this letter finds you well and happy.

We're having a string of accidents here. Anybody can tell you that there are accidents in the military. It's always been like that. And it's worse in wartime. Some units suffer as many casualties from accidents as they do from enemy action. Our unit is usually not like that. I run a clean, safe camp. But still, things happen. Guys get careless. They think too much about who they're missing at home or about how many days they have left in their hitches, and while they're distracted they do something stupid. Sometimes they do it on purpose so they can get sent home. That's really not an accident but it goes down in the records as one.

So anyway, yes. We've had several accidents lately. More than our usual per cent, though we're still better than a lot of units. But three in just a few weeks. First it was Morrison. I wrote you about him. Then Wilcox somehow got his hand run over by a Jeep, believe it or not. And then two days ago Hackenschmidt had a case of rations fall on him. Broke his collarbone and sliced a chunk out of his left cheek.

Lieutenant Alberto is furious because you wouldn't believe the paperwork he has to do each time something like this happens.

Don't worry. I'll get the lid back on things. Just see if I don't.

I send you hugs and kisses.

Your Stefano

* * *

July 20, 1969

Dear Auntie Violetta,

I hope this letter finds you well and happy.

So it has finally happened. Men walking on the moon. Hooray for America! Of course it would never have happened except for all those Nazi scientists we brought back from Germany after the war. And that would never have happened if an Italian hadn't discovered America in the first place. You never get to the end of things when you start trying to trace history. I learned that in my GED classes.

Anyway, I can see you all there at the salon watching it on TV. How I wish we could have watched it, too. We were able to listen to it on the radio here in camp, but of course that's not the same.

I went outside last night but I couldn't see the moon. There were too many clouds. Sikorsky told me I was a fool thinking the moon would look different now. But he's the fool. The moon will always look different now that men have been there.

I send you big hugs and slurpy kisses!

Your Stefano

* * *

August 1, 1969

Dear Auntie Violetta,

I hope this letter finds you well and happy.

More bad luck here. We were out on patrol two days ago and took some fire. Nothing serious. Just what they call a "minor skirmish". But I got hit. Not bad at all. Just a scratch. Really, it barely broke the skin. Got to experience Corpsman Bentley's work first hand. Boy, he's good. Had me stitched up lickety split. Didn't even bother reporting to the field hospital. It's healing up nicely. Be 100% in just a few more days. One more scar for Stefano.

And one more Purple Heart.

I send you kisses but no hugs. Shoulder still too sore!

Your Stefano

* * *

August 9, 1969

Dear Auntie Violetta,

No! Honest to God! I swear by the Blessed Virgin herself. Bentley took out the stitches and there's only going to be a tiny scar, if that. Remember when Cousin Arianna's little Rodrigo fell on the monkey bars at kindergarten? Less than that, even. May God strike me dead if I'm lying to you.

Three more men have gone home. Blakely, Jefferson, and Quitmeyer. Their replacements are O'Donoghue, Kurbweiler, Robinson, and Adams. Quitmeyer was such a huge guy I guess somebody decided we needed two men in exchange for him. Seriously, he was almost as big as I am. Can you imagine such a thing?

No more accidents around here. Isn't that lucky?

I guess they're saying in the news back home that we're all on drugs over here. Just one more of their lies.

Auntie Violetta, if Father Michael gives any more sermons like that one you wrote me about, you have my permission to put rat poison in his coffee. God Himself would thank you for doing it. You really must not take him seriously. An Italian priest would not say such things, ever. It isn't decent. Don't let him upset you. Or I may have to go to the Vatican and kick some butt.

You know I'll do it.

Big kisses and hugs, hugs, hugs!

Your Stefano

* * *

August 17, 1969

Dear Auntie Violetta,

I hope this letter finds you well and happy.

Yes, Bentley did receive your *birthday card*. No, it hadn't been opened. He was extremely amused, since his birthday is not until December. He was also a little troubled by it. Who exactly is J. Robinette of Staten Island? Did you just make up that return address, or is that a real person? I can see you riding out on the ferry to mail it from there wearing a trenchcoat and a fake mustache.

Auntie, promise me! No more little practical jokes like that. He gets his mail just like the rest of us these days.

And remember. You can fool all kinds of people, but you can't fool Stefano.

I send you hugs and kisses.

Your Stefano

* * *

August 26, 1969

Dear Auntie Violetta,

I hope this letter finds you well and happy.

Two days ago Bentley saved Frederickson's life. What's the big deal, you ask? He's a medical corpsman. It's what he's there for. Yes. You're right. But Bentley had been wounded himself. He had lost a lot of blood and he must have been in a lot of pain. But he hardly took his eyes off Frederickson the whole time. And it was a long wait for the chopper because we were pinned down by sniper fire for a while.

When Frederickson was hit I hustled over there as fast as I could. It was tricky, because like I said, we were taking fire. Bentley was already with Frederickson. He had a wad of gauze on the wound. He was pressing down on it really hard. There was blood everywhere.

"Take over, Sarge."

I got my hands in position so the second he moved I could put my weight on the wound.

"He's not gonna make it if we don't get this bleeding under control."

I held on like that while Bentley shot Frederickson up with morphine and got a bag of plasma going into him. I heard the radio operator calling for a chopper. We hunkered down over Frederickson. Fire was still coming in all around us. I noticed that Bentley was unbuttoning his shirt.

"What?"

"Check something out."

He got his shirt off and that's when I saw he'd been hit. It was bleeding pretty bad. Too high up on his shoulder for a tourniquet.

"Jesus, Bentley."

"Keep the pressure on that wound, Sarge."

"How bad is it?"

"Real bad. We've gotta try and keep him alive until the chopper gets here."

"I don't mean Frederickson."

He didn't answer me. He just shoved a couple of wads of gauze against his shoulder with his good hand and held them there. I could see blood seeping through the gauze and running down his arm. Every few minutes he'd check Frederickson's pulse and remind me to keep pressure on Frederickson's wound.

The chopper finally got there. By then I could see that Bentley was in pretty bad shape himself. But he never said anything about it. When we got to the hospital, they took them both away and I went off to clean up and scrounge some food.

I was dozing when one of the doctors sat down next to me.

"Your boy Frederickson's going to make it."

"That's good."

"He ought to be dead right now. That's some little medical corpsman you've got."

"Bentley? He's one in a million."

"Tough bastard that one. Half dead himself by the time he got here."

"But he's O.K?"

"Got a couple of units of blood into him. He'll be right as rain by day after tomorrow. Clean little wound. Hardly be a scar. Bled like a mother fucker, though."

"Guess I'll try and get a ride back to camp."

"Hell, Sergeant, I'll have them find you a bed for the night. We'll send you back with Bentley in the morning."

When we got back to camp yesterday just before lunchtime, Lieutenant Alberto told me those intelligence guys had been snooping around asking questions about Bentley again. I felt like killing somebody.

I send you hugs and kisses.

Your Stefano

September 4, 1969

Dear Auntie Violetta,

I hope this letter finds you well and happy. I was excited to hear about Rosa and Joey's baby girl. How nice of them to name it Stephanie, after me. Make sure they get a real nice present, O.K?

Lieutenant Alberto finished his hitch and is headed back home. Our new guy is Lieutenant LeDoux. Another one just out of college. First thing I noticed about him, other than that he looks about sixteen, was his cornball accent. He told me he's from some little place in Mississippi.

"No kidding? Our medical corpsman is from Mississippi too."

"How about that?"

"Name of Bentley."

He got a real funny look on his face when I said the name.

"It couldn't be."

"What?

"First name wouldn't be Tristan, would it?"

"Matter of fact, it is."

"The hell."

For some reason, he didn't like hearing that one bit. He just walked away. I asked him about it the next day and he made some excuse about them having been rivals on the football field. And something about some girl. I didn't believe a word of it.

Bentley didn't show any interest at all when I told him who the new lieutenant was. He just said they'd grown up a few miles apart and he had gone to high school with some of LeDoux's cousins.

You would think that two guys from the same neck of the woods would be excited to run into each other over here. War sure is strange sometimes.

I send you hugs and kisses.

Your Stefano.

September 12, 1969

Dear Auntie Violetta,

I hope this letter finds you well and happy. You really shouldn't let those protesters upset you. After all, all they really want is for the killing to stop and for all us guys to come home safely. That's what you want yourself. And so do all of us over here. At least almost all of us. So really, we're all on the same side whether we realize it or not. That doesn't excuse them if they are obnoxious or rude about it, but their hearts are in the right place, I'm sure. You see, Father Michael and I disagree once again.

The new lieutenant is settling in O.K., I guess, but I'm afraid he's kind of a hothead. And he really does have a bee in his bonnet about Bentley. I know that sounds like a nursery rhyme, but it's true. His second day here, he pulled me aside. I thought he wanted to ask me for a pointer or two. I've always got some of those ready.

"I want you to keep an eye on that man, sergeant."

"What? Bentley?"

"Yes, that prettyboy Bentley. I don't like prettyboys. And I won't have him causing trouble around here. Do you year me? I won't have it."

"Bentley, sir? Bentley never causes trouble. Bentley's a model soldier."

He looked at me like I was some kind of idiot.

It's very strange. Like he thinks he knows things about Bentley that I don't. And maybe he does. But what I know about Bentley is what I need to know about any soldier. Whether he can be trusted or not. Whether he's solid. Whether he'll freeze under fire or freak out. I can't imagine what Lieutenant LeDoux thinks he knows about Bentley that's more important than things like that.

I'm sure the lieutenant will understand that once he's been here for a while.

I send you hugs and kisses, Auntie Darling.

Your Stefano

September 20, 1969

Dear Auntie Violetta,

I hope this letter finds you well and happy. Yes, I do think you should go spend a month with Ysabella in Florida. You'll be back in time for Thanksgiving, and it will do the girls at the salon good to have to run the place on their own. Also, I think it would be bad for Ysabella to be down there by herself so soon after she lost Jerry. The first time is probably the hardest. And by going, you'll keep her sisters from showing up and bothering her. You know what freeloaders they all are. They have always taken advantage of her, and she really does deserve better. So by all means just pack your bags and go.

Seriously Auntie, when is the last time you had a real vacation?

Things are a little tense around here. It's not the brass breathing down our necks, and it's not even Charlie. There is some serious bad blood between LeDoux, our new lieutenant, and Bentley. LeDoux practically breathes fire any time Bentley's name is mentioned. Bentley pretends to ignore the whole thing. But the men are all talking about it, which is never good. It would be comical except that this is a war we're in, and these are grown men.

I'm trying to decide how to handle this. I think I must do something before the situation becomes serious. Say an extra prayer, *cara*, that I will have patience, if nothing else.

I send you hugs and kisses.

Your Stefano

* * *

September 28, 1969

Dear Auntie Violetta,

I hope this letter finds you well and happy. You must be getting ready for your trip. I wish I could see you and Ysabella leaving for the airport. She'll have as many bags as she can fit into the taxi, and you'll have that one tote of yours. Auntie, you could go to the moon with that trusty old tote bag. God knows how you are able to get everything into it, but I've never seen you travel with more than that, God bless you.

No worrying about the plane. I forbid you to be nervous. Flying to Miami is nothing like flying all the way to Rome. Besides, when you went to Rome that time there were not even jet airliners. You won't believe how fast you'll get there or how smooth and pleasant the flight will be. So I tell you again. No nerves. The tail won't fall off.

I got a message last week to report to company headquarters to speak with Colonel Winterbottom. I had met him before. He's a lifer, like me, and really, for a colonel, a hell of a good guy. He has NCO's in to see him all the time. He's one of those senior officers who think we have ideas worth hearing. And is actually willing to listen to them. When I got there, he wanted to talk about Bentley.

"Got this paperwork from your Lieutenant LeDoux. Can't make heads or tails of it, tell you the truth."

"Sir?"

"Now, Fabiani, you and I have had words about this Bentley before, haven't we?"

"Sir."

"Some kind of saint-slash-hero. Walks on water. You're not the only one I've heard that kind of talk from."

"No sir."

"So what is this, then? This request from Lieutenant LaRoux?"

"LeDoux, sir."

"Right. Wants to have your man Bentley transferred to another unit."

"No idea, sir. News to me."

"Bullshit, Fabiani. There isn't a sergeant in the whole damn army better at keeping track of his lieutenant than you are."

"Sir."

"Keep 'em on a real short leash, you do. And that's as it should be."

"Sir.

"Never said that, of course."

"No, sir."

"Well?"

"What I meant to say, sir, was that Lieutenant LeDoux never said anything to me about trying to get Bentley transferred."

"But you know something about this, Fabiani, or I'm the man in the moon."

"No, sir, you're just a colonel. Until they promote you."

"So what's it about?"

"Best I can tell it's some personal beef."

"Really."

"They grew up a few miles apart. Small town rivalry kind of thing. Football. And some girl or other."

"That's it?"

"Sir."

"That's what all this is about?"

"As far as I know."

"Those two idiots don't know any better than to leave that kind of shit stateside? That what you're telling me?"

"It's not Bentley, sir. It's pretty much all on LeDoux's side. Bentley won't engage in the dispute. Just ignores it."

"Good for him."

"Except that LeDoux is the type of guy who doesn't take kindly to being ignored that way."

"He needs to learn that there's no place for that kind of bullshit in the service."

"Sir."

"I'm losing this paperwork, Fabiani."

"Yes, sir."

"Not enough medical corpsmen in the army as it is. Hell only knows where we'd find a replacement. Not going through all those gyrations just because LaPew has the vapors. But you've got to help me out here."

"Sir?"

"Keep the lid on things at your place."

"Sir."

So that's what I'm doing, Auntie. Keeping the lid on things between LeDoux and Bentley.

Have a great trip! Spend lots of time on the beach!

I send you hugs and kisses.

Your Stefano

* * *

October 4, 1969

Dear Auntie Violetta,

I hope this letter finds you well and happy. I hope this letter finds you on the beach sipping some bright colored drink with a baby umbrella sticking out of it.

Things here are like this—I'd appreciate a really good run-in with Charlie right now. It would make a nice change. It would be like peace breaking out. The good lieutenant heard about my visit with Colonel Winterbottom. He is not pleased.

"What the hell did you think you were doing?"

"Sir?"

"Insubordinate bastard, going over my head to that colonel."

"Sir, all due respect, sir, Colonel Winterbottom called me in. Can't just duck out on it when a colonel says he wants to you drop by. Doesn't work like that."

"Like I believe you, Fabiani."

"Check with his office, sir. Sure they'll clear it up for you."

"I'm sure they will. Brown nosers like you always cover your tracks, don't you?"

"Sir, you really don't want to make this personal. No good ever comes of that."

"Sergeant, don't even think about telling me what I do and do not want to do. No good ever comes of that."

"Just trying to help, sir."

"Right. And I suppose that's what you were doing when you went over my head trying to protect your little boyfriend."

"All due respect, sir. . ."

"All due respect, my ass. What did you tell that colonel?"

"Sir, I'm afraid I can't tell you what we talked about."

"The hell you can't."

"Doesn't work that way, sir. The colonel is my superior officer, sir. If he wants to share our conversation with you, that's his place, not mine."

"Fuck that regular army shit, Fabiani. Spill it now or spill it later. But nobody under my command is going to go talking out of school."

"Sir. Understood sir."

"You haven't heard the last of this."

That's what they always say, Auntie. But I'm guessing that LeDoux is as bad a poker player as he is an army officer.

Please eat a big plate of shrimp for me, Auntie. You know how I love shrimp.

I send you hugs and kisses.

Your Stefano

October 11, 1969

Dear Auntie Violetta,

I hope this letter finds you well and happy. I'm sure Ysabella really appreciates having you there with her. I know you miss New York. Just keep eating shrimp and the time will go quickly.

After my talk with Colonel Winterbottom, I knew I had to get to the bottom of the thing between LeDoux and Bentley. And after the crazy way LeDoux had talked to me, I didn't figure I'd get anything sensible out of him. That left Bentley.

"What's his beef with you Bentley?"

"Beef with me? What do you mean, Sarge?"

"Aw, Bentley, don't play dumb. Everybody knows he's permanently on your case. And it started just about the minute he got here."

"So?"

"So it was before you had a chance to piss him off. What gives?"

"Ancient history, Sarge."

"Bentley, I'm Italian. To me, ancient history means Romulus and Remus. You've gotta do better than that."

"You really don't want to know about this."

"It's not about what I want. I've got a baby lieutenant losing his marbles because you're his medical corpsman and a colonel telling me to keep the lid on the pot. I need you to help me understand the situation."

"O.K. Since you put it that way. But I'll be real surprised if knowing what I'm going to tell you helps any."

"Try me."

"It happened back home. The summer before my senior year of high school. My daddy was killed and our house was burned down."

"Jeez, Bentley. That must have been rough for your family."

"It was."

"But what's that got to do with LeDoux? It's not like he did it."

"He knows who did."

"Well, sure he does, Bentley. I mean, everybody would know that by now, right?"

"Wrong, Sarge. The case is unsolved. None of the guys who did it ever saw the inside of a jail cell."

"You're shitting me."

"'Fraid not."

"Bentley, you don't really think LeDoux. . ."

"I think it was some of his buddies, actually. He just helped them get away with it. And he knows I know. Or at least he believes I think I know. So all this idiotic shit is because of his paranoia."

"That could be dangerous, Bentley."

"You think I don't know?"

Now, Auntie, I have to tell you, there's simply no way Bentley was lying to me. So I've got a bigger problem than I realized.

But don't worry. I've had worse things to deal with. Like Charlie.

I send you hugs and kisses.

Your Stefano

October 19, 1969

Dear Auntie Violetta,

I hope this letter finds you well and happy. You shouldn't worry about what's going on back at the salon. That's no way to enjoy your vacation. You're supposed to be a woman of leisure. That's what you have employees for, after all. They should work at least as hard as you do.

I really thought that Lieutenant LeDoux would cool off about me and Colonel Winterbottom, but there's no sign of it so far. He rides my ass constantly about Bentley. It's Bentley this and Bentley that. He keeps saying he wants me to write things up. But there's nothing to write Bentley up for. Unless I make something up. And I won't do that. He can't order me to.

It's weird, really, because Charlie isn't very active right now. There's not much going on. And we should be resting up and getting our strength back, but the lieutenant has to go finding things to be worked up about.

I do hope the weather where you are is better than here, though. But at least it keeps the snakes away.

I send you hugs and kisses.

Your Stefano

* * *

October 27, 1969

Dear Auntie Violetta,

I hope this letter finds you well and happy. You will be home from Florida soon with your glamorous tan that will make all the girls at the salon crazy with envy. I'm sure you look just like a movie star, sitting by the pool at Ysabella's apartment complex, wearing your sunglasses and your big straw hat.

Lieutenant LeDoux apparently went to see Colonel Winterbottom to complain about Bentley's transfer. The colonel's aide told me about it. Unofficially, of course, but we're old buddies. I guess the colonel hardly gave LeDoux the time of day.

Anyway, when he got back, LeDoux was really furious. He'd court martial Bentley and me both if he could figure out how. But he's really put himself in a bad position with the colonel, and nothing good ever comes from that.

You think you miss the autumn leaves there in Florida. I could tell you a thing or two about that, believe me.

And no worry about the plane. The tail is no more likely to fall off on a north-bound flight, so just relax. Think about Renata and Sergio and baby Desdemona waiting to greet you. That will help the trip go faster.

I send you hugs and kisses.

Your Stefano

* * *

November 3, 1969

Dear Auntie Violetta,

Happy Birthday to me! Happy Birthday to me!

Yes, today is my birthday. Thank you for the card. And thanks to the girls for the amazing birthday treats. The men were extremely impressed and appreciative. They wish I had a birthday every month!

So now I am thirty-five. That seems pretty old, though I don't feel old at all. But it does seem like a long time ago that I was a scared fifteen year old who had just enlisted (illegally!) in the service. You and Father Rodrigo certainly knew what you were doing. I can't imagine what would have happened to me if I hadn't come into the army. There have been lots of adventures. Trying not to get killed in Korea. Helping keep the Russkies out of West Germany. My tours here in 'Nam. I have spent almost my whole nineteen years and eight months in the service away from the States. Like somebody important doesn't want me on American soil.

That's almost over now. I'm planning to be in America for my next twenty birthdays at least. And when you think of all the things I've done and all the adventures I've had, thirty-five doesn't seem old at all.

Thanks for having the accountant send copies of all the statements. They certainly make interesting reading. People would be shocked to know what a Wall Street shark you are, Auntie. It's amazing how you've made my paychecks grow like that. I bet there are not many thirty-five year olds with that kind of money lying around. You will have to help me think of things to spend some of it on. Though of course I know you want me to keep most of it invested for my old age. Just think. I may actually live to be an old man. How many people would have believed that back when I was a schoolboy with "behavior problems"?

You are certainly right when it comes to money.

Anyway, Happy Birthday to me!

I send you birthday hugs and kisses.

Your Stefano

* * *

November 11, 1969

Dear Auntie Violetta,

I hope this letter finds you well and happy.

There's a lot to think about this Veteran's Day. After all, wasn't World War I called "The War to End all Wars"? How funny, when you think about it, that people could ever have believed in such an idea. Here we are over fifty years later and there's still no peace. All that changes is the location of the fighting.

Your Father Michael probably thinks it's a good thing. Otherwise Stefano would be out of work and back in Brooklyn getting up to no good. I know how those priests think. They're Men of God, of course, but that doesn't stop them from being crazy.

I'm sure that now you're there to take charge of things, Baby Desdemona will shape up. Paulina is lovely and sweet and I don't doubt that she took the very best care with the doggies while you were gone, but remember how she was with her boys? Especially Rocco? She's lucky they didn't end up in prison. You, on the other hand, know all about how to discipline unruly youngsters. Tell Desdemona for me that if she's not careful she'll end up in the military.

I send you hugs and kisses.

Your Stefano

* * *

November 17, 1969

Dear Auntie Violetta,

I hope this letter finds you well and happy. Now that New York has had some bad weather, you're probably extra glad you're in Florida. But I know how much you love the holidays in New York. Just be careful about skating at Rockefeller Center. I don't want you hurting yourself. Make sure if you go, you take someone with you just in case.

Lieutenant LeDoux just keeps getting crazier. He's riding Bentley's ass unmercifully. I do what I can, but it's getting really ugly. It's like that Captain Ahab going after the white whale. It is not making LeDoux any friends among the men. In fact, it's like watching Bentley stand up to everything he dishes out is making Bentley into kind of a mascot for the rest of the guys. They're starting to get really protective of him. They know what a great medic he is, and they don't want anything happening to send him away. I hear them talking among themselves, and I don't like what they say.

I have to play this very carefully. I have to support LeDoux because he's our lieutenant, but I have to support the men, too, because the unit can't fall apart. And I have to support Bentley because so much depends on him.

Don't stop praying for us, Auntie. I need to know that you are praying for us.

I send you hugs and kisses.

Your Stefano

* * *

November 24, 1969

Dear Auntie Violetta,

I hope this letter finds you well and happy. And tan! You should be back from Florida by now, and I'm sure you're as golden brown as an Egyptian princess.

There is much to be thankful for this year. I will think of you on Thursday, sitting down to the holiday table with all your friends and those members of our family who truly appreciate you. The others hardly matter. Do not forget that.

And don't worry about us out here. There is one thing you can depend on about the army. No matter where you are on Thanksgiving or Christmas they will find you and make sure you have enough turkey and all the trimmings to eat to sink a battleship. Our food is always plentiful, if not particularly tasty, but the holiday meals are the one time that the army cooks really do it up right.

Have a wonderful, holiday, Auntie darling!

Of all the things I am thankful for this year you are at the top of the list, as always!

I send you hugs and kisses,

Your Stefano

* * *

November 30, 1969

Dear Auntie Violetta,

I hope this letter finds you well and happy. I bet you're still eating leftovers from Thanksgiving dinner. What I wouldn't give for one of your turkey sandwiches right now. Don't get me wrong. We ate good for the holiday. But there's just something about the way you make a turkey sandwich that nobody else in the world can match.

The day after Thanksgiving we were ordered out on patrol. You should have heard the guys grumble. There's nothing like a holiday dinner to make you forget you're in a war. Sooner than should have been possible, we were deep in the boonies. That's when LeDoux's usual luck kicked in. If you can call it luck. Sometimes I think he does it on purpose. He's got this crazy idea about becoming some kind of legend out here. Which would be great if he were freelance. But unfortunately he's got us under his command. And being a hero the way he thinks of it usually means putting the rest of us in harm's way. Anyway, on this patrol he led us right into an ambush. Except "led" is really the wrong word because he was back behind almost everybody. Most of the guys managed to pull back out of the ambush, but I was on point and Bentley was with me. We ended up pinned down for several hours.

I have to say this for Bentley. He didn't panic. He didn't get the jitters. He just sat quietly and waited it out with me. We fired our weapons only when we had to because we had no idea how long our ammunition had to last. But we managed to hold Charlie off. Eventually they pulled back and some of our guys were able to get to us. I was really happy to get on that chopper when it finally showed.

And the whole thing was for nothing. Worse than nothing. LeDoux misread the map coordinates he'd been given. We were nowhere near where we should have been. He just about got Bentley and me killed through sheer stupidity.

This isn't the first time LeDoux has put Bentley in a really bad spot through some mistake of his. It's inexcusable. The men have noticed it. They're talking about it among themselves. If it doesn't stop it's going to be really bad for morale. The men need to have confidence in their officers. They need to know that they're not going to get killed because of some college boy's idiot mistake.

There's just so much I can do to protect them.

I send you hugs and kisses.

Your Stefano

* * *

December 8, 1969

Dear Auntie Violetta,

I hope this letter finds you well and happy. I am glad you approve of the new priest. I never really thought that Father Michael was the right priest for St. Anselmo's. I don't think he understood the people and the traditions of the parish.

I am sure that having a real Italian priest will make all the difference. But if Father Gaetano is as handsome as you say he is, you will need to protect him from some of the women.

Last week we celebrated Bentley's birthday. His grandmother and sisters had sent a very nice parcel, and we made quite a party. Twenty-two years old, but what a mature, serious young man he his. All the men like him. With one exception, unfortunately. But we didn't let the lieutenant's absence ruin our celebration. I know Bentley noticed, but he didn't mention it.

Perhaps LeDoux should have attended the party after all. If he had known what was about to happen I think he might have. Because the very next morning he was shot by a sniper. Right outside his hooch. He was dead before he hit the ground. Now the last memory the men have of him is that he skipped out on Bentley's party. Several of the men took off into the brush to try and find the sniper but there was no trace of him.

I hope our new lieutenant will be smarter. And a better listener.

It is certainly very sad.

The holidays are coming soon, and that will take the men's minds off of it.

Do not worry about me, Auntie. I am always very careful.

I send you kisses and hugs.

Your Stefano

* * *

December 16, 1969

Dear Auntie Violetta,

I hope this letter finds you well and happy. I am glad Baby Desdemona has taken my advice. Her namesake didn't come to a very good end, as I remember. She doesn't want to take unnecessary chances.

Our new lieutenant is named Breitkopf. He's one of those Midwestern farmboy types. He's all business but not in a stupid way. In fact, he seems pretty smart. I think I'll be able to get through these last few weeks without him giving me any trouble.

I got a little note about him. It wasn't signed, but I know a certain colonel's handwriting. Breitkopf is his hand picked boy. Kind of a thank you gift for putting up with LeDoux and keeping things around here from going completely to hell. It's nice to be appreciated, even unofficially.

You wouldn't believe how much better everyone is getting along around here now. Bentley is still pretty jumpy but getting better. I'd rather have him jumpy than too calm. Calm gets guys killed.

I can't help it. I still feel really bad about LeDoux. It would have been better if he could have had a chance to outgrow some of his stupidity. Everybody deserves that. But we don't always get what we deserve. Especially in a war.

But I still think it's very sad about him.

I send you hugs and kisses.

Your Stefano

* * *

December 23, 1969

Dear Auntie Violetta,

I hope this letter finds you well and happy.

Yes, we are counting the days around here. The men are all excited, just like little children. You would think that Santa Claus was real. You would think he was immune to the missiles Charlie uses to shoot down aircraft. You would almost think there is no war. It has been very quiet around here. It is always quiet in the days leading up to our one, very special day.

Even thought it's quiet, we don't let down our guard. That's what Charlie wants us to do. But someday, either Christmas itself or on Christmas Eve, Charlie will try to present us with his own holiday surprise. I have been here on enough Christmases to know and I will make sure we are ready.

What worse tragedy could there be, really, than to have some terrible thing happen to you on Christmas? How sad for your loved ones always to have the holiday spoiled for them.

But enough talk of sad things. Every day at mail call there are more parcels for the men. Yours arrived two days ago. Yours and several others from the girls at the salon. It is overwhelming to see them stacked in my hooch, waiting for the big day.

Next year, dear Auntie. Next year we will be together for Christmas.

I send you hugs and kisses.

Your Stefano

* * *

January 1, 1970

Dear Auntie Violetta,

Happy New Year! Happy New Decade!

First of all, tell all the girls they are our heroes. You all really outdid yourself. The men cannot believe the goodies. And the socks, Auntie Violetta, the socks! Really, you are a band of angels. You and the girls made Christmas very special, not just for me but for all of the men. *Mille grazie*!

Of course many of the men received parcels. And everyone was very excited and happy to share what had come. Bentley especially. His sisters and grandmother sent a parcel almost as spectacular as yours. But do not worry. Not quite. He was so proud, though, passing around his treats to all the men. Such a smile on his face. It will be a long time before I forget that sight.

A new year. A new decade. And for me, very soon, a new life. In just a few more days, God willing, I will have finished my work here and I will be on my way home. And not long after that I will leave the army forever.

A new life, Auntie. Just think of it! It is almost impossible to imagine, after twenty years, what it can be like to be a civilian. I wish I could tell you that I have all kinds of wonderful plans for my new life. But I don't. I hardly think of it at all. It is as if I'm afraid to. As if imagining my future might somehow lead to misfortune.

There will be plenty of time for us to talk of such things when I get home.

Only keep praying, *cara*. Just a little while longer.

I send you extra special kisses and hugs.

Your Stefano

* * *

January 16, 1970

Dear Auntie Violetta,

I hope this letter finds you well and happy. I know my handwriting is a mess. It's the drugs. I'm still having some pain, but it gets better every day. I don't let it stop me. I'm up walking around. When the weather's not too bad I go outside. The grounds here are beautiful. In one direction you can see the Golden Gate Bridge and in the other you see the skyline of downtown San Francisco. The doctors say I'll be released in a few days. But I don't know where they'll be releasing me to, since there are just a few weeks until my separation date. I'll keep you posted.

I don't remember much about what happened. I lost consciousness just a few minutes after I was hit. All I remember is Bentley being there with me. They say he stayed with me for several hours under extremely heavy fire and that it's a miracle he was able to keep me from bleeding to death until help came. It wasn't a bad wound but the bullet nicked an artery. Because of the location of the wound it wasn't possible to apply a tourniquet. Somehow he was able to apply enough pressure to control the bleeding. I'll never understand it. Bentley is just a miracle worker, that's all.

I don't know what happened to Bentley after that. It was supposed to be the last patrol for both of us. He already had orders for someplace in New Mexico. Or maybe Arizona. When I'm feeling better I'll put out some feelers and see what I can find out.

I don't regret anything I did over there. I know I'm supposed to. I know there's not really a different set of rules just because you're in a war. I know that taking a life is taking a life. It's something you can never atone for because it's something that can't be undone. If you steal, you can always give back what you've taken. If you tell a lie, you can go back and tell the truth. But if you kill, there's no going back. There's no fixing things.

You do what you do because it seems certain that if you don't you'll die yourself. Or someone else will. Someone who needs protection. The problem is the guy you're killing is probably in the same position you are, thinking the very same thing you're thinking as he gets ready to pull the trigger. You can't be at war for very long without understanding that.

But every once in a while you run into a man who seems to be operating according to a different set of instructions. That's what makes him your enemy. Not the color of his skin or the language he speaks or the kind of food he eats or where he's from. He could be exactly like you in every way except for the rules he's chosen to live by. And you can just stand by and let him do what he's going to do because you'd have to kill him to stop him and that would be wrong. Or you can stop him even though it means turning into someone like him. Choosing that other set of rules. Just that one time.

I did what I thought I had to do at the time. I know that's no excuse.

I didn't shoot to kill. I shot to wound. When you have the best damn combat medic in the army on duty, you don't have to kill a man to neutralize him. But you can never guarantee what's going to happen after you pull the trigger. It's the risk you take, and you know you're taking it.

I can't take it back. That's not how it works. I'm not even sure that I would if I had the chance.

And I wouldn't be here today writing this to you if I'd done things differently. I had to save Bentley so he could save me. In a way that makes it self defense.

Pray for me, Auntie Violetta. I try to pray for forgiveness. But you have to be sorry for what you did, don't you? And I'm not sorry. I'd do it again it I had to.

So it's up to you, Auntie Violetta. Only you can do this. Pray that God will forgive me.

Your Stefano

Part Three

Geronimo

Southern Arizona: Spring, 1970

I

"You can go in now," the corporal behind the desk said, putting down the phone. It sounded like he was pronouncing sentence on a felony.

Major Wallace was one of those small, wizened men who look old before their time but whose aged appearance is belied by an irascible vitality. He wore his sparse gray hair in the severest possible crew cut, his jawline could have been carved in granite, and his chin was pugnacious. His nose had been broken more than once, under God only knew what circumstances. Looking at him, I thought of an aging miniature schnauzer with a ferocious temper and a criminal record.

"Bentley, is it?" he barked as I stood in front of his desk painfully conscious of my threadbare, oversized fatigues and willed my backbone to be straighter.

"Sir."

"Just back from Southeast Asia."

"Sir."

"Infantry unit, it says here."

"Sir."

"See lots of action, did you?"

"Yes, Sir."

"Save lots of lives, did you?"

"Some, Sir, I suppose."

"Yes, I'm sure. All you boys see lots of action before they send you here. You see lots of action and you do a lot of things and through sheer dumb luck some soldiers survive your ham handed attempts at treatment just long enough to get to the field hospitals where the real doctors patch them up properly, so you think you're heroes who've saved a lot of lives and that makes you believe you actually know what you're doing. Which is extremely unfortunate for everyone who encounters you. Because you come back thinking you're practically doctors. But you're not practically doctors. Are you, Bentley?"

"No, Sir."

"That's right. You're not practically doctors. You're not even practically nurses. Not even that."

"No, Sir."

"What you are is practically useless. Worse than useless, actually, because you think you know things. You think you can diagnose and treat. You think you know how to use instruments and write prescriptions. You think you know everything a doctor knows. But let me tell you, you know nothing. Absolutely nothing about medicine or how a real, modern hospital works. So please don't think while you're on duty here. Or if you insist on thinking, think about the dishonorable discharge you're about a heartbeat away from getting. Think about that every minute, do you hear me? And otherwise, just do what you're told. Don't try to figure things out, don't check other people's work for mistakes, and for God's sake don't have ideas. And don't tell the nurses or the other corpsmen or the doctors or heaven forbid any of the patients about them if you do. Because any idea you might have will be a bad one and will almost certainly do people harm. Because despite what you undoubtedly believe, You Don't. Know. Anything."

"Yes, Sir."

"And whatever you do, don't go anywhere near the emergency room or the operating theaters. You'll just get in the way and cause trouble, and I won't have you getting in the way and causing trouble. I won't have any of that in my hospital. I'll have your balls served to me in aspic on toast points first. Understood?"

"Yes, Sir."

"All right. You either understand or you don't and we'll find out which it is soon enough. We do have a stockade here at Ft. Geronimo just in case the answer to that question is no. You won't be the first medical corpsman to spend time there."

"Understood, Sir."

"I'm putting you on the three to eleven shift. Report to Lt. Reeves on Ward Six at two forty-five sharp."

"Yes, Sir."

"And I mean today, Bentley."

"Yes, Sir."

"I don't care what fucking time your plane got you into Tucson and what fucking time the bus from the airport got you here. You sleep when I don't have anything better for you to do."

"Yes, Sir."

"Dismissed."

So much for the thanks of a grateful nation for the last twelve months I'd spent in the vestibule to hell. It appeared that even the army itself didn't give a damn about what we'd been doing over there. It was exactly what I'd been told to expect. I should have listened more carefully.

A tall, lanky man a few years older than me was waiting in the outer office. A stethoscope was slung across the shoulders of his spotless lab coat. He stared at me out of slightly bloodshot, pale gray eyes for an instant like he'd seen a ghost, or perhaps something slightly more prosaic than a ghost though still fairly exotic. Whatever had caught his attention, in an instant he recovered himself.

"The thing to remember about Major Wallace," he said, grinning like the junior class president in a posh boys' school, "is that his bite is far worse than his bark. Isn't that right, Corporal Stein?"

There wasn't a scintilla of irony in his tone or body language.

"Yes sir, Captain Cox," Stein smirked. "Everybody knows that."

"Don't forget now," Cox instructed, squinting at my name tape, "Bentley."

"No, Sir."

"Just back from 'Nam, Bentley?"

"Yes, Sir."

"Infantry unit, I'll bet. Front line infantry medics always have that haunted look, don't they, Stein?"

"If they're even alive," Stein chuckled.

"Am I right, Bentley?"

"Yes, Sir."

"Like working in a slaughterhouse, I've heard. That'll seem like a picnic compared to working here."

So I had an assignment. In 'Nam it had been exactly as Major Wallace described. I'd been a doctor in all but name, treating the sick and injured with surprising success considering my meager training and the circumstances. This led to a growing confidence that had me daydreaming at least once a week of medical school. The men in my unit believed I was a miracle worker and had sworn that once I had my diploma they'd travel thousands of miles to have me treat them, and I guess their adulation had gone to my head.

At James W. Calhoun Army Hospital, Fort Geronimo, Great Stinking Desert, Arizona, USA, it seemed ordained that I was to spend my life as an orderly or even a janitor. I hadn't expected to be treated like the conquering hero, but emptying bedpans and finding clean ashtrays for colonels' wives admitted for nothing more serious than inoperable neuroses seemed the dreariest possible comedown from the wretched but somehow glamorous life of a beloved front line medical corpsman in the boonies. How was I going to adapt to a situation in which boredom loomed as the greatest threat?

Boredom, indeed, was more dangerous than it sounded. I might have time to think. I didn't need a Major Wallace to warn me about the dangers of that. I already knew all about it.

I had arrived at Fort Geronimo the previous sundown after a long, nightmarish flight across the Pacific crammed into a chartered 707 with about half a million drunken, riotous grunts. That prologue to the apocalypse was followed by the briefest of layovers in San Francisco, which I was barely able to glimpse through the fog, a shorter but no less surreal flight to Tucson, which I barely glimpsed among the cactus and mesquite, and a bone jarring ride on a rattling, wheezing Army bus through the mountains and desert to my new, and hopefully final, posting. The place had looked depressing enough as the bus rattled through the main gate just as the winter twilight was falling. In the glare of desert midday, its drabness was overwhelming. I choked back tears as I practically raced from the hospital back to my barracks, certain that I had exchanged one anteroom to hell for another.

* * *

"Yes, operator," Uncle Gunnar said. "I'll gladly accept the charges."

Finding him at home seemed nothing less than a miracle, what with his schedule. Perhaps God had decided to be on my side for once.

"Go ahead," the operator said.

"Tristan, where the hell are you?"

"Arizona," I croaked.

"Thank God."

"You might not say that if you could see this place. Turns out Arizona has boonies, too."

"Maybe so. But at least you're alive and there shouldn't be anyone shooting at you."

"Let's hope."

"Have you called your grandmother?"

"I wanted to talk to you first."

"Good thinking. She's awfully upset that you didn't come home on leave."

"I don't want her seeing me like this."

"Like what? Is something wrong? Are you hurt?"

"Not hurt. Just pretty fucked up. I'm not fit company for man nor beast."

This wasn't melodrama. I had only ever been in a state this bad once before, and I hadn't gone running to Grannie then either.

"You know I can't tell her that. She'll be on the first plane out there."

"I know," I said. "Will you please explain to her that by skipping leave right now I'll be eligible for my discharge thirty days earlier? I wrote a letter to her and Papa telling them about it, but she may have forgotten. Or misunderstood."

"All right, T. I'll see what I can do. Now be honest. Do you want me to come out there? Would that help? Because you know I will. On the very next plane."

"I know. Thanks. But no. Later on, maybe. Right now, I think I'd best be on my own."

"O.K. On one condition."

"What's that?"

"Call your grandmother. She's really in a state over you, and she's taking it out on your uncles. Understand?"

It was not until I returned from my first shift that night that I met my new hoochmates. They had been away on weekend passes when I arrived. They were listening to "Stairway to Heaven" and rolling joints when I entered the spartan four bunk room we were sharing. They looked up just long enough to decide that they already knew everything they needed to know about me and went on with their business. Bone tired and jet lagged as I was, I was perfectly happy not to engage them in conversation. And since they were both on the seven to three shift, it was several days before we had a chance for anything more than an exchange of distracted nods and exhausted smiles. They were medical corpsmen as well, also recently returned from the war. I had known them both by name and reputation over there but had never actually crossed paths with either one. You would have thought we'd have a lot in common, but as I was a draftee and they had enlisted, they weren't short timers like I was. It was even conceivable that they could be sent back for an additional tour. No, not merely conceivable. It was highly likely given the chronic shortage of medics in the army, and they seemed to think that if they went back they'd surely die, as well they might given the stratospheric mortality rate of corpsmen attached to infantry units, so their gloom was near suicidal and as far as I was concerned completely justified. They tried to relieve it with copious doses of rock and roll and pot, but to my eyes at least these efforts were unavailing. In any case, I resolved to treat them the way Major Wallace had instructed me to treat everyone else—keep my mouth shut and mind my own business.

Jones was a stocky, raspy voiced little cracker from Georgia with freckles everywhere and a head covered in wiry reddish fuzz. A bundle of nerves, he twitched and wriggled like a two month old beagle puppy even in his sleep. Jefferson was a regally effeminate, six and a half foot tall black man from Boston. Aristocratic as a duchess and erudite as a Jesuit, he'd have been the headmaster of an exclusive private school in a world where justice prevailed. Their shared misery bound the two of them together like a couple of Chekov's sisters pining for Moscow. After determining that my separation date was a scant few months ahead they could barely bring themselves to speak to me. I was a walking, talking reminder of the mortal danger they were in.

Fort Geronimo had been established in the 1880's as a base for U.S. attempts to pacify the Apaches in the otherwise empty territories along the Mexican border. The necessity for this could only have been apparent to Washington desk jockeys who had never seen so much as a photograph of the territory. Anyone with first hand knowledge would have left it to its original inhabitants. The task accomplished, the fort was more or less abandoned. Pancho Villa and the Zimmerman Telegram made its remote location appear strategically important again during the years around World War I, but in the Twenties the place had fallen on hard times once more. Its entire history had been one of boom and bust. During World War II it had flourished as a site for basic training. During Korea it had been once again a beehive of activity. Then another somnolent decade had passed during which it became little more than a graveyard for the careers of second and third rate officers, many of them alcoholic. For whatever reason, the Viet Nam mobilization had bypassed it. Buildings sat empty, their windows boarded over. Whole sections of the base were like neighborhoods in a ghost town. Grass grew up through cracks in the runway at the seldom used airfield. Jeeps and deuce-and-a-halfs dozed away months and even years covered with dusty tarps and sitting on flattened tires.

The place might as well have been a thousand miles from civilization. To the east of the fort, an enormous valley slumbered under the harsh glare of the desert sun. Beyond it, a range of mountains shimmered in the distance like a mirage. Jones had told me the peaks were twelve thousand feet in elevation and only appeared as small as they did because they were forty miles away. I couldn't imagine being able to see anything that distant, but Jackson assured me it was true and that the dense green line snaking across the valley floor was indeed a tree lined river. They pointed all this out from our second floor window the first morning we actually spoke to each other, all the while mummifying themselves in caps with fur lined ear flaps and field jackets and gloves and scarves as if the trek to the mess hall led across an Antarctic waste.

"Elevation here on base is nearly seven thousand feet," Jones explained. "It won't get over twenty-five degrees until lunchtime. And about that time it'll just turn around and start getting colder again."

I knew this already from bitter experience, but didn't interrupt. It was strangely comforting listening to a man complain about something of no more consequence than the climate.

"We're in the foothills of a mountain range fourteen thousand feet high," Jefferson said, referring to the other line of peaks, the one rising just west of the base. "Hell, for all I know there might be glaciers up there. It sure feels like it when the wind blows."

"And the wind blows all the time," Jones added. "You're really going to hate it here."

"When the weather warms up, we gots snakes," Jefferson said, making a stereotypical face. "And you have to shake your shoes out every morning before you put them on on account of the scorpions. The only thing we don't have around here is folks shooting at us."

"Yet," Jones said.

My second Monday at Fort Geronimo I woke from sleep that had only been interrupted twice by nightmares. This constituted a major improvement on the recent average, and I felt almost rested. A quick trip to the can brought the welcome and long awaited news that I might be starting to win my ten month long battle with diarrhea. I was almost giddy at these portents. "Caesar shall go forth," I muttered to myself as I lingered over breakfast while my comrades in arms rushed off to report for their daylight duties and the mess hall emptied. I finally felt up to something more than going back to bed until time for my shift.

The scales in the weight room mocked me. One hundred thirty five pounds. Unbelievable, but all too true. No matter how many times I stepped off and back onto them, the same number came up. It didn't seem possible that I'd lost sixty pounds since reporting for basic training eighteen months earlier, but the first barbell I attempted to pick up was all the proof I needed. I went for a much lighter one and even struggled with it. Thank God there were no witnesses. I was finally discovering an advantage to working the three to eleven shift. I had the gym to myself. Forcing my reluctant muscles and joints through the reps and sets, I approximated the kind of workout that wouldn't have made me break a sweat even in junior high. Chalk it up to eighteen months of rotten food, twelve months living in primitive conditions in a tropical climate, that diarrhea that nothing had been able to cure, subsequent total exhaustion, and the local altitude to which I hadn't yet adjusted. But I didn't want a list of excuses no matter how convincing. I wanted my body back, and God only knew how long that would take.

I had better luck in the library, where once again I was the solitary patron. I came up with copies of *Mrs. Dalloway*, *Howard's End,* and *Berlin Stories*. It was like running unexpectedly into a group of old friends and being invited to join them for coffee and gossip. My enthusiasm seemed inexplicable to the PFC manning the circulation desk that morning. He yawned repeatedly while stamping due dates into the flyleafs. I assumed that his occupational specialty, like those of practically everyone in the whole army, had been carefully selected to avoid utilizing any skills or aptitudes he possessed or any education he had received prior to being drafted. Looking at him, I judged that he'd probably make a pretty fair heavy equipment operator if anyone ever gave him a shot at it. The idea that anyone could possibly spend his whole hitch in the army working in a sleepy stateside library was mind boggling. How different my life would have been if I had drawn a duty like that.

II

I was sitting in the hospital cafeteria staring into my tea mug where a wedge of lemon floated like a dead goldfish; staring so hard at that symbol of mortality that I didn't notice Captain Cox walk up. When he spoke to me I jumped like I'd been shot. I hadn't seen him since my first day on base, and as much as being jarred from my reverie I was surprised he remembered me.

"Sorry," he grinned, "didn't mean to startle you."

"I'm a little preoccupied," I grunted.

"Mind if I sit down?"

"'Course not, Sir."

"Let's dispense with the 'sir' stuff, O.K? Call me Andy."

I thought he must be out of his mind. Or perhaps just a twisted officer who liked to trick grunts into committing insubordination.

"What's wrong?"

"I'm not sure I. . ."

"Don't worry," he winked. "I won't tell anybody if you won't. It'll be our little secret."

I didn't like the sound of that. No more than I liked the look in his eyes, which was the same as I recalled from my first morning at Fort Geronimo when he had joked with me outside Major Wallace's office. But he was an officer, so I figured I'd best tread lightly while I worked on figuring him out.

"On break?"

"Uh huh," I said. "How about you? Late rounds?"

"Something like that."

Either it was late rounds or it wasn't. I didn't see any need for him to insist on being cryptic. Or maybe it was the way he stared at me that made me edgy.

"Sick of emptying bedpans and mopping floors yet?" he asked.

I shrugged.

"Come on," he chuckled. "Forget I'm an officer. Tell the truth."

"The truth."

"Just, like, man to man."

"Oh well, in that case, I was sick of my job after the first ten minutes."

"And it's what, now? Six weeks?"

"Five," I said, sure to the marrow of my bones that he knew exactly how long I'd been on base but didn't want to cop to it.

"Seems like longer," he mused, in a fashion too offhand to be anything but calculated.

"Yeah," I said, "like five years."

"So come to work for me," he suggested.

So that's what this was about. My suspicions suddenly seemed ridiculous.

"I don't know the first thing about pediatrics."

"But I bet you're a quick study. Nothing complicated about it, really. Just basic nursing skills. You can take vital signs, write up charts, and give injections, can't you?"

"Sure."

"So that's it. I'll drop Major Wallace a request for your transfer."

"You can do that?"

"Uh huh. I'd have done it sooner but I had to wait until he had a new victim to torture."

"Madison," I nodded, recalling the gaunt little medic who'd materialized a few days earlier, obviously just back stateside.

"Now that Wallace has his teeth sunk into that one, I can spring you."

"All right."

"I can get you a single room, too. That is if you're not too attached to Jones and Jefferson."

"If you can do that," I told him, "you've got yourself a deal."

* * *

When I showed up at Major Wallace's office two days later to be reassigned, he looked like he had never laid eyes on me before and didn't care one way or another whether I spent the rest of my hitch mucking out the men's medical ward or performing brain surgery. And my new housing assignment sailed through just as easily. Either Captain Cox knew what strings to pull or things here at this somnolent backwater of a base were more casual than I'd yet realized. Crawling into bed that night in my new, single room, I reflected that dealing with several dozen sick kids in the clinic the next day was a small enough price to pay for such luxury. Not to mention, I'd finally be on day shift. I hated the hospital at night. I'd never been easily spooked but somehow those late shifts managed to do it to me.

"Just lay him down right there," I told the enormous sergeant. In my first two days working in the pediatrics clinic I hadn't seen anything more dramatic than a runny nose, but this was obviously different. The little boy was hanging onto his father like a shipwrecked man clutching a life preserver.

"No," the little boy shrieked.

"It's all right, buddy," the sergeant grunted.

"No, Daddy. Hold me."

"What's your name, little guy?" I asked, frantic to get on his good side.

"Danny."

"I'm Corpsman Bentley. Nice to meet you."

"Say hello, buddy," the sergeant said.

"Hello."

"O.K., Danny. We need you to lie down here so the doctor can examine you and find out what's wrong," I told him.

"No," he wailed.

"How about if you lie down but your daddy holds your hand?" I suggested. "How about that?"

The kid kept sobbing but he didn't say no. The sergeant gave me a grateful look as he set the boy onto the examination table. O'Malley, the fatigues proclaimed now that the little boy had released his death grip on his father's chest.

"All right," I said. "How's that?"

"It hurts," the boy whimpered.

"I know it does," I told him, "but the doctor will be here soon, and he'll make you feel better. Now, Sergeant O'Malley, what seems to be Danny's problem?"

"I don't know," O'Malley grunted. "His mother's out of town, so a neighbor has been looking after him when I'm on duty. She called me about an hour ago and said Danny wasn't feeling well and I'd better pick him up and bring him in here. When I got there he was screaming bloody murder. She said he hadn't fallen or anything like that. And there wasn't any blood anywhere. All he could tell me was that it hurts."

"I see," I said. "Danny, can you tell me where it hurts?"

"Tummy," he sobbed.

"Can you point to exactly where in you tummy?"

A chubby little finger pointed in the general direction of his appendix. Bingo.

"Have you thrown up any, Danny?"

"Oh, hell," O'Malley said. "She mentioned he wouldn't touch his lunch."

"Did you, Danny?"

"A little."

"Did you tell Mary Margaret?" O'Malley demanded.

"No," Danny whimpered.

"You didn't tell her you threw up?"

"She'll be mad."

"Jesus, Mary, and Joseph," O'Malley muttered.

"Nobody's going to be mad at you, Danny," I said. "It's not your fault you're feeling so bad. Now Dr. Cox is going to need to examine you with your shirt off. Can you help me take your shirt off?"

He nodded, and I gingerly started unbuttoning.

"You be sure and tell me if I hurt you."

"What do you think it is?" O'Malley asked.

"Dr. Cox will be here in just a minute, I'm sure," I told him, slipping Danny's arms out of the shirt sleeves.

"But what do you think?"

"I'm sorry, Sergeant O'Malley. Army regulations. I'm not allowed to think."

"Can Daddy come with me in the operation?"

"Sorry, little man," Captain Cox said, "daddies have to wait outside."

"I want Daddy," Danny began to whimper.

"Danny, listen to the doctor," O'Malley said.

"Tell you what," Cox said. "What if Corpsman Bentley comes in with you? Would that be O.K?"

"O.K." Danny whimpered a little more, but nodded.

I stared at Cox, dumbfounded. I hadn't been in an operating theater in months.

"He won't leave me?" Danny asked, staring up at me with terrified eyes.

"He'll hold your hand the whole time if you want," Cox said. "You'll go to sleep and I'll do the operation and when you wake up he'll be right there. And then in a little while your daddy will be able to come in and see you."

"Corpsman Bentley?"

"How about if you call me Tristan?" I suggested, squeezing the tiny hand.

"Corpsman Tristan?"

"Yes?"

"You won't go away?"

"No sir, little buddy."

"Good morning, Bentley."

I looked up from my filing. Sergeant Gabriel O'Malley loomed at the nurses' station counter like a force of nature.

"Morning, Sergeant. Something wrong with Danny?"

"Right as rain," he grunted. "Kid bounced back like nobody's business. You can't tell lookin' at him he's ever had a sick day in his life. If I'd had an emergency appendectomy two weeks ago I'd probably still be flat on my back."

"Three year olds are pretty resilient. Thank God."

"No," O'Malley shook his head. "Thank you."

"I think you should really be thanking Captain Cox."

"Oh, sure," he said, "the doc's great. But you're the one who knew how to talk to my boy so he wasn't scared out of his wits."

"Honestly," I insisted, "I had no idea what I was doing."

"That's not what it looked like to me. And Doc told me you really did stay with Danny right through the operation. I figured once they put him under you'd check out. Said you sat in the recovery room with him, too. Danny talks about you all the time."

"Does he?"

"All the time. Says you're his best friend."

"That's sweet."

"Got kids of your own?"

"No."

"Well, you'll make a great pop one of these days."

"Thanks."

"So listen," he said, looking over his shoulder as if he thought we were being watched, "how long you been back stateside?"

"Couple months."

"Saigon?"

"The boonies. Infantry unit."

"Figures," O'Malley nodded. "Couldn't have been that many medics over there named Bentley who came back when you did."

I had no idea what he was getting at.

"So I guess that makes you the guy who saved Big Steve Fabiani's bacon."

Hearing that particular name on his lips made me a little woozy.

"Just doing my job," I croaked.

"Way I heard it you kept him from bleeding to death for several hours under heavy fire."

I shrugged.

"You know, I've done three tours over there. I know how it works. Ninety-nine out of a hundred medics would have bugged out on him and nobody ever would have known the difference. Guy all but dead and everything."

"He saved my ass about a thousand times," I said.

"Still."

"I had no idea you knew him."

"Hell, the army isn't that big. Not for career NCO's like Big Steve and me, at least. Lotsa people know him. He's one of those real solid guys, you know? Type you could trust with your life. Without even thinking about it. I guess you're like that too."

"Oh, I don't know," I protested. "He's a tough bastard. He really didn't want to go. That's what kept him alive."

"Way I figure it," O'Malley said, "I owe you two big ones. One for my boy and one for Big Steve. You ever need a favor, you just let me know. Don't care what it is, and no questions asked. Got that?"

"Thanks."

I had spent pretty much every waking minute since that chopper took off into the tropical haze trying to forget I'd ever heard of Sergeant Stefano Fabiani. I'd been doing a pretty good job of it until O'Malley rattled my cage that morning. The shock of being reminded completely unnerved me. I knew I wouldn't be worth a thing the rest of the day. I might even make a mistake and kill one of our patients. When I told Captain Cox I wasn't feeling well and needed to leave, he didn't bat an eye. He told me to get some rest and not to come back on shift until I was good to go. Not that inactivity promised any cure for what was ailing me.

Back in my room I locked the door and then barricaded it with the dresser. On top of that I stacked my footlocker. I don't know what I thought I was protecting myself from doing all that. The situation was way too serious for such a b-movie gesture, but when you're half crazy all kinds of things make sense to you that would make a sane person shake his head. Like what I'd done that early morning while some far off medical team was getting Sarge ready to medevac to Japan.

Once I felt like I was safe, I got out the packet of letters. Sarge always got several letters a week. I had watched him reading them and there was no question of their importance though he'd never said who they were from. And there had just been so many places he could keep them. So that morning, the minute I'd gotten back to camp and with his blood still caking my fatigues, I sneaked into his hooch to find them. It hadn't taken long. They weren't hidden at all. What did he need with concealment? Nobody in their right mind would have messed with his stuff. I shoved them inside my shirt and left. Back in my own tent I'd packed them quickly into my duffle. My tour was up that day. I was due to leave and most of my packing was already done.

I hadn't looked at them since putting them away here in my new place.

The letters were identical. The stationery was flimsy and expensive. The handwriting of the addresses was almost calligraphic. They were postmarked Brooklyn, where I knew Sarge was from. The name on the return address was Violetta della Torre. Little Violet of the Tower. What a perfect name for a fairy tale princess, which I didn't doubt for a moment she was. Because who else could she possibly be? Who else would write letters that looked like that? In handwriting like that? Who else would be waiting back home for a guy like Stefano Fabiani? No ordinary woman, that was for sure. So despite my curiosity, I didn't look inside a single envelope. Suddenly it didn't seem decent, and I was horrified at what I had done. Sarge must be somewhere wondering what had happened to them. I should try and find out where he was so I could send them to him. I stared at that name on the envelopes until I was practically crosseyed. Then I tied the bundle back up and put the letters away.

That evening I hit the gym. I had gained back some weight but not very much. I didn't like the way I looked at all. I stayed on the far side of the weight room from the seriously big guys there. I figured they took their bodies as much for granted as I had mine once upon a time, and rather than calling attention to myself as a pencil neck I made every effort short of leaving to remain invisible.

Halfway through my workout a guy came in I hadn't seen there before, though all the big boys greeted him like he was a regular. Not that you'd have mistaken him for anything else even if the place had been empty. He was five feet ten or eleven and weighed well over two hundred pounds. And though he was massive, he was breathtakingly proportioned. It was the same general idea as my uncles. But his build wasn't the only thing that got me. He was movie star handsome. His coal black hair was longer than the army really preferred and slicked into place. His jaw was square and his chin was firm. Deep slashes of dimples canyoned his cheeks, and even from clear across the room I could see that his eyes smoldered. I couldn't stop looking at him.

III

I was on the last page of *One Day in the Life of Ivan Denisovich* when there was a knock on my door. My alarm clock read almost midnight, so I decided to ignore it. Probably some drunk soldier who'd gotten lost looking for his buddy's room or had forgotten the directions to the guy on the floor below who sold weed. But the knock came again, more insistent this time, and now my curiosity was aroused. I pulled on a pair of sweatpants and went to answer it.

"Good. You're awake," Captain Cox said. He was dressed for the Officers' Club, but his demeanor was all business. "I need your help."

"What's up?"

It couldn't be official business or there would have been somebody on duty he could call on. What could a straight arrow like Cox be up to? Plotting to steal a fellow officer's stamp collection? I wasn't sure he was up to even that level of criminality.

"We'll talk about it in the car, O.K?"

"I guess," I said, reminding myself that I owed him for getting me off that horrible bedpans and mop buckets duty. When I thought about it, it seemed surprising that he'd taken so long to call in the marker. "Just give me a minute to dress."

That should have been his signal to step back into the corridor and give me a little privacy. Ordinarily he was the most considerate of men, and my curiosity ratcheted up another notch or two when he just stood there. I dressed quickly, trying my best not to think about him watching. A couple of minutes later we were in his Volvo.

* * *

It was a gynecological examining room. The woman was in her late thirties, I guessed. Everything about her said officer's wife. Her hair was blond but the roots were a couple of weeks overdue for a touchup. Under other circumstances she'd probably have been reasonably attractive. Captain Cox didn't introduce us. I wasn't certain whose anonymity he was protecting. Around us, the obstetrics clinic was dark and silent.

"Now I'm afraid I can't give you a general anesthetic."

"Yes, Doctor," she said, "you already told me that."

Her Mississippi accent gave me the creeps. I wondered if we had grown up in the same part of the state. I wondered if I sounded like that to Captain Cox.

"This injection will sedate you sufficiently that there shouldn't be too much discomfort. If there is, you must tell me."

He gave her the injection and we waited for a few minutes for it to take effect. Then he began the procedure. There was really nothing for me to do except stand there and watch. In the car on the way to the hospital he had explained everything that would take place, including what he would need me to do if something went wrong and I had to help out. But there were no complications and it was over with before I knew it.

The next morning before we saw our first patient of the day, he motioned me into an empty examining room.

"Thanks for helping out last night," he said. His eyes were not as bright as usual, but that was no surprise. I was sure I looked no better than he did.

"I didn't do anything."

"Except help clean up," he nodded, "but you might have had to. There's always the possibility. Only a fool would go into something like that without backup ready. I appreciated having someone there I could trust."

I wasn't sure why he believed he could trust me. Worse, I wasn't sure I liked the implications of his trust.

"You understand that you can't say anything about it," he murmured.

"Certainly not," I said, finally looking him in the eye. "It's illegal."

"Right. I don't do those very often. I'm not sure I really approve of them unless it's a case of medical necessity. But I owed someone a very big favor."

"You don't have to explain."

"I want you to understand that it wasn't just some casual thing."

"I didn't think it was."

"Tristan, this is very important to me."

His use of my first name jarred me. Its implication of a greater familiarity between us than I believed existed made me uncomfortable. It felt like a commanding officer taking an inappropriate liberty, but even if I'd known who I could safely go to about it I wasn't sure I wanted to. He'd been nothing but decent to me and I didn't want ingratitude added to the long list of my shortcomings.

"All right," I said.

"I know helping me like that could have gotten you into serious trouble. And I'd never expose you to such a risk if it wasn't really important."

"I've been in trouble before," I told him. "You don't have to worry about me."

"I'll tell you anything you want to know."

"What's there to tell? Some major's wife gets knocked up by the guy she's seeing on the side. She's terrified of the repercussions if her husband finds out. You ride to her rescue on your white horse. I'm guessing, of course. But I'm not stupid. I know people get into all kinds of scrapes. I don't need you to tell me all the details. If I know anything for certain, it might start to get complicated."

"I'm not sure you should trust me so much."

I wasn't either, but he didn't need to know that.

"I can take care of myself."

That night, the huge, black haired guy at the gym caught me staring at him. I had been trying my best not to be obvious about it, but God help me I couldn't keep my eyes to myself. I could as easily have flown to the moon. Still, I knew it was inevitable. Sooner or later he was going to notice. He'd have to be blind not to. I expected him to call his buddies' attention to the skinny little homo, but he didn't. Our eyes met across the weight room, and I was the one who looked away first.

When I got back to the barracks after my workout, I found a note taped to my door. Uncle Gunnar had left a message for me to call him. Bone weary, I trudged back down the corridor to the pay phone, terrified that something had happened to Grannie or Papa. He answered on the first ring as if he'd been sitting right by the phone, but he accepted the long distance charges in a breezy tone of voice that calmed me immediately. Uncle Gunnar had many talents, but hiding his feelings was not one of them. Nor was breaking news gently. If something was wrong back in Chattanooga, I'd have known it from the way he spoke to the operator.

"What's wrong?"

"Nothing, you ninny. Can't I call you without something being wrong?"

"So everyone's O.K?"

"Fine. Couldn't be better."

"It's just when I got the note that you wanted me to call, I was afraid perhaps. . ."

"Sorry, bud. Guess I should have thought of that. No, I was just so excited I couldn't wait for your regular Tuesday night call."

"Excited about what?"

"I'm coming to see you."

"You're coming here?"

"Are you deaf? You work at a hospital. You'd better see a doctor about it. I have to be in L.A. on business for a few days and I thought on my way back I'd swing by."

"L.A? What kind of business do you have in L.A? More commercials? I thought you hated doing them."

"Sure as hell don't hate cashing the checks, though," he laughed, "but it's not commercials this time. I don't want to talk about it right now. Might jinx the deal. I'll explain it all when I see you. Which will be weekend after next. Is there any chance you can get some time off?"

"I should be able to swing it," I said, thinking that Cox owed me a favor and this might as well be it. Besides, I hadn't had a weekend pass since I got back stateside. "There's just one thing. There's really nowhere for you to stay around here."

"There must be a hotel somewhere."

"Closest decent one is in Tucson. That's about ninety miles."

"Tucson it is, then. I'll rent a car at the airport and drive over to pick you up."

"No need," I said. "There's bus service from the base. You can pick me up at the Greyhound terminal in Tucson."

"All right," he agreed. "Call me Tuesday at your regular time. I'll have it all worked out by then. Can't wait to see you, T."

The army bus made a stop at the airport a few miles outside the city. A dozen or so GI's got off. Some were going on leave. Some were catching transport to San Francisco where they'd board flights for Southeast Asia. Two were celebrating their discharges by wearing civvies. The rest of us were in uniform. I envied those boys on their way home. They had survived the ordeal. After the airport, there were only a couple of us on the bus for the ride in to the Greyhound depot. Tucson wasn't much to look at except in comparison with everything surrounding it. I stumbled down the steps after the two and a half hour ride and there was Uncle Gunnar climbing out of his rental car. Since I had seen him last, he had entered the 1970's by forsaking pomade and letting his hair grow out into a shaggy mop that made him look more like a Viking chieftain than ever. I wondered if Uncle Lars and Uncle Tor had followed suit. It was hard to imagine one of them doing anything without the other two copying him.

"T.," he yelped, hugging me and pounding on my back like someone trying to save a choking victim. "Damn, it's good to see you, boy."

I blinked back tears and stared at him. He looked so damn normal.

"Here, give me that," he commanded, grabbing my duffel and striding off toward the car. "Don't you have any other clothes?"

"Active duty personnel aren't allowed to change into civvies until we're off army property. And the bus counts as army property."

"Stupid fucking military," he muttered, slinging my duffel into the back seat while I got in on the passenger's side. "Worse than pre-season camp. What's wrong?"

"I can't get over the spectacle of you behind the wheel of a Plymouth," I chuckled.

"They don't have any Jaguars in the rental fleet. At least not around here, they don't. I checked."

"I wish I had a camera."

"Like I'd let you take that picture," he said, starting the engine. "Don't take this wrong but you look like death eating a soda cracker. And I'm not talking about the clothes."

"You should have seen me when I first got back."

"You mean it was worse?"

"I've gained back nearly fifteen pounds."

"You must have looked like a concentration camp survivor. No wonder you didn't want to come home on leave. You'd have given Mom heart failure."

"I seem to remember explaining that to you at the time."

"So you did," he nodded, "but I assumed you were exaggerating. Army guys are as bad as fishermen, the stories you all tell. Seriously—you been checked out? You don't have any tropical diseases they should be treating you for?"

"Fit as a fiddle. I'm feeling better every day."

"Working out?"

"How do you think I gained back those fifteen pounds?"

"You better be telling the truth," he said, honking at a driver who'd just cut him off, "'cause you know I'll have to give Mom a full report. If you're lying, it'll eventually catch up with you."

"Speaking of full reports, how did things go in L.A?"

"All in good time," he said. "All in good time. Get you to the hotel. The pool's heated. We'll have a nice swim and think about dinner. You know of any good restaurants here?"

"You're kidding, right?"

"No. Why?"

"We GI's don't spend a great deal of time hanging out in swanky joints."

"Well, we're going to take care of that this weekend."

For as long as I could remember I had thought of my three uncles as the ultimate in manhood. College football heroes and later professional athletes, they embodied everything my friends and I had aspired to as boys. They were the next thing to giants. Everything about them was manly, from the thunder of their footsteps upstairs when I visited my grandparents and the smell of after shave and hair oil which hung in the house, to their loud, gruff voices asking for dishes to be passed at the dinner table. In comparison, my father—their brother-in-law—seemed a member of a different species, and though I had adored him beyond words it was hard to think of him in anything like the same terms. My uncles were as handsome as they were boisterous and as happy go lucky off the playing field as they were fiercely competitive on it. To my young eyes and ears at least, they were as elemental as the earth and sky.

My parents had carefully taught me to appreciate things my uncles knew or cared little about: literature, music, art, and philosophy. They inculcated in me beliefs about politics, social responsibility, and justice I could never have outgrown even if I wanted to. They had done everything in their power to civilize me in a way my uncles would never be civilized. But my parents had never been able to acquaint me with anything that could compete with the attraction presented by those three huge, laughing, blond men. As I grew older and it became more and more apparent that I was more my mother's son than my father's, my unmistakable physical resemblance to my uncles made me even more determined to emulate them in every way possible. That my uncles themselves did more than anyone to temper this obsession was testimony to their respect for my parents as well as their own good sense and fundamental—though unquestionably simplistic—morality. If I was going to grow up and become a fourth musketeer, or more accurately, Nordic warrior, they seemed determined that I'd have pounded into my head in any way necessary a clear understanding that their brand of manhood entailed more than just good looks, big muscles, athletic notoriety, and braggadocio. The code they lived by was a simple one, its tenets having to do with honesty, hard work, generosity, consideration for others, and perhaps most importantly, a refusal to take themselves too seriously. At every opportunity they let me know in no uncertain terms that they expected me to cultivate those virtues as conscientiously as they had.

All that came back to me that evening as my uncle and I lounged by the hotel pool. Gunnar had only been ten years old when I was born, and at age thirty-two could easily pass for five years younger. His chest, shoulders, and arms were as huge as ever, and you could have laundered shirts on his abdominals. Alcohol and tobacco had never been given the least chance to ravage the smooth, clear skin or bright eyes of his Eagle Scout's face. Physically, he was everything I had ever wanted to be, but it was his essential gentleness, unexpected and consequently all the more compelling for it in such a specimen, that I focused on that night, hoping that in spite of the things I had witnessed and survived I had been left similarly unscathed.

We settled on the hotel dining room that night owing to the limitations of my wardrobe. I got nothing but family talk out of him until we were more than halfway through our ranchers' cut prime ribs. While I appreciated hearing about the accomplishments of my sisters, the exploits of Lars and Tor and the antics of Grannie and Papa, I was half delirious with curiosity about his trip to Los Angeles.

"O.K." he grinned when I mentioned it again. "You've been awfully patient. Ask away."

"Are you signing with the Rams?"

"The Rams?" he chuckled. "No, this trip had nothing to do with football."

"What else is there?"

"Here's a hint. Hollywood."

"You're joking."

"Nope."

"You're going to be in a movie?"

"That remains to be seen. But I did do a screen test."

"What movie is it?"

"It's a remake of one of those old Steve Reeves things."

"Hercules?" I yelped.

"That's right."

"You'll be fantastic."

"Whoa there, partner. I'm not the only guy they're looking at for the role."

"But you're perfect for it."

"Says you. But those Hollywood types don't necessarily look at it the way you do. I figure it's not more than a fifty per cent chance."

"It's going to be so great," I enthused. "You'll see."

"Today," he informed me over breakfast, "we're going to go out and buy you some decent clothes."

"What do I need clothes for? I never leave the base."

"Tonight I'm planning to take you to a fancy restaurant the front desk told me about. And if you show up in blue jeans and a t-shirt they'll send you to the kitchen to scrape potatoes and wash dishes. Got the name of some fancy, preppy type clothing store, too. Gonna get you outfitted."

"But. . ."

"No arguments, young man," he said. "Now finish that omelet. Time's a wasting."

Five hundred dollars later, I had a navy suit, two additional pairs of dress pants, half a dozen dress shirts, a pair of black loafers, a belt, a selection of ties, and enough new underwear to make doing laundry unnecessary for two weeks at a stretch. I deplored this expenditure, as I was determined to outgrow at least the suit and shirts within a matter of months, but Uncle Gunnar shrugged off this objection, and I had to admit I looked almost as resplendent as he did when the *maitre d'* seated us at a prime table in what I had been told repeatedly was one of the finest establishments in Tucson.

We shared appetizers of shrimp cocktail and oysters on the half shell while he recounted the televised antics of Lars and Tor, who had turned up their noses at the NFL after graduation and had become professional wrestlers instead. Our salads had just been served when an all too familiar face suddenly appeared at our table.

"Bentley, is that you?"

"Captain Cox," I stammered, rising awkwardly from my chair. In a navy blazer and khakis he was all but unrecognizable.

"Well, this is a pleasant surprise," he said, staring at Uncle Gunnar. "I didn't expect to run into you this weekend."

"No, Sir."

"Cut the 'sir' stuff, please. We're nowhere near base, and we're both out of uniform. Now why don't you introduce me to your. . .uh, friend."

"This is my Uncle Gunnar," I said. "Gunnar Ingebrittsen. Uncle Gunnar, this is Captain Andrew Cox. I work for him."

"Gunnar Ingebrittsen?" Cox asked. "The quarterback?"

"I'm afraid so," Uncle Gunnar laughed, getting to his feet and extending his hand. "Tristan's told me about you."

"And he hasn't said a thing about you," Cox said. "Looks like I'm going to have to give him a stern talking to when he returns from his weekend pass."

"Good," Uncle Gunnar grinned. "His family has always found it challenging to keep him in line."

"Seriously," Cox said, "you must all be very proud of him. He's a fine man and a good soldier. I know his hitch is about up but I'm hoping we can convince him to re-enlist. We need more like him. He's practically my right hand man."

"Captain Cox is exaggerating," I insisted.

"Not at all," he said. "Well, I won't presume on any more of your time. Nice meeting you, Mr. Ingebrittsen."

"Pleasure was all mine."

"Interesting man, your Captain Cox," Uncle Gunnar observed in the car on the way back to the hotel. "What do you know about him?"

"Nothing, really. I mean, he's an officer and I'm a GI. We don't exactly mix."

"I suppose. It seemed a little strange to me."

"What did?"

"Oh, all that talk about how you're his right hand man and he's hoping you'll re-enlist."

"What's strange about that? Is there any reason you find it unbelievable?"

"Not at all. But if you're so good, why's he trying to keep you in the army? Seems like he should be encouraging you to go to medical school."

"Never in a million years," I laughed. "Once my hitch is up, I never want to see a sick or injured person again."

"So you're not considering staying in?"

"Not on your life."

"Thank God," he said, tapping his fingers on the rim of the steering wheel impatiently while we waited for the traffic light to change. "Your grandfather and grandmother won't stand for it, you know. They're terrified that the army will find a way to keep you and send you back to the war."

"That's probably the first thing that would happen if I re-enlisted. I know I've been through a lot but I'm not crazy enough to want that."

"Of course not. So what plans have you made for when you get out?"

"Hell if I know. I can't seem to think about it very clearly."

"That's probably not surprising after what you've been through. Promise me something?"

"What's that?"

"When you're discharged, come back to Chattanooga. Just for a while to try it out. If you don't like it you can go wherever your heart desires, but just give it a chance, O.K?"

"What the hell would I do in Chattanooga?"

"You just said you don't have any plans. You might as well be aimless and lacking in ambition in the bosom of your family as anywhere else."

"All right. I get the point."

"One other thing."

"What's that?"

"Watch out for that Captain Cox."

"Why?"

"I can't say exactly. There's just something funny there. I'm not sure I think you should trust him."

Captain Cox had written me a three day pass, so it was late Monday afternoon when I arrived back at Fort Geronimo. I ditched my duffel bag at the barracks and headed for the gym. Three days in the company of Uncle Gunnar had left me more determined than ever to get my old body back, but the real reason I was in such a hurry, though I hardly admitted it to myself, was that three days without so much as a glimpse of the black haired muscle guy had left me practically salivating. I was half afraid he'd be there and half afraid that during the last three days he had disappeared.

He was just arriving at the gym himself. As I rounded the corner of the building, I saw him getting out of a green Mercedes roadster. I stopped dead in my tracks, not wanting him to see me. I stood and watched as he locked the car and went into the gym. Somehow a Mercedes didn't seem quite right for him—not sufficiently operatic to complement his turbulent masculinity. I would have figured him for something more extroverted, like a Corvette or a Cobra. As I walked past the car I noticed that the base registration tag on the windshield was in blue lettering, which made him an officer. I wouldn't have guessed that, either. The officers I had encountered, even the young ones, were bloodless and washed out, like pedigreed dogs or decadent European aristocrats. This guy seemed too red blooded to be one of them.

Captain Cox showed up at my door just after midnight. I was in bed but not asleep when I heard the knock.

"You need help?" I asked, seeing him there in the shadowy corridor.

He nodded.

"I'll just be a minute."

In the car he explained that a friend of a friend had attempted suicide. I wondered, but didn't ask, why whoever found the victim hadn't just called an ambulance. Probably for the same reason that somebody's pregnancy had needed to be terminated on a hush-hush basis a few weeks earlier. Secrets had to be kept. The truth was complicated. It was a harsh, troublesome thing. It created difficulties. My hunch about this became a near certainty when we pulled up in front of one of the big old houses on Colonel's Row. Nothing enlisted men did seemed to make any difference to anyone but the individuals themselves, but for all practical purposes officers lived in fishbowls. Something like this could end a career.

I followed Captain Cox up the walk. Just before we reached the front door, he motioned me to a corner of the porch well out of earshot. He watched me and didn't knock on the door until I was clear. From what I could see the door only opened a crack, and whatever discussion took place only lasted a few seconds. Then he waited for a moment before motioning me to follow him inside.

There was no sign of anyone in the entry hall. Whoever Captain Cox had spoken to didn't want to be seen, which was fine with me. Perhaps that person had already left the house by the back door. The less I knew about who and what, the happier I was. I had been very careful not to look at the house number. The colonels' quarters along this block were all identical. In daylight, I'd never be able to tell this house from its neighbors, and I'd never have to know which of them I'd been to. I followed Captain Cox up the stairs. We found the woman lying on the bathroom floor, unconscious. Someone had wrapped wet towels around her wrists and tied them in place with shoelaces. Blood was just starting to be visible seeping through the terrycloth. Captain Cox took her pulse at the carotid artery and then listened to her chest with his stethoscope. He pulled open her eyelids and glanced at the pupils.

"Stay with her," he said. "I'm going to go call for an ambulance."

He was gone for several minutes, and the woman never stirred. When he returned, I handed him the empty pill bottle I'd found in a corner behind the toilet.

"Good man," he gave me a grim little smile. "I was told she had taken something, but not what it was."

"We still don't know how much she took."

"Unfortunately."

He knelt to check her pulse again.

"How is it?"

"A little ropy," he said. "We'll have to pump her stomach. Probably give her a unit or two of blood as well. She'll pull through. When the ambulance gets here, I want you to step into the bedroom next door and wait until I give you the all clear. Nobody needs to know you were here."

"Our friend is going to be fine," he told me the next morning when I got to the clinic.

"That's good."

"I'll tell you anything you want to know."

"Let's see," I said, scratching my head. "That would be nothing."

"You aren't the tiniest bit curious?"

"Didn't you hear? That's what killed the cat."

"You're not a cat."

"I'm human, which means I don't have nine lives."

"Suit yourself."

"You know the word is already out," I told him. "I saw one of the emergency room nurses on my way in. She's a real blabbermouth. You can't keep people from finding out about something like this."

"No, but you can protect the person who found her like that."

"I figured it wasn't her husband who called you."

"You're too smart for your own good," he laughed.

"I've never believed that was possible."

"You know, I meant what I said to your friend the other night. I really am hoping you'll re-up. I know you're worried about having to go back to Viet Nam. I can fix it so you'll stay right here."

"Really."

"Honest to God. So think about it. O.K?"

"I will," I said, not because I had any intention of doing so but because only an idiot goes out of his way to make his boss unhappy.

Later that morning I was filing charts when Sergeant Gabe O'Malley appeared at the counter.

"Brought you something," he grunted, holding out a manila envelope.

"Thanks," I said. "How's Danny?"

"Open it."

"Oh, jeez."

"He says it's a horse. Did it at nursery school."

"It could almost be a horse," I chuckled. "I never really got the hang of finger painting either. But it's so sweet of him to make this for me."

"I'll tell him you liked it."

"Yes, please. Tell him I sent him a big thank you hug."

"Will do."

He seemed reluctant to leave.

"Listen," he said, lowering his voice, "word is you're down to pretty short time."

"Ten weeks."

"The vultures'll be circling soon," he nodded, "if they aren't already."

"What?"

"You know better than I do how hard it is for the army to keep enough medics around."

I shrugged.

"Don't be surprised if people start crawling out of the woodwork to try and get you to re-up."

"I'm listening."

"They'll promise you anything, but watch out. The one thing you want they can't promise you. 'Cause the war isn't about to be over, and they need you over there a lot worse than they need you stateside."

The logic of this was blindingly obvious. It was exactly what I'd been thinking about ever since Captain Cox had mentioned my possible re-enlistment.

"Anyway," O'Malley said, looking over his shoulder to make sure we weren't being overheard, "you don't want to go and do something stupid, O.K?"

"What about you?" I asked, thinking it would be a shame for Danny to lose his dad. Or even do without him for another tour overseas. Kids that age needed to have their fathers around.

"I'm out in another two months. I just have to keep my nose clean a little longer."

"Well, don't worry about me. I can't imagine anything that would keep me from leaving all this behind the second I'm free."

"Good man."

I was mopping up the remains of my spaghetti sauce with a slice of garlic bread when he appeared out of nowhere, setting his tray down across the table from me and sitting down with a grin best described as piratical. It was like having a Greek god materialize out of thin air.

"Seen you at the gym," he said. The accent was pure Brooklyn. Up close he was even bigger than I had realized. Prettier, too. He was wearing corporal's stripes. "You got really good form. Whoever taught you to lift sure knew his stuff."

"My uncle," I stammered. "He's in the NFL."

"Yeah? What's his name?"

"Gunnar Ingebrittsen."

"No kidding?" he stared at me. "I see the resemblance."

"Right."

"Joe Cortese," he said, offering a beefy hand across the table.

"Tristan Bentley."

"So what kind of grunt are you, Bentley?"

"Medical corpsman."

"Been to 'Nam?"

"Got back recently."

"You poor fucker."

"You?"

"Ain't been and ain't goin'."

"Nice work if you can get it."

"No trick to it," he laughed. "I'll show you how if you want."

I shrugged.

"So what they got you doin' here? Emptyin' bedpans?"

"Actually I'm working in the pediatric clinic."

"Do tell."

Unlikely as it seemed, I didn't dream of Cortese when sleep finally came that night. It was Violetta Della Torre who waited there for me. I saw her bent over a tiny, delicate looking writing desk, her hand moving gracefully across a flimsy page, pouring her love onto paper. Her beauty was luminous, like that of a princess in a Pre-Raphaelite painting. It was the beauty of sunrise, of moonlight on the ocean, of dew spangled roses. It was all those kinds of beauty and a thousand others, yet it transcended them all.

When I woke, I knew exactly why Sgt. Stefano Fabiani was still alive. It had nothing to do with me. What had kept his heart beating that afternoon wasn't anything I did for him. It was his knowledge that she was back home waiting for him that wouldn't allow him to breathe his last.

IV

When I got to the gym the next day, Cortese motioned me over to where he and his buddies were working out. He introduced us, and then asked me to spot him on his bench presses. He ground out a set of twelve reps with over twice my body weight on the bar. If he had actually gotten into trouble with me spotting, I'd have been precious little help. I watched breathless as his muscles bulged and his veins popped and his skin glistened with a film of sweat.

"Your turn," he gasped after his last rep. "How much do you want on the bar?"

I told him, sure that he would laugh. Or at least the onlookers would. But there wasn't so much as a stifled snicker. A guy named Rick loaded the bar and I lay down on the bench. Cortese got into position to spot. From that angle, he was overpowering. Although the weight I had asked for was pitiably small it was substantially more than I had been handling. I hoped to God I wasn't about to make a fool of myself.

The next day, he picked me up at the clinic and drove me to the gym. I wondered what had happened to the Mercedes roadster I had seen him in before. But an Alfa-Romeo was a perfectly acceptable substitute. I wondered how it happened that a corporal always drove expensive cars with officer's registrations.

Friday night he showed up at my door slicked up for anything but a trip to the gym.

"Whatcha doin'?" he asked, pushing past into my monk's cell of a room.

"Writing to my grandmother."

Standing there in my jockey shorts on account of the impossibility of adjusting the radiator properly, I had never felt more naked. That was silly because we showered together every day after our workout, but this felt completely different.

"That's nice," he said.

I shrugged.

"You're a nice guy, Bentley."

I gulped. I felt myself blushing.

"So where does grandma live?"

"Chattanooga."

"Figures," he said. "You got that southern accent thing."

"I thought you were the one with the accent."

"Yeah," he laughed. "You would think that."

I laughed too. I wondered if he could tell I was faking it. If he figured out what was going on in my head, I'd better plan on being beaten to a pulp. And he couldn't be as unaware as he appeared. Nobody could, short of a dead man.

"Hot in here," he said. He set the brown paper bag he'd been clutching on my dresser and started unbuttoning his shirt. For some reason this took him a long time. He hung the shirt on the back of a chair. He looked at me.

"You any good at your job?"

"What are you talking about?"

"Takin' temperatures. Usin' those doohickeys for blood pressure. Stuff like that."

"I guess."

"Ever give shots?"

"Sometimes."

"Little kids cry when you do?"

"I try to be careful. I don't like to hurt them."

"Right. That's on account of what a nice guy you are."

"You keep saying I'm nice."

"Anybody can tell," he said. "I hear people talk about what a nice guy you are."

I didn't believe that for a minute. I'd be willing to bet that nobody on the base gave me a second thought. He picked up the brown paper bag. He pulled out a syringe and several ampules.

"Say a guy needed a shot. Like a buddy of yours, you know?"

"Are you sick?"

"Yeah, right," he laughed. "You know what this stuff is?"

"I'm not sure I want to."

"Juice," he said. "Muscle juice, you know?"

"Steroids?"

"Sure."

"Where did you get it? It's next to impossible to find a doctor who'll write you a script for it."

"Next to impossible for some guys, maybe," he said. "Me, I got a guy beggin' me to take it off his hands. So are you going to shoot me up?"

"Are you sure you want me to? That stuff could be dangerous."

"Oh, hell, Bentley. What? Did you just fall off the turnip truck or somethin'? Look at me. I didn't get this way just thinkin' about it. I been on the stuff for years. It ain't hurt me any yet. And this friend of mine ain't gonna pass me any junk. It's A-one. Guaranteed. So ya gonna help a buddy out, or what?"

"If you're sure."

He unzipped his pants and pulled them down. He wasn't wearing any underwear. He stroked his cock absent mindedly, tugging on the foreskin.

I tore my eyes away. I picked up the syringe.

"How much do you take at a time?"

"Two of those little glass thingies."

"O.K." I said, filling the syringe. "Turn around."

He turned.

"Bend over a little."

He leaned on the dresser.

I told myself this was no different than giving some kid at the clinic a shot of penicillin for his tonsillitis. I told myself there was no reason to be nervous. I willed my hand not to shake.

"Hey, you're good," he said, straightening up and grinning at me. "Hardly felt a thing."

V

At Fort Geronimo, non-commissioned officers and their families lived in their own enclave behind and up the hill from Colonels' Row. The bungalows were lilliputian compared to the dwellings of the commissioned officers, the neighborhood itself a relic of the World War I mobilization. Nestled among tall, ancient looking oaks and elms, surrounded by velvety lawns that were as ridiculous in that desert climate as icebergs would have been moored in Honolulu harbor, they were neat, cozy looking, picturesque. Their quaintness seemed a distillation of everything that typified small town America. I had grown up in that America and knew how deceptive its prim and placid appearance could be. But the Saturday afternoon after Memorial Day, I couldn't manage to feel haunted. I had been invited to help Danny O'Malley celebrate his fourth birthday, and, incidentally, his father celebrate his impending retirement. I was bearing gifts. During Danny's hospitalization I had learned that the tiger was his totemic animal. The base exchange stocked a very limited supply of items that could be construed as suitable gifts for children, but a friendly clerk there had helped by ordering from a semi-legendary "warehouse" somewhere on the east coast and so I was equipped with a rather magnificent stuffed tiger and an elaborately colorful picture book of all things wild and feline. I wasn't bringing anything for Sergeant O'Malley, who had issued the invitation in person and had forbidden it.

"There'll be enough liquor to float an aircraft carrier," he said, when I offered, "and plenty to eat, so bring your hollow leg."

The bungalows differed in one respect from those you'd have seen in any Norman Rockwell reverie. They were identical to one another, as uniform as deuce and a halfs, rifles, mess hall trays. I had no reason for anxiety about finding the right one, however. Everyone on the whole block was in the one back yard.

Danny had five older siblings, all boys. Danny himself was the quintessential Rockwell redhead, pale skinned, freckled, blue eyed. His brothers, however, had wavy black hair and eyes like onyx. They ranged in age from seventeen to ten. Gabe, Jr., the oldest, and Patrick, the second boy, were famous, I learned, as starting and second string quarterbacks respectively at the local high school. A year apart in age, they were virtually indistinguishable from each other. They had their father's looks, which on teenagers were devastating. The next three boys were of the same overall type. As a group, they were what is generally described as "all boy". They were rackety, charismatic, physical. It was obvious Danny was their absolute pet.

He was the only child of the second Mrs. Gabe O'Malley. The first Mrs. O'Malley had died of a massive hemorrhage at the time of ten-year-old Rory's birth. She had been a Yugoslav war bride, an orphan from Dubrovnik whom Gabe had met in Trieste and brought home after an acquaintance of a few days. I tried, and failed, to imagine the kind of man who could have stood up to the tragedy of losing his wife while serving overseas. The boys had stayed with his parents on their farm in Wisconsin until Gabe and Gracie had married.

Gracie was a gorgeous red haired tomboy just a few years older than me. She seemed exactly the kind of girl who'd be able to take on a widower with five sons and never break a sweat. She'd make a terrific farm wife, I thought, when they returned to Wisconsin in a few days, after Gabe, Jr.'s graduation.

I learned everything about the O'Malleys without having to ask a single question. I kept my eyes and ears open, and their friends and neighbors provided me with all the exposition I could possibly need. I felt like a stranger in the midst of all the celebratory clamor, but not for long. I heard the women murmuring "that's Corpsman Bentley, the one who stayed with Danny when he got sick"; the men grunted "that's

Bentley, the corpsman who took care of Big Steve Fabiani the last time he got hit. Yes, *that* time". After that I was left in no doubt that I was a member of their tribe for life. I had saved the life of their brother in arms. I had comforted one of their suffering children. I needed no other ticket of admission, then or ever. Warriors clapped me on the shoulder and roared my name. Women pressed my hands, their eyes brimming. To the younger children I was no object of curiosity. I was merely the stalwart adult presence that invariably materialized in times of threat. This was no miracle but simply the way the world worked. It was no more surprising than a sunset. To the older children I was just another grownup, as inscrutable as the rest, worthy of no more interest than any other.

All around me the vision unfolded. Hordes of neighborhood children rampaged laughing across the unfenced back yards. The womenfolk exchanged recipes, gossip, and knowing glances. The men laughed, smoked, drank, told stories. This was the world of Sergeant Gabe O'Malley, a world of snug little houses, station wagons that were washed every Sunday afternoon, laundry hanging to dry on backyard clotheslines, faithful dogs snoozing on porches, ironically worshipful wives who tended flower beds and baked, children whose resemblances to their parents were unmistakable and infinitely comforting. This was the world to which Big Steve Fabiani must have returned by now, the world where Violetta della Torre patiently awaited him, her heart pure, her soul serene, and her imagination teeming with visions of hearth and home. Big Steve was still young enough to father children, a whole tribe of them. True, it was hard to reconcile that man tossing a baseball in the back yard with the warrior I had known back in the boonies, but each father there in the O'Malleys' back yard shared a similar body of experiences. As bizarre a set of juxtapositions as these might appear, they were commonly held and understood. And what did warriors do between epic battles, after all, but replicate themselves?

It was a world I had turned my back on long since, not by an act of will or any impulse to non-conformity, but through the simple acknowledgement that I could never inhabit it authentically. It was not in my nature to give myself over to fathering children and providing for them, to devotion to their mother, to allegiance to the domestic ideal. It was not that I was too selfish for this. At least I didn't think so. Instead, I recognized that I was incapable of it. I would always be dissatisfied with that life, drawn away perpetually from it as surely as the great oceans were tugged onto and back off of the world's shorelines by the moon.

I understood that about myself. I regretted it but saw no escape, at least none that would leave me whole. I accepted it and set off resolutely on my own path. I did it willingly because I knew it was real and true for me, and I rarely looked back. But that world had never seemed so seductive as it did that night in Sergeant O'Malley's back yard.

Deep into the evening, Gracie O'Malley came to tell me that Danny would like to say goodnight to me. I followed her into the small house and upstairs to Danny's room. There, enrobed and enthroned like a miniature prince, he greeted me with the elaborate punctilio of a tiny aristocrat. I assumed he had been coached, but then again in that household good manners were probably not something reserved for Sunday mornings and audiences with grandparents. I sensed them in the air.

"Corpsman Bentley, thank you for coming to my party."

Earlier, he had thanked me effusively for his gifts.

"Thank you," I said, "for inviting me. It was a terrific party."

"Would you read me my tiger book?"

This was how children expressed the truest gratitude for the presents you brought. They offered to share them with you.

"I would love to read you your tiger book, buddy."

I sat down next to him on the bed. He snuggled against me instinctively, like a child of my own body. The volume was both brief and comprehensive in that ingenious manner typical of the best children's non-fiction. I read to Danny of all those wild felines: lions, leopards, cheetahs, cougars, mountain lions, bobcats, lynxes, and his beloved tigers in their Bengal, Malay, and Siberian incarnations. As I read, his small forefinger indicated the relevant illustrations without ever quite touching the vividly colored pages. The satisfied gleam in his sleepy eyes expressed his devout conviction that these beasts had exactly three purposes in life: to prey fiercely and tirelessly on every animal they encountered, to fearlessly protect and lavishly provide for their young, and to passionately and exuberantly declare their friendship and allegiance to Danny on the day of his eventual meeting with them.

My voice as I read to him was, I realized, the voice of my father and my uncles as they had read to me in my boyhood. I had fallen instinctively into those distantly remembered cadences and intonations. But it was also, Danny's serene countenance asserted, the voice of his own father and brothers and untold other men. Further still it was the voice, commanding yet infinitely gentle, in which he would speak to his own children one day.

"Will you come to my birthday party next year?" Danny asked when we finished the book. He was barely awake by then. "We will be at the farm then. I'll show you all the animals. They're going to be my friends."

"We'll see, buddy," I told him, taking the liberty of kissing him on the forehead. "Goodnight now."

"Thank you so much," Gracie said, standing in the doorway of the tiny room, "for everything."

"Thanks for inviting me," I said through the lump in my throat. "He's a great little man. You and Sergeant O'Malley are terrific parents."

Then I went out to the back yard to say my goodbyes.

VI

"You want what?"

"You heard me," Cortese grunted, absent mindedly fondling his left nipple. There was something about that left nipple. It was just enough larger in diameter and plumper than the right one for it to be noticeable if you paid close enough attention. I tried not to. But I failed every time. Cortese had been practicing poses that evening after our workout. He smelled of baby oil and good, honest sweat. I had been lightheaded long before he made his request.

"We're doubling up on the dose."

It was several days since I'd seen him the afternoon before the O'Malley's party.

"You sure you know what you're doing?"

"Sure I'm sure," he said, unzipping his pants and sliding them down his massive thighs. "The rate I'm going I'll never make Mr. America next year. Can't be wastin' time like this. Gotta do somethin' radical."

I knew, of course, because he talked about it almost incessantly, of his plan to win the Mr. America title. But I hadn't taken it that seriously. I had thought it was just so much guff. That was how I preferred to think of him, as someone not to be taken seriously. I hadn't convinced myself so far, but I remained committed to the idea.

"This syringe won't hold that much."

"So hit me with it twice."

"Just so that you know."

"You're a nice guy, Bentley," he said, bending over and leaning on my dresser, "but you worry way too much. Anybody ever told you that?"

"No."

"Unbelievable."

I filled the syringe. I gave him the injection. I shot the juice right into that smooth, firmly muscled buttock. The buttock I had shaved for him the night before. I filled the syringe again. I gave him the second injection on the other side.

"Oh, that's good," he said, straightening up. When he turned around, I could see that he was partially erect. "Man, oh man."

"Tell me something."

"What's that?"

"What happens if your guy stops supplying you?"

"He won't."

"But what if he does?"

"If he does I don't let him suck my cock any more is what."

"Oh," I said, unable to meet his grin.

"Now don't go gettin' any ideas. Guy's got to get off somehow. The broads in town are all ugly trash and the women on base are too stuck up to live. Not a one of them can give a guy a decent blow job. Not one. But this guy, he's some kind of expert let me tell you. Enjoys givin' it as much as I enjoy gettin' it. So he's not gonna pull any tricks. And if he still feels like givin' me trouble after I stop lettin' him suck on it, I'll just let him know I'm ready to start tellin' people he's been suckin' it. Nothin' to worry about."

"Oh."

"You know," he said, "I see you workin' so hard in the gym. And you've got terrific bone structure. You could get bigger real quick. I know this guy'd help you out, too. Hell, I know I'm not the only guy he's servicin'. Not as crazy about it as he is."

"I don't think. . ."

"Now Bentley, it wouldn't make you queer or nothin', lettin' a guy suck your cock in exchange for somethin' like that."

I didn't go with him that night to meet his benefactor, though he seemed anxious for me to. It was as if he wanted an audience. Like it wasn't enough having some guy begging him for sex—he needed me to witness the transaction. As if that would prove something, though I couldn't imagine what. He left only after I promised that I'd think seriously about his suggestion. But I wasn't as nice a guy as he thought. It was a promise I had no intention of keeping. I knew there was practically nothing I wouldn't do for him, but I also knew I could never let him find that out. I was crazy enough just from working out and otherwise hanging around with him. I could hardly think of anything else, and I couldn't imagine doing something that could only make it worse. Still, imagination can be even more powerful than reality, and I couldn't help wondering what I'd have seen if I'd gone with him.

There were two possibilities. First, Fort Geronimo was only a few miles from the Mexican border, though an actual crossing was over an hour's drive away. I had heard that in the *farmacias* you could come by just about anything if you only knew what to ask for. Written prescriptions were an unnecessary formality. Anyone with a mind to could buy what Cortese was using and bring it back across for him. But it was the second possibility that intrigued me. Because if it was a doctor getting it for him through American channels—and those syringes he brought along each week were army issue as sure as God made little green apples— it could feasibly be someone I worked with. Of course a civilian doctor from the town was a possibility as well, but it was hard to imagine a civilian doctor with certain inclinations ending up in a place like this. A military doctor seemed much more likely.

I didn't know what any of the other staff doctors drove, but Captain Cox had a Volvo sedan. I would have to scout the physicians' parking lot for the green Mercedes roadster or the more recent Alfa-Romeo, though I knew the guy Cortese was getting the drugs from and the guy whose car he was driving didn't have to be the same person.

Why go to all the trouble of figuring it out instead of just tagging along with Cortese the next time he asked me? For the simple reason that as desperate as I was to know, I didn't want either Cortese or his friend to know I knew. As long as they didn't know I knew, I wasn't really involved. That was the theory, at least.

Meanwhile, I made little or no progress with Violetta's letters to Stefano. I repeatedly requested an Italian grammar and dictionary, but the base librarian seemed completely disinclined to help. The Latin grammar and dictionary I had checked out earlier led me down innumerable blind alleys, but they were all I had. I slaved away for hours on end but had yet to satisfactorily translate even a sentence of the very first letter. The words and phrases taunted me—I read and reread them phonetically until they took on the character of incantations. But as the days passed, I knew no more of her, or of them together, than I had before I read her name on the return address of that very first envelope.

That didn't make the secret any less tantalizing. I needed to discover it like a man overboard needs to find a life preserver. Every time I heard Cortese's rumble counting out reps or felt the pressure of his beefy hand on my shoulder, which seemed to burn all the way to my toes, or shaved his chest or oiled him up to practice posing, I felt myself sinking deeper. Before I realized it, I was so far down I wasn't sure I would ever break the surface again. I had no idea where the bottom might be. I tried not think about it.

I slaved away at Violetta's letters as if I thought they might contain some roadmap to salvation. Somehow, the sheer perfection of every single unintelligible word was a clue in itself. A woman whose penmanship was so exquisite seemed bound to have all kinds of miraculous qualities. Perhaps among them was the power to heal.

"They think I'm too big," Uncle Gunnar's voice crackled out of the phone.

"You're joking," I gasped.

"'Fraid not."

"How can anybody be too big to play Hercules? That makes no sense."

"That's what my agent asked. Then she reminded them that I'm a big star in the NFL. The film would benefit from that tie-in. Immediate name recognition. But they weren't having any of it. I'm just a big, musclebound galoot. Apparently somebody out there has mistaken Michelangelo's David for the Farnese Hercules."

"It's unbelievable."

"Not really."

"How can you say that?"

"I met them," Uncle Gunnar grunted, "and those Hollywood types, they're from another planet."

"There are always other parts."

"If I can't get cast as Hercules because I'm too big, it's hard to see what I might be more suitable for."

"Don't talk like that," I insisted. "When have you ever given up on anything?"

"When I didn't give a damn," he said, "and in this case, I don't think I do. I mean, sure, it would have been fun. And you'd be crazy to turn down the money they were talking about paying me. But I really have no ambitions in that direction. This is just one more reason not ever to set foot in that hell hole again."

"Well anyway," I said, "preseason starts soon. That'll take your mind off things."

"There's not going to be a preseason this year."

"Of course there is."

"Or a season, for that matter."

"What are you talking about?"

"I'm retiring."

"What?"

"You heard me."

"Why? You're in great shape. You could go on for years yet."

"Sure I could. But I want to go out while I'm at the top of my game. And while my knees are still in working order. Not to mention all my other parts. I don't want to be forty years old and dependent on pain killers just to get out of bed in the morning. I know lots of guys like that, you know. And getting to play for another season or two just isn't worth the risk. I've had a better than average career and now I'm moving on."

"But to what?"

"We'll talk about that when you get home."

"Aw, hell, you can't do that to me."

"Yes I can. And watch your language. Your grandmother will wash your mouth out with soap if you come home cussing. You are coming home, aren't you?"

"Sure."

"'Cause she's afraid you're going to skip out."

"I promised I'd come."

"And I'm going to hold you to it. Lars and Tor, too. The whole posse'll mount up and hunt you down if you try anything funny."

I wasn't crazy about the idea. I had never actually lived there, just visited. There was nothing wrong with it as a place. But I couldn't see myself living there. How could a man like me ever fit in? I figured I'd go for a few weeks or even three or four months. Just long enough for everyone else to realize I didn't belong there. After that? Well, that was the question I was mulling over early the next evening. Cortese had mysteriously disappeared two days before and I was at loose ends. I'd already been to the gym, and I was afraid if I went to my room and tried to read or work on translating Violetta's letters I'd explode. So I went walking. I was just exiting the main gate of the base onto the main drag of the town when Captain Cox's Volvo rolled up next to me.

"Where you off to?" he called out the open window.

"Nowhere, really."

"Have you eaten yet?"

"No."

"Hop in. We'll go get a pizza."

"I'm not sure that's a good idea."

"Come on, Bentley. Don't be so regular army. I'm a doctor. Everything's different for doctors. The brass don't care what we do as long as we put them back together when something works loose. Besides, it's the weekend. And you're off duty. That practically makes you a free man."

"Sure it does," I snorted.

"Will you please hop in?" he laughed. "You're holding up traffic."

"What do you want on the pizza?" he asked, beaming across the table at me in a way that I found nearly intolerable.

"Doesn't matter. Whatever you want."

"Let me rephrase that. Is there anything you don't like on your pizza?"

"Not really. I mean I'm not crazy about that pineapple and Canadian bacon thing some people rave about, but other than that anything goes."

"Even anchovies?"

"Never saw the harm in them."

"Seriously?"

"Seriously."

"I can't remember the last time I met a man who'd eat anchovies on a pizza with me."

I shrugged. It didn't seem like that big a deal.

"We'll order the special. That has a little of everything on it. Now what about something to drink?"

"Coke's fine."

"You don't want something stronger?"

"Not really much of a drinker. Don't let me stop you, though."

"Shouldn't really," he said. "I'm on call."

"You know, Bentley," Cox said, cutting his pizza with a knife and fork just like Mama had made me do when I was little, "you're a really hard man to get to know."

I wondered why it mattered. Did captains actually need to get to know grunts?

"Like for instance, we've never talked about your family or what you did before you got drafted. Much less your interests."

"I have no interests."

"Pull the other one," he grinned. "I know that you visit the base library several times a week. When you're not there, you're at the gym."

"Hire a private detective, did you?"

"Fort Geronimo isn't a big place," he said, "and there's not a lot going on. Minding other people's business gives us all something to do. When a guy's as intent on fading into the woodwork as you seem to be, it makes people curious."

"Who's curious?"

"Well," he said, looking sheepish, "I'll have to admit, you've had me wondering."

"Wondering what? I'm just a GI on short time. Trying to keep my nose clean and my ass out of the line of fire. You must know that story."

"Maybe."

"What does that mean, 'maybe'?"

"Maybe that's all it is. Maybe it's not."

"Listen," I told him, "there's no mystery about me, so don't go trying to make one up. I'm just a guy who got drafted, got sent to 'Nam, managed to get back in one piece, and is now counting the days."

"I thought you were considering re-enlistment."

"My grandmother won't let me."

"I almost think you mean that."

"Believe me, I do."

"You're what? Twenty? Twenty-one?"

"Twenty-two."

"You must have gone to college."

"Uh huh."

"Why didn't you stay in?"

"I graduated."

"Grad students get deferments, too."

"I'd rather not talk about it, thanks."

"All right," he said.

And I mentally kicked myself for making him even more curious about me.

"So you're twenty-two and you still let your grandmother call the shots."

"Actually, this is the first time I've ever let her have her way. I'm only doing it as a favor to Uncle Gunnar. You met him that night in Tucson."

"You mean that really was your uncle?"

He seemed astonished.

"Of course he was my uncle. Who did you think he was?"

"I don't know," Cox blushed. "He just seemed. . ."

"What?"

"Too young to be your uncle, I guess."

Which wasn't what he'd been thinking at all.

* * *

"Put your wallet away," Cox said.

"No, really," I insisted. "Let me pay my share."

"Bentley, this is my treat."

"But. . ."

"No buts. If it really bothers you that much, you can pay next time."

Next time. Right.

"Come on," he said, laying some bills on the table. "Let's get out of here."

I followed him outside.

"Want to come over to my place?" he asked. "I'll make a pot of coffee and we'll listen to some music."

"Listen, Captain Cox."

"I'm not listening to a thing unless you call me Andy."

"Listen, Andy," I said, nearly choking on his name, "I appreciate dinner. And your taking an interest in me and everything. But this is making me real nervous."

"Why? Is it something I said?"

"Nothing like that," I lied. "It's just, I've got less than two months to go. I don't want to do anything that might screw that up."

"Tristan, I've told you lots of times. You don't have to worry. I won't let anything happen."

"Maybe some other time," I said, hating myself for conceding even that much, "but would you please just take me back to the barracks?"

It wasn't just my imagination. Captain Cox was getting more insistent by the day. Like Cortese, but in a totally different way. It was like being the rope in a tug of war. On the face of it, Cortese, with his physique and his looks, should have won hands down and ended up dragging me away with him. But Cox had a kind of pull that was, in its way, even more dangerous if not as strong. His power was the kind only an officer could wield. He had the whole United States military pulling along with him, and thus his efforts trumped any exertion Cortese could muster. All I could do with either of them was play for time. Somehow I had to find the will.

VII

Off Main Street, the town was sleepy at all hours. At night it was practically a ghost town. A few porch lights always burned but many of the houses were completely dark, and it seemed as if the same dogs barked every time I passed, the same cats streaked in front of me, the same kids were practicing the same pieces on the same invisible pianos, the same cars slumbered in the same driveways. Every time I walked down Main Street itself, I half expected to see some familiar face or other behind the plate glass windows of some shop or restaurant. And it wasn't army personnel I was thinking of. I had grown up in a town almost as sleepy as the one outside the gates of Fort Geronimo and I knew all too well how fragile an illusion that somnolence could be, how easily and instantly it could be shattered. I knew, too, exactly where the fault lines lay, so my meanderings through those quiet streets avoided certain spots like the plague.

I was very careful not to call attention to myself as I walked those silent streets night after night. I didn't whistle or hum as I walked, and I kept my footsteps as muffled as humanly possible. On the rare occasion when I met anyone I avoided eye contact. And in the almost unheard of event that someone voiced a greeting, I kept my answer monosyllabic.

A few nights later when I got back to the barracks from one of these walks, the door to my room was standing wide open. I thought at first I must have been robbed, not that I had anything anyone could possibly want. A split second later it occurred to me that this might signify some snap inspection, and I hoped the sheets on my bed were taut enough and their corners regulation sharp.

I stepped inside and found Cortese reclining bare chested on the bed and my heart started to pound in a way it hadn't in the weeks that he'd been gone. The world lurched vertiginously one time as if something elemental had happened, which I supposed it had. Until I saw him there, I'd convinced myself I would never see him again.

"Got somethin' to show ya," he said.

I watched his abdominals flex as he sat up.

"Close that door."

"Where have you been?"

Had his nipples been that fleshy and prominent the last time I had stared at them?

"On leave. Didn't I tell you?"

"No."

"Musta forgotten. Might want to lock that door, matter of fact."

I did, and he stepped across the small room and picked up a manila envelope off my dresser. He opened it and pulled out a stack of photographs. Eight by ten glossies, in color.

"Here, take a gander."

They were of him performing bodybuilding poses. I knew the sequence by heart after seeing him go through it dozens of times. Front biceps. Rear lat spread. Side triceps. Side chest. All the others. I couldn't pretend any longer that he was just some huge, built galoot. The camera didn't lie. In a strange way the photos insisted that he was a god even more clearly than did his physical presence in the room.

These were no snapshots. They were unquestionably the work of a professional photographer, or at least a very skillful amateur possessing the best equipment. That wasn't the most striking thing about them, though. There were two shots of each pose. One with Cortese wearing his perennial navy blue posing trunks, and another with him nude and his erection unflaggingly at high noon.

"Who took these?"

"A friend."

"What friend? The one who gets you the juice?"

"Don't ask boring questions, Bentley. Who shot them doesn't really matter, does it? It's what's in the pictures that matters. Right?"

"He must have his own darkroom. You can't get stuff like this commercially developed."

"No kidding. And if you think those are hot, get a load of these."

He handed me a second stack of photos. In the first of them he was once again nude and rampantly at attention. A slutty looking blond woman with dark roots and breasts so large they looked like they couldn't be real crouched beside him. Her stiletto sharp, blood red fingernails were splayed across his thigh as she embraced it, meanwhile puckering her lips and staring rapturously up at him. I leafed through the photos quickly. They were amazing. It seemed to me, though my experience was admittedly limited, that every possible activity was depicted. And somebody had been there to witness it all.

"Go ahead," Captain Cox said, grinning sheepishly in at my door. "Say it."

"Say what?"

"How about, 'oh no, not again'?" he suggested, "or perhaps you'd prefer the ever popular 'we've got to stop meeting like this'."

"Just a sec," I grunted, already pulling on pants.

"Not an ounce of poetry in you, is there, Tristan?"

"I don't believe in it."

The boy was sixteen or seventeen. He might have been—almost certainly had been—a classmate of the O'Malley boys. He had the build of an athlete. His blond hair was matted with sweat and his blue eyes were red and puffy. Every now and then he sobbed involuntarily or shuddered. When he moved to wipe his nose with the back of his hand, I grabbed a wad of tissue and handed it to him.

I tried not to think who he reminded me of. I told myself it was just a coincidence, and that the resemblance was only superficial in any case. It was a common enough type. But my skin still crawled.

"I'm all right," the boy insisted. "Really. It's just a little blood. There's nothing to make a fuss over."

It had been serious enough to make him cry like a baby. It had been serious enough that he was teetering on the razor's edge of shock. Whatever it was, it was serious enough that someone had insisted on calling in Captain Cox.

"That's what we're going to find out," Captain Cox said, readying his apparatus. "This may hurt a little."

"It was my fault," the boy insisted. "I didn't know how to do it right. If I had just known how to do it right, this wouldn't have happened. He really didn't mean to hurt me. He's just so big, and I'd never done that before. I'll die if he gets into trouble."

Cox began his examination. I stood with my back to the wall and watched. Once again, I wasn't doing a damned thing. Cox always insisted on having me with him for backup but he never needed any assistance. I felt increasingly that he brought me along for some other purpose.

"Listen to me," Cox said, straightening up, "I'm pretty sure there's no serious damage. But there could be if you let anybody do that to you again any time soon. It's really important for you to be careful the next week or so. You're going to have to take it easy. No physical exertion. No running, no working out. Absolutely no swimming. And no baths, either. Showers only. If the bleeding doesn't stop in the next couple of days, or if it gets worse, you have to call me immediately. Understand?"

"Yes."

"I mean it. You say you don't want anyone getting into trouble, but the only way I can guarantee that is if you do what I tell you. You're just lucky he didn't hurt you any worse or I wouldn't be able to keep this quiet. And until you're sure there's no more bleeding, you're going to have to pack toilet paper inside your underwear."

"All right," the boy said. "I'll be good, I promise."

"I don't care what he tells you. You don't do that again."

"All right, yes," Cox said the next morning, standing in the very same examining room and shuffling his feet. "That young man was underage."

"I don't remember asking."

"And that particular act would be illegal in this state even if he wasn't."

"What act? Was there an act?"

"I expect you're wondering if I'm going to report the matter to the authorities."

"I'm not wondering anything," I said. "Don't you get it?"

"Get what?"

"I don't mind helping you out," I said. "You can always depend on me in a medical emergency."

"I know that, Tristan," he said, his voice a little husky. I felt like running out of the room but I'd have had to go through him to get to the door, so I didn't. "Believe me, I do. I can't tell you how much I appreciate it."

"I just wish you'd spare me the post mortems," I said.

"I feel the need to explain."

"To me? Why?"

His shrug was more eloquent than anything he could have said. Seeing it, my heart sank even further. So it was like that. I knew exactly how that felt. But though it helped me understand, it didn't make me feel sympathetic. I couldn't afford to let it. This was every man for himself.

"O.K." I said. "Here goes. Correct me if I get any of it wrong. You're not going to report anything because that boy won't testify. You're a doctor, and they'd have to take your medical evidence seriously, but if the boy won't identify the other person, they can't nail anybody for anything."

"I'm with you so far."

"Anyway, what's the point? You blow the whistle and perhaps they grab the man and send him to prison for a hundred years or so, but what really happens is that now that boy's parents know what happened and his friends know and his teachers know. Everybody in the whole county knows. And even if somehow somebody convinces him to testify that it was an assault, in the back of all those people's minds they'll be wondering if maybe it wasn't an attack, really. Maybe he encouraged the guy. We both know what kind of hell that kid would go through, and there's only one way to keep it from happening. I'd do the very same thing in your position."

Of course I didn't want to believe that I'd ever let myself get into his position. I didn't know whether he was some kind of Good Samaritan everybody in the area knew to come to when they got into a scrape or whether he just happened to have one particular friend who was a walking catastrophe. I had my suspicions, but if I didn't ask I didn't have to know.

"Nobody has to explain anything to me," I went on. "Nobody has to justify anything or apologize for involving me or anything like that because I don't want to know any more than I already know, and I don't care, and I'm not involved."

Which house was it? I wondered that night as I walked the streets of the town. Had I already passed the house where that boy lived? Or was it on one of those streets where I never went? How was he feeling? Were his minor abrasions and contusions starting to heal? Had he managed to keep his underwear clean enough that his mom wouldn't have a nasty shock next time she did laundry?

What was he thinking about as he did the dishes or took out the garbage? Was he having trouble concentrating on his homework? Did he regret what he had done? Or was he writing a certain name over and over on a piece of college ruled notebook paper and counting the minutes until he could do it again?

What stupid questions. I had seen that look in his eyes. I knew what a look like that meant like I knew my own name. I was exactly that lost myself.

Cortese was waiting in my room when I got back. His hair had never been slicker, shinier, or more fragrant. His skin had never glowed more seductively. His eyes had never been so bright. His strength as he wrestled me onto the bed was terrifying. But the brief spanking he administered apparently wasn't the main event. He soon let me back up.

"You ready for this?" he asked, panting a little and hauling a fistful of ampules and several syringes out of the paper sack he had brought.

"What the hell is all that for?"

"Ain't takin' no for an answer," he said. "I'm shootin' you up."

"But. . ."

"Hold it right there," he said, slapping a massive paw across my mouth to silence me. "Nothin' to worry about. My buddy showed me how to do it. Can't guarantee I'll have as soft a touch as you do. But I'll try my best not to hurt you too much."

"But. . ."

"My buddy says there's no way it can do you any harm. And anyhow, we're startin' you off with a dose so small it probably won't do a thing. Just to see that you're not gonna have any strange reaction or nothin'."

"Cortese, I can't do this."

"'Course you can. When you put on another twenty or thirty pounds and really start to look like somethin', you'll thank me. Now are you gonna drop 'em, or am I gonna rip 'em off you?"

I unzipped my pants and let them fall. Then I pulled down my briefs. I could feel myself blushing all over. I watched as he filled the syringe. He'd been practicing. I thought about the blond boy.

"Turn around and bend over," he commanded.

God help me, I did. It was all over in a second. There was just the tiniest sting in my butt as the needle went in. It was the rest of me that hurt like blazes.

"Good boy," he chuckled, giving my other buttock a hard slap. "My turn now."

I pulled up my briefs and pants.

"O.K.," he grinned. "Tonight we're shootin' the moon."

"What?"

"We're doublin' the dose."

"We already. . ."

"We're doublin' it again."

"But. . ."

"But shit. You saw me on the scale today. Finally broke two-fifty. Now I got to get the cuts. Most guys get cut, they end up all puny. Not gonna make that mistake."

"You know this means I'll have to inject you three or four times."

"Bentley, just shut up and get busy, huh?"

I did. When he turned back around, his erection was red and throbbing. I could see a tiny iridescent pearl glistening in the slit. He dabbed it with a finger and held it in front of my face.

"Want a taste?"

I pushed his hand away, desperately pretending he meant it as a joke though I wasn't fooled.

"No thanks," I croaked.

"Just checking. . .oh, no."

His ejaculation was astonishing. The force of it seemed nothing short of supernatural. Stream after stream shot onto my pants leg. I stood staring at it, unable to move.

"Don't matter," he grunted when it was finally over. He pulled open a drawer of my dresser, took out a t-shirt, wiped himself clean with it. "Plenty more where that came from."

VIII

After Cortese left I couldn't settle down. Whether it was the drug itself making me want to crawl out of my skin or the blatancy of his approach or the spectacle that followed his own injection, I couldn't be certain. What I really couldn't get out of my head as I paced from wall to wall was the feel of his hands on me, or rather my hunger to feel his hands on me again. Finally I couldn't stand it any longer. I left that tiny room like it was on fire. The summer twilight was a faint glow silhouetting the mountains. Toward the east, the valley was already in deep shadow. The lights of the town glimmered in the still air, and I plunged toward them. Anything to distract me.

My aimless blundering along the shadowy streets eventually led me to the one place I had been avoiding like hell itself ever since I'd first caught sight of it. All that red brick and white wood trim—it looked like nothing so much as a miniature Monticello. It couldn't have seemed more out of place in that desert village. But it wasn't its architectural incongruity that had caused me to give it such a wide berth. It was the tall white steeple. I knew all about Baptists. I had been one, after all.

As I approached the building I remembered it was Wednesday evening, which meant that choir practice must be going on inside. It was the sound of the organ drifting out the open windows that finally stopped me in my headlong flight. They were rehearsing an anthem that was painfully familiar. And by the worst possible luck, it was based on the hymn that had been my father's favorite. Not for him the sentimental ditties about Gentle Jesus. This was a text smack out of that militant, almost socialist Anglicanism of the late nineteenth century, all about personal responsibility and building the Kingdom of God right here on earth with our own hands, about justice, about peace, and with hardly a word about religion.

The organist finished the introduction and the voices of the choir swelled up. Two phrases later, I was sobbing.

That was how Captain Cox found me when he came out of the sanctuary, heaven only knew how much later.

"Tristan. My God, what's going on?"

His unexpected appearance astonished me into silence. It was about the last place I would have expected to find him. But that made no sense, because knowing him like I believed I did I shouldn't have been surprised. What better camouflage?

"What are you doing here?"

"Nothing," I stammered.

"Don't give me that. You're obviously very upset. What's happened?"

"I told you. Nothing. I'll be fine."

"Come on," he said, grabbing me by the elbow. "My car's over here."

"No. Please just leave me alone."

"You don't really mean that," he said, opening the passenger side door and shoving me inside, "even if you think you do. I've finally seen through that independent act of yours. What you really want is someone to take charge of you."

By then the motor was running and he was backing out of the parking space. For a moment I considered opening the door and jumping out, but by the time I'd actually registered that thought we were going fast enough that I could be certain it would really hurt. Somehow I couldn't make myself feel quite that desperate. Maybe he was right. Maybe what I wanted was somebody to just tell me what to do.

"Feeling better?" Cox asked.

"Yes, thanks."

"Can I get you something else?"

"No."

"I wish you'd tell me what's wrong."

"I'm sorry," I lied. "If I could talk to anybody about it, it probably would be you."

"Thank you."

His smile made me feel even guiltier.

"You go to that church?" I asked.

"Yes."

"Sing in the choir?"

"Uh huh."

"Baritone, I bet."

"How did you know?"

"Always been a churchgoer?"

"My dad's a preacher back in Missouri," he said looking a little embarrassed, like it was the worst secret I could have uncovered about him.

"But you're all grown up now."

"Is that supposed to mean something?"

"I don't know."

"Wait a minute," he said, "is that what this is about? Are you having some kind of spiritual crisis?"

"That's not what this is about."

"I'm not so sure."

"Listen, Captain Cox. . ."

"You mean, 'listen, Andy.'"

"Andy," I relented. "I meant what I said, but right now I just want to lie down in my own bed and not think about anything."

I had left Violetta's letters lying on out on my desk. They had been there when Cortese arrived earlier, but he hadn't paid any attention to them. They were, however, the first thing Cox noticed when we walked into the room. He picked one up and stared at it. Then he noticed me watching.

"Sorry," he said. "Didn't mean to pry."

"It's all right."

"Violetta," he said, his voice suddenly husky. Seeing him close to tears was excruciating. "So it's a girl, Bentley? Is that what's got you so upset?"

For a moment I didn't follow him. Then I remembered that the greeting to her letters never said "Stefano", but merely began "Caro" or "Tesoro". Cox apparently thought they were letters to me.

"You're blushing," he said. "It is a girl."

I couldn't lie, but I was damned if I'd tell the truth.

"My God," he said, incredulous. He stared at the desk, shaking his head. "It's a girl and she writes to you in Italian."

He set the letter down and picked up the Latin dictionary that was now disastrously overdue from the base library.

"And you apparently don't read Italian," he mused. He turned to look at me. His upper lip trembled almost imperceptibly. "You don't read Italian, do you?"

"No."

"I guess it all makes sense," he said, shaking his head slowly. "I should have known. I can usually figure it out."

"Thanks again," I said. "For everything."

"You should have told me about her."

I shrugged.

"You should have, Tristan," he insisted. "I could have helped you."

"You've done enough," I said. "Really."

"I'm not just being nice," he shook his head. "I really mean it. I have a friend who's Italian. I bet he'd make short work of those letters."

"My buddy Captain Cox says you have some letters," Cortese said in the shower after our workout the next afternoon, ostentatiously soaping himself.

"I didn't realize you knew him."

"Oh, hell yes."

It wasn't that I hadn't figured it out. Still, I was strangely unmoved by this revelation. The sky didn't fall, the seas didn't engulf us. I only felt a little sicker to my stomach than I had all day.

"So," he said, stroking his cock thoughtfully. "Want me to have a look at them?"

"You read Italian?"

"Some. It depends on the dialect. May not be able to help. Happy to give it a try."

"Sure."

Not that I felt I had any choice. I knew Cox would have been insistent. And Cortese's own curiosity had apparently been aroused. If he could read them at all, he'd soon figure out the letters hadn't been written to me. I cringed inwardly at the thought of Cox's reaction when Cortese told him and he realized I had lied to him. The trap I'd been in since my very first day at Fort Geronimo kept getting tighter.

"Can't do it right now," Cortese said. "Got to see somebody after dinner. I'll stop by later."

It didn't seem possible, but he got better looking every time I saw him.

"Jeez," he muttered as he entered my room, "how do you live in this oven?"

He slipped out of his shirt and tossed it onto my bed. The sight made me light-headed. I had been hoping all along that if I spent more time with him I'd eventually become immune to his looks. It hadn't worked.

"So, how's about these letters?"

"They're over there."

"Must be pretty important."

"I don't know. I haven't been able to read them."

"Don't do it, Bentley," he chuckled. "Don't try to bluff me."

"Am I bluffing?"

"'Course you are. Bet you're hopeless at poker. So who they from?"

"Her name's Violetta."

"That I already know. What I mean is who is she to you?"

I shrugged.

"Important enough that it's drivin' ya crazy not bein' able to read them."

"Really?"

"Uh huh," he grinned. "There you go again."

"See for yourself," I suggested.

"No so fast," he shook his head.

"Oh?"

"You haven't said what you'll do for me if I tell you what's in them."

"What do you mean?"

"What I mean," he said, stretching his arms over his head and giving me a flash of freshly shaven armpits, "is what's this favor worth to you?"

"Oh."

"'Cause I mean I know we're buddies and all, but, well, you know."

"Do I?"

"Yes, Bentley, I think you do."

"I thought you said you weren't even sure you'd be able to read them."

"Don't know until I try, do I? And we don't know for sure I'm even gonna do that."

"Oh."

"Look at me," he said, fondling his left nipple.

"What?"

"Wouldn't make a guy queer," he said, "sucking off a guy like me."

"Oh."

"Look at me. What do you think?"

"I don't know."

"Yes you do," he said, starting to undo his pants. "Who's gonna say no to this?"

Which was the question, all right.

"Or say," he mused, "maybe suckin' me off wouldn't be enough, you know? Maybe somebody should be thinkin' about lettin' me fuck him in the ass."

"But. . ."

"Don't worry," he said. "I'll do it nice and slow. Won't hurt a bit if you just relax. I'll make you feel real good. You'll see. Then we'll have a look at those letters."

Part Four

Lodestar

1970-71

VEGA

What Vladimir was trying his best not to listen to was the silliest possible of arguments. Semi-articulate posturing at best, as if Preble (not his real name) and Rancik (not his, either) had come to some agreement independent of him whose terms specified that never again would the two of them agree on anything, no matter how inconsequential. Vladimir couldn't believe, or rather didn't want to believe, what he was hearing and focused his attention instead on the scene outside the shattered windows. The huddled groups of demonstrators were perpetually in motion, shuffling their feet in the snow, clapping their mittened hands together, hugging each other in elaborate pantomimes of affection and solidarity—anything to keep themselves warm or at least provide the illusion of comfort as they played their assigned roles in the drama. They were held at bay on the opposite side of the street by the long lines of National Guardsmen, who all too obviously would much rather have been at home watching this scene on their televisions, bottles of beer ready to hand and pizzas fragrant in their ovens. The exhalations of both groups rose, mingling into a cloud only slightly less substantial than the leaden mass looming only feet above them. Just whose idea had it been, smashing every window in the building with subzero temperatures in the forecast?

Preble and Rancik continued to argue, their expressions intent but their voices betraying their fatigue. Or was it merely boredom? Who wouldn't be bored? Those two put trivia on one pedestal and egotism on an identical one beside it. They worshipped those idols. How appropriate. How bourgeois. It was impossible for Vladimir to tell whether the two of them truly cared about anything any more. Everywhere he went these days he encountered these idiots, these juveniles, grunting and farting like apes in the rain forest, intent on nothing more meaningful than proving themselves the most radical, most defiant, most committed, most fearless, most intrepid of all, as if the movement he had dedicated his life to half a generation ago were all just some spectacle of one-upsmanship and the future of humanity wasn't at stake. Each planning session he attended, each march, each demonstration, there were new ones, younger ones, stupider ones, their shrillness in inverse proportion to their tiny intellects, their theatricality calculated more to gain them individual notoriety than to advance the cause, to bring peace nearer to reality, to move the revolution forward.

The cause? What cause? "*I am the cause*", he heard the subtext in their bleating, just like some doomed and deluded autocrat of centuries past. "*La cause, c'est moi!*" Meanwhile the industrialists and bankers and policitians daily increased their iron fisted control here at home, and their lap dogs in the media applauded them for it, and everyone else looked the other way, and across the Pacific jungles burned and boys died.

One boy died. Vladimir shuddered involuntarily. One boy. The same boy. Always the same boy, over and over in the nightmares that assaulted him whenever he slept and haunted his waking hours like film loops playing over and over again on banks of flickering television screens in some demented pop-art installation in some inexcusably bourgeois loft in Manhattan that styled itself as a temple of radical chic but was neither chic nor radical by any reasonable set of criteria. One boy. That one boy. Vladimir couldn't save that one boy, much less the whole world. He couldn't, not because he wasn't capable of it, but because he couldn't bring himself to do what the task required. What failure could be more bitter than that—a totally unnecessary one?

One boy. That one boy. That name he couldn't even whisper to himself. Because, as events had proved, he was unworthy to. That boy he'd never been able to forget. Remembering him was a penance. Except that as a revolutionary Vladimir was an atheist, so the concept of penance was inadmissible. It was a bourgeois sentiment grounded in the opiate of the people. But he couldn't help himself. Remembering that boy was a penance because he needed to atone for what he'd done and, as the Catholics put it, what he had left undone. A lapsed Jew could certainly understand that concept.

These fools, these cowards, these charlatans chanting their trite slogans and waving their signs and taunting the National Guardsmen as if it was some reinvented pep rally. These idiots, their eyes constantly peeled for the news cameras, for the adoring glances of the hordes of young girls who showed up for the excitement, the romance of the scene, but for the attention most of all of their rivals. *"Look at me, I'm Che!". .."I'm Red Rudi!". . ."I'm Konrad!"* Oh, the absurdity of their aliases. One of them actually asked Vladimir where he had come up with his own. *"Vladimir? Like for one of those Old Bolsheviks or something?"* "It's on my birth certificate," he had growled, and the kid turned away thunderstruck. That's how much they knew. Wherever they were, whatever they were protesting, pretty soon it all devolved into performance and self-promotion. Into theatre. And the politics and authenticity were gone, lost, tossed aside as the drama of the event took on a life of its own, and the historical opportunities and necessities were left glimmering like stars in the night sky over an arctic landscape, brilliant but unwitnessed by human eyes and thus for all practical purposes invisible.

Outside the shattered windows, a kind of soundtrack to futility, he could hear the faint sound of dispirited, non-rhythmic chanting and the unintelligible squawking of bullhorns. Nothing was happening out there and nothing was going to happen. That dismal tableau outside was the extent of what they'd accomplish. Behind him, in the freezing shadows, Rancik's whining drone and Preble's rasping bark wove in and out of each other, lines converging, diverging again, at times running briefly parallel, never actually intersecting. What kind of argument was it really, when neither party ever heard a word the other said? There was no dialectic without the actual confrontation between ideas.

It hadn't always been like this. Vladimir remembered different times, different faces, different voices. It hadn't been about personalities then, but goals. It hadn't been theatre. It hadn't been about "sending a message" or heaven forbid "raising awareness". God how he hated those clichés. More than the clichés themselves he hated the way they had become ends in themselves. No, back in the days he increasingly found himself recalling, the focus had been on achieving results. Remembering those times only made him feel colder and deepened his despair. As if he would go back to them even if he could. History had only one direction, and that direction was inevitable. That's what Grandpa Zitronblatt had drummed into him. That and its corollary. Memory was counterproductive self-indulgence. But still, shouldn't one seek and accept instruction from the past? Wasn't that, too, part of the dialectic?

Two sharp yelps erupted from Preble, followed by a punctuating squeal from Rancik. Then silence. A dog and a pig, except not so smart. No. Vladimir couldn't insult honest animals with such an association. He listened to the long pause and heard in it a seething resentment that echoed through the room, ricocheting off the walls, the ceiling, the debris clotted floor. Nothing had been settled. Their dispute wasn't over. They were catching their breaths in preparation for the next round, which would be equally futile. It was that knowledge that impelled him, the moment the next word was uttered and he realized that he could practically recite the arguments of both Preble and Rancik for them—and more articulately by far than either of them was capable of doing—to rise from the folding metal chair he'd been slumped in and stumble wordlessly through the piles of garbage on the floor out the doorway into the corridor and without a pause, without a glance backward, toward the east stairwell.

They had occupied the building four days earlier, a scant dozen of them in the first wave, storming in from the snowy twilight, shocking a couple of custodians just starting their Friday evening shifts and terrifying a secretary they found working late in one of the top floor offices. These people they released immediately. There was no thought of holding them hostages. This wasn't terrorism but an act of liberation. Their demands deserved to be met on their merits, not as a result of coercion.

After that it was routine. Barricading the entrances so that only their reinforcements and suppliers could enter, ransacking filing cabinets, tossing furniture out classroom windows, smashing anything of value they could find. Word spread quickly as they had known it would. Hordes of students gathered from all parts of the campus, but they allowed only a few inside, pre-selected according to the usual criteria. Amateurs were always a problem because they tended to be politically unreliable and their behavior was unpredictable at best. They had no notions of revolutionary discipline. Worst of all they brought with them the perennial threat of informers. The FBI had more plants on university campuses with every passing week. These operations never worked out if they deviated from the plan. Their rule had to be that nobody they didn't know could be trusted.

With the students came the police. Campus security first, followed later by city forces. By midnight the entire area was cordoned off, the lawn in front of the building cleared, the throngs of students—peaceful at least for now—pushed back across the street onto Founders' Square. Saturday morning the first camera crews arrived and took up their positions. This was the cue for Preble, Rancik, and Vladimir to emerge briefly from the building, Preble's raspy bark having previously been chosen to give voice to their demands. The cameras rolled, the police officers clenched their jaws and their nightsticks, the students cheered. Then it was over and they went back inside to wait. Sunday passed like a week in purgatory. On Monday morning, the National Guardsmen arrived and relieved the exhausted, half-frozen cops.

By nightfall Tuesday the entire campus, one of the largest in the Midwest, was completely shut down. Negotiations with the university administration, the police, and ultimately the governor of the state, frenzied at first, had long since reached impasse. And the initial exhilaration had died, replaced by a sort of dumb inertia. Vladimir had seen it dozens of times. These people, his purported comrades in arms, had no staying power. They devolved from near hysterical fervor to zombie-like lassitude almost instantaneously. Then the operation slowly began cannibalizing itself. It started with whining. Bickering followed. Then accusations and recriminations, painstakingly prepared beforehand, were trotted out. And finally came the collapse, first of their solidarity, an ephemeral thing at best, later their organization, and eventually the plan itself until nothing remained but confused fumbling, disguised ever so thinly by whatever face saving flourishes they were able to execute in the course of their headlong retreat.

He was so tired of it, the wasted time, misguided effort, and soul destroying futility. He had started out as the truest of believers. It was in his DNA, after all. Now he was an agnostic at best and veering dangerously close to the revolutionary equivalent of atheism. Apparently Americans just didn't comprehend the historical necessities. They had sold out their original radical tendencies—the ones that empowered them to take on and defeat the wealthiest, most powerful empire on earth at the time—to jingoism, materialism, conformity. To bread and circuses. Worst of all, to that blackest of bourgeois seductions, "affluence". And the minority in the country who hadn't, who still felt the impulse to rebel, either didn't know who to rebel against or had no idea how to go about it. Because it wasn't just their shallow, boring, middle class mommies and daddies they need to depose but their whole culture, it turned out. And how did you accomplish that? By acting out and shouting "look at me"? Hopeless and inexcusable, given the ready availability of appropriate revolutionary examples in this land of free, comprehensive public education.

Weaving through a maze of huddled bodies on the stairs—drunk, stoned, sleeping, or merely spaced out—Vladimir reached the basement. Since Friday evening the only way into or out of the building had been through a maintenance tunnel inexplicably left unsecured by the authorities. He fished the Red Army flashlight from the pocket of his field jacket and turned the beam toward the tunnel entrance. Once inside the tunnel, he aimed it at the floor directly in front of him. With all utilities to the building shut off, condensation had frozen on the curving walls and floor, making the footing treacherous.

Vladimir was not merely stretching his legs, taking a break to clear his head, going to buy cigarettes—all those excuses employed by the dozens of defectors he had heard mumble them over the years in preparation for their departures. He was finally washing his hands of it all. Behind him in the tunnel bridges were burning. There would be no going back. No more crouching in the freezing darkness grinding shards of glass into the linoleum with his boots, waiting for the debacle to unfold. No slow, miserable ride back to New York with Preble and Rancik in the garishly painted, rust disfigured Volkswagen van, breathing the noxious amalgam of carbon monoxide from the broken exhaust and hash smoke and sodden clothing and unwashed bodies. No enduring the purgatory of endless, inconclusive, and self serving post mortems. Tired to death of the constant failures and the unending futility, he was done.

That silliest possible of arguments, deplorably inconsequential as Vladimir had deemed it at the time, nevertheless achieved a sort of bizarre significance, gravitas even, through its one and perhaps only material consequence, however unintended. He didn't die. He was miles away on a bus heading east when the building exploded.

He wasn't among the injured, much less the deceased. And he was farther away still when he learned about it, in a bus station in a small town in Pennsylvania, the headlines screaming at him. Reading them, he imagined the building in rubble, the campus thrown even deeper into chaos. Three people were dead, Preble, Rancik, and an as yet unidentified male. At least forty had been admitted to area hospitals. Some of the injuries were described as life threatening. The authorities continued their search for additional survivors or possible human remains. The death toll was expected to rise. Vladimir was identified as one of the ringleaders and described as missing. The implication couldn't have been clearer, he thought.

This was not in the plan. Blowing up the building had never been mentioned. It wasn't the way their group did things. They practiced non-violence as advocated by Gandhi and King. Though it had to be admitted Preble and Rancik did love throwing things out windows, the things in question had never been alive. Vladimir wouldn't have agreed to a bombing under any circumstances. Even if he hadn't been philosophically opposed, there was the question of technical expertise. Vladimir had kept his experiences in bomb disposal while serving with the IDF the deepest of secrets. None of the rest of them knew anything about making things explode. He would never have come along on this trip if he'd known they were planning an action of that nature. Bloody fools, Preble and Rancik. What a monumentally stupid thing to do. The proof of that was all over that front page. Photos of the wreckage and the dead, quotes from the injured. It served those two right, Vladimir thought, for their idiocy. But to have killed that third man, to have put all those others in the hospital? Why should anybody else have to suffer? And how could they have thought a bombing would advance their aims?

Still, his revulsion and disbelief were tempered by curiosity. How had they done it? And why? There was no conceivable advantage to be gained by such an act. The American public, for all its glorification of and fascination with violence in movies and on television, was invariably repelled by violence in real life. More to the point, how had they pulled it off without him knowing about it? It seemed all but impossible, but the newspaper headlines were no hallucination. He couldn't come up with a satisfactory explanation.

It wasn't the time for pondering every question that occurred to him, however; to stand clutching the newspaper in trembling hands with his heart racing and his temples beginning to throb, avidly devouring the scanty account over and over. As the son, grandson, and great-grandson of radicals, Vladimir knew instinctively that he must act and act quickly. Thanks to that heritage he knew exactly what steps to take. He'd been preparing for something like this since boyhood.

The next late afternoon found him several hundred miles away aboard another bus headed in a completely different direction, his long, curly raven hair shorn to a scant inch all over his skull and bleached almost white, his prophetic beard shaven to reveal the smooth skin of a child, his wire framed Trotskyite glasses discarded—causing him to squint slightly—and his army surplus store wardrobe abandoned in a dumpster, replaced by a completely different, unmistakably thrift store sourced one. No matter how effective it was, he knew a disguise was not something that could be depended on indefinitely. It was a poor substitute for a new identity. Which was what he now required. Well schooled by his forebears, he had a contingency plan. He knew the steps by heart. Given a few weeks he would be a new person. If his disguise was good enough, if he had covered his tracks skillfully enough, he would have the time he needed.

The bus growled on toward the sunset, and he slept.

"I don't trust him," Preble grumbled.

"Only an idiot would," Rancik concurred.

"That haircut alone. . ."

"But people are taken in."

"Stop it, you two," Marytza laughed. "You almost sound like you really mean it."

Vladimir watched Preble and Rancik exchange a meaningful look. He watched Marytza choose to ignore the evidence of her eyes. He knew the truth she chose to ignore. They did mean it. Really.

"Konrad is sure he's an FBI informant," Rancik said.

"That haircut," Preble said.

"Konrad's never wrong," Rancik said. "Has anyone ever known Konrad to be wrong?"

"Really, you two," Marytza protested. "That's enough."

But really it wasn't. It never was. Vladimir had long since recognized their enmity for what it was. Jealousy. Well, fine. God only knew Tristan was awfully easy to be jealous of. At least if you didn't know him as Vladimir did. Or believed he did. No, it was more than belief; far more of course. But still, he could understand so easily why they made up the lies, spread the gossip; why they hated. It was abundantly clear that neither of them could hold a candle to Tristan and that their preeminence in the group resulted solely from Tristan's refusal to take a leading role himself.

It had to be admitted that Tristan was far too bourgeois in his sensibilities and his habits. He actually supported himself by holding a job, for instance. What true revolutionary would willingly slave away waiting tables in an expensive restaurant? Kowtowing to the plutocrats for tips? Especially when there was an unending parade of rich hangers-on whose class guilt could be exploited? Vladimir understood exactly how retrograde it appeared while at the same time secretly applauding it. Then there was Tristan's abstention from what all the other men in the group held as their revolutionary right, the steady supply of all too willing young females. The girls found his apparent chastity chivalrous, romantic, and all the more enticing. In the boys it aroused profound suspicion. That their suspicions were correct only Vladimir knew for certain. That knowledge, and his own highly ambivalent relationship to it, kept him dumb when a truer, or at least braver, friend might have defended Tristan's reputation. The boys' grumbling had only one practical effect, really. It further increased the girls' fervor as they trailed Tristan through the streets or listened, rapt, to his contributions to the group's discussions or even, merely, when he was a topic of conversation.

As for the way Tristan wore his hair, as far as Vladimir was concerned this criticism was ridiculous. What is revolution for, anyway, if not to assert true and radical freedom of personal choice? And what business was it of anyone's if Tristan chose a style which brushed against neither his ears nor collar and which occasionally necessitated the employment of discredited grooming agents? All right, so it made him look like the enemy. Wasn't there something elegantly subversive about that? The only possible problem Vladimir could identify with such a statement was its subtlety.

Outside the apartment windows, Greenwich Village basked in the sunshine of early May. Vladimir caught Marytza staring at him and smiled back, tuning out as best he could the infuriating drone of Preble and Rancik with their almost Dostoyevskian gloom and ineffectual ire.

"Complain about the president we're going to get if somebody doesn't do something," he growled at them. "Complain about Tricky Dick."

"Don't those idiots realize that if the FBI wanted to infiltrate us, Tristan's the last person they'd pick?" Vladimir muttered.

"If anyone's a stoolie," Marytza giggled, "it's Konrad himself."

They were in bed, finished but cuddling. Late afternoon sun slanted in at the windows. Down the hall, someone was listening to the Rolling Stones. In the kitchen someone else was attempting something which employed lots of garlic and lots of oregano and would ultimately prove to be inedible.

"Stoolie?"

"I know, I know," Marytza admitted, "but those guys. I mean, really. Their dialogue comes right out of some horrible radio script circa 1937."

"Agreed. But Konrad? You can't seriously think. . ."

"I know I can't seriously think," Marytza said. "After all, as I'm constantly having pointed out to me, I'm just a girl."

"Come on, Marytza. Not now."

"I just think it's funny that it's always Konrad sniffing around for traitors. Nobody else seems that concerned. But if I didn't know better I'd say he's paranoid."

"Maybe he is paranoid."

"Or maybe he's an informant himself, trying to deflect suspicion—shift it onto others."

"Now who's paranoid?"

"You have to admit it's a possibility."

"You know," Vladimir mused, "I'm not sure the FBI is really that interested in us."

"You're joking," Marytza gasped.

"Everything's different now."

"You bet it is. We shut down the whole damn university. Nothing will never be the same."

"But look who got all the credit. The SDS and all those black groups. It's like we don't exist any more."

"Well if that's what the FBI thinks, they're sadly mistaken. They haven't heard the last of us."

* * *

She must have repeated this conversation, or at least described its substance, to Preble and Rancik because almost immediately Vladimir began overhearing garbled versions of what he had said in conversations all over the building, which by that point was all but devoid of actual, paying tenants. If the landlord had been anybody other than his Uncle Yevgeny, a dyed in the wool radical himself, they'd all have been evicted long since. Soon the sentiment Marytza had expressed transformed itself into a kind of mantra. *Make the Man take notice.* Various proposals for bringing that to pass were floated.

Looking out the bus windows as he crossed yet another state line, Vladimir contemplated his new, unsought notoriety. The Man had noticed, all right.

He pushed the coin through the slot. The tone sounded. He dialed the number. He waited three rings and then cut off the call before anyone could answer. He repeated this sequence twice more. Then, studying the hands of his wristwatch intently, he waited exactly seven minutes, fed the telephone yet again, dialed the number again, listened to the ring tone on the other end.

"Hello."

"*Yit'gadal v'yit'kadash sh'mei raba.*"

"I'm sorry," an accentless voice said, "I believe you have the wrong number."

"*B'al'ma di v'ra khir'utei.*"

"I regret to inform you that that synagogue has closed."

"*V'yam'likh mal'khutei b'chayeikhon u v'yomeikhon.*"

"Unfortunately, Rabbi Korngold is retired now, but if you really must speak to him, I believe he can be reached at. . ."

"*Uv'chayei p'khol beit yisrael.*"

The voice on the other end spoke a telephone number, which Vladimir repeated and the voice confirmed. Vladimir hung up. The area code was for Boston, so he knew he was meant to call Chicago. And since this was his first contact, he knew he was supposed to add one to each digit of the number he had been given. He waited exactly one hour before calling it.

When that telephone was answered, he skipped the first line of the Mourners' Kaddish, beginning instead with the second. The telephone number he was given this time had a New York area code, so he knew he was to place a call to Omaha. This was his second call, so he subtracted two from each digit of the number he had received. It was too dangerous to stay in once place any longer, so he bought a bus ticket to a city he could easily reach by the next day plus two hours.

So far so good.

To be fair to Preble and Rancik, though Vladimir didn't know why he felt that was necessary or even how it could possibly matter now that they were dead, Tristan's politics had been deplorable. Though those two had of course been completely wrong on the question of where his loyalties lay, they had been right about that much. Still, it had to be acknowledged. Tristan had been no Marxist. Hardly a radical, even. Unless, of course, you counted utopianism as a radical position, though in that case you might as well consider "Goldilocks and the Three Bears" a political manifesto. Tristan's politics had been derived largely from *Leaves of Grass* and the book of *Isaiah*. Nothing reliable there. No theory to speak of. No system at all. Just a fuzzy vision of a perfect world. Well, fair enough. Tristan had been far from alone in that dream. It had, for all practical purposes, constituted the *zeitgeist*. There had been fuzzy thinking all around. There had been grandiose visions aplenty. The movement had probably been doomed from the first by its lack of appreciation for the intellectual side of things. Americans thought of themselves as intensely practical. Tinkerers. Shade tree inventors. Suspicious of theory. At the very least, they had little patience for theoretical speculation, for the development of conceptual frameworks. Paradoxically, this anti-intellectual approach made practical action more difficult to achieve. Cause was constantly mistaken for effect, and vice versa. Lack of conceptual clarity and contextual understandings made organized efforts largely a matter of who could shout the loudest in meetings, not what actions were most likely to have the desired effects. No, you couldn't call Americans practical at all, despite their protestations, their often expressed regard for "hands-on" and "grass-roots". Those were merely rhetorical tropes, the activists' equivalent to inserting "like" after every sixth word they uttered. They had no more meaning to the people who spoke them than the words of those ancient prayers in that unintelligible language that lazy bourgeois Bar Mitzvah boys learned to repeat phonetically. What Americans truly loved was not practicality but emotionalism. What they were good at was not direct action but political theatre.

He had been able to get Tristan to understand that. It hadn't been difficult. Tristan's early training hadn't been particularly helpful in this regard, but his natural intellectual bent had made up the difference. He had the makings of a fine revolutionary of the old school. Vladimir's Uncle Yevgeny had seen it immediately. With the right reading list and appropriate encouragement Tristan could have become a clear thinker and a truly reliable operative. But Vladimir had never been able to get him to take that last, crucial step. Perhaps it had been too much to ask of a sixteen year old. At least an American sixteen year old. Israeli teenagers could accept the necessity of such a thing. It was a matter of national survival. Teenagers of the Eastern Bloc apparently had no difficulty falling into line with party dogma. But American teenagers grew up with radically different assumptions. Primary among them seemed to be the belief that individual happiness trumped everything else. If anything was the pre-eminent imperative that was. Tristan could never become a true revolutionary because Tristan never would agree that the political was more important than the personal and the welfare of the group counted for more than that of any individual. He grasped the point of self-sacrifice well enough, but he rejected it on any other than voluntary terms. Indeed, he had somehow formed the opinion that the political was only meaningful to the extent that it validated the personal, which as far as Vladimir was concerned didn't make you a revolutionary but an anarchist.

And not an anarchist of a particularly useful sort.

At a pay phone Vladimir found a couple of blocks from the current bus station, he fed coins into the slot. He followed the prescribed sequence exactly and timed each step to perfection. He was eventually rewarded by the sound of a voice on the other end of the line.

"Hello."

"*Sim shalom tovah u-ve-raha*"

"I'm sorry, but I believe you have the wrong number."

"*Hen vachesed ve-rahamim aleinu ve-al kol yisrael amekha*"

"That is correct. Rabbi Rappaport will be making a trip to Toronto on Thursday."

"*Barkheinu Avinu kulanu ke-ehad be-ar panekha*"

"Until then, he can be reached at. . ."

The voice gave Vladimir a telephone number, which he repeated. The area code was for Kansas City so he knew he was to call Little Rock. And since this was his third contact, he was to multiply each digit of the number he had been given by three. In the event that the product turned out to be a two digit number, he was to use its second digit only.

The message about Rabbi Rappaport indicated that a contact would be available to help him cross the border at Windsor, Ontario on either of the next two Wednesdays. This was not an instruction, he knew, merely an option he was being given. He would indicate his response by choosing one or the other of two prayers which he would repeat when he made his next call, twenty-seven (twenty-four plus three) hours later.

At each stop on his trek, Vladimir scoured the bus terminal for abandoned newspapers. He had to keep up with developments. With no end in sight to his wanderings, he could ill afford to spend money on non-essentials. Fortunately, Americans were slovenly. He didn't once have to reach into a trash receptacle. He just picked papers off chairs, the floor—anywhere, really. As the days wore on, however, little additional information found its way into coverage of the event. Apparently the authorities were keeping journalists on a very short leash.

One thing every article agreed on was that the "manhunt" for the "terrorist radical" who had "masterminded" the bombing continued unabated. It was surreal, reading this and knowing he was the target. The FBI was said to be leaving no stone unturned. Vladimir had never doubted their determination to run him to ground, but he found it deeply gratifying that his physical description continued to be repeated exactly as it had in the first hours after the event. The long, wavy hair like in those paintings of Jesus. The steel rimmed glasses like those worn by the revolutionaries of 1917. He saw no profit for the feds in continuing to circulate these details if they knew them to be outdated. His disguise remained effective.

The situation he had found himself in was his own fault, at least partially. Not the current situation, with him on an endless bus ride though regions of America he had only been vaguely aware of the existence of until now, but the orginal and fundamental one that was the basis and context for everything that had happened during the years leading up to this bus ride. Vladimir was finally ready to acknowledge his share of the responsibility for all that. In the beginning, not realizing what was at stake for both of them, he had led Tristan on. There was no point in denying it any longer. It was easy enough to admit it now that there was no one to address the admission to. Some would add his belated willingness to make this confession to the tally of his guilt, and who was he to say that they were wrong about that? He had done everything wrong, both from a political and personal perspective. He had luxuriated in the hero worship, for what could be more seductive than the extravagant adulation that had been offered him by such a brilliant, breathtakingly handsome young man? When it happened he had already been well aware of his propensity to be seduced by this particular combination of qualities. Tristan was far from being the first such admirer he had attracted. By the time Vladimir realized that it was something far deeper and more complex than in any of the previous instances, it had been too late for both of them. He had been as powerless over his emotions as Tristan had been over his own. Vladimir had never been in such a position before. Indeed, he had never imagined being in such a position, not because Tristan was a young man rather than a young woman but because Vladimir had never considered it possible to lose himself so completely in emotion, to be propelled beyond the limits of rational thought into a domain he had previously considered mythical. It was the first time in his life that he had been able to identify to any extent with the experiences and preoccupations of the bourgeoisie. He valued that insight for what it was but at the same time found the idea revolting. Being in love threatened to transform him into the sort of person he had vowed never to become, and on returning to New York with Tristan in tow at the end of that tumultuous summer he knew he had no choice but to break things off. It was the hardest thing he had ever done because it was the first time in his life that he was conscious of being willfully cruel.

America appeared to grow larger with every passing mile. It expanded in all directions. The distances were stupefying, the emptiness incomprehensible. The fields stretched on forever, except when replaced outside the windows of the bus by forests or mountains. There appeared to be no end to it, but, paradoxically, nothing outside the windows seemed to offer him the sort of refuge he required. The days crept past with the engine grumbling distantly, the tires hissing on the pavement, the utility poles flickering past outside the windows, and the white center stripe strobing underneath like some cryptic code. The nights passed even more slowly. Vladimir had nothing with him to read. And before long he had more than caught up on his sleep. There was nothing to do but think. And there is nothing worse than having excess time available to devote to that.

On the bus with him during each leg of the journey were exactly the sort of people he had dedicated his life to liberating. Theoretically they were noble sons and daughters of the working class and thus his allies, his natural element of humanity. But up close and in person they seemed dirty and deplorably unrefined and uneducated. They wouldn't do at all as heroic figures in the great struggle for the future of the race. He could hardly stand to be around them, and he supposed that to his betrayal of Tristan had to be added the hypocrisy inherent in his disdain for these fellow citizens. It was the sort of criticism Tristan had leveled all too often at many of their associates, and the memory of this stung.

In the towns and cities the buses of his flight rumbled through, life went on uninterrupted. The sun rose and set. Rain fell. Clouds parted. People woke, went about their business, lay down to sleep each night. Each fleeting image through the deeply tinted glass confirmed the passage of time and the continuation of every conceivable human activity. On the buses themselves, the faces constantly changed—not only new passengers at every stop but a parade of drivers. Their uniforms never varied, but everything else about them did. By comparison with all the activity around him, Vladimir felt almost inanimate. He might have been an article of freight.

He thought of his great-grandfather and great-great uncles on those endless train journeys from St. Petersburg to their Siberian exiles and the scenes that had passed before their eyes, the endless forests and endless snow. The more things changed the more things stayed the same. Their journeys had been no more nor less voluntary than his. A hemisphere and seven decades separated them, but the plight of the revolutionary never changed. Czarist Russia, Imperialist America—completely different to the eye yet identical in their essentials. The injustice, the inequality, the exploitation, the enslavement, the profound misery of all but the few and the limitless guilt of those fortunate ones. Even now, the same conditions were evolving somewhere else, South America perhaps, or in parts of Asia, which would necessitate the perpetuation of the struggle. Vladimir might never have sons of his own—that seemed increasingly unlikely—but somewhere on the planet, some undetermined number of years or decades into the future, his nephews or great nephews would almost certainly find themselves in similar circumstances, riding on some conveyance or other toward a destination not so much geographical as existential, totally different from his in every detail but the significant ones. Perhaps Marx had been wrong in one crucial aspect. Perhaps history was not progressive but cyclical. In that case, revolution was nothing but one more item in an infinite list of names for doom.

Breaking off with Tristan had been easier said than done. Vladimir's painstakingly constructed arguments shattered like the flimsiest glass against the stone walls of Tristan's implacable convictions. That's how Vladimir had been forced to describe

Tristan's position in his own mind, though he would never have voiced such sentiments aloud. Acknowledging their conflict would have constituted a confession in itself. It would have been an admission of the fallibility of the revolutionary ideal, if nothing else. An admission as to the nature of the conflict was even worse. Unthinkable, really. By which he meant that he literally hadn't been able bring himself to think, much less speak, words such as love or passion. He had been horrified at the sight of the young man he had so idolized turning into a bundle of seething, uncontrollable emotions. Tristan didn't clamber down from the pedestal Vladimir had placed him on; he dove from it with a recklessness, an impetuosity, that almost drove all thoughts of affection from Vladimir's mind. Almost. Because when all was said and done Tristan was still Tristan and not some monstrously debased stranger, and Vladimir couldn't help but suspect that it was he, not Tristan, who was the debased and corrupted one. Tristan, misguided as he was, was at least honest. He was attempting something more than Vladimir could bring himself to do, to live authentically.

Vladimir's objections remained exclusively political. As far as he was concerned, homosexuality per se wasn't the problem. He could accept it in Tristan and he could very nearly accept it in himself, at least theoretically. It was disloyalty to the revolutionary ideal, to the discipline necessary to any successful movement, that was his sticking point. That's what Vladimir had insisted, both to himself and to Tristan as they argued it out night after night, week upon week. It was their single and perpetual argument. The revolution couldn't succeed, Vladimir maintained, if homosexual men were seen to be at its vanguard. The masses, the people they were ordained to liberate, wouldn't stand for it. They wouldn't follow cadres thus constituted into the radiant future that awaited them. Instead, the movement would cannibalize itself and eventually collapse. Any reasonable individual could see that, could understand the impossibility of what Tristan proposed.

Tristan's repeated response was the only response Vladimir's logic could have failed to answer. What good is a revolution if it liberates only some and not all? If men like themselves were to be left out?

Canada was certainly the easiest, the most logical answer. It had been in the back of his mind from the first. From before the first, actually. The group had always thought of Canada as a sort of lifeboat. Many of their number were already there evading the draft. The country was a sort of platonic ideal, what America could have been, if only. The people were unfailingly polite, staunchly egalitarian, less invested in materialism than their southern neighbors, and seemingly immune to demagoguery or jingoism. The danger of the place was that to the impressionable its existence seemed to make the notion of revolution unnecessary. Still, Canada had one compelling argument in its favor as a destination. From there, the whole world would be within reach. Vladimir could settle in Montreal or Toronto, reach out to his former associates already living in the country, and eventually develop channels of communication with the remaining radicals of America. He could continue to influence events. He could maintain his usefulness to the cause. And if none of those things was to materialize, Canada would at least make it possible to travel anywhere else he might choose. Europe. Israel. South America. Australia. New Zealand. Only America would be off limits.

Staying in the United States, on the other hand, was problematic. At the very least it would entail establishing a new identity. This was well within the capabilities of the people whose aid he was depending upon, but it had to be accepted as an irrevocable step. It would require all kinds of alterations to his way of life, including, most crucially, refraining from any and all political activities more or less for the rest of his days. He didn't know if he could do that. It would require a degree of self discipline he wasn't certain he was capable of even as a matter of self preservation. At the same time, he didn't know what else he could find to devote himself to that would engage him to a degree sufficient to give his new life any significance. It was as unthinkable, in its own way, as Tristan's allowing himself to be drafted.

Canada. A simple crossing of the world's least threatening border. Even with the authorities presumably on alert for his attempt, there was no doubt the people he was in touch with could bring it off. Those people were, after all, completely above America's suspicions. If anything, they were regarded as being among America's staunchest, most reliable allies. Their assistance had nothing to do with his politics. It was neither because of nor in spite of. It transcended all political notions. It was based on an identity far too ancient and profound to be affected by such trivia.

The whole thing couldn't be easier or safer, and it was hardly worth considering alternatives.

Except that he had never been able to formulate a satisfactory answer to Tristan's perennial question. In their disputations he had, certainly. But on those very occasions when he was most vociferous, when his eloquence moved him almost to tears, his heart had always told him that Tristan was right and he was wrong. In Canada he could only hope that someday the two of them might be reconciled through the random, unanticipated workings of fate, not that fate was something a true revolutionary would ever allow himself to believe in. While if he remained in America. . .

No, it wasn't even safe to entertain the thought. But his resolve was clear, and so was the path. And so for only the second time in his life he prepared to follow the dictates of his heart in contradiction to everything else.

Another telephone booth a few blocks away from another bus station somewhere else in America. Vladimir wished he had put more effort into learning about American geography. He fed coins into another slot, followed the sequence exactly, timed every step precisely.

"Hello."

"*Sh'ma Yisrael, Adonai Eloheinu, Adonai Ehad.*"

"I'm sorry, I didn't quite catch that. Could you repeat it, please?"

"*Sh'ma Yisrael, Adonai Eloheinu, Adonai Ehad.*"

"You're quite certain?"

The first utterance so far that wasn't in code.

"Quite certain."

"Very well. Here is the address."

The voice gave him an address in Denver, which Vladimir knew really meant someplace else entirely. It was farther than he had hoped and in a direction basically opposite to the one he had been traveling in. The prospect of further days on the road dismayed him, but he realized that he had made his choice a long time ago.

Seeing his picture on the cover of *Newsweek* was a greater temptation than he could resist. He parted with coins he could ill afford to spend and shoved the magazine into his bag for later perusal. The surrealism of the scene, being greeted "good morning" by the man at the newsstand and exchanging pleasantries as if Vladimir wasn't the man glowering at the camera in that cover shot was something he would never forget. The regret he experienced at having no one to laugh about it with was excruciating.

"Biography of a Revolutionary" was the title of the extensive article, and reading it, Vladimir's bemusement only increased. The reporters had done extensive research, it was true. But they had blindly accepted all they had been told. The resulting account was no more Vladimir's life story than it was Christ's or the man in the moon's. What hope was there for America if its "journalists" were so easily bamboozled? The article proved definitively that they were capable of nothing but the propagation of lies.

It had to be admitted now. Tristan had been right all along. Personal fulfillment couldn't be held in abeyance indefinitely in the name of some great, comprehensive transformation of material reality. That path was ultimately dehumanizing, and it led nowhere Vladimir had any desire to go. On a more practical note, it had to be accepted that the revolution was dead for the foreseeable future. Recent events had simply driven the nails into its coffin. Americans wouldn't cast their lot with people they considered terrorists. It would be a generation at least until the ideal might be resuscitated. Vladimir's generation wouldn't do it. Vladimir's generation had proven itself unworthy. Vladimir, with his conceptual frameworks and his theoretical expertise, had been the utopian one after all. It was Tristan who had truly respected the dialectic of the material universe and had attempted to live within it. Even now Vladimir's salvation depended not on solidarity with his Marxist brothers but on a persistent, seemingly irrational fervor based in the mythology of his forefathers. It was difficult to imagine anything more retrograde than that, yet it offered his only hope of salvation.

Tristan had known. Tristan had understood and accepted.

As he slipped yet again into unquiet sleep, Vladimir could almost hear Tristan's voice declaiming the words of that most bourgeois of all English poets, Matthew Arnold:

Ah, Love, let us be true
To one another! For the world, which seems
To lie before us like a land of dreams,
So various, so beautiful, so new,
Hath really neither joy, nor love, nor light,
Nor certitude, nor peace, nor help for pain;
And we are here as on a darkling plain
Swept with confused alarms of struggle and flight,
Where ignorant armies clash by night.

By the time Vladimir took his seat in the shadows of the tiny sanctuary, his stomach was growling so fiercely that he was certain everyone present could hear it. He hadn't eaten in several days. He had had to save every remaining cent for bus fare just to get there. He was actually lightheaded from hunger. He had always wondered what that felt like. It was worse than he had imagined. If anything went wrong at this juncture, he was truly helpless.

It was well past time for evening prayers to begin but there wasn't a minyan present, so they waited. Finally, just as Vladimir was beginning to despair of his ordeal's ever ending, a young man entered and sat next to him. This made up the required number, and at last the prayers got under way. Perhaps it was his lightheadedness, but to Vladimir the young man's beauty seemed to eclipse that of any other person had ever seen. In his addled state, it seemed like a sign.

At the end of the service, the young man departed without a word. Or even, really, a glance at him. Vladimir slipped the parcel the young man had left behind into his pack without looking at it.

He made his way to a diner he'd seen on the way to the synagogue and ordered a meal. Only when he had a few bites of food in him did he dare to look inside the small parcel. To his enormous relief there was money there. Plenty of money, in easily negotiable small bills, with enough larger ones interspersed to make buying additional bus tickets convenient. He wouldn't starve and he'd be able to continue his journey. If he was careful, he'd be able to make it last for several months. But really, the money was the least of what he'd been hoping to find, and his hopes hadn't been in vain. There were documents. Not anything as elaborate as a fake driver's license or passport. That wasn't how these things were done. Fake documents such as those would never be anything but fake. They would have been fine if he was trying to escape the country, but they couldn't be relied on long term. It had to be assumed that the longer he held onto them the more likely they were to be detected. Instead, the documents he had received were the very ones he would need in order to apply for a genuine driver's license and a genuine passport when the time finally came. He looked down at them, at the name he might actually go by for the rest of his life. There was nothing special about it at all. It certainly wasn't the kind of name anyone would ever make up. It was simply a name on a genuine birth certificate. The name of a child lying in a graveyard somewhere. A male child who had been born within a few months of his own birth and who had been chosen to give Vladimir his name because, presumably, in addition to his appropriate age and gender, his family would, for whatever reason, never pose a challenge to Vladimir's new identity.

And staring at that name he realized how totally that new identity would differ from his old one. His benefactors had made themselves invisible in choosing it. They had totally obliterated his association with his heritage.

Bellatrix

Marytza heard about it the same way the rest of the country did. It was all over the newspapers and television. Breathless, grim faced reporters babbled semi-hysterically into microphones as they stared wide eyed into cameras. It was the big deal of the week and its ramifications looked like they might proliferate even beyond Saturday and Sunday. Little had she known.

"Student radicals occupy university building," she muttered under her breath as she waited in line at the subway turnstiles. "Whatever next?"

Of course it couldn't be Vladimir and company, she had thought on hearing that first news of the action, the occupation of that building, though she had no way of knowing this for certain. Almost immediately she had found out differently, and suddenly, without meaning it to happen, she was in the middle of it. At least by association. Everyone in the house knew her history. And they weren't subtle women. Most of the time it was like the second act of *La Boheme* with her housemates as the chorus. One of them had to have said something to somebody. It wasn't the kind of secret which could be kept. She held her breath and waited. But no consequence materialized. Something should have tipped her off to the approach of fate. But there had been no furtive telephone calls, no quiet muttering that stopped the second she entered a room, no meaningful eye contact in the kitchen, none of the usual clues. Nothing at all to feed her paranoia, which starved but wouldn't die. All she had to go on were her instincts about how to best deconstruct this media frenzy swirling on unabated. As usual, establishment disinformation constituted the bulk of the coverage. No surprise there. The free press was probably Amerika's most enduring myth. The tense days as the standoff between radicals and the rest of the universe stretched mind numbingly on drove her nearly out of her mind. It was so much like all the other times that both sides seemed to know the script by heart. Didn't anybody have any imagination these days? And then, almost the instant she'd formulated that critique, the final, horrific denouement. Talk about burning your bridges. Once upon a time she'd have been in on it up to her eyes, but she'd had no inkling. And as the days passed and her housemates still betrayed no interest in her beyond the usual and no word came from any direction, she realized just how completely she had become a non-person. That was her fate. She had wanted to disappear—be careful what you ask for. The FBI didn't even bother interviewing her.

Well, fuck them. The FBI of course, but Vladimir and company as well. Fuck them all. "A plague on both your houses," she muttered, as the line slowly inched its agonizing way through the turnstile. She must have missed two trains already.

"And good riddance," she muttered a few minutes later, hanging onto a pole as the packed train lurched out of the station. She even thought she meant it. At least for a second. But of course she didn't, really. As angry as she'd been—as she still was—she had never wished any of them dead. Even Vladimir. Like it or not, it was beginning to look suspiciously as if he'd been the great love of her life. Talk about tragic. It was worse than *Anna Karenina*.

When Marytza left Vladimir, she joined a feminist commune in deepest, darkest Yorkville. She left no forwarding address, no telephone number where she could be reached. She avoided all contact. And though her vanity and paranoia both insisted that Vladimir wouldn't just let her disappear like that, there had never been any sign to the contrary. Nothing in all that time. Nevertheless, she was not surprised, not one bit, the afternoon a few weeks after the final catastrophe when she got home and found the message that Vladimir's Uncle Yevgeny had called. The Zitronblatts knew everything, including, it seemed, how to find out anything they weren't already aware of.

She considered not returning the call, but the Zitronblatts were as persistent as they were omniscient. Not to return the call would merely be to put off the inevitable. She might as well get it over with. And besides, she had always had a soft spot for Uncle Yevgeny. He had always treated her like Vladimir didn't. Or wouldn't. And that was worth something. So she called. What did surprise her was the way the sound of his voice on long distance made her weep. But not until she was safely off the phone, thank God. He said he would be in town for a few days visiting friends in Brooklyn. He would like to buy her lunch. Against her better judgement she assented. As always when dealing with a Zitronblatt, she regretted it as soon as she hung up. But she didn't call him back. Simpler, really, just to stand him up.

Of course when it came down to it she couldn't do that. She supposed he'd known it. She was pretty sure he had also known she'd at least consider it. She wondered if he'd had a backup plan. No, she knew he'd had a backup plan. Zitronblatts had backup plans like everybody else had navels. She wondered what it had entailed. She stepped off the bus on an April day that felt like November into a street that could have been Warsaw before the war or Tel Aviv right that minute. Hebrew script everywhere she looked and the few words spelled in Roman alphabet were either proper names or words in something that obviously wasn't English. Her forebears had terrorized neighborhoods like this back in Krakow and Katowice. They'd done it for entertainment as much as for hate. The thought made her shudder. The restaurant was easy to find. "You can't miss it," Uncle Yevgeny had assured her, and he was as good as his word. The Zitronblatts were absolutely trustworthy when dealing with matters of no consequence. The more trivial something was, the more you knew you could depend on them. Talk about perversity. When she stepped inside, he was already at a table sipping tea.

"Marytza, darling," he smiled, rising to kiss her on both cheeks.

"Yevgeny."

Why couldn't Vladimir have been like this? Elegantly dressed, distinguished looking as a French diplomat, charming, gentle. Why were nice clothes and refined manners dismissed as intolerably bourgeois? What revolutionary purpose was fulfilled by dispensing with things like those? The family resemblance was striking. She felt uncannily as if she were looking at Vladimir himself, circa 1992. Not that she expected to live that long, even if his death hadn't made the proposition absurd.

"I ordered lunch for us," Yevgeny said. "I hope you don't mind."

"That's fine."

Their food came almost immediately, a fragrant chicken and vegetable soup almost as thick as stew. Her grandmother had made soup like this. Perhaps all the grandmothers in the world carried the recipe for it in their DNA.

"So I suppose it's true," she said, several minutes later.

"You mean Vladimir?"

She nodded, hardly able to meet his gaze.

"So it would seem."

The ambiguity of the statement was as loud as an explosion. She looked around the dining room half expecting to see the other patrons cowering under their tables. Bastards. So Vladimir was alive and they'd let her go on all these weeks mourning him. Well, not exactly mourning perhaps, but something close enough to it that the difference hardly signified.

"Was there a funeral?" she asked. What she really meant was, *why wasn't I invited? And why did you wait all this time to let me know the truth?* But of course she'd never get the answer to either of those questions out of him. The Zitronblatts were strict "need to know" types. She suspected it went far beyond revolutionary discipline.

"You know our family are atheists."

"Yes, but even in the Soviet Union there are funerals."

"It would not have been his wish. Or that of his parents."

Fine. But if they really were faking Vladimir's death, it seemed to her that a public funeral would be awfully effective window dressing. Of course, it would mean too many of them in the same place at the same time. The feds would have a field day. That was undoubtedly the reason they'd forgone the opportunity for verisimilitude. It was good news, actually. Now she could stop grieving and get back to nursing her anger. Anger was infinitely more satisfying. She finished her soup in silence. She wondered where Vladimir was. Canada? Israel? Timbuck-fucking-tu? She wondered if Yevgeny even knew. It didn't matter. At least it shouldn't matter. Officially dead meant she'd never see him again. And she didn't want to see him again, ever, so why did the idea of it make her feel like she was about to cry?

"There's just one thing," Yevgeny said.

There it was. The real reason for this meeting. For the love of God, these Zitronblatts never stopped asking too much.

"What?"

"I thought you might want to go back to the apartment before I close it up. I'm going to be renovating the whole building. Gutting it completely."

"Why would I want to do that?"

"You might have left something behind."

"It's been almost two years since I left there, Yevgeny."

"Still. You never know what you might have forgotten. Vladimir always said you left there like the place was on fire."

"I didn't leave anything behind."

"You might have."

She got ready to argue but held her tongue. What he was obviously worried about was what Vladimir might have left there. She saw the point. Who knew better than she what skeletons were in those closets, or even where all those closets were located? Who else could he ask? His eyes said all this. But they also said how sorry he was to have to make this request. True or not, she admired the gallantry of it. That was what convinced her.

"Perhaps I did," she said, as if making an admission. "It's true I was in a hurry to get out of there. I hardly knew what I was doing."

"The building has been under surveillance from time to time," he said, sliding a pair of keys across the table. "They may still be watching it."

Of course.

"I know what to do."

She borrowed a long black wig from Sue Morgenstern and a pair of galoshes from Ruthie Maustro. She bought a ragged old house coat at a thrift shop. The kind nobody under the age of fifty would be caught dead in. It looked like rats had gnawed on the hem. The satchel she already had. Whoever she looked like at least wasn't her. It wasn't a great disguise. It wouldn't fool anybody who looked at her twice, but she was really hoping it would keep her from being noticed at all. All she had to do was get inside the building in the first place. That particular block in Greenwich Village was busy any time of the day or night. They could have a dozen or more people watching the entrance and no one would be any the wiser. But after three months, and with Vladimir officially dead, it didn't seem likely they'd bother with more than a token presence. The disguise only had to fool one or two watchers at most, probably just street level informants at that, and only for a few seconds.

If she wasn't up to that she might as well hang up her six shooter and spurs.

Come to think of it, if she wasn't up to that, she deserved whatever she got just for saying yes to Uncle Yevgeny in the first place.

The flat looked like it had been hit by a tornado. She had always hated that cliché, but there was no other way to describe it. The sheer chaos took her breath away. It must have taken them hours to disarrange and destroy so thoroughly. It wasn't vandalism. It was annihilation. It wasn't so much ruthless as calculated. The initial shock almost sent her immediately back out the door. There couldn't be anything left to find, so why risk another second in the place?

But then reason reasserted itself. No matter how thorough they'd been, they were strangers. Fascist strangers into the bargain, which meant that no matter how smart they were they lacked imagination. It was an old building and it had been renovated repeatedly and not always expertly. There were all kinds of nooks, crannies, and hidey-holes that they might have missed. She'd lived there as long as anyone except Vladimir himself. She knew every last one of them. She went room to room, searching systematically, and by the time she was through the shopping bags she had packed into her satchel were crammed and so was the satchel itself. God help her getting it all home. She'd have to resort to a taxi. It was a good thing she'd brought all that cash with her.

She was shocked that no one stopped her as she left the building. In all her planning, she had identified that as the most dangerous moment. All this apparent good fortune told her was that there was a chance she was being followed home. That would be a much quieter street to snatch her from. But her arrival there passed also without a hint of trouble. She took no comfort in this, however. The minute she got inside she squirreled her treasures away all over the house, hiding them all as well as it was possible to hide anything in a feminist commune, with its bizarre notions about privacy and personal property.

For days afterward, every time she left home, to go to classes, to go get groceries, or just because of her mounting claustrophobia, she expected to be grabbed off the street and taken away. That she might actually have gotten away with it only occurred to her gradually. Too gradually, really, for it to feel like a relief.

Most of the stuff she had retrieved was trash. She went through it methodically nevertheless, piece by piece, just to make sure. But acting like an archaeologist sifting through the rubble at some exotic dig didn't alter the facts. And some of the guys had had such unimaginitive taste in pornography she didn't know whether to laugh or cry about it. It almost made her want to go into the business herself, just to show them the possibilities. Some revolutionaries. They'd hardly make good Girl Scouts. Still, she had to dispose of it carefully. Every night when her housemates were finally asleep, she'd troop down to the furnace room and feed the day's harvest to the flames. She couldn't imagine why any of it had been stashed in the first place. It wasn't incriminating, merely sad and stupid.

Finally there was nothing left but Vladimir's things. Stupid her. She had left them for last. As if they mattered more than all the rest. As if the fact that they were his things made them more significant. One small box yielded an array of items she didn't know the names of but recognized as artifacts of a Jewish boyhood. So much for his atheism, but then his mother had been the heretic in the household, and everyone knows about Jewish mothers. Marytza had always suspected that his religious skepticism had been no more genuine than her own. Here was possible proof. Whatever the case, she was sure his family would want these things.

A larger box contained several old fashioned leather bound diaries, the typewritten manuscript of what looked like a novel, and a bundle of letters tied up in the lace from a sneaker. This, obviously, was what Yevgeny had sent her there to find. As a matter of principle, she hated to prove him right.

The next morning she hadn't been to sleep, but she had read the novel. As a work of fiction it was abysmal. Like something an emotionally needy, socially awkward ninth grade girl might have written. As a social document it had a certain fascination but broke no new ground that she could discern. As an artifact providing insight into Valdimir's psychology and character, it was completely useless, though highly entertaining in a bizarre way.

It was the story of a brilliant and dedicated young revolutionary, his even younger, indefatigably faithful sidekick, and the glamorous tomboy they were both in love with, told in perfect 1930's Soviet Socialist Realism style. To anyone in the know, what it was really was a *roman a clef* of Marytza, Vladimir, and Tristan, but as they should have been and not as they actually were. In the telling, Vladimir had managed to turn them into cardboard cutouts, stereotypes of perfect young student radicals without a discernable flaw, a single drop of red blood flowing through their veins, or an ounce of living meat on their bones. They might as well be a heroically posed art deco sculptural group in a station of the Moscow Metro except they lacked even that much dimension. A painting, then, but only in the most muted tones. Only a twelve year old girl—preferably the daughter of a Politburo member—could have read it without snickering. The mystery was that Vladimir had been capable of writing five hundred plus pages of such drivel. Surely he must have known far before he reached the ending that the entire thing was no more than mental masturbation of the most juvenile variety. Marytza almost hoped they would be reunited some day so that she'd have an opportunity to deplore it to his face.

Initially, the diaries defeated her. The first volume was written in Hebrew, the second in Russian. But her impulse to leave no stone unturned was rewarded halfway through that second volume when Vladimir suddenly shifted to English. Beginning to read, she was transported in just a few pages to the day the two of them and their friends arrived in New Jerusalem, Mississippi. By the time she reached the end of that volume a couple of hours later, Vladimir and Tristan were madly in love. Yes, with each other. Thunderstruck by this development, she leafed back to the entry about their first meeting, to see if there had been any clue.

July11, 1964

At the gathering this evening I met the son of a prominent local clergyman, Daniel Bentley. The most *prominent local white clergyman, I should say. For many years, he has enjoyed the status of a sort of unelected mayor of the town. That's the influence and prestige white pastors enjoy in these communities. He has just been dismissed by his congregation after informing them of his intention to join us in our work here. The blacks are apparently not surprised at this development. They have long known Daniel as an ally, if a quiet one, and they had been halfway expecting this. The whites, on the other hand, are as horrified as if the world were ending. And I suppose it is, from their perspective. Their anger at his "betrayal" is of a magnitude that is difficult to convey in writing. If I had not witnessed it myself, I would not have believed its intensity. It is a testimony to something which I am not certain whether to label courage or extreme foolhardiness on his part. We have seen white clergymen in the throes of such crises of conscience in every town we have visited, but never an actual defector. He apparently had the foresight to send his wife and daughters away for the summer, but not his son. Tristan—the son—is, at first glance, the archetypal All-American boy. He's sixteen but physically quite mature. He could pass for several years older than that. He's apparently a very big deal around here: star quarterback, captain of the wrestling team, etc., not to mention alarmingly handsome. He belies the stereotype of the high school jock with a ready wit as well as obvious intellect. He converses intelligently on a wide variety of topics one wouldn't expect to be of interest to a young man of his age. His parents have obviously taken a great deal of care to supplement his formal education with a curriculum of their own. He gives the impression of being completely at ease socially. At least until the topic of conversation turns to him, at which point he becomes self conscious and rather guarded. I can't imagine that his schoolmates understand him at all.*

Not exactly a declaration of love at first sight, Marytza mused. Read in isolation, there was nothing especially suggestive about it. But given the content of later entries, it turned into a pretty close approximation of one. "Alarmingly handsome" was certainly a red flag. Perhaps "physically mature" carried a similar message, though she had to say in each case the descriptions were accurate. Whatever his motivations in putting this down on paper, there was no denying that despite Vladimir's political and intellectual biases, he had always been a sucker for a pretty face. He was never more heated than when denying such accusations. The fact that Tristan had possessed plenty of the qualities Vladimir claimed to value more highly than good looks had probably made the attraction irresistible. Except, of course, that Tristan was not a girl, but a young man. That was the part that was difficult for Marytza to accept. She recognized that homosexuals existed, of course. She knew several. She could almost see Tristan as one if she squinted hard enough. Not that there had been any obvious indication of course. More a question of temperament than any overt sign. But Vladimir? It was like a plot twist in a science fiction story written by an author addicted to heroin.

Which, she supposed, proved the point. If nothing else, Vladimir's unpredictability had been vividly reaffirmed over the past weeks.

She skimmed back through the entries she had already read with the aim of identifying the crucial moment when boy meets boy had ignited in such an unexpected conflagration. She finally fixed on an entry which described an incident that had taken place not long after the murder of that poor Mercer Swinford, the notorious town homosexual of Tristan's somnolent native village. She recalled the incident in question as both Tristan and Vladimir had recounted it at the time, but in Vladimir's diary it took on a completely different tone. His description of the two of them taking cover in a ditch while an unseen gunman shot at them with a high powered rifle was riveting enough, but crucial details seemed to have been omitted which made the young men's subsequent behavior baffling. As Marytza recalled it, the two of them had barely spoken for well over a week after that fateful encounter. Indeed, they had hardly been able to be in the same room, yet just a few pages later everything was suddenly violins and roses.

But the violins and roses disappeared soon enough.

September 2, 1964

Back in New York at last. There were many times during our work in Mississippi that I wasn't sure any of us would return in one piece. Thus, I had expected returning to the city to be a relief but seem to have made a serious miscalculation in planning for it. T. apparently assumed that when I invited him to move into the apartment with me I intended for us to live here as a couple.

The heartbroken expression on his face as I showed him the room I had decided was most suitable for him—the old maid's quarters at the rear with its private bathroom and window overlooking the garden—was almost enough to break my own heart as well. But really, what other course is there? There is far too much work yet to be done to allow myself to go down that path. It's not just the cause of racial justice in this country, though it may take decades yet to bring that to fruition. All the signs are that the conflict in Southeast Asia is becoming more intense and that American involvement there is almost certain to increase beyond imagining. So to issues of racism we have to add issues of disarmament and pacifism. How can I be of service in this monumental and rapidly intensifying struggle if I'm recognized as a homosexual? If that happens I can give up any hope of contributing to our cause in the way my experience and training qualify me for. I'm not sure I could survive such a disgrace. I know some would say that's inexcusably bourgeois of me, but I'm really just being practical. To face the end of one's work—for that? Dr. King has men close to him who have made the same choice in this matter as I am making. The same sacrifice of their personal happiness in the service of the cause of justice. History, I know, will regard such men as heroes. I can do no less. I have tried explaining all this to T. He says he understands, but his eyes tell me he thinks I am making a wrong choice, not just for myself but for him.

And of course it just got worse from there. Subjecting herself to the rhetoric Vladimir employed in the next several diary entries was one thing. Imagining the actual discussions between him and Tristan was nearly unbearable. The young man had just lost his father and been uprooted from his boyhood home. He'd been in no mood to listen to reason, though she wasn't sure that was what he was hearing from Vladimir. The emotionalism between them could not have been sustained. Something had to give. And it did. Not long after their group reassembled in New York, Vladimir swept Marytza off her feet. She had thought of it at the time as the miracle she had been hoping for, but the diary gave his extravagant courtship of her a totally different significance. He was desperate to establish himself as heterosexual and keep Tristan at a distance. He obviously had no genuine feelings for her at all. Stupid, gullible Marytza. She had swallowed the whole thing. Just like a giddy, brainless young schoolgirl or the simpering princess in a fairy tale. She couldn't recollect Tristan's reaction to their love affair, but there must have been one.

Then, only a few weeks after she moved into the apartment as Vladimir's acknowledged companion, the news came of Elizabeth Bentley's cancer diagnosis. By November, she was dead.

November 16, 1964
Just back from meeting Tristan at LaGuardia. It seems that his uncles have become quite affluent as a result of their athletic careers. Typical capitalism, lavishly rewarding the trivial, and typical America, with its ridiculous notions of what constitutes heroism. They paid for his airline tickets for the trip. Greeting him on his return from his mother's funeral with a manly handshake rather than the embrace I knew he longed for was the most difficult thing I have ever had to do. I ached to take him back to the apartment, to my own bed, to comfort him in the only way I knew would really matter to him. But of course that was not possible. Indeed, it would only have made things worse. I knew that and that I had to be the one to think of the long term, to be responsible to our cause. Still, how cowardly I felt to leave him so wounded and vulnerable, and how deceitful it was of me to make Marytza's presence in the household the convenient excuse for not doing what I so easily could have done. Simply force him to confront the reality, once and for all, that we can never be more than friends and comrades. In failing to do that, I let us both down. He says he loves me beyond reason. How can I possibly be worthy of that? Especially knowing that I have no intention of making things right between us in the only way that can satisfy him. So many times during his absence I found myself daydreaming about an air disaster which would take him instantly and painlessly and deliver me from this horrible predicament I have allowed myself to fall into. That's how completely lacking in moral character this impossible love of ours has made me.

Marytza read on. Betrayal followed betrayal. When Vladimir wasn't betraying Tristan he was betraying her. Often he betrayed them both simultaneously. Sometimes physically, with some young woman they all knew, but more often simply by inattentiveness or inadvertent cruelty. And, most poignantly, each time he betrayed one or the other of them he was betraying himself. He at least had enough self awareness to recognize this, and more than one entry in the diary was devoted to his castigating himself accordingly. But not all of his anger was turned inward. Arguments she had forgotten all about showed up in the diary in newly comprehensible forms. Everything that had gone on in that wretched apartment month after month and year after year somehow originated in that first horrible betrayal. She had recognized Vladimir long since as a failed human being, but she had never understood the nature of the flaw behind his perversity. Now that the mystery was revealed, she found no satisfaction in the knowledge of his duplicity and cowardice.

March 23, 1965
Another argument with Tristan. He says that I don't really love Marytza; I'm only using her for camouflage. Using her in what he describes as an inexcusable way. As if he knows what my true feelings are. As if he could. He's so blinded by jealously that he's incapable of seeing what's right in front of him, of making objective judgments. And he'll say anything that might help him gain an advantage in any argument between us. Of course I love Marytza. In my own way. Our relationship is something Tristan could never understand in his current frame of mind. But really, all he needs to do is ask her. She'll set him straight. She's certainly happy. There's no mistaking that. And our sex life, regardless of how dubious he may be on that particular subject, is deeply satisfying to both of us. My great fear continues to be that he might say something to her. When you believe those around you are living in a house of cards—yes, he actually said that!—you might consider yourself justified in doing or saying almost anything. When you're insane with jealousy, there might not be any limits to what you'd be willing to attempt in order to get your own way.

This, Marytza thought, was certainly the pot calling the kettle black. Tristan, as it turned out, had been right about pretty much everything. But he had kept his mouth shut about all of it. He had, apparently, just hung on and hoped for better times. It was cowardly in its own way, but it was far less objectionable than Vladimir's corrupt manipulations. So much for Vladimir's questions as to Tristan's character.

The diary wasn't exclusively about their infernal triangle, of course. Vladimir had been extremely busy that year teaching courses at the university, finishing his dissertation and preparing for his oral defense, attending meetings and rallies, planning actions of various kinds. Many of the diary entries didn't mention either Tristan or Marytza, as if both of them disappeared from his life for weeks at a time. Except that neither of them ever did.

May 28, 1965

Tristan graduates from high school next week. He has been accepted at NYU. Of course, he can hardly afford to attend any university. He could easily get the money from his uncles, but he says that asking them for help would be "exploiting the bourgeoisie"', and he refuses to do it. He feels it would be beneath him, which is a bourgeois sentiment in itself. A true revolutionary would never think in such terms. He believes he can make enough money waiting tables to pay tuition and living expenses. He also proposes to move out and get an apartment of his own. He says he must, that it is the only way he can get free of me. And he says that he has to be free of me since I continue to insist that we have no future other than as friends. I have absolutely forbidden him to move out on his own He just might be able to scrape together money for tuition and books, but rent as well? Impossible. He'll live under this roof as long as he needs to. I insist on it. If he's not attending college, the minute he turns eighteen they'll draft him. The situation in Southeast Asia is deteriorating by the week. It's unthinkable that he could be caught up in it simply because he's too proud to ask for financial help. That can't be allowed to happen. I feel responsible for him, after all. Marytza says this is not altruistic on my part but merely that I'm determined he continue to be dependent on me. Of course, she understands nothing—at least nothing important—about our friendship. But it is hurtful of her to ascribe such motives to me.

Marytza understands nothing. How arrogant of him to say a thing like that. That really stung. How could she have understood with both of them concealing from her everything that mattered? Was she supposed to be a mind reader? She could just about forgive Tristan. He'd been trying to honor the wishes of the man he was in love with, and in comparison with that he owed her very little. Nothing at all, really, considering she was his rival—however unwitting—in romance. But Vladimir? No, she couldn't forgive Vladimir. He had used her. There was no question about it. She had recognized that long since. She had only lacked an understanding of how completely he had used her and what his motives had been. Now she had that as well. How she wished she could make him pay for it.

August 7, 1965

The first anniversary of those horrific events in Mississippi. No one has called attention to this date, but I know it weighs heavily on Tristan. His suffering is horrible to witness. And at this point, unnecessary. Almost to the point of self indulgence, though I would never say so to him.

Instead of confronting it, I'm attempting to help him past it indirectly. I have been trying to encourage him into the same direction I have taken. There are several young women attached to our group who would be more than happy to offer him comfort and consolation. Indeed, I know that they have made this quite obvious to him time and again. It is tricky, though, because the least indication that I approve of this idea will undoubtedly send him running away from it as fast as he can go. Why can't he see that such a relationship needn't mean anything that he doesn't wish it to? It would have no significance whatever except for the comfort and companionship it could provide him day in and day out. It would simply be a source of comfort and support. Utilitarian considerations such as these are far more relevant in our current situation than the kind of bourgeois notions of "true love" and "finding one's soul mate" could ever be. Things like that really have no place in the life we live, which, if our struggle is successful, will ultimately be the life everyone lives. Sex and affection are good things in themselves, regardless of where or with whom they originate. There is no politically defensible rationale for shutting himself off as he does. It's egotism, the most pernicious poison of the bourgeoisie. Surely, with the example of Marytza and myself before him, he will soon come to this understanding and give up his folly.

Marytza remembered all too well the competition which had been more or less perennial among the girls. Tristan had been friendly and correct with them all but had favored no single girl in preference to any of the others. At the time she had chalked this up to his upbringing and good manners, not to mention a certain natural diffidence in him that she had been aware of from the first. But how self serving of Vladimir the whole thing was. It wasn't just that "curing" Tristan of his proclivity was the correct thing to do from the point of view of revolutionary politics. Its real importance to Vladimir was that it not only promised to get him out of a relationship he had convinced himself he wanted no part of—except on his own terms—but at the same time validated his own choice and left him more or less guilt free. By this time Marytza had read and recalled enough that she was no longer in any doubt about Vladimir's own sexuality. What she had excused at the time as a lack of ardor, not just physical but emotional, caused by his tireless efforts "for the people" she now understood as being no more nor less than a complete lack of interest in the opposite sex. Which meant that she had wasted years of her life, or, more accurately, had allowed years of her life to be wasted for her, in aid of Vladimir's self delusion. How many boys she had turned away out of her loyalty to bourgeois notions of fidelity.

And for what? This ridiculous chimera, this illusion that Vladimir had manipulated her into sharing even though he hardly believed in it himself.

But more important than the efforts of Vladimir to maneuver one or the other of those young women into Tristan's bed was his recognition of the basic pattern of his relationship with Tristan. That pattern had been established very early on, Marytza now saw. It was a pattern of Vladimir's perpetual insistence on control and Tristan's determined subversion of it. Every fight she had been witness to had been that same fight. Right up to the last fight of all. And in a fight like that there could never have been a clear winner.

Marytza herself was rarely mentioned in the diary. When she was it was never in isolation. Invariably she was little more than a pawn in Vladimir and Tristan's ongoing dispute. This more than anything else, she believed, was emblematic of her true position in the household.

June 12, 1967

Huge fight—I will not dignify it by calling it an argument—with Marytza last week. I had, it seems, forgotten her birthday—again. What a silly thing to fight about. As if a card or some flowers could communicate her importance to me. What better way to trivialize her, I thought, than by treating her like some bourgeois young girl when she is a powerful revolutionary woman? She did not appreciate hearing this critique with its "implied accusation of retrograde tendencies" on her part. But really, if she didn't possess such tendencies she wouldn't have cared about her birthday and she woudn't have needed my intended compliment explained to her. The fight didn't resolve anything, and she hasn't spoken to me in nearly a week now. When I complained of it to Tristan, he took her side. I pointed out that I had never done anything in particular to acknowledge his birthday, and he said he knew that all too well (!?!). He went on to inform me that since I seemed to have forgotten it, women are different! *I pointed out that from a revolutionary perspective this was a ridiculous idea. He said that it would take more than a revolution to alter something that had existed since the beginnings of human civilization, and that I had better find a way to accommodate it. I told him I considered that beneath me as a revolutionary. He said that while he could certainly understand that reluctance, nothing was "beneath the true revolutionary"—yes, throwing my own words back at me—and that he had little sympathy with it because the solution was obvious. If I didn't want a lover with feminine characteristics, I shouldn't insist on being with a woman. How like him, to turn the argument into a discussion of his dissatisfation with me instead of Marytza's unreasonableness. As a revolutionary, he has no right to adopt such a stratagem, which is right out of the bourgeoisie's playbook. He invariably does this, and I have to say, it's becoming intolerable.*

After reading that, she decided that she hated them both. She tried very hard to hate them equally, but as usual she couldn't. She and Tristan had both been victims of Vladimir's monomania, and that inevitably swung things in Tristan's favor.

December 4, 1967
My beautiful, brilliant, darling boy. You are twenty years old today. And you are no longer a boy but all too surely a man. I would give anything, anything under the sun, to be able to take you in my arms and cover you with kisses. To worship you with my body as my heart has silently worshipped you all these years. If only we had met in another time and place where such a thing were possible. That is our tragedy, though, it has to be said, "tragedy" is a bourgeois concept. But that imagined world is not the world we live in, the world which we are working so passionately to remake in a better, truer form. Oh, my dearest, dearest one, you know as well as I do that you are my beloved, my soul mate. You are the love of my life. I wish I could promise you that someday we will be together in the way you dream of, but the struggle we face is so enormous and threatens to last so long that such a promise could do nothing but raise false hopes. So although nothing else may ever be yours, my own darling, my heart will, always.

Even in a moment of what he would have called weakness, when he was able at least to admit to himself the nature and depth of his feelings—because Marytza was as certain as it was possible to be that Tristan was never actually intended to see those words that had been addressed to him—Vladimir had still been unable to accept and live by them. Which as far as she was concerned truly made him a lost soul.

February 19, 1968
Tristan has been reading Carpenter and Hirschfeld and—my God!—Kinsey, and insists that if the world is to be remade, it must be remade by men such as ourselves in order to insure that in its renewed form it will guarantee us the same rights and freedoms enjoyed by everyone else. As if it were that simple. I remind him over and over again that politics is the art of the possible.

But he insists that we only learn what is truly possible through attempting the impossible. He will not listen to reason. I suppose it must come from his religious upbringing. He insists that he has turned his back on that, but it has left its mark in the form of a belief in the possibility of miracles, a pernicious sort of "magical thinking" that makes things possible which are impossible in a universe governed by the principles of materialism. I've got to get him focused on reading Marx and Hegel again, not these ridiculous anti-intellectual, bourgeois sentimentalists!

Over time, Tristan's position, which had started out as a largely instinctual one, evolved into an informed and even sophisticated stance, albeit too eclectically based to pass muster among orthodox revolutionaries. Marytza could almost imagine him standing in front of St. Patrick's Cathedral nailing his theses to the door. Meanwhile Vladimir remained preoccupied with "larger matters" and could only respond to Tristan's arguments by increasing his volume. Over and over again, they played the game to that same, infernal stalemate.

May 1, 1968

An auspicious date for our movement, though it is hard under this morning's circumstances to think of it in that way. The action at Columbia is finished, it seems. Crushed by the authorities and, it has to be said, sold out by some of our so-called allies. We achieved some of our goals at least. For a few days, more than that seemed to be possible and it brought us all together in a way that recalled times long past. Marytza, Tristan, and I—once again at the barricades. Of course that's a metaphor. Tristan wasn't there. I felt betrayed that he didn't come along with us as we occupied that building. But then, in the darkest hours there, to learn that he was on the outside working tirelessly, supporting us behind the scenes. He was, I've been assured by many reliable revolutionaries, nothing short of heroic, though he never mentioned it himself. Learning about it after the fact was tremendously gratifying. Really one of the most wonderful things imaginable. I sense somehow that this marks a turning point in the relations between us, that he has finally reached a level of maturity that will make it possible for us to enjoy the kind of friendship I have been envisioning for us all along, free from the emotional undercurrents that have kept us in such turmoil these months and years. Even now, I can think of no one I would rather have by my side than this stalwart, brilliant, beautiful young man. I know Marytza loves him as I do. Together we will go forward, and the future we build together will be as glorious as I have always hoped. Oh, to see it all finally becoming possible.

But of course there would be no future of any kind for the three of them, because of the three of them Vladimir was the one who hadn't changed.

May 17, 1968

Tristan graduates from NYU soon. Just think—a bachelor's degree with High Honors in only three years. While waiting tables the whole time, not to mention all the other odd jobs. It is a remarkable achievement, though, it has to be said, a quixotic one as well. It's heartbreaking when I think of it. So much unnecessary effort. It could all have been avoided if he had just allowed people to help him. There's no dishonor in accepting help from likeminded individuals. And Tristan's always one of the first to offer help when it's needed, so why should he make such a fetish of refusing it when it's offered? It's anti-revolutionary, a terrible breach of our solidarity. It constitutes a kind of bourgeois narcissism that I know he recognizes for what it is. It's not accidental but by choice. He's willfully perverse, that's all one can say. Everything he does seems calculated to prove me wrong. It's as if that has become his primary goal in life. He has been admitted to a graduate program. I am hoping that the intellectual disciplines of graduate work will help him finally achieve some clarity about his situation. It seems tragic that he has been stuck for these three years at the same point in his development, but surely a change will come. Surely he will realize the futility of the course he has chosen. It's no dishonor to be somewhat confused in youth, but he's rapidly approaching the age when he must finally put all that behind him and move forward. He received his draft notice yesterday. This occasioned great hilarity among the members of our household. The idea of Tristan in the service is completely absurd. He won't go, of course. One of our sympathetic doctors will have him declared 4F and that will be that. Anything else would be unthinkable.

But it hadn't been unthinkable, because Tristan committed the unforgivable sin of having a mind of his own. The arguments had been horrific. Marytza remembered being stunned by their ferocity. Knowing what she now did, it seemed obvious that only two people who were deeply in love with each other could have fought that violently. Vladimir himself had been caught completely off guard by Tristan's implacable determination to go his own way. Especially after the golden days he believed they had experienced during the recent action at Columbia. This shock had undoubtedly been the cause of his fatal miscalculation. The most serious one of all.

He had fallen into the trap of believing that issuing an ultimatum can ever be a show of strength.

June 17, 1968

Tristan left last week for basic training. I still cannot believe that his motivation in allowing himself to be drafted is anything but self centered and spiteful. He is trying to get even with me for never letting him have his way about us. He is trying to make me sorry. Such manipulative behavior is the opposite of true revolutionary spirit. He is willing to turn his back on every principle I ever tried to teach him just to prove a point. What a petty, disloyal child he has turned out to be. And now Marytza has left me, too. I have no idea why she has done this or where she has gone. Her explanation was, if anything, even more irrational than anything Tristan said prior to his departure. The last time I spoke to her on the telephone, all she would say was that if I wanted to know where she was I should contact a private investigator. What have I done to deserve such disloyalty from the two people I have shared more of myself with than anyone? It really makes one question one's faith in humanity. This is why revolutions fail—unworthy behavior on the part of "revolutionaries". Can there be anything more bitter than what I am experiencing?

She didn't bother reading the rest of the diary. There didn't seem to be any point. Whatever had happened after she left the apartment had nothing to do with her. It was heartbreaking to read the things he had written. They were the thoughts and feelings of a man who had for all practical purposes dug his own grave with the shovel of his own arrogance. It didn't seem to matter to her any more whether he was actually dead or living, because the life he had chosen for himself wasn't a life at all.

Marytza had always believed that if she had just fallen in love with Tristan instead of Vladimir everything would have been different. She had often daydreamed of leaving Vladimir and running away with Tristan. On more than one occasion she had been on the point of seducing him. He had been everything Vladimir was not.

Considerate, patient, nurturing, always interested in her, always respectful of her opinions. The contrast between the two men had driven her to distraction. She had never imagined that the root cause of all her heartache with Vladimir had been anything other than his single minded devotion to the revolution. Now she knew the truth: that his political obsessions were merely an escape from personal realities he refused to deal with. What a fool she had been. Even if she had succeeded in luring Tristan away from Vladimir, the result would have been the same—hooked on a man who could never give her the devotion she wanted. Because Tristan, true and perfect a friend and confidant as he had always been, was just as unattainable in his own way as Vladimir. It could never have happened as she had envisioned it. She knew that now, thanks to Vladimir's diary. It was enough to give a girl a complex. Women she knew had ended up in therapy over far less.

* * *

So she came finally to the bundle of letters. She had hardly paid attention to them before. For some reason she had had the idea that it was just miscellaneous correspondence. But when she realized what they actually were she blessed the strange providence which had kept her focused elsewhere. She wasn't sure she'd have bothered with Vladimir's stupid novel or the insane rantings of his diary if she had known.

The letters were all from Tristan, all postmarked since his departure for the service, all addressed to Vladimir. Not a single one of them had been opened. Talk about burning your bridges. That damned fool.

* * *

It was exactly as her housemates had told her when she first showed up on their doorstop, furious and sputtering. At the time she had argued with them, accusing them of being paranoid manhaters. This dispute had continued uninterrupted right to the present. If a couple of lesbian residents hadn't developed crushes on her, Marytza would probably have been tossed out of the commune long since.

Now, finally, she had to admit that the sisterhood had been right all along. The revolution was nothing but a boys' club. For all their protestations about justice and equality, Vladimir and his pals concerned themselves shockingly little with the social condition of their female counterparts. They saw women as tools or toys—in most cases both—but never as equal partners in the great enterprise. What better proof could she have found than all that drivel, written in Vladimir's own hand? Some revolution—making the world safe and just for a bunch of bourgeois white males. Talk about a waste of time.

* * *

Following protocol to the letter, over the next few days she made a series of calls requesting a meeting. When she stepped off the bus in Brooklyn it was with a sense of déjà vu. Yevgeny had at least taken the precaution of selecting a different restaurant on a different block, but they might as well have been identical. Even the soup they ate seemed exactly the same as the time before.

"So? You found something at the apartment?"

"Very little, actually," she said, conscious that he could tell she was lying. She had decided that the manuscript, diaries, and Tristan's letters were not to be surrendered to anyone who hadn't lived through the events.

"Really?"

"Well," she relented. "Several things that belonged to me. You were right about that."

"I was quite certain of it," he smiled.

"But hardly anything of Vlad's. Just these few things I've brought. I assume that the FBI either didn't recognize them as his or didn't consider them significant."

"Nothing else?" Yevgeny asked, opening the flaps of the box and surveying the contents like a child on Christmas morning who feels Santa has cheated him.

"I told you," Marytza said, "the rest belongs to me."

Sine Nomine

Afternoons there wasn't any action worth the trouble. Trolls and tourists: that was it. Both groups meant more hassle than they were worth—they represented desperation, basically. Afternoons there were plainclothes cops around, too. Naturally. But they were easy enough to avoid if you kept your eyes and ears open. They went for the easy collars—the guys who worked drunk or high. If you stayed reasonably sober you didn't have to worry. They were more of an annoyance than anything. Still, they made afternoon work less than desirable. Someday he might be that desperate, but he hadn't had to work the streets in daylight since his first few weeks in the city. He'd figured it out fast. It had either been that or starve. Some choice.

Nightfall was the start of his working day, nightfall until midnight his regular shift. There was plenty of action then. Unless the weather was absolutely terrible there was more action during that stretch than he could take advantage of. He was still young enough and cute enough that he did just fine without having to put in longer hours. He was a hot enough commodity that sometimes he actually turned gigs down. That was usually in really good weather when the johns were as thick on the sidewalks as the rats were in the alleys. Nightfall until midnight. Much later than that and all there was out looking were creeps and crazies. The one time you needed undercover cops on the street they weren't there. Someday he might be desperate enough to work that shift, but he didn't seriously expect to live that long.

He slept late, of course. The guys all did. Some of them right through until sunset. Mostly those were guys who took the really heavy drugs. Occasionally one of them wouldn't wake up at all and the other residents of the loft would drag him down the stairs to the street and leave him to be found by passers-by or the police.

One of the more experienced guys said this was the equivalent of burial at sea. He still wasn't sure whether that was meant to be a joke or a tragic comment on their lives. But he didn't sleep as late as that. He didn't even when the nightmares didn't wake him. He was almost always up by noon, sometimes earlier.

Every now and then one of the guys would bring home a television someone had abandoned on the sidewalk and for a few weeks or months until it broke down they'd have that for entertainment. That and fighting about what to watch. The arguments were wasted breath on all sides. There wasn't anything on worth fighting over. He was no intellectual, but he knew stupid when he saw it on the staticky screens of those orphaned sets. They always broke down sooner or later and then the guys only had themselves for entertainment until someone dragged the next one home. Afternoon television was the worst of the worst. It provided no diversion at all. He couldn't imagine being that desperate, though it was hard to imagine anyone more desperate than he was. He preferred staring out the window. There was always something worth watching down on the street. Something happening, about to happen, or being cleaned up after. Almost invariably whatever went on out there was stupider than anything on the television, but it was at least real. It was real, the reception was good, and he didn't have to listen to any ridiculous dialogue. He could make up his own or he could just watch the way movie audiences had done during the age of silent films.

That's how he happened to see her. If his routine had been different he'd have missed her visit to the building across the street. He was staring out the window as usual that afternoon and there she was. He'd have known that walk anywhere. It wasn't that her walk was especially distinctive. He just had a thing about watching people walk. He had a theory that you could tell a lot about a john by the way he walked up to you. It had saved him lots of grief and a couple of arrests, and over time he extended it to take in civilians as well. So by now he was kind of an expert on people's walks and he recognized hers from his catalogue. The disguise she had on didn't fool him for a second. He was used to people in disguises. Most often it was the raincoat, dark glasses, and hat pulled down over the eyes of the johns. They thought that getup hid them but it really did the opposite. They were anonymous, all right, but only as individuals. As a group that disguise made them conspicuous as hell. The plainclothes cops were no better at disguises and even more conspicuous. So much for "professionals". Marytza's disguise that day was a little better than the usual on that block but she still made the mistake of relying on a stereotype. And it was the wrong neighborhood for that particular one. The clincher, however, was that though she'd taken quite a bit of trouble to disguise her appearance, she did nothing to disguise that walk. It was a typical mistake, and he'd have expected better from her. He spotted her the second she rounded the corner of the block and didn't take his eyes off her until she stepped inside the building.

The building he and the guys squatted in was directly across the street from the one where Marytza and her crowd had lived. It was the reason he'd insisted the guys choose the place over several other vacant properties in the neighborhood. By then he had already thought of Marytza as a friend, and that wasn't his only, or even strongest, motivation in advocating the location. It hadn't mattered to anyone else. At least that's what he'd thought at first. Later on, he realized that he'd done someone else's work for him. But by then it had hardly mattered. At the time, he hadn't had to explain it at all. He'd simply said "hey, this is as good a place as any." And to be fair, it had turned out better than any of them expected. They'd been there for nearly two years now. They could hardly believe their luck. Usually landlords got wise and had them rousted in about two weeks. It was as if somebody in their group—and calling it a group was stretching the point, really, since the membership was so fluid—had been the beneficiary of some weird karmic dispensation. That was how one of the more experienced guys explained it—the same guy who referred to burials at sea, actually. That guy was really quite a philosopher.

He was more inclined, actually, to suspect that Mr. Philosopher was the long rumored FBI informant that bunch across the street had always been so paranoid about. That probably explained the hustlers' immunity from eviction all this time. Whoever their landlord was was being encouraged to ignore their presence in his top floor loft so that the FBI could keep their informant in place. For all he knew, the FBI might even be paying rent on the place to keep the landlord happy and their informant viable. If that was the case, their days on this block were probably numbered. There hadn't been any activity across the street since the big raids back during the late winter. Surely by now their presence in the neighborhood as a cover for Mr. Philosopher had outlived its usefulness. What good was a spy if there was no one to spy on? The guy wasn't around that afternoon, so it was probably safe enough for Marytza to make her visit. Still, he hurried downstairs and stationed himself on the front steps where he could pretend he was sunbathing and keep an eye out. He could be across the street and inside the building in seconds to warn her if it looked like there might be trouble.

It was the least he could do. He owed her and he'd never had a chance to pay her back.

He'd only been in the city for a few days when he first met her. It hadn't taken him long to get the lay of the land. He'd known there was only one way for a guy in his situation to survive, and he quickly figured out the times, places, and how to's. But the local talent hadn't been particularly welcoming. It was dog eat dog on the street and he was one of the smaller dogs, barely a puppy. He'd gotten off the bus almost starving, and he was making just enough money to keep his stomach from getting any emptier. He couldn't remember the last time it had truly been full. And then that afternoon he'd been beaten up. They'd left his face pretty messed up and they'd taken all his money. They hadn't meant to hurt him badly, just make him unmarketable for long enough that he'd have to give up. Or at least move to another location. He had no idea what he'd do then. Probably just lie down in an alley and wait for the inevitable.

That's when he saw her for the first time. Through tear blurred eyes, blood still seeping out of his nose, wounds stinging, there she was. He was pretty sure she wasn't real. Those guys must have hit him hard enough in the head that he was seeing things. She looked like Grace Kelly playing a college girl out for an afternoon slumming. She looked happy and carefree. She was movie star skinny but looked like she never missed a meal. Her clothing was clean and as new as a girl her age could get away with, fashionwise. He couldn't help himself. Seeing her like that, he started to sob. That's probably what got her attention.

The next thing he knew he was wearing a borrowed bathrobe, sitting at a kitchen table and eating chicken soup.

"How old are you anyway, Hank?"

She was standing at the kitchen counter making a ham and cheese sandwich to go with the chicken soup. Hank wasn't his real name. She obviously knew it. She wasn't stupid. He heard the quotation marks in her voice.

"Seventeen," he lied.

She obviously didn't believe that, either, but let it go.

"You want pickles with this sandwich? What kind?"

"Whatever you've got is fine," he said.

"Where do you live?"

"Me and some of the guys have a squat over on Barrow."

It was before they moved in across the street.

"Well, you're not going back there," she said.

"The hell."

"Not until your face heals. You can't work looking like that, and I bet there's nobody there to take care of you while you're laid up."

He thought it was interesting that she didn't try to talk him into getting a real job. That's what he would have expected a girl who looked like that to do. They had such ridiculous ideas about life. He assumed she didn't bother because she considered him a lost cause.

She was inside the building for a long time. He wasn't surprised. She must have come looking for something. Why else would she have taken the risk? She probably wouldn't find it, whatever it was. He'd been in there himself since the raid. Several times. He hadn't been looking for anything in particular, but the mess the feds had left was astonishing. A junkyard was more orderly. He slouched on the front steps and imagined her annoyance, her mounting desperation, surrounded by all that trash. He'd go inside, but there was nothing he could do to help. He was more use here on the lookout. Branch (aka Mr. Philosopher) might show up any time. And if he really was an FBI informant it woudn't matter if he recognized Marytza or not. Just the fact that someone had been inside the building would be enough to bring them all back with their anonymous sedans that were conspicuous as hell and their dark glasses and walkie talkies and shoulder holsters and what all.

She'd have to come out eventually. There was no electricity in the building. He hoped she wouldn't leave it too late. She could hurt herself in there in the dark.

When she finally emerged, she had bags and bags of stuff. He couldn't believe she'd found anything worth salvaging. But, he supposed, unlike him she'd known where to look. He almost ran over to help her wrangle it all into the cab that miraculously appeared just as she hit the sidewalk. But he didn't want to spook her. He knew some of that crew still undoubtedly thought he was the informant himself. She had always said she didn't believe it, but everything else had changed so maybe that had, too. He was desperate to speak to her but it couldn't be like this, out on the street. He might as well set off fireworks. A guy like him talking to someone like her—nobody would believe it. He watched the cabby stow all the stuff in the trunk and memorized the cab number.

The official occupant of the room where he stayed that couple of weeks while he recovered was a guy named Tristan. Tristan spent the first three nights of Hank's visit sleeping in the big armchair in the corner. Hank didn't plan it that way. The first night when Marytza bedded him down he didn't realize that the room belonged to anyone. When he woke up the next morning there Tristan was, curled up in the chair. It looked pretty uncomfortable. Hank felt guilty. When he asked about it, Marytza told him that Tristan got off work very late most nights. The next night he curled up in the armchair himself so that when Tristan came in he could have the bed. But that didn't work. Sometime about one-thirty he felt himself being lifted out of the chair and carried over to the bed and very tenderly tucked in. Just like when he was a little kid. He thought he was dreaming until he woke up the next morning in the bed and looked over and saw Tristan in the armchair.

"Listen," he said the next night, having waited up for Tristan to get home, "this is stupid. The bed's big enough for both of us. I won't tell anyone if you don't."

"You're supposed to be recovering from your injuries," Tristan said.

"And you're a working man who needs his rest. Let's not argue about it."

One of the guys who lived in the loft wasn't a hustler but a purse snatcher. There were always purses lying around the place like the pelts of dead animals. He grabbed an expensive looking one and headed back downstairs. Rush hour on the subway and then three different buses meant it took over two hours to get where he was going.

"Help you?" the cab dispatcher asked.

"Saw a lady drop this getting into one of your cabs. I tried to chase them down but I couldn't catch up."

"Yeah?" the dispatcher sneered. "You sure you didn't just grab it from her?"

"I'm sure."

"What am I supposed to do about it?"

"Help me get it back to her."

"How's that supposed to happen?"

Hank told him the cab number.

"That'll be Otis. He won't be in until late."

"I'll wait."

"No need," the dispatcher said. "Just leave the bag with me. We'll get it back to her."

"I'll wait."

"Not supposed to have people hanging around, you know?"

Hank pulled a twenty out of his pocket.

"Wouldn't want you to get into trouble over it," he said, handing the man the bill.

"You must be expecting a pretty big reward," the dispatcher said, "'cause Otis'll have to have something, too. I mean, he's not just going to give out an address for free. Even supposing he took her home. He might have dropped her anywhere."

But he was pretty sure Marytza wouldn't have just gone larking around the city with all that stuff. She'd head for safety with no wasted moves.

"Don't worry about it."

"Hate to see you come out on the short end, is all. Some of these rich women is real tightwads."

He was starving by the time Otis rolled in at the end of his shift. He hadn't left the whole time. The dispatcher hadn't been very clear on what time Otis's shift was supposed to be over, and he didn't want to give those two an opportunity to confer. He handed over another twenty and got the address Otis had taken the fare to.

It was too late to go there. He'd have to wait until morning. By then it might be too late. If Branch or somebody he'd deputized had seen Marytza that afternoon, the FBI might be there already. They could trace a cab number with a phone call. There wasn't much hope, really. But it was the the only hope he'd had in a long time.

He'd known who Tristan was even before ending up in his bed. Tristan was the flash of shining hair halfway down the block. Tristan was that pair of muscular shoulders streaming with sweat as he jogged past on Hank's first afternoon in the neighborhood. That deep, hairless chest bouncing just so with each stride. Tristan was perfection on two sturdy legs, enough to deepen his already bottomless despair yet at the same time inspire almost infinite hope. That's who Tristan was.

Tristan was also the big, strong, unexpectedly gentle guy who slept beside him every night for the rest of his stay before Marytza finally let him head back out to the street. The guy who never tried anything. The guy who made him want to never leave the apartment. But he had to. He had to make a living. It wasn't just his immediate need for cash. When you were off the market you were forgotten. You had never existed. You had to start from scratch cultivating your customer base. You had to make it up to your regulars for your absence.

Yorkville might as well have been New Haven. It was practically to Connecticut and hardly seemed like the city at all. He stood across the street from the address he'd been given wondering what to do. He was pretty sure that Otis had pulled one over on him. It didn't look like the kind of place that a dyed in the wool revolutionary would end up living in. But he didn't have anything else to do, so he found a place to sit where he could watch the entrance to the building. He watched the street, too, in case the bad guys showed up.

Just when he was about to give up, she appeared. She'd never stopped reminding him of Grace Kelly. It was ironic, because of all the women in the world Grace Kelly was the one his crazy dead mother had most wanted to be like. She died her hair to the right shade. She bought the clothes. She faked the accent. But she only fooled that one guy. And look how it ended up—both of them dead in his parents' bed and his dad dead in the front yard. At the last minute, Dad had chosen suicide over flight. This verson of Grace Kelly stepped out the front door of the building and he could tell immediately that she believed she was being watched. He knew she wasn't thinking about him. She couldn't possibly know he was there. It was someone else that she was looking for, presumably the feds. So, frantic as he was to speak to her, he held back. If she was under surveillance he couldn't afford to show himself. The last thing he wanted was to get involved in all that mess. As much time as he'd spent in that apartment, he'd never paid much attention to what went on there. He'd known it was way too heavy for a simple street hustler to deal with.

It had been Tristan who brought him back to the apartment over and over again.

Oh, sure, the free meals had been nice. And the attention. Marytza had been a true friend. No question about that. But it had been Tristan. Each time he'd entered that front door and trudged up those stairs had meant a chance to spend time in that glorious presence.

So no, he didn't dare speak to her. But he couldn't let the opportunity slip away completely. She set off down the street, and stealthily as he knew how he followed her.

It hadn't taken him long to figure out that some of Marytza's gang were suspicious of him. That's when he stopped using the front door. As paranoid as they all were, they seemed completely ignorant of the fact that the building had a fire escape. Some revolutionaries. Outsmarted by a thirteen year old. Getting onto the bottom of the thing took some scrambling, but once there it was a straight shot up the backside of the building to Tristan's window, which was always ajar. That crack between the sash and the window frame was like a welcome mat. Once a week or so, when the weather was bad or the cops were especially fierce or he just couldn't take it any more, he'd sneak into Tristan's bed.

Nothing ever happened. Tristan wasn't the type for funny business. What Tristan did was hold him until he stopped shaking, until the terrors subsided, until he fell asleep. Sometimes when he woke up in the morning Tristan was still holding him. Tristan was the big brother he'd never had. Tristan was like Dad had been until Mom made him go away and then he came back and everything turned rotten. Tristan was strong and gentle and kind and patient. He was handsome as a movie star and built like some guy in a book about mythology. He was everything good in the world. He was the man Hank would have tried to be if he'd had any idea how to do that. Hank was very careful not to wear out his welcome.

He followed Marytza for a full week. He was waiting outside the building each morning when she left, and he trailed her everywhere she went. All day long, each day. Mostly she was in classes or the library at Columbia. This was welcome, because it took him inside and there were restrooms handy. Then there was the bookstore where she worked part time. He didn't go inside there. It was too small. He'd certainly be noticed. Through the big windows he watched her waiting on customers and shelving stock and sitting down occasionally with a sandwich. A full week, and there was never a sign of any of the others from the apartment. Well, there wouldn't be, he reasoned. They'd scattered to the four winds long before the raid. The feds were probably still pissed that they'd showed up after the party ended. Marytza's buddies might be keeping in touch with each other, but they certainly weren't meeting. There was no sign, either, that she was being watched by anyone but him. He was her solitary shadow.

The week passed like a dream. No johns. No tricks. No cops. No fights. And no money coming in, but plenty of money going out. All those bus tickets, those rides on the subway. Those meals gobbled down from street vendors. He was about to run out of money, and no money meant no more time.

So finally, Friday evening just half a block from her building, he caught up with her, grasping her ever so lightly by the elbow. He'd been giving signals since they emerged from the subway station so she wouldn't be completely surprised that someone was behind her.

"How did you find me?" she muttered.

"I never really thought you were working for the FBI," she said.

They were sitting on the bench across the street from her front door. The bench he'd been sleeping on all week.

"I think I know who the real informant was," he said.

"That dark haired guy," she nodded, "squatting with you guys and pretending to hustle. Never actually saw him pick anyone up. Nobody did. Rookie mistake. Stuck out like a sore thumb. That and he was always too clean. Thought even a low level FBI informant would do better maintaining cover. Had to be him, right?"

"Right."

"I can't believe you're all still in that place. It never crossed my mind when I was planning my trip down there that any of you were around."

"It's a good location," he said. "Business wise, you know?"

"You know what I mean," she said. "You all should have been tossed out on the street a long time ago."

"That's what made me suspicious of that guy in the first place. That whole arrangement doesn't make sense otherwise."

"Tristan always trusted you, too," she said.

At the sound of that name on her lips, he started to cry.

"Come on," she said. "Let's get inside."

"You really have to find another way to make a living," she said, watching him wolf down the soup. "You should get a real job."

"Right," he said. "I didn't even finish seventh grade. Who's going to hire me to do anything but wash dishes and mop floors?"

"That would be a start," she said. "It would at least be safe. Not to mention indoors."

"When did you turn all bourgeois?"

"I guess I really never was anything else," she smiled.

"Some revolution you guys put on."

"You're right about that. No better than little kids playing dressup."

"Graduation is in a couple more weeks," she said, making up a bed for him on the sofa.

"I'm not sure I'm staying," he told her.

“I’ll be sure for both of us,” she said. “Where would you go? It’s raining buckets out there.”

“Graduation, huh?”

“Ph.D. in Humanities,” she snorted. “Can you think of anything more useless than that?”

“I don’t even know what Humanities is,” he said. “Are. Whatever.”

“Neither does anybody else,” she said.

“I mean, what kind of job do you get?”

“You can work part time in a bookstore,” she said.

“You already do.”

“Exactly.”

“Sounds like you’re not any better off than I am,” he said.

“You might think that,” she nodded, “but I have big plans, don’t I?”

“Do you?”

“I’m moving back to Boston,” she said. “I’m starting law school next fall. Harvard.”

“I bet you can get a good job with that.”

“I certainly hope so,” she said. “You sure you had enough to eat?”

He was still hungry, but he didn’t want to accept any more of her charity than necessary. He really should have left already. The rain meant nothing to him. But there were still all those unanswered questions. Now that he was right there with her, he couldn’t bring himself to ask them.

“I’m O.K.” he said. “Soup was really good.”

“Restaurant leftovers,” she said.

He remembered her trip out to Brooklyn. He’d watched her eating lunch with that man who looked like Vladimir.

“Tasty,” he said.

“You really should go in and take a shower,” she said.

“Do I smell that bad? Sorry.”

“No, you don’t smell,” she said. “You’ll sleep better. That’s all I meant.”

"You've always been so nice to me," he said. "I wish you'd let me make you feel good. Free of charge, I mean. Just this once. All this time you've never let me."

It was Tristan's last night in New York. He was leaving for boot camp the next day.

"I'm not like your johns," Tristan said.

"Everybody likes to feel good."

"I didn't mean that," Tristan said. "I guess what I meant was I'm in love with somebody."

"And she's in love with Vladimir," he said.

"It isn't Marytza," Tristan said.

"No?"

"No."

"If you're in love, why are you always alone? Why am I the only one ever in bed with you?"

"Yes," Tristan said. "That's a mystery all right."

A guy as spectacular as that—lovesick. It made no sense. All these people around and nobody in love with Tristan. It was like Dad all over again. More evidence that the world was totally fucked up.

He had intended to clear out before sunrise. But the unaccustomed comfort made him oversleep. He woke to the smell of bacon. Pulling the top sheet around him like a toga, he went into the kitchenette.

"Morning, sleepyhead," Marytza said. She was already dressed. She probably had to work a long shift on Saturday.

"Morning."

"Have a seat at the table," she said. "This is almost ready."

"Not sure I'm staying."

"About that," she said.

"Don't worry," he said. "I'll be clearing out as soon as I'm dressed. I won't be bothering you any more."

"Actually," she said, "I've been doing some thinking."

"Oh?"

"You should come to Boston with me."

"Why?" he asked.

"I'm not the only one who needs a fresh start."

"Is that what I need?" he asked. "I hear the johns up there are really stingy and the climate sucks. In the winter you either starve to death or freeze. Plus the cops are meaner than the ones here. If you can believe that."

"You won't be staying in that line of work."

"No?"

"You're going to go to school and get your GED. Then who knows? Maybe community college."

"You tried this once before," he said. "You and that guy. . .you remember that guy. You mentioned him last night. What was his name?"

"Tristan," she said. He could tell she knew he was pretending he couldn't remember. He was pretty sure she knew why.

"Yeah, that Tristan guy," he said. "The two of you tried to get me off the street."

"We did."

"Didn't work."

"I'm older and wiser now."

"Really."

"My grandfather left me enough money to get through law school. We'll share an apartment and I'll pay all your living expenses as long as you stay in school."

"That's crazy," he said.

"I always was," she smiled, reaching over and touseling his hair.

"Why would you want to do something like that?"

"I'm a revolutionary," she said. "We want to change the world."

"I think I'd better get dressed now," he said. "It's time for me to go."

"If you leave," she said, "you'll have to go wearing that sheet."

"What are you talking about?"

"I burned your clothes last night while you were asleep."

"You didn't."

"I took them downstairs and threw them in the incinerator."

"What the fuck?" he sputtered. "Marytza, why the hell would you do that? I hardly have any clothes as it is."

"I'll buy you new ones. But only if you agree to come to Boston with me."

"Why are you doing this?" he asked, his desperation rising. "Why won't you leave me alone? That's all I want."

"No," she said. "That's not what you want."

"Who says it isn't?"

"Why else are you here?"

"I wanted to make sure you were O.K."

"Tristan never forgave himself, you know. It was his one regret when he left for boot camp. His one last piece of unfinished business. You were still out there on the streets. That was the last thing he wanted for you. And I won't forgive myself if I let another chance slip by."

"Tristan, huh?" he shrugged as if the name meant nothing to him. "This plan of yours is all his fault?"

"If it helps you to think of it that way, so be it. Now there are a few conditions."

"Let's hear them," he said. He could always change his mind later.

"No drugs," she said.

"Never take them anyway."

Except for smoking a joint occasionally, it was true. He couldn't afford that shit.

"No turning tricks," she said. "You can have all the sex you want, but as long as you're living under my roof it better not be for money."

"All right," he said. Actually, not having sex would be a relief. Maybe by the time he turned thirty he'd be in the mood to try it again. "That all?"

"No," she said. "There's one more thing."

"Uh huh."

"You have to tell me your real name. I know it's not Hank."

"My real name," he said. "Afraid I'll have to think about that one."

Regulus

I first met Ford Hopkins the day his mother invited me to their home for dinner after Sunday morning services at Faith Presbyterian. I had been in Chattanooga nearly a month at that time, living in Uncle Gunnar's guest cottage and placating Grannie Ingebrittsen's maternal impulses by attending church with the family every week. These were Presbyterians, I silently lectured myself, not the despised Baptists who had killed Daddy, but sitting in that pew every week, listening to the sounds and smelling the smells, I found the distinction fuzzy almost to the point of invisibility. And in the moments when it threatened to vanish altogether I would fight off my mounting discomfort by comtemplating the back of Ford's head, four rows forward of us in the family pew. On Sunday mornings, his board straight shock of raven hair was perfectly groomed. Staring at that hair, at the square shoulders encased in that immaculate suit of navy wool, at the cool white of the shirt collar just visible through the silky black fringe, I could will my pulse to slow and my blood pressure to fall and my bowels to unclench. The pure aesthetics of the moment were enough to rout those demons, at least briefly.

I couldn't have not known who the Hopkinses were. Ford's maternal grandmother, Henrietta Armstrong Ford, had been Grannie Ingebrittsen's high school classmate. I had heard of the Hopkinses in myriad connections over the years and knew all the highways and byways of their lineage. I also knew that it wasn't the back of Ford's head I was meant, and understood, to be staring at those Sunday mornings but that of his fraternal twin, Isabella. It was on her behalf that the dinner invitation had been extended. Isabella, better known as Belle, had reached the ripe old age of twenty-six in an unmarried state, so nothing would suffice but that a fiance be found and a wedding planned. And here was Tristan Bentley home from the army and apparently unscathed. How fortunate. For Presbyterians, just as for Freudians, there are no accidents. Predestination, whether divine or set in motion by the unconscious, is the driving force in all things. Belle's progress toward matrimony and motherhood had been retarded by a master's degree in art history and a stint in the Peace Corps, but back home and safely under the influence of her mother, aunties, and grandmothers, she was on the true path at last. And Tristan? Obviously a case of being in the right place at the right time. I knew the entire congregation believed this, though I didn't entirely understand why I had to be the chosen one. It was a large congregation and an affluent one, and I knew there had to be other candidates, and from my perspective better qualified ones. Scanning the sanctuary each week, I could pick out likely looking young men sitting with their families. I knew, too, that these represented the tip of the iceberg, because irregular church attendance didn't necessarily constitute a disqualifying factor in itself.

I eventually settled on my uncles as the cause of all the focus on me. Well into their thirties, they had completely avoided marriage thus far. Uncle Gunnar, newly retired from the NFL, had more or less immediately disqualified himself by hiring an agent and staying busy reviewing scripts and flying back and forth to Hollywood for auditions and doing every conceivable thing that might advance his anticipated career. He would eventually achieve sporadic notoriety in B movies. My Uncles Lars and Tor, younger but earlier defectors from football, graced the southern professional wrestling circuit with their antics. Thus they had no fixed address and no career worthy of the label and couldn't be considered appropriate prospects. None of them was likely to marry any time soon, if ever. And if one of them eventually did, it was inconceivable that the bride would be one of those demure church girls. It seemed obvious that I had been singled out to pay for the community's pent up frustration with the Ingebrittsen brothers and be offered up to the gods and goddesses of matrimony as a living sacrifice.

With his sleek raven hair, eyes the color of black coffee and perfectly trimmed mustache, Ford's appearance was rakish, but this was overlaid by well scrubbed wholesomeness like a model in an advertisement for men's dress shirts. He and Belle were obviously siblings. She shared his features, coloring, and smooth hair texture.

She was his exact height, average for a man and tall for a girl. What she lacked were Ford's dimples and his irony. At least I believed she lacked this last characteristic in the beginning.

Sunday dinner featured exactly the same menu Grannie Inebrittsen was serving. The subtle variations in seasonings and presentations enlivened it, but the dishes themselves anchored me amid the swirls of surrealism at the table. The members of the family all seemed such cartoons. Grannie Henrietta with her grin and knowing glances which seemed to imply that she understood me much better than I did myself; Mrs. Hopkins, whose overly solicitous chatter seemed both morbid and faintly manic; Judge Hopkins, notorious for the sarcasm which he indiscriminately unleashed at defense attorneys, prosecutors, defendants and witnesses alike yet scrupulously fair in his rulings, snorting sardonically at the faux pas of his wife and mother-in-law; and Belle, apparently as ill at ease as I was, giving what I sincerely hoped was an inaccurate impression of eccentric preoccupation. I left that day thinking that of the whole bunch, Ford, with his air of mild amusement and those glinting eyes which seemed to miss nothing, was the only remotely normal one in the household.

There was a second Sunday dinner two weeks later, identical in all respects except the color of Ford's necktie, and a third the week after that. I was being designated an official suitor, and by that time I knew that for whatever reason there were no rivals. I suffered acute pangs of conscience at this. I knew exactly what my intentions were, or rather that I had none. Except, that is, a generalized resolve to sleepwalk my way through the remaining decades of my life. I should have refused to have anything more to do with the Hopkins family on general principle, but I wanted nothing more or less than a life without principles. I wanted to forget not only the fiasco at Fort Geronimo but my time in Viet Nam and my "bohemian" years in New York. Most of all I wanted to forget the upbringing which had taught me those damned principles which had made me care about truth and integrity and standing for things. Those principles which inevitably and unfortunately led me constantly to sit in judgment of myself.

I aspired to be a sleek young Presbyterian like those handsome, self-satisfied young men I saw at church on Sundays, not forgetting their absent brothers and cousins, those men I considered far more appropriate suitors for Belle Hopkins or any of the other young women of the parish precisely because they had no principles whatever. They needed none. They had church and family and social convention to guide them and had only to do as was expected and father another generation of Presbyterians and not interfere in their upbringing as mine had been interfered with. Surely there must be a way I could slither back into that particular Eden and partake in its smug oblivion.

In other words, I can't claim any kind of integrity in what I was doing when I accepted that fourth invitation from Mrs. Hopkins, not to Sunday dinner this time but an altogether more intimate Saturday evening. No integrity. Nor ignorance either. I knew the rules as well as anyone, even though I had never played by them. I was being offered an opportunity to declare myself. And though I did so only in the most oblique and noncommittal of ways, I did it, and I knew what everyone involved made of it.

Despite my dithering and my ruminations on the bucolic attractions of "normality", I did not then or ever seriously entertain the notion of marrying Belle Hopkins. I had no intention of marrying anyone, ever. If this was not as a matter of principle—which it should rightly have been—then at least it was a matter of preference. I was as clear as could be on that but only in my own mind. I let people believe I was at least considering it. I let Belle believe it, and I knew I risked both her disappointment and embarrassment. I risked those things willingly. I did all that, and I knew exactly what I was doing, and I did it anyway: the last words of a scoundrel.

I had a choice to make. I could have refused Mrs. Hopkins' overtures and insisted to Grannie Ingebrittsen that I be exempted from the marriage sweepstakes until later at least. It would have hurt her feelings but no more than they were destined to be hurt in the long run. Because the whole thing started with Grannie's tacit approval, if not at her instigation. I could have adopted a less confrontational approach, graciously refusing that fateful fourth invitation and positioning myself to repeat the process with a succession of young women ad nauseum until at last everyone got the idea. I could have refused to attend church at all, which would at least have been spiritually honest. As a last resort, I could have left Chattanooga as resolutely and defiantly as my furious sixteen year old self had left my hometown. But any such response to the situation would have required resolve and worse than that, exertion. And I simply wasn't capable of either. I told myself as much, as if that might excuse not only what I was participating in but every possible consequence. I knew it was inexcusable. I was too morally lazy to care. I just wanted to be left alone.

So I arrived at the Hopkins' Greek temple revival home that Saturday evening having given more than usual attention to my appearance, fully aware of the enormity I was committing. I remember a particularly exquisite pang of chagrin on hearing that Ford had other plans for the evening. I sat with Belle and her parents and grandmother at dinner and in front of the television afterward. Grannie Henrietta excused herself for the evening at what seemed a ridiculously early hour and Judge and Mrs. Hopkins weren't far behind her. Belle and I were alone, face to face for the first time.

My uncles had pooled their resources and bought a car dealership. They considered themselves frightfully clever. Three Swedish brothers selling Volvos. Uncle Gunnar was the "smart" one, the one with "a head for business", and so served as titular general manager, though the real managing was performed by staff inherited from the previous owner. Lars and Tor contributed nothing but capital, except for appearing in a series of increasingly bizarre, madcap advertising spots which appeared late at night on local television. The franchise included, almost as an afterthought, Jaguar cars. I had gone to work for my uncles after arriving in Chattanooga, and I was loitering in the Jaguar corner of the showroom the next Tuesday afternoon when Ford came in, apparently playing hookie from the law firm where he was putting his recent J.D. degree to its intended use. He greeted me with the elaborate, highly calculated casualness with which young southern manhood of a particular class addressed its equals and intimates, and requested a test drive in the latest model Jaguar roadster.

We put the top down, I handed him the keys, and we were off. It was high summer, muggy and stifling, but he somehow mananged to look crisp and cool behind the wheel. With the slipstream plastering his hair to his scalp, I thought he was reminiscent of those dashing aces of the Western Front, flying open cockpit against the Red Baron or somesuch Fiendish Hun.

Far later than we should have returned, he steered us back into the dealership drive. I anticipated catching forty-seven varieties of homemade East Tennessee hell from the floor manager, who, to his credit, never cut me the tiniest slack for whose nephew I was. But Ford fended off any such eventualities by brandishing his checkbook and insisting that a deal be written up. I didn't know what I was most astonished by, that what had appeared to me to be no more than a lark had ended that way or that a young man more or less my own age could afford to pay cash for such an expensive vehicle.

What I absolutely refused to give any thought to was how attractive I found him.

My first real date with Belle took place a few nights later. We went to a movie. I insisted she select it. I couldn't imagine her having a good time on a date with me, so it only seemed fair that she at least have the opportunity to see a movie she would like. Smart, beautiful, charming, poised, she sat next to me in that darkened theater as the images flashed in front of us. I couldn't figure out for the life of me what I was doing there. I couldn't imagine what I had to offer a woman like that, so complete, so self possessed. It was like sitting next to the Sphinx, a giant riddle I couldn't begin to answer. All our subsequent dates left me with that same profound befuddlement. She was terrific company and our times together were full of conversation and laughter. I was crazy about her in my own inept way. But I had no idea how it was all supposed to happen and I had no inclination to learn. All I knew was that I absolutely didn't see us as a couple in the sense everyone around us understood the term.

Belle's many attractive qualities were the same ones Ford possessed. Fraternal twins aren't supposed to be alike to the extent identical ones are, but Belle and Ford were amazingly similar. The same sharp wit and gift for badinage spiced their conversation. They shared the same tastes and prejudices, the same irony, and the same irreverence. Their identical eyes flashed with the same sparkle. I quickly became devoted to them both, and almost as quickly the three of us were inseparable. I saw Belle two or three times a week for movies, dinners, and the occasional night in front of the television. Ford I spent more time with, as young men of that time and place did. I joined his gym. We did outdoorsy things together. We engaged in long, philosophical discussions. My work schedule was chaotic as the newest member of the Ingebrittsen Volvo-Jaguar team. My hours averaged sixty per week. Belle and Ford monopolized my remaining time to the extent that I only saw Grannie at church. When Uncle Lars called her discontentment at this state of affairs to my attention, I retorted that she had no one to blame for it but herself.

Almost immediately upon starting to work, I was informed by Uncle Gunnar that I should consider myself a member of the cast whenever a new commercial for the dealership was produced. At first this entailed changing into casual clothing and pretending to be a customer while Uncles Lars and Tor, in full Viking warrior drag, helped me select my new car. Since this was all performed to run under Uncle Gunnar's voice over, there was no dialogue to worry about. My biggest challenge was self-consciousness. But upon viewing a rough cut of my first spot, I realized that my uncles' extravagantly displayed physiques and wrestling ring histrionics made me more or less invisible. After that I was a great deal more relaxed in front of the camera. We made a succession of these commercials during the summer and early fall. Eventually I was able to watch them without cringing. But when talk turned to planning something special for the holiday season, I couldn't help having some misgivings.

Since Uncle Gunnar was insistent that the spot go into rotation by Thanksgiving, it had to be filmed in October. This in itself was surreal. Decorations for the showroom had to be planned and acquired and suitable music selected, all well before Halloween. It was hard to take any of it seriously. The first section of the commercial was filmed in Uncle Gunnar's master bedroom, where I portrayed a customer "lying all snug in his bed/while visions of Ingebrittsen Brothers' Volvos danced in his head". The second section, where, tousle haired and pyjama clad I found my bow festooned new car by the Christmas tree in the middle of the showroom, accompanied by glamorous young women in the skimpiest imaginable elves costumes, Uncle

Gunnar's three long suffering Labrador Retrievers wearing fake reindeer antlers, Uncle Gunnar in white tie and tails, Uncle Lars as a bare-chested, clean shaven Santa surrogate, and Uncle Tor as the Viking Warrior of Christmas, was a major production. The showroom had to be prepared after closing on a Saturday evening and the shooting took place on Sunday, the only day of the week when we were not open.

The production company arrived from Atlanta on Saturday afternoon, and it included, in addition to gaffers, camera men, production assistants, a director, a costumer, and a sound recordist and his assistant, a makeup artist. This tall, slender gentleman was one of those walking stereotypes that represented the general public's entire understanding of homosexuals. The traditional code word "flamboyant" didn't even begin to describe him. I found my uncles' reactions to him—or rather their absolute lack of reactions to him—illuminating in the extreme.

Uncle Gunnar, as one would have expected, was all business. His experiences in Hollywood had no doubt accustomed him to this type to at least some extent, and he paid the man no more attention than he would have to any other member of the production company. Uncle Lars, always the clown, behaved exactly as was his habit, no more nor less. It was Uncle Tor whose reaction I was most interested in. Uncle Tor, the largest, most ruthlessly gymmed out of my uncles, was a rather cryptic figure, monosyllabic, deliberate in his movements, and rather opaque as to personality. There was, to be honest, no family consensus to the effect that he actually possessed one. Despite the fact that I was substantially smaller than he was, I was said to resemble him more than I did my other two uncles, but that was a merely physical observation. Though he was unfailingly affectionate to me and remarkably and unexpectedly gentle with my sisters, I found his quietness more than a little menacing. Indeed, his wrestling persona was that of a taciturn, edgy killer—unusual for a "good guy" but there it was. It seemed almost like type casting.

He was, almost inevitably, the target of the makeup man's most outrageous flirtation that afternoon as we prepared to shoot the scene set in the showroom, and I found myself watching uneasily as the man flapped and fluttered, getting Uncle Tor's luxuriant blond mane teased out just so and oiling his stupefyingly muscled chest. I wasn't the only one focused on this spectacle. Out of the corner of my eye I could see the director looking a little queasy, and several of the elf girls were whispering about it more or less at the top of their lungs. Finally the tension of this interaction reached such a pitch that even Uncle Gunnar noticed it and his conferring with the sound recordist trailed off, while Uncle Lars' ordinarily non-stop clowning halted more or less in its tracks, leaving him simply agape. I watched breathless, certain that Uncle Tor would at any moment snap the willowy gentleman like a twig, leaving us to clean up the mess and deal with the legal complications.

What he did instead was take the man's head in his beefy hands, pull it up to his own face, and stop that chattering mouth with a kiss. And not just any kiss. It was full on, deep and long, and appeared to include substantial tongue action. Indeed, it was the most pornographic act I had witnessed in my life to that point. It made me positively lightheaded. Around them, the whole room had gone silent. There wasn't a pair of eyes in the place that wasn't fixed on that kiss. Even the Labradors stood stock still. After what seemed like an eon, Uncle Tor pulled back.

"You talk too much," he quietly told the astonished makeup man, who was blushing like a mishap in a neon light bulb factory.

That was Uncle Lars' cue to make some wisecrack nobody quite heard but everyone found hysterically funny.

After that, we all got back to work.

Before I knew it it was Thanksgiving, and we were rushing headlong into the holiday season. All around, evergreen trees were being decorated, presents were being purchased and wrapped, cookies and fruitcakes were being baked and stored against the myriad parties, family gatherings and invasions by carolers which would soon ensue. The holiday season was also, of course, a time when proposals were made and accepted and rings were slipped onto young women's fingers. I knew what was expected of me even after so brief and half hearted a courtship. I read the expectation in the faces of Grannie Ingebrittsen and the host of church ladies every Sunday at services. I read it in the smile of Rev. MacPherson as he shook my hand each week as Belle and I exited the sanctuary together. I read it in the expressions of our fellow parishioners as Belle and I took our seats in the Hopkins family pew. I read that expectation everywhere except in the faces of Belle and Ford themselves, where I adamantly refused to look for fear of seeing it there as well.

I could play the amiable buffoon for everyone but them. I could risk the disapproval of all the others. But the good opinion of the twins had become the air I breathed, the water I drank, the safe and comfortable spaces I inhabited, the sun I labored under, and moon and stars I slumbered beneath by night. I couldn't imagine willingly disappointing them. I might, just might, brazen my way through the holidays and emerge unencumbered, but that would leave me staring Valentine's Day in the face. It wouldn't be any easier then to remain a holdout. It would become more and more difficult to maintain an independent position. Time would pass, the seasons would change, but the pressure could only intensify until I eventually spoke those two tiny, momentous words—"I do".

So I had at least half a mind to get it over with.

"We insist," Belle laughed, the Sunday morning after Thanksgiving. "Ford and I positively insist on taking you out to dinner for your birthday. He feels like spanking you for not telling us it was coming up so soon."

So later that week, on the only night I wasn't on evening shift, we piled into her Volkswagen. Ford had made a reservation at a new restaurant, an upscale spaghetti joint located in a renovated Victorian downtown, the height of cosmopolitanism given the parochial nature of the local cuisine. The occasion was a delight, not so much because of the stated reason as that I had them both there as my companions, which provided, I believed, insurance against awkward scenes and sensitive topics of conversation.

We ate, drank wine, laughed and enjoyed ourselves. The twins fought over the check, and Belle won. It was the nearest I could remember to a truly perfect evening. This made me pensive and even slightly abashed. Who was I to deserve such kindness, such friends? I with my reluctance to do what was so obviously expected? My expression must have alerted them to the possibility of something less than festive in my mood, because the next thing I knew Ford said "look here, man, we need to talk," and I felt my blood run cold.

"Let me," Belle said, reaching for my hand across the oilcloth covered table.

"What?" I asked with an audible tremor in my voice. I wondered if she could feel my hand shaking. She had to. And what must she think?

"You've got to be hearing the same talk we are," she said.

"I'm not sure what you mean."

"The old folks can't mind their own business," Ford growled.

"Please don't take this wrong," Belle pleaded, "but I'm not interested in you as a husband. I'm a fool not to be, I suppose. God knows you're the most wonderful man in the world."

"Hear, hear," Ford agreed.

"I know a girl would have to be out of her mind not to want to marry you. But guess what? I'm truly out of my mind. I do love you—I hope you believe that—I do, truly. In my own way. But marriage? I don't know if it's something I'll ever want."

"But. . ."

"I know," she nodded. "You're too much of a gentleman, I guess. I have no idea, really, if you've been considering it—um—us, like that or not. But those old biddies just won't leave it alone. And if they're working on you even half as hard as they've been working on me—oh, Jesus, I'm making such a mess of this. Please just say you don't hate me for not wanting to marry you. Even if it's not true."

"I could never hate you," I said, dazed but incredibly relieved. "Either of you."

"If we present them with a united front," Ford proposed, "they'll have to leave us alone about it."

"And you thought I might be the weak link?"

"We weren't sure," Belle said. "You're not an easy person to read."

"He is, too," Ford insisted, in one of their rare disagreements. "You just haven't learned the signals."

"All for one and one for all," I said. "And in that spirit, shouldn't we have more wine?"

The next morning I was giddy with relief. But on reflection I grew concerned that the situation had resolved itself far too easily. I could recite Uncle Gunnar's skeptical commentary without having to hear it. Additionally, I realized that I didn't know either of them as well as I had thought. I had been so absorbed by my own anxieties, so preoccupied with my own ambivalences, that I had mistaken what was essentially a casual relationship for something deeper. I was at a loss. All I knew for certain was that my misgivings wouldn't allow me to accept the new state of things at face value.

At the gym a couple of days later, I raised the issue—extremely gingerly—with Ford.

"Oh, hell, T.," he grinned. "She's as serious as a heart attack. She has no intention of settling down. It's a shame, really, because God knows when or where she'll ever find anybody to equal you."

I winced at that.

"And boy would I love to have you for a brother-in-law. But really, there's no chance."

"None at all?" I asked.

"Believe me, if there was any hope whatsoever you'd be the first to know."

"I see."

"I didn't tell you this, O.K?"

"All right."

"She's actually a little bit afraid that if she were to offer you any encouragement, you'd decide to wait for her to change her mind. And you really shouldn't think of doing that."

I was speechless. I had always considered myself completely transparent, and here, the two people I felt I knew best actually misunderstood me that profoundly.

"Buck up, pal," Ford said, flashing that grin again, "and try not to take it too hard. We both think the world of you, you know. We don't want anything spoiling our friendship. I believe you're too big a person to let that happen."

"I'm not at all convinced that you have an accurate estimation of my character," I protested, "but you can both relax."

"I knew you'd come around," he said. "I told Belle."

"You two," I laughed. "You think you're so smart."

"What do you mean?"

"We've all been suckered in by the church ladies."

"I don't understand."

"I never had any intentions."

"Come on. You expect me to believe that? The way you've been all serious and dramatic on us the last couple of weeks?"

"I couldn't figure out how to get by without proposing to Belle. I was afraid I was about to hurt her terribly. I was convinced she was expecting it."

"No," Ford insisted. "You didn't really think that. At least you wouldn't have if people hadn't interfered."

Conscious of Grannie Ingebrittsen's impending disappointment, I went out of my way to be the ideal grandson during the remainder of the holiday season. I took my sisters Christmas shopping. I spent hours listening to my grandfather's rambling ruminations and reminiscences. I helped trim the tree. I did my part to stock it with brightly wrapped presents. Uncle Lars and Uncle Tor were on tour right up until their rambunctious arrival on Christmas morning itself, but Uncle Gunnar was around constantly, taking note of my efforts and giving off unmistakable signs of approval. And as I sat beside her in the candlelight service on Christmas Eve, the tear blurred smile Grannie gave me said that though she couldn't for the life of her understand why I hadn't presented her with a granddaughter-in-law elect for Christmas she could almost forgive me the lapse.

The perils of the holiday season behind us, Belle, Ford, and I entered what I thought of as our "Three Musketeers" period. This was somewhat of a misnomer, however, since during the next months we rarely did anything as a threesome. I saw Ford nearly every day at the gym, but on weekends it was mostly Belle and me on our own, as more and more he was spending his free time visiting a friend in Atlanta. I assumed that friend was a young woman, and that Ford sooner or later would sit me down to speak of his engagement. It seemed ironic that after so enthusiastically approving of my evasion of matrimony he was headlong on that course himself, but our situations were obviously different. I tried to worm some information about it out of Belle, but all she would do was give me what she referred to as her Mona Lisa smile.

Still, threesome or not, we were unquestionably all for one and one for all during that brief period. And the prospect of its ending as a result of some new arrangement involving Ford didn't distress me unduly. In this I took my cue from Belle, who evidenced no qualms about it whatsoever. Why should it concern either of us? Ford, with his looks and charm, could only be considered rampantly eligible. Indeed, his marriage seemed as inevitable as gravity.

I didn't comprehend my uncles' dealings with women. The reasons for this were obvious enough. My upbringing had been extremely sheltered with regard to such matters, and upon leaving home I had ended up living in the most bohemian circumstances imaginable, where the normal rules of male/female interaction didn't apply. Then it was off to the army. I had no first hand experience and very little observation of "normal" behavior to guide me. Then there was my orientation, which seemed to completely disqualify me from getting the way things worked. Even so, my uncles seemed to go about things in a particularly unorthodox manner. Uncle Gunnar was perhaps the least *outré* of the three. Though there was never anything like a girlfriend in the picture, there were legions of young women who were his friends. They were like paper dolls, all cut to the same pattern and ruthlessly two dimensional. They were constantly showing up at the dealership whether he was at work—or even in town—or not, dropping off lunch, cookies, handmade greeting cards, potted plants, bizarre little knickknacks, all manner of tokens of their affection which I interpreted as fairly pathetic pleas not to be overlooked. When I saw him with those girls he was courteous in the extreme, a kind of archetype of the southern gentleman. His manners would have made them swoon even if his looks and physique didn't. That he knew how to dress, was exemplary in his grooming, and had serious money did nothing to blunt his attractions. Yet his courtliness and genuine warmth signified little and perhaps nothing at all in the usual scheme of things. Although he was often to be seen in the company of one or the other of them (though it had to be said that he usually traveled in the company of two or more at a time) at some restaurant or other or at the country club where he was a member or at the functions which constituted the "social calendar" of the city, I knew to the marrow of my bones that every last one of those statuesque beauties was barking up the wrong tree. I knew this for the simple reason that Grannie Ingebrittsen was completely unaware of their existence from first to last and it was inconceivable that given this crucial fact the least significance could be ascribed to any of these attachments. Uncle Gunnar was, for all his eccentricities, the consummate Mama's boy. And until some young woman inveigled herself into Grannie's consciousness at the very least, not to say her approval, no one needed to take any of Uncle Gunnar's adherents seriously.

Uncle Lars and Uncle Tor were even more disorganized in their habits. Gangs of nubile, big haired young persons trailed in their wakes like tribes of forlorn Amazons, yet neither of my uncles seemed capable of remembering even the simplest biographical details—names, for instance—of these admirers. The idea that one or the other of them might become embroiled in some entanglement or other stretched the imagination to the breaking point and beyond.

Or so I thought.

The one way in which all three of my uncles could be considered exemplary was their refusal to discuss their activities except among themselves. I was certainly never a party to anything that went on. Except for that one time.

"You seem to be the kind of guy," Ford mused one evening, "who learns about life primarily through observation."

"What's that supposed to mean?" I asked.

"Learning from other's mistakes is infinitely preferable to having to learn from one's own."

"Yes, certainly," I said, "but what the hell are you talking about?"

"Nothing in particular," he said, in a tone that left no doubt that there was something very particular on his mind indeed.

I didn't pursue it and he offered no further explanation. This conversation took place on a Friday evening at his apartment while we were waiting for Belle to arrive and join us for takeout, and by the time I left for home at the end of the evening I had forgotten all about it. But Monday morning when I arrived at the showroom, Uncle Gunnar motioned me into his office and shut the door behind me. He'd just arrived home from another of his forays to the west coast, and I assumed he wanted filling in on the latest.

"You've undoubtedly heard that Tor's been a very bad boy," he said.

"Oh?" I had heard nothing of the kind, but suddenly Ford's insinuations recalled themselves to me.

"Haven't you?"

"Not that I know of."

"If you had," Uncle Gunnar said, "you wouldn't have to think about it."

"Then I haven't."

"That would make you the only man in Chattanooga," he said, "with, I sincerely hope, the exception of Papa."

"That doesn't sound good."

"All right," he said, smoothing his already perfect hair and mustering an expression of grave disapproval. "It appears there's a young woman."

"'Appears' hardly seems an appropriate word," I pointed out. "There are squadrons of them. Regiments."

"Yes, T., but there's one particular one with whom Tor apparently has crossed some Rubicon or other."

"That could mean anything from going steady to filing for dissolution of their secret marriage," I said. "It's hard to know how he may have gone wrong when you never have the least idea about anything he does."

"What it means in this case," Uncle Gunnar said, "is twin baby girls. Eight months old."

"What?"

"And you have to be my eyes and ears with your grandparents. They are not to know anything of this until we've arrived at some resolution."

"Twins," I marveled. "I can't believe it."

"Neither can I," Gunnar said. "Quite literally."

Those last two words seemed strangely chosen, but I didn't remark on them. I simply promised to find out as quickly and surreptitiously as possible what Grannie and Papa Ingebrittsen might have heard on the subject and report back.

What they had heard, I quickly learned, was everything. Uncle Gunnar was thunderstruck by this piece of intelligence, but he shouldn't have been. Church ladies hear all and have never been known to keep their knowledge to themselves. Unless their knowledge involves themselves, which in this case it didn't.

"They must be devastated," he said.

"Not as much as you'd expect," I said.

"No? Why would that be, do you suppose?"

"They simply don't believe it," I said. "They are of the opinion that the young woman in question must be making the whole thing up."

"Why, that's wonderful," Gunnar said. "That's absolutely the best thing."

"How can you say that? Won't it make things even more difficult when the truth comes out?"

"Why would it?"

"Well, you said it yourself. They'll be devastated when they realize they're wrong."

He said nothing and gave me one of his cryptic looks.

"You knew," I said to Ford at the gym later that afternoon. "You had heard the story and you didn't tell me."

"Wasn't my place," Ford insisted.

"Hell it wasn't," I said. "You're my best friend."

This was something I hadn't said to him before, and the moment threatened to become awkward.

"Am I?" he grinned. "I'm tremendously honored that you think of me so highly. But really, something like that—it was only right for you to hear about it from family."

"I suppose."

"Besides," he said, "just between the two of us, I'm not sure I believe that girl."

"Why not? The way he and Uncle Lars carry on, seems to me it's nothing but a miracle that something like this hasn't happened before."

"Suit yourself," Ford said. "It's just a feeling I have about him."

"What kind of feeling?"

There was a long silence. I found it a little surprising, since Ford was seldom at a loss for words. I only thought of it as awkward in retrospect. Finally, as if having made a decision of some kind, he spoke.

"He'd never have gotten into a position like that."

This was more or less the sentiment my grandparents had expressed. They waited as avidly as anyone in the city for the results of the tests. With Gunnar back in Los Angeles, they, Belle, and Ford constituted the miniscule local minority that expected Uncle Tor to be exonerated. I, on the other hand, sided with my fellow citizens and assumed the worst. I envisioned an improbably busty young woman with hair chemically fried to match Uncle Tor's taking her place at Grannie Ingebrittsen's holiday table the next Thanksgiving, her small daughters having been ruthlessly trained to call him daddy.

"How did you know that Tor wasn't those little girls' daddy?" I demanded the first time I saw Ford after Tor's paternity test came back negative.

"I just knew," he shrugged.

"Seriously."

"Seriously," he said.

"Tell me, counselor," I said, "when you say you just knew, are you talking about a strongly held opinion? Or something more definitive?"

"If I tell you it was more than just a strongly held opinion, will you believe me?"

"I'll certainly try to," I said, "but I still won't understand."

"It's not that hard to explain," he said. "I run into Gunnar now and then, you know. You'd have to say we're acquainted. But I don't know Lars and Tor from Adam's housecat. I readily admit it. So you might think I have nothing to go on. Still, Chattanooga's not that big a place. You hear things."

"What things?"

"Nothing in particular," he said too quickly, so that I wondered what it was he wasn't willing to tell me. "It's just that the three of them have been local celebrities for a long time. Since they were in high school really. And they've got a reputation."

"I'll say."

"No," he shook his head. "Not that kind of reputation."

"What other reputation could they have?"

"Well, simply put," he said, "the Ingebrittsen boys don't make stupid mistakes."

"I see."

"Anyway, shouldn't you be having this discussion with Gunnar? I know he was just as convinced as I was."

"I've already talked with him about it."

"What explanation did he give you?"

"He didn't explain it at all," I said. "He told me that the real question was why I hadn't been on board with the rest of you."

"Interesting. Did he offer you an answer to that question?"

"He said my problem is I only see Lars and Tor as characters."

Belle, Ford, and I spent a week in Florida that April. Careful to avoid any of the traditional spring break lunacy, we adjusted our dates and accommodations accordingly. The idea, as Belle and Ford explained it, was to relax, soak up the sun after a cold and dreary Chattanooga winter, and enjoy ourselves. There was no agenda beyond that. But my long time fear of inactivity made it difficult to contemplate. I bought a couple pairs of swim trunks, stocked up on tanning oil, and bought a book on meditation which I never read and ended its life as a wad of pulp after being repeatedly soaked at the beach.

Our route south would take us through Atlanta, and I mentioned to Belle that a brief stop there might be anticipated. It seemed the perfect opportunity for Ford to introduce us to his "friend", or as I thought of her, his intended. Belle greeted this suggestion with a look of utter bafflement, as if I had spoken in Serbo-Croat. I couldn't fathom this but was too embarrassed to pursue the matter. Still, as we loaded up the Volvo station wagon I had borrowed out of the dealership's used car inventory for our journey, I was full of anticipation. I sensed that both of them had things up their sleeves and that I was in for at least one major surprise.

It was a long, monotonous drive lengthwise across Georgia, across northern Florida to the coast at Jacksonville, and south along the coast to our final destination. We passed the time playing the games I remembered from road trips as a child, "what animal does that cloud remind you of?" and "how many different state license plates on passing cars can you list?" We made puns out of highway signs. We ate sandwiches that Grannie Ingebrittsen and my sisters had packed for us. We talked nothing but trivia, and we laughed a great deal.

At the motel, Ford and I shared a room and Belle had her own. Each day we rose late, breakfasted copiously, and headed for the beach. The local tourist attractions held no interest for us. Nor did shopping, apparently. I never heard either of the twins express the least desire for anything but the sun, the sand, the surf. Initially awkward, I soon left behind my inhibitions about applying tanning oil to their backs, even when Belle loosened the strap of her bikini to give full access. Ford sported a tiny garment which barely qualified as a g string, and I was shocked at how little attention this attracted, though truth to tell much of the time we had large expanses of the beach to ourselves. This, I was given to understand, was no accident. Ford had done his homework.

The two of them tanned rapidly to deep, satiny tones. They credited some distant, unnamed Cherokee ancestor for this. My pale Scandinavian skin took longer and required more caution before I was able to attain a shade I considered sufficient in such company. Ford, especially, seemed completely in his element. He was a god of the surf. His beauty grew more dazzling by the day. And back at the motel in the evening, when he showered and then anointed himself against dry skin with some unfamiliar but redolent emollient, I found myself entertaining thoughts I had promised myself I wouldn't. But such was the blessed lassitude granted us by the sea and the sun that even this failed to present more than a passing annoyance incapable of darkening my mood.

Days spent at the beach. Nights devoted to long, languid dinners, moonlit conversation, and wine. It was, I repeatedly mused, the closest to thing to heaven that I had ever experienced. I didn't want it to end.

* * *

I expressed that sentiment aloud over dinner on our last night along with a hope that we would repeat the visit before long. Perhaps during the summer? Granted, the weather then would be hotter and it might be more crowded, but surely? They seemed to have enjoyed themselves as much as I had. I saw no possible obstacle to another blissful week spent in such glorious surroundings and ravishing company. They gave me identical smiles but made no reply. The silence greeting my suggestion grew protracted enough to become noticeably awkward. I felt like I had passed gas noisily in church.

"You haven't told him," Belle said finally.

"No," Ford shook his head.

"You really should have."

"I didn't want to spoil his mood. He's been so relaxed all week. So contented. It didn't seem fair."

"Told me what?" I asked, sensing that now was the moment he would finally explain about the young woman in Atlanta. Was I about to be asked to stand up as best man?

"It's like this," Ford said. "Some friends of mine have taken a house for the summer on the French Riviera. Outside Nice. A place called Cap Ferrat. I'll be leaving just after Memorial Day. Belle's coming with me."

"For how long?" I stammered.

"I'll be back by Independence Day," Belle said.

"I'll be staying on indefinitely," Ford said.

"Can you just do that?" I gasped. "I mean, how were you able to fix it with your firm?"

"Oh, the firm didn't pose a problem," he said.

"How can that be?"

"I've resigned," he said. "I never meant to be a lawyer, really. I only did it to please Mother and Daddy. I've shown them that I can do it and do it well. They'll never be able to say that I was too lazy for it or couldn't cut it. But I truly despise practicing law and I have no intention of spending any more of my life that way. So I'm off to France."

"I'm astonished," I said.

"You certainly look it," he laughed. "Buck up, buddy. It's not the end of the world."

"It's the end of something," I said, very nearly heartbroken.

"Every ending is a beginning," Belle smiled gently. "You'll see. In fact, it's probably time for you to go on an adventure of your own."

"I'll second that," Ford said, raising his glass. "To adventures."

Over the years, I heard from Belle a few times. Christmas cards, mostly. She sent news of her husband and children and not much more. I never had the courage to ask about Ford. Even the most innocuous question about him seemed as if it would be a confession of something. My new life occupied all my time and attention, and a wide gulf seemed to have opened between us. It was the gulf between past and present, but I believed it was also the gulf between straight and gay, a gulf that seemed all but unbridgeable in those days.

Then, one evening over a decade later—

We were hosting a party, though not our usual kind. We entertained often enough in those days, but more typically on a much smaller scale, intimate gatherings of our closest friends. For whatever reason, that evening the crowd was large and random. I felt less like a host than a maitre d'.

A sudden shriek drew me to the study. Not that a sudden shriek was in any way unusual in a large gathering of gay men, but this was a shriek I couldn't identify, and mildly curious, not to mention a little bored at my own party, I went to investigate. I found a man there I knew by sight only, the friend of a friend of someone's cousin I think he was, a nondescript gentleman teetering on the brink of middle age but dressed in a defiantly youthful fashion that screamed "GAY!!!!!" and unflatteringly emphasized both his age and his unfortunate girth. I hate stereotypes but I don't necessarily dislike stereotypical individuals, so I had no objection whatever to his presence in my home. I do, however, detest that stereotypical shriek, no matter who utters it, no matter where or when, and our close friends either censor themselves in my presence out of respect for my sensibilities or, more likely, share those sensibilities themselves, so it was an extremely rare sound within our walls.

The gentleman was staring at one of the framed photos on the mantelpiece, and as I moved closer I realized which one. He sensed my presence, and turned.

"You," he said a little tremulously. "You know the Hopkins twins."

The photo had been taken by a German tourist we met on the sand at Daytona Beach on the final afternoon of our trip. In the photo, I was squinting stupidly in the sunshine, flanked by Belle and Ford. They were sporting their identical grins. They never looked more alike either before or since. That shot captured the effect to perfection. Ford was wearing that ridiculously skimpy garment alleged to be a swimsuit, the one Belle had constantly tried to induce him to replace with something more modest.

"I met them on the Cote d'Azur" the man explained. "It must have been the summer of 1971."

I nodded. He had the date right.

"He was living with the son of a German industrialist at the time."

I didn't speak. I didn't want it to be true, but I couldn't help but believe it.

"Oh, my," he sighed. "He was such—a divine creature. But you obviously know all about that."

"Our families were close," I offered by way of explanation. Or was it a disavowal? I wasn't sure. The ambiguity of my response wasn't lost on him.

"You mean you weren't?" he stared at me and then back at the photo, mildly surprised. "No. You wouldn't have been. He always had to be the pretty one."

Once again, I didn't speak. I didn't want to shape or in any way influence the narrative I sensed glimmering like a tropical isle just beyond the horizon.

The man exhaled profoundly.

"You know, it was the most amazing funeral I ever attended. Monte Carlo, I ask you. A flock of white doves was released at sunset and after dark there were fireworks over the harbor. It was like he'd been a prince, or. . ."

He paused, and I waited.

"No," he shook his head, correcting himself. "It was like an opera."

He stared at the photo, obviously moved.

"They said it all cost the boyfriend a quarter of a million."

He paused again, and still I waited. Finally he turned to face me.

"You knew him."

"It was a long time ago," I shrugged.

"Yes," he said. "I remember that swimsuit."

The question I refused to ask loomed between us like the threat of severe weather.

"You didn't know he was sick, did you?"

"No," I admitted. "We weren't in touch."

"Not even with Belle?"

"No."

"This damned disease," he muttered. "The funeral was Bastille day, 1984."

"Thank you."

"He was. Just. The divinest. Creature."

Creature, I thought. Not *man*. *Creature*.

"Just. . ." He shook his head slowly, and I left him there. I left the room looking for a friend, any friend, or most preferably my husband.

So just that suddenly I was confronted with the reality that Ford had gotten on the plane in Chattanooga a respectable young Presbyterian attorney, however former, and had disembarked in France a divine creature, the transformation having apparently taken place high above the Atlantic. I had watched him walk up the steps of that plane biting my tongue, wishing I had the balls to say, "No! Don't go!", and very nearly ready even to say the rest. To explain why.

That close. Had I had the one word on the tip of my tongue which could have changed everything? The man in our study that night apparently believed I must have. And maybe, just maybe, he was right. Not because he had any special insight into that particular situation. He couldn't have. It was merely because he was that eternal gay type, middle aged, single, sharp tongued and flamboyant, obsessed with romance. Maybe there had been a moment on any one of those sunny afternoons, misty mornings, crisp autumn nights, while riding with Ford in his Jaguar, sweating beside him in the gym, sharing pizza and beer in his living room floor with the big game on the television. There had been a hundred moments like that. Or a thousand.

A stronger or braver or merely less repressed man than I was in those days might have attempted it, but that's not the point. Because we're talking about me. About me and about Ford and about another time and place, a time and place that made it impossible regardless of any other considerations. It could never have happened that way then, there. He had to go to France, after all, to become that divine creature. And I had to go almost as far to become whatever I eventually became. So the alternative being suggested subtly but oh, so insistently in my husband's study that night was not and could never have been anything other than the fantasy of a moment, experienced by a sad but brave queen well on his way to a bittersweet, almost inevitably lonely, old age.

The truth of it was that I could no more have spoken that word than I could have flown to the moon. Because that time and that place ordained that I had never detected the least sign that having heard it Ford wouldn't despise me. He had, I suddenly gathered, been at least as guarded during all those months as I had myself. He was all surfaces. Even his sincerity was an act. Not an act of deceit, but an act in the sense of something an actor says or does in the course of a portrayal. That's what our lives were that few months. Performances. If there was one thing that could have made that parting even more unbearable—well, that afternoon I found it impossible to see how I could live without his good opinion or at least the recollection of it, whatever lies I was compelled to tell to protect it. There are just some risks you don't dare take.

That's what I thought that day, staring after his plane and then staring at that empty sky.

I would learn about risking everything later on and two thousand miles away. There is no way of knowing what lessons Ford learned or how he learned them. How does one apprehend the consciousness of a divine creature?

The Sunday after Belle and Ford left for France, I went to church with Grannie and my sisters as usual. I sensed the twins' absence acutely. With only their parents and grandmother sitting there, the Hopkins family pew seemed desolate as the Gobi Desert. They had made their escape and I must find a way to make mine. Chattanooga was no more home to me than it was to them. I loved my family passionately, but I couldn't let that love hold me hostage. I hated the thought of letting everyone down, but that seemed inevitable. It was just a question of now or later.

As we made our way up the aisle at the end of the service, Francine Murchison's mother, Alice Rae, invited me to their house for Sunday dinner. Grannie's eyes flashed with an excitement I hadn't seen in them for months as she waited to hear me accept. I had hoped to avoid for a while longer the moment when I would disappoint her again, but I wasn't being given any reprieve.

"Thank you so much," I told Alice Rae Murchison just as graciously as I could and making sure to smile as I spoke, "but I'm afraid I won't be able to join you today. I'm not feeling very well."

The light in Grannie's eyes blinked out like someone had turned off a switch.

I didn't set foot in that church again until my sister Ondine's wedding, nearly ten years later.

Interlude

"I'm leaving."

"Of course you are," Uncle Gunnar said, turning the steaks on the grill.

"You aren't surprised?"

"Ask a stupid question," he smiled. "What else were you going to do? Hand me that bowl of marinade, please."

"I seem to remember you insisting that I come home and go to work for you," I told him. "You're in bad shape if you can't recall something that happened just a year ago. Must be all those concussions you got playing football."

"T., you were in no condition to make decisions about your future when the army first turned you loose. You needed family looking out for you. You needed time to pull yourself together."

"I don't feel pulled together."

"Time to take those ears of corn off the grill," he said.

"Aye, aye."

"Let's put it this way. You're a hell of a lot better off than you were. That time I visited you out in Arizona you really gave me a scare."

"Rather not talk about that, thanks," I said.

"That's how much better you are now."

"You're not angry? About me leaving?"

"It's your life."

"I just feel bad about Grannie," I said.

"Mom understands."

"Uh—no, she doesn't."

"She does," he said. "Same way she understands everything else."

"You're going to have to explain that."

"I'm too busy running my empire and plotting my Hollywood career to think about settling down. Tor is too sensitive to get along on his own and too shy to find someone to take care of him yet too stubborn to accept help. Lars is a hopeless mess."

"Sounds like chapters from an unpublished science fiction novel," I said.

"It's not as crazy as you think it is. She makes up these stories for herself because they help her understand things that would make no sense to her otherwise. All women do that. It's one of the main things that makes them different from us. I'm surprised I have to explain it to you."

"I'm not sure I agree. It makes a good theory, but it doesn't sound like Mama at all."

"You're right. Elizabeth was an exception to the rule. She was an exception to most of the rules of womanhood. If you'd been older when she died, you'd understand. But that's my point. She was an exception. Most women are much more comfortable making up stories about the world than actually living in it."

"Just like the ancient cavemen made up stories about gods living in the forests and lakes," I said. "I get it. So what's Grannie's story about me?"

"Belle Hopkins broke your heart and you can't go on living in a place that constantly reminds you of that disappointment."

"You're joking. She has to know better than that."

"You'd better take advantage of it and get out while you can."

Leaving wasn't difficult, even though it included saying goodbye to Grannie and my sisters. Figuring out where to go was the hard part. It didn't seem possible to plot any kind of future until some things had been settled. My only certainty was that I had unfinished business. And so, at least for the time being, there was nothing to do but head for New York. Airplanes reminded me of those nightmare flights across the Pacific. I'd do anything not to get on a plane. Taking the bus had an additional advantage. It meant I could approach the city gradually. It gave me time to gather my wits; to contemplate the past but not get trapped in it.

So I left Chattanooga the way I had arrived, and I relished the symmetry. It was rainy that morning, but the forecast for the eastern United States was sunny.

I couldn't just show up on the doorstep. I had no idea what I'd say. Should I beg for forgiveness or offer it? Should I plead insanity or make that my central accusation? Anyway, whose doorstep was I thinking of?

Contemplating the city through the deeply tinted windows of the bus was like watching a coin spinning in midair, sunlight dancing off both head and tail, the outcome suspended in gravity and light.

Arriving on a muggy early afternoon, I established my headquarters at the Y. Contrary to the expectations I'd been nursing during my journey, time seemed to slow down. I fell into a kind of lassitude, a loss of will. Everything was unresolved but nothing clamored to be settled *right now!* This was all the excuse I needed to put off not only the future but the present. What I lacked, I told myself, was context. History had continued without me. I went to the library.

Catching up on three years worth of the *Times* ate up several days. But it gave me context in spades. All those momentous events. Vladimir missing, presumed dead. That "presumed" was impossible to swallow. The unidentifiable corpse was too convenient. I didn't believe in it for a second and I was sure the feds didn't, either. It didn't explain anything, least of all my dozens of unanswered letters. Even if

Vladimir truly had departed the land of the living, that hadn't happened until I was already back in the States. Had the feds truly intercepted all that mail, or had Vladimir made good on his threat?

No newspaper could answer any of these questions. Another mode of investigation was obviously required.

The loss of Preble and Rancik presented no obstacle. They would never have spoken to me even if they'd been alive. But there were others who might. And how hard could it be to find them? My first stop was obvious. A short subway ride and then a few blocks' walk through the familiar streets.

The building stood behind construction fencing. The windows were completely boarded up. I couldn't manage to be surprised. What better way for Uncle Yevgeny to cover any remaining tracks than by a complete renovation of the property? I was momentarily stymied, however. Whatever work might be in progress was at a standstill that day. There was no one in sight.

I spent three more days chasing down possible sources of information. Carpenter had gone "straight" about a year after I left and was in graduate school in San Francisco. Greenberg was on a kibbutz. Winkelmann had fled to Montreal on receipt of his draft notice. Conte was in jail. Riseley had disappeared without a trace, as had Hutton and Dewes. Browne was said to be living on a commune in Vermont, so drugged out that his claims not to know anything about anything were generally accepted as factual. Sansome was either in Costa Rica or Belize—or perhaps Alaska. Richardson had gone home to St. Louis, married an heiress, and was working in his father's bank, of all bourgeois things. Even that teenaged hustler who had called himself Hank, never actually part of the group but constantly present (more than once in my own bed) had managed to disappear without a trace.

Marytza O'Connor, whom I had considered my best hope, had apparently left the group under much the same sort of cloud as I had only a few weeks after my departure for boot camp. She was said to have moved back to Boston to enter law school. Boston wasn't that far. I could be there in a day. I knew her family. We had always been on good terms. There was no reason to believe she'd refuse talk to me. She'd easily been the sanest one of us. There was nothing stopping me at all.

But the coin seemed to have landed. It had come up tails.

I was traveling light. I had left almost everything in Chattanooga, ready to ship as soon as I settled. But I had Stefano's letters with me. I didn't know how to find him, but I knew how to find Violetta. My years in Manhattan had habituated me to the island almost as well as if I had been a native. But Brooklyn might as well have been Bucharest from all I knew of it.

I rode the subway and then two buses. If time had seemed to slow down before, now it absolutely stood still. I felt like I could die of old age before reaching the return address on those envelopes. But finally I was there. It was a block of shop fronts with, presumably, apartments on the floors above. There was nothing out of the ordinary about the scene I was about to enter. No portentous clouds hovered overhead and no dramatic music played in the background. I had the letters and I had my curiosity.

I found the address with no trouble at all. What I had assumed would prove to be an apartment was a business. Violetta's Tower of Beauty. Of course a woman named Violetta della Torre would have named a beauty parlor after herself. That much I could easily fathom. But the idea that Stefano Fabiani's One True Love could be a beautician was as impossible to imagine as sitting down at a table in a restaurant and being waited on by armadillos. This incongruity was nearly enough to send me back to the bus stop.

But I had come too far not to see it through to the end. And I couldn't accept that neither heads nor tails had won the toss.

Altair

I knew who he was the instant he appeared in the doorway. In the snapshots Stefano had sent from the war everyone looked like a ghost. So that was of little help to me in recognizing him. But Stefano had described him perfectly. "*Un angelo molto muscolare*", "*Occhi triste—molto bello*". His hair was as blond as Stefano had said. More to the point, it was exactly as blond as Stefano *hadn't* said and perhaps hadn't consciously realized. There was no mistaking that shade. It could only be a sign from God, that hair color. His eyes were indeed sad. They were as blue as the Adriatic. His young face was heartbreakingly handsome. Oh, my Stefano—*caro mio*. The nuns had despaired of teaching him poetry. Teaching him anything at all, come to that, though he had a natural talent for arithmetic. They never discovered his talent for poety, the nuns. But I knew it slumbered deep within him, waiting for the right subject to awaken it. And there it was in Stefano's letters when he wrote of this young man.

There are gifts God gives us which we do not discover in elementary school, not even with the holy sisters hovering over us like the heavenly host. And we certainly don't discover them fidgeting in drafty barracks classrooms on desolate army bases as we earn our G.E.D.'s. But the gifts are nevertheless there, waiting. And one day an exquisite young stranger appears in the middle of our jungle, in the middle of our war—not our first wilderness or our first war, far from it, actually. He appears like an angel of light, "*un angelo di luce*". And having seen the vision, we begin to speak in a strange new tongue. It rushes from us like an underground river bursting to the surface, its waters sparkling for the first time ever in the sunlight. When the day finally comes that we sit down to write about the unprecedented event, describe it to our loved one, we write, "Dearest Auntie Violetta, it was like being at the opera."

To anyone but an Italian this would sound ridiculous, or at the very least ironic, but I, Stefano's Auntie Violetta, sitting at my kitchen table reading the letter (The nuns succeeded in one thing at least. His penmanship was irreproachable. Now, finally, he had a topic worthy of it.) I understood. This young man appeared, this very young man standing in the doorway, and in that instant my Stefano became a poet. An angel, indeed. No mere mortal. . .

Obviously not. Still, he was mortal enough. As are we all. Mortals die, and before we do certain things must be experienced in order to complete us. Simple as that.

"I'm looking for Violetta della Torre," the young man said, still half inside, half outside. A Saturday afternoon. Sweltering June. The salon was packed but suddenly silent, more silent even than during a high mass at St. Anselmo's. More silent than at the opera just before the crucial moment unfolds itself and the chorus bursts into song. An expectant silence. There was no mistaking the expectancy of everyone in the room. This was something—what? Worthy of their rapt attention, at least. True, men enter Violetta's Tower of Beauty frequently enough. Husbands checking to see when their wives will be ready to leave, young men of the neighborhood meeting one of my girls for a date, boys making deliveries, even, occasionally, men lost and asking for directions. But not men like this, men who look like they have just stepped off a movie screen or descended from the heavens. Every eye was on him, every tongue silenced in mid-syllable, every ear tuned to the subtlest vibration. Indeed, Stefano's description of the moment of Bentley's arrival in the jungle had been perfect. This arrival, too, was truly like being at the opera.

"I am Violetta della Torre," I said. "How may I be of assistance to you this fine day, good sir?"

Even from across the room, I saw the flicker of surprise and curiosity in his eyes—"*occhi triste*" indeed. They seemed to contain all the tragedies of Shakespeare in them and more, though the alabaster smooth face revealed nothing. I noticed his surprise and curiosity only because I knew to look for it. His assumptions had been as predictable as sunrise.

"My name is Tristan Bentley," he said. "I served with Sergeant Fabiani. In Southeast Asia."

Only then did I move toward him, extending my hand, welcoming him inside. Face to face I saw that his skin was indeed flawless. It was the skin of a young girl. His hair was combed to the side, the line of the part as straight and precise as the blade of a knife, held in place that humid afternoon with just enough pomade to give it a slight sheen. My nose identified the brand, a lesser known one chiefly sold, I believe, in the southern states. I am Violetta della Torre. I know all there is to know about hair, even men's hair. We never touch men's hair here, not even the downy fuzz on the heads of the treasured grandsons of old, old friends when it is time for the very first haircut. Not even when the old, old friends beg, plead, or threaten. No, not even then. It would not be decent. And even if it were, I would never take business away from my second cousin Alfredo in the next block, who I knew would swoon to see this particular head of hair. But still, I, Violetta, know men's hair.

At any second the salon would erupt into rejoicing and pandemonium because everyone there, every last soul, revered the name of Sergeant Stefano Fabiani and knew this young man's name, too; had heard over and over again the story of that miracle of all miracles, the one by which the life of our Stefano had been preserved. But it was not yet time for the celebration. I had things that I must tell this young man first, and he had at least one thing to say to me. So "not yet" I signaled them all with the tone of my voice and the perfection of my posture.

"You must come upstairs, Mr. Bentley," I told him. "I will make tea."

Standing at the kitchen counter, letting the tea steep, I saw him eye the plate of biscotti hungrily. With a physique like his, he must require constant feeding. Who understood such necessities better than I?

"They are for eating, Mr. Bentley," I laughed. "Not for staring at. Please, help yourself. The tea is almost ready."

He turned those sad, brilliant eyes toward me.

"I've done a terrible thing," he said. "I'm ashamed to be here."

"You mean the letters."

He nodded.

I poured the tea. I placed his cup in front of him. I sat down across from him and pushed the plate of biscotti toward him, just another inch.

"These are biscotti, Mr. Bentley, not communion wafers. It is not necessary that you receive absolution before you partake."

He didn't move. Those eyes. My God, those eyes. If he ever learned what to do with them, he would be extremely dangerous. Even now in his innocence they had a power. All the more reason for me to do what must be done and waste no time about it. Those eyes were brimming, almost liquid.

"And really," I continued, "there is nothing for me or anyone else to absolve you of. Your intentions were pure. There can be no possible doubt of it. Certainly not, now that you are here. What other proof could be needed?"

"My intentions," he muttered.

"Yes. Your intentions. You are Protestant, presumably. So for you, I suppose, the intention does not matter, only the deed. What a harsh thing it must be to be judged only by what one does and not by what one feels. Intentions, Mr. Bentley, are everything in a case like this. Stefano had been wounded. He had been evacuated to the hospital. For all you knew he might be dead. And even if his life had been spared, you knew your base could be overrun by the enemy at any time. And him not able to look after his things. In fact, I believe I heard that is exactly what happened. Very soon after you left."

"Twelve hours," he nodded. "I was lucky not to be there."

"What would have happened to the letters if you had not taken charge of them?"

He shrugged.

"You are thinking that this strange woman is trying to be kind. Trying to supply you with a rationalization. You are too hard on yourself."

He shrugged again. It was as Stefano had warned me. He was determined to blame himself.

"You knew the letters were important to him. So you took them for safekeeping. Of all the things that could possibly have happened to them, this was by far the best. Surely you must see it."

"I have no right to expect you to understand that."

"It is absurd to speak of what right one does or does not have and what another person does or does not understand in the same sentence," I told him. "Under such circumstances, during wartime, such fine moral distinctions simply aren't reasonable. Only a fool would think so. Or a madman. Even a Jesuit would agree with me, so you might as well. Anyway, if your intentions were not of the best, you would never have come here. You would not be facing me now at my own kitchen table. This much is obvious. So please eat."

"I have them right here," he said. "In my bag. I've brought them back to you."

"You have read them?"

"Certainly not," he said, beginning to blush.

So he had tried. Well, what of that? It proved his humanity. That was the significance of the act. And it was significant. He might look like an angel, might have been mistaken for one more than once, but for the task I was to set before him only a man of flesh and blood would suffice. So it was significant that he had tried to read the letters and it was good. There had never been any threatening intention, and there had never been any risk. It would have taken a miracle, even for an angel of light, to decipher them, written as they were in such an obscure Italian dialect. Most Italians in America had come originally from the south, from Sicily or from the region around Naples. But our family came from the far north. Practially Austria. I could speak and understand the dialects of my neighbors and in-laws, but my own, the one in which I wrote to Stefano, was Greek to them. And how could Bentley, how could anyone, have resisted his curiosity about my Stefano? Who, as anyone with a soul could understand knowing the story and seeing the young man now, was Mr. Bentley's destiny.

"Stefano is my nephew," I said, ready to tell my story now that he had eaten three biscotti. Eating two biscotti is good manners. Any decent human being knows this. Eating three shows true commitment. Eating three biscotti indicated clearly that Mr. Bentley was prepared to hear whatever I had to tell him, that he was sufficiently engaged in our *tete-a-tete* that I need have no fear my story might fall on insensitive, unappreciative ears.

God in heaven, those eyes, that hair, that face. Let alone the rest of him. There was no hope for either of them unless I did what must be done. That is how opera works. The plot must be propelled forward by whatever means the drama necessitates. Father Ferelli would never understand. But does any priest truly understand the matters of the heart? Much less the flesh? Unless he is a priest who is well on the way to turning his back on his vocation, no. And in that case he wouldn't need to be told, he would guess. He would guess and understand and I wouldn't need to defend my actions, or even confess them. Opera and the church are in the same business, that of redeeming lost souls. That they go about the task in such radically different ways is one of the glories of creation. What civilized person could do without either of them?

"Stefano Fabiani is my nephew, my brother Antonio's child. My only brother Antonio's only child, orphaned not long after his birth, and I, his widowed auntie, raised him. You did not know these things."

"No," Bentley said.

"It is of no consequence that he did not tell you. Stefano is a very private person. That is all. Really, you should attach no significance to it beyond that. None whatever. It is no secret, yet there is no shame in not having been told. So, we were a small family. Very small. Mama, Papa, Antonio, and Violetta, the little sister. Papa was a longshoreman. You know what that is?"

"Yes," Bentley nodded.

"Very hard work is what it is. Very, very hard. But Papa was a strong man. A huge man. Strong, huge, gentle, and so, so patient. He was a saint, truly. He had come from Italy looking for a better life. To this day I could not tell you, Mr. Bentley, whether or not he believed he had found it. He worked very hard every day but never got rich. He never learned to speak English well. But he raised two children who were never cold and never went to bed hungry like they would have in Italy. So he must have been satisfied at least, and he always seemed happy enough. And because he always seemed happy it was easy for the rest of us to be happy, too, living here in this very apartment."

"Here?"

"Yes, Mr. Bentley, here. I know it doesn't seem like much."

"That's not what I meant," he protested. "I'm just surprised that after all this time. . ."

"Indeed," I said. "It is somewhat surprising when you think about it. It is like those families in Europe who live in the same castle for centuries on end."

"Please," he said, "you misunderstood."

"No, my young friend," I told him. "I don't misunderstand you at all. It is you who misunderstand me. I simply make a little joke. To show you, you see, that you have nothing to fear from Stefano's harmless little old Auntie Violetta. That is all."

"All right."

"It is true, you know. No one living under this roof will ever harm you. Understand?"

He nodded, but I was not sure I had gotten my point across.

"Now my brother Antonio was the handsomest boy in the world. Everyone who ever met him recognized it. It was undisputed fact. Like—like gravity is not arguable, yes? And as he grew toward manhood, it was clear that he would be at least as huge and strong as Papa and probably more. He was not brilliant in school, mind you. He didn't have the head for that. I do not mean to imply that he was stupid. The subjects at school simply did not speak to him. But he never gave the nuns anything to complain of. He might not have been smart but he was good and kind and obedient. Diligent at his lessons, even though he found the material hard. And oh, so dear to me he was, to his little sister Violetta. His shy, quiet little sister. You wouldn't believe it to hear me now, but in those days I rarely opened my mouth. I spoke only when required to by Mama or the nuns. But shy as I was and unlikely as it seemed, I had many friends. Many, many friends. I had more friends than I knew what to do with. But I was not stupid. I knew which of those friends were true friends and which were pretend friends who only liked me because it provided them with an opportunity to visit our home and be near to Antonio. That is how it is in families sometimes. It is unfair, of course, but God in His mercy ordains it and we shy, quiet sisters accept. But Mama and Papa were very wise, even though neither of them ever learned to read, and they knew how to make it into a joke so that I never felt sad about it. And Antonio was always so kind to me that nothing else mattered. So kind, so gentle, so strong, so handsome. What more could a little girl have asked for in a big brother, I ask you?"

"I have sisters," Bentley said. "Four of them. Younger than me."

"Then you know."

"I'm not sure I've ever been that good a brother to them."

"Of course you have, Mr. Bentley. I'm sure that if they were here they would agree with me."

He shrugged. It was as if he were incapable of believing anything good about himself. That was what lay behind them—*occhi triste*.

"Trust me on this, please. And eat more biscotti. You will please let me know when you are ready for more tea."

He got up from the table and poured himself another cup. Then he brought the kettle over to the table and filled mine. I was astonished by this. I, Violetta della Torre, have never seen a man wait on himself like that. And certainly not on a woman. Except for one man, that is. One man, Luciano della Torre. My lucky star. He was lucky only for me. He had no luck himself, but that was different story. Stefano—he doesn't count because I trained him to do it. But no other man. And I took this for a sign. I didn't need a sign particularly. I already knew what I knew. I knew what needed to be done, and I knew I was going to do it. I had the strength of the saints and angels in me, and I had no fears at all even though I knew there were many, many among my friends and neighbors and customers and fellow worshippers at St. Anselmo's who would insist that what I was planning to do was the gravest of sins. I did not need a sign, no; but it was a comfort nevertheless to have it revealed to me in that small way that I was right and they were wrong and that Bentley's happiness, beautiful, exquisite young Bentley, and Stefano's happiness were in the right hands. The only possible hands, really, because who else could God have chosen for the task He Himself had ordained?

"By the time Antonio had finished sixth grade it was clear that there was nothing for him to gain by staying in school, so Papa got him a job down at the docks. You should have seen how quickly he grew up after that. We had thought of him as big and strong and handsome before, Mama and I, but he just shot up and broadened out, and his voice grew deeper and he had to start shaving, and people seeing Papa and him on the street would call out, 'Hey, Pietro. . .'—that was Papa's name, Pietro—'I didn't know you had a kid brother.' Papa loved it when they said that. And Antonio loved it, too. It became the family joke. Antonio was Papa's little brother who had just come over from the old country to join us. Of course, when the people of the neighborhood said all this, they said it in Italian, you understand?"

"Yes," Bentley nodded.

"So, there was one girl in particular. Not one of my friends. Not from the neighborhood, actually. She was from several blocks away. She was the most beautiful girl any of us had ever seen. Really exquisite. She was not one of us, you understand. Not Italian. Her family was Finnish. I have no idea how a family of Finns ever got to that part of Brooklyn. It is as much of a mystery to me now as it was all those years ago. But there it is. Among us there was this amazingly beautiful girl. You would see her on the street every now and then and you would rub your eyes to make sure you were not dreaming. And you would think to yourself 'she is just like a girl in the movies', or 'she is just like a princess', or 'she must be an angel sent from heaven to reveal to us what true beauty looks like'. She was the talk of the neighborhood even though she was not actually from the neighborhood. Boys of the neighborhood followed her around and of course the girls of the neighborhood were jealous and began making up stories about her. Bad stories, terrible stories, you understand?"

"Yes," Bentley nodded.

"How else were they to defend themselves? And they had to defend themselves from her. A girl like that could annihiliate you with a word, a glance. It was inexcusable, yes. Yet you must excuse them because such beauty as she possessed is a terrible power, especially in the service of, well, never mind. You shall hear what it was in the service of."

I had to give Bentley credit for his patience. He couldn't possibly see the point of my story and young men of his age are so easily bored, but he never acted like he was losing interest and he never fidgeted and he didn't sneak any glances at his wristwatch as if he wanted me to think he was expected somewhere else and must leave soon. He just listened. He listened silently. Really, I found his silence quite surprising. It was not silence of the voice, merely. It was silence of the spirit. The only silence of course that truly means "I'm listening". There he was, a young man who had seen war and heaven only knows what else, a young man accustomed to tumult of all kinds, sitting quietly drinking tea and listening to an old woman ramble.

"They gave her a nickname, actually, those girls," I said. "They called her *La Puttana Svedese.* The 'Swedish' was because of her blond hair of course. And because up to that point we knew nothing about her or her people. She was a beautiful blond princess from a fairy tale, and Swedish seemed to explain all that. So that was it. *La Puttana Svedese.* Mama and Papa were furious about this. 'How can people talk about her that way?' Mama would ask. 'She's just a young girl like any other. It's unjust to call her such a name. It's evil.' So you see, when Antonio started going around with her, Mama and Papa were very, very careful to be kind to her. To make up for the bad manners of all the neighbors. And because they loved Antonio so much and it soon became obvious that he was deeply in love with her. Deeply, deeply in love. But unfortunately, the girls of the neighborhood had been right about her from the first, though they had no way of knowing it. It had just been jealousy and spite, but in some strange way they had hit on the truth about her. Which was that she truly did have the heart of a whore. Soon she refused to have anything to do with Antonio because he didn't make enough money on the docks. That's exactly what she told him. 'Get another job. Find a way to make more money so that you can give me the things that I want.' And what could poor Antonio do? He was in love, after all. It made him sad. More than sad, it made him desperate. Mama tried to tell him that no decent girl would ever say such a thing and he must not mind it so much but instead should put her out of his heart. And Papa told him he must listen to Mama because she was unquestionably right. But I don't know if Antonio could ever have put that girl out of his heart. Even if fate had not intervened, you understand? I am telling you, you see, that perhaps there never was any escape for Antonio. Perhaps what happened was what had to happen, sad as it is to consider a thing like that. Sometimes things are because they must be—that is all. It is important never to forget that. Sometimes things are because they must be. In a case like that, no other explanation is required.

"Now there were men around the docks all the time looking for boys like Antonio. Yes, I call him a boy. He was still only seventeen at the time this happened. And I'm sorry to have to tell you, but no matter how big and strong and handsome you are, when you're seventeen you're still a boy. Because 'boy' is not in your arms and shoulders, it is in your heart, right? And the heart changes from boy to man in its own time. There are many men who are never more than boys, and this is why. Well, these men, these particular men, were boxing promoters. Antonio knew nothing about boxing, but he was enormous by then. He was a giant. That was all those men needed to know about him. They said they had people who would teach Antonio everything that was necessary about the sport and that he would surely become a sensation. Papa and Mama didn't like it at all. But to start, Antonio only had to go to their gym in the evenings after work to train, and they gave him a little allowance and bought his equipment for him, and it didn't seem so bad.

"Mama cried every time he came home with a new scratch or bruise. And believe me, there were plenty of those. But Antonio just laughed. And when Mama was really upset, Papa would show off his scars from working on the docks and tell her how silly she was being. Because each of Antonio's little marks—that's what Papa called them, 'little marks'—was worth a lot more money than Papa had ever been paid for his injuries. Finally, several months later, Antonio got his first booking. Oh, he was so excited to have a bout on the card. Papa and his friends all planned to go to see him fight, but Mama absolutely refused. I wanted to go too, but Mama wouldn't let me. Boy, did she ever put her foot down. Usually you could hardly hear her around the house, so soft spoken she was. But that time? Jesus, Mary, and Joseph, you should have heard her screech. I had never heard her like that. Papa was afraid she had lost her mind.

"The night finally came, and off they went, Antonio, Papa, Papa's friends, and about a hundred boys from the neighborhood. Mama and I stayed home. Mama wouldn't even listen to the radio. I don't mean that the fight was on the radio, you understand? It was a local bout, far too unimportant to be on the radio. But for something to do while they were all gone, you know? Listen to some music to help us not be so anxious. But Mama wouldn't. She lit candles and she prayed. I tried to get her to drink some tea and nibble on some biscotti. But no. She was certain her baby Antonio would be killed. Or scarred for life at the very least.

"How they all laughed at her when they got home. Antonio had won by a knockout in the second round. He was a hero. There wasn't a mark on him. He was as beautiful walking back in the door as he had been walking out. More beautiful, really, because he was a winner then. And being a winner transfigures a boy like Antonio. He was just beaming.

"After that there were more and more fights. He won every one of them, and there was money. Oh, the money he brought home. He would throw piles and piles of bills on the kitchen table in front of Mama. He would laugh and throw that money up in the air and let it fall down all over the living room like confetti. But nothing would stop Mama's crying. Papa was proud, but Mama just cried.

"And that girl, that *puttana*. He bought her gifts. Gift upon gift. He bought all of us gifts. He bought Mama new pots and pans for the kitchen. New dishes for the table. New lamps and rugs for the living room. And he bought Papa a new watch and sooner or later a Buick. It was a used Buick but it was very nice. We had never had a car before. Papa had to go get driving lessons. He and Antonio both did. Antonio bought himself a little Chevrolet roadster. You should have seen the two of them, Papa with the Buick and Antonio with that sporty little Chevrolet. They would take us for rides around the city on Sunday afternoons. Oh, it was lovely. Those were wonderful days. At least Papa and I thought they were wonderful. Mama never stopped worrying. Sooner or later her Antonio, her beloved Antonio, would be killed or at the very least crippled for life, and how would we stand the sadness then?

"Then Antonio asked the girl to marry him. And miracle of miracles, she said yes. It wasn't a very big wedding because times were still hard. But mostly because she wasn't an Italian girl. Her family had no idea how things were done. So it was a small wedding and there were lots of hard feelings because all kinds of people thought they should have been invited, and Mama just hung her head. She stayed in the house all the time for the shame of it. She wouldn't even go to Mass at St. Anselmo's because she was so mortified. The *puttana* just laughed.

"You notice, Mr. Bentley, that I have never told you her name?"

"Yes," he said.

"And I never will. I never speak that name aloud. All these many years since the tragedy happened, and it has never passed my lips. It is an evil name because it is the name of an evil woman, and a decent woman such as I could never dirty herself by speaking a name like that. You understand?"

"Yes."

"You will hear the name when Stefano speaks it to you."

"*If he speaks it to you*," I added silently. Really, that would be the ultimate test.

"I understand," Bentley said.

Did he?

"Well, soon enough that girl, that wife of Antonio who had so dishonored our family by the way she had gotten married—not even in a church, mind you, just standing before a judge—she was expecting a child. And really, you know, that should have been enough to cheer Mama up. To make her take an interest in life again. Because what is more important to a woman than a grandchild, Mr. Bentley? Nothing, that's what. Nothing in the universe. So it should have been a happy time, getting ready for that baby. But Mama would have nothing of it. Nothing at all. She had nothing against the child. But she had everything against the mother. 'Just you watch, Violetta,' she would say to me. 'Just you watch. Sooner or later she will show her true colors again just like she did about the wedding. And then my Antonio will be sorry. And it will be too late.'

"Antonio kept fighting and winning and making more and more money. He and that girl had gotten a beautiful apartment, and he wanted us to move into the same building to live downstairs from them. Papa and I were so excited. It was a beautiful building on a very nice street, and I could hardly wait. Antonio had taken Papa and me to see the apartment he had picked out for us, and oh, such a beautiful bedroom I was to have. It was a young girl's dream of a bedroom. I was wild over it. But Mama refused to leave this place. She and Papa fought and fought about it. Oh, those fights. They were horrible. Horrible, I say to you. Fighting like the end of the world. My huge, strong giant of a Papa and that tiny little woman yelling at him and stamping her feet. And when she got really wound up she'd throw something at him. A plate or something. Oh, the crashes. The broken glass I had to clean up. And Papa being bossed around like that. Truly, it was like the end of the world. How else could Mama and Papa have fought so terribly? Finally we gave up on the idea of moving into their building. And do you know, I think that girl was happy about it. I don't believe she ever wanted us living so near to them. I think she would never have been happy with us around. As long as they lived over there in that beautiful building on that lovely street, she could pretend that Antonio's people were wealthy people. I know that's the kind of thing she was telling everyone. But with us around she could never have gotten away with it.

"Finally the baby came. Antonio had a bout that very night and he showed up at the hospital with a little bandage over one eye where he'd taken a punch. He had won his bout handily, but he'd gotten a little cut, you see? And it made Mama frantic. Waiting for the baby to come and then seeing Antonio like that. She became so upset that she actually passed out. The nurses had to find a bed for her and a doctor had to come and examine her and make sure she wasn't seriously ill. But it was just her nerves. And then the baby came. They called him Stefano, after Mama's father back in the old country, and she finally came back to herself. Oh, how she loved that baby. The minute she laid eyes on him, all was forgiven. But she never did go see Antonio in one of his fights. The girl, she went to every one of them except when she was giving birth that night. Not two weeks after Stefano was born she was off to see Antonio in another of his fights. She left Stefano with us that evening. Her own mother wouldn't have anything to do with Stefano. She hated us all because we were filthy Italians, so the girl couldn't leave Stefano with her. But Mama was in heaven. She wouldn't let me listen to the radio because she was afraid it would wake the baby, but at least I didn't have to spend those nights lighting candles with her and praying."

"Shall I make more tea, Mr. Bentley?"

"I wish you wouldn't go to so much trouble."

"Hospitality is never any trouble," I told him. "Hospitality receives as much as it gives away. If you would like more tea or something more substantial than those biscotti, you must say so."

"I'm fine, really," he insisted.

It wasn't just that Bentley was gorgeous to look at. His manners were beautiful as well. His demeanor was so quiet and thoughtful. Dignified, really. He seemed strong yet at the same time vulnerable. A light, a pure soft glow, seemed to emanate from deep inside him. Stefano had said it himself, and it was true. *Un angelo di luce*. Really, his mother had done a wonderful job. Staring down at him from heaven—because Stefano had told me the poor woman was dead—she must be profoundly gratified at what she saw, must be proud, justifiably proud, of her accomplishment in raising such a son. And his grandmothers must be beside themselves that he was out on his own like this without a woman to take care of him. So strong, so wise, yet such an innocent. How could he be expected to find his own way? Some woman or other must step in. And who better than I, who knew so well the other side of the story?

My duty could not have been clearer. And I have never backed down from doing my duty. No one who has ever known me could accuse me of that, despite my many flaws and failings. I did my duty then just as I had done it with my poor darling Luciano.

Downstairs, as we talked, preparations were being made for the celebration. I knew they had begun the minute I escorted Mr. Bentley upstairs. I knew exactly what dishes were simmering on what stovetops, baking in what ovens; what party dresses were being ironed, what suits and ties were being aired out. I knew which young women of the neighborhood were already planning to set their caps at him for his beauty and his muscles even though he was not Italian. And good luck to them, for such a thing was not his destiny. He of course did not know any of this and he probably would not have believed it if I had told him. He would certainly be surprised when we went back down the stairs and he walked into a full scale Italian feast in his honor. Surprised and embarrassed. Because there was one thing I was absolutely certain of. He had no understanding whatever of the significance of what he had done for us in saving Stefano's life. Stefano was not just any man and he was not only my nephew. He belonged to us all, everyone in the neighborhood. And that made Bentley a neighborhood hero of the greatest magnitude, indeed, in a class with Stefano himself. There's destiny for you.

"Well," I told him, "soon it came. The opportunity Antonio and Papa had been waiting for. A bout against a truly worthy opponent. A man all New York had heard of. If Antonio could defeat him, his fortune would be made. We had seen nothing yet. This was the big moment. There was rejoicing all over the neighborhood at the prospect. Antonio redoubled his efforts in his training. He took weeks off from his job at the docks to devote himself entirely to his preparations. He seemed transformed. Each day stronger, each day more handsome, each day more confident.

"Each day hungrier. He lived with that girl in that fine apartment in that beautiful building, but still he took all his meals with us. He trusted no one else to feed him. Only Mama's cooking was good enough to ensure his continued health and strength. Oh, the mountains of food he could work his way through. I have never seen anything like it to this very day. And Mama slaving away in this tiny kitchen, the happiest of smiles on her face. This was what she lived for, to fill the stomach of her beloved son. She even returned to services at St. Anselmo's. The family's honor had been restored. She could once again expect to be treated with respect. All was well and all would be well because surely the angels were living among us and doing their blessed work, protecting and guiding and making all things possible for her Antonio and for his most wonderful son the gorgeous baby Stefano. Mama was even kind to the girl on the few occasions that we saw her. Truly, I never saw my mother happier than in those weeks before the big fight.

"And Papa? Well, that smile on Papa's face never wavered, not a flicker, until that last afternoon before the fight. By then he knew what none of us did and he was terrified, broken hearted already. Because the promoters had told Antonio that he must throw this fight. There was very big money involved. The betting, you understand? He must throw this fight, just this one. They had promised him that if he agreed to take this one solitary loss they would give him the world. They could do that. And really, they said, after this one loss all the subsequent victories would be even sweeter and the rewards even greater. This one loss would somehow make the rest seem even more miraculous. Papa knew all this, but he said nothing. He sat in his Buick weeping because he didn't want us to see it. We only learned of it afterward, when everything was lost. But really, what good would it have done if he had shouted it from the roof of the building? If he had called on God and all his angels to help Antonio it would have changed nothing. What was to happen was already ordained. Nothing on earth or in heaven could stop it.

"The promoters had told Antonio to throw the fight, but Antonio did not throw the fight. He beat his opponent, a man who had never been defeated, by a knockout in the second round. That was Antonio's trademark. Always a knockout in the second round. It was a sensation. It was a miracle. It was a tragedy. Because not even a man as big and strong as Antonio was big enough to stand up to them.

"They had him ambushed and beaten as punishment. He fought back, of course, but there were too many of them, and they were armed. It wasn't supposed to go as far as it did, but the violence of his resistance surprised and frightened the attackers, and he was gravely injured. He was only supposed to be frightened into submission. The promoters had so much invested in him. And they were no fools. They had done the same kind of thing dozens of times before to dozens of young men. It was just another part of the business. But they had never before tried to bring such a man as my brother Antonio to heel. I am not certain that they realized such a young man as my brother Antonio had ever existed. At least in modern times. In ancient days, in the times of the heroes, certainly, though it was exceptional even then. But they were not educated men. They had no knowledge of that. They didn't even know who Antonio's heroes were, so how could they have predicted his reaction or the nature of the force that would be required to subdue him?

"We were called to the hospital, but they wouldn't allow Mama or me to see him. Only Papa and the priest. That is how bad it was. We sat in the waiting room and wept and prayed. The doctor came and told us that all might be well, that Antonio might possibly live, but that he would never be the same again. His injuries were too severe. In time he might walk again; with great patience and much help he might even learn to speak again; but he would be helpless. We would have to care for him like a child has to be cared for, for as long as he lived.

"And we would have done it, Mr. Bentley. We would have done it. I swear to you by the Almighty. As He and His angels are my witnesses, we would have done whatever we had to do to give Antonio whatever sort of life he might have had."

"I understand," Bentley said.

I watched as a single tear ran down his cheek. He didn't reach up to wipe it away. He allowed that single, exquisite tear to fall however it might, as gravity and the Good Lord willed. And that precious tear told me more than his words that he did truly understand. His soul had been touched by some tragedy I knew nothing of, and because of it he understood all tragedy.

"So it was a mercy, really, when, on the third day, Antonio had a massive seizure of the brain and left us. It was God's mercy. I will always believe that. Though Mama didn't see it that way.

"The girl brought Stefano to us. She didn't say it but we knew that she was never coming back for him. She was going away to be the woman of one of the promoters and there was no room in that life for a baby of any kind, not even one as divine as Stefano. Certainly not the baby of a discredited boxer. A few years later there was a fight. She was with a different boyfriend by then, but I am quite certain it was the same fight that she always had with her men. Because that's the kind of woman she would always be. At least until she grew old and lost her looks and could no longer find a man to have such a fight with. In the fight she fell and hit her head. At least that was the story they told about it in the newspapers. Perhaps it was true and perhaps it wasn't, but at any rate she was dead.

"A few months after we lost Antonio, Mama died. They said it was an anyeurism in the brain, but I knew and Papa knew that it was nothing more or less than a broken heart. So that left the three of us, Papa and Stefano and me. As small a family as you could imagine. But Stefano, that divine little Stefano, brought joy back into this home of ours. He gave us a reason to live and he forced us to find the strength to live it. And we did as well as we could for as long as we could. But life is never easy, and anything can happen at any time. Papa died in an accident on the docks that would never have happened if Antonio had been working at his side, but at least Papa died quickly. He never even made it to the hospital. By then it was the war, and I was able to find a good job in a defense plant. I made artillery shells, and they paid me very well. Every now and then some girl I worked with would blow herself up, but I was too careful for that. I had Stefano to take care of, and I couldn't let an accident like that happen. I couldn't let him be orphaned. So I called on all my strength and all my cunning.

"Yes, Mr. Bentley, cunning. I am smart, clever, calculating, brilliant, Machiavellian even, because I have had to be. I was a young, single woman of very little education and hardly any understanding of the world, and there was this child, this beautiful, glorious, divine child who had been entrusted to me, and I had to be all those things and more. And I never blew myself or anyone else up except the Germans and Japanese who were the intended targets of those artillery shells, and I kept Stefano safe and healthy and warm in the winter. And he was never hungry, and to the extent that it was in my power to make it so, he was never sad.

"I had married my Luciano after Papa died, but he went to the war almost immediately. And thus I never bore him the child he should have had. My Stefano was my consolation.

"The war ended and the defense plants closed. And with the men coming back from overseas jobs were very hard to find. So I took the money I had saved, because I had foreseen all those things, and I got myself trained and I opened my salon. And I did everything within my power to take care of my Stefano until the day inevitably came that I knew the job had become too much for me. He was too big, too strong, too handsome, too charming. He had his father's physique and his mother's beauty, God help him. God help us both. And the whole neighborhood knew him and saw what he was becoming and every day I could see more clearly the tragedy beginning to unfold once again. For the world either hates strength and beauty and wants only to destroy anyone they appear in, or it desires strength and beauty and will stop at nothing to possess whomever they appear in. So unless I could find a way to save him, my Stefano was doomed.

"I couldn't allow it, Mr. Bentley. I had to stop it. I thought about it and prayed about it. I was only one small, weak woman, and the whole world was against me and there was no other way. I had to send him to a place where such a horrible thing could not happen again. Not to him. I knew how dangerous it was. I knew that a thousand, thousand things might happen to him there, and that I would be powerless to stop any of them. But as long as he was not here where the original tragedy had taken place, he might be saved from repeating it. I trusted in that because it was all I had to trust in besides Almighty God Himself, and I enlisted the aid of our priest, Father Rodrigo, and we took him to the recruiters and lied to them about his age. Stefano was big enough and strong enough that they did not doubt what we said for a moment. And he was obedient enough not to question what I was doing as we signed his enlistment papers.

"Twenty years, Mr. Bentley. Twenty years he served in the military, and every day I prayed for his protection. Every day I went to St. Anselmo's and lit candles. And every day he was safe. Every single day. Until that one day, Mr. Bentley, that terrible day I had always dreaded, when my prayers were no longer enough and the candles were no longer enough and my faith was no longer enough and God's back, for whatever reason, was turned for just that single, horrible instant. And when that moment came that I had been fighting to prevent for all those years, there you were my divine, my beautiful, my brave, my strong, my pure Mr. Bentley, there you were—his guardian angel, you see, you understand?"

"No," he said, looking into my soul with those eyes of his, those eyes of infinite sadness, and shaking that exquisite, perfect head of his ever so slowly. "It wasn't like that at all. I was just doing my job. Any other corpsman would have done the very same thing."

Which, I thought, proved my point exactly.

"We will go downstairs together now," I told him, once I had had a few moments to compose myself. I had already warned him what to expect. "We will go downstairs, and I know I do not have to tell you to be gracious to them all."

"I'll just leave the letters here on the table," he said.

"You will not," I said.

"But. . ."

"They are not mine, Mr. Bentley. They are Stefano's. I wrote them to him, I mailed them to him. They are his. You surely cannot leave them here with me. If they are to be returned to him, it is your hands he must receive them from."

POLARIS

My birthday. My twenty-fourth. The day gave no impression it might be an auspicious one. It had been raining off and on most of the afternoon. There was one of those San Francisco chills in the air that made you think of the city as an arctic capital. The Thanksgiving turkeys were long gone except for leftovers lurking here and there in people's freezers. As I walked around the city, signs of Christmas were inescapable. Unsurprisingly, my grandmother's demands had grown more insistent as the ultimate holiday loomed. Thanksgiving had been dreadful without me. Worse than dreadful. How could I think of deserting my family at Christmas? Over the months since my departure from Chattanooga she had sustained the belief that my sojourn in San Francisco was an extended vacation. Now it was time to get back to real life. My uncles had kept a place for me at Ingebrittsen Jaguar-Volvo. My sisters missed me terribly and couldn't wait for my return. My grandfather wasn't mentioned, but I knew I was supposed to imagine him sitting on the front porch wearing his Swedish fisherman's hat and smoking his Swedish fisherman's pipe, looking taciturn and scanning the horizon for signs of my approach.

The subtext of every letter she wrote was "I have girls lined up." A whole slew of them, I was certain. She wasn't about to allow another fiasco to occur like the one with Belle Hopkins. She still thought Belle's treatment of me and my resulting disappointment and humiliation were what had propelled my flight. What she was saying was, "get back here and get to work. I have to have great-grandchildren." She was falling behind too many of her friends in that ultimate matriarchal sweepstakes. I knew that as mild mannered as she was, she was as competitive as my uncles Lars and Tor in the wrestling ring. And I knew for a fact that she could be pushed too far. That was true of every woman who ever lived.

My birthday. Even in earliest boyhood I had never been able to celebrate it without soul searching. But that stereotypically gloomy day I was especially pensive. I had finally realized that I would never know for certain whether Violetta della Torre was a prophetess or a loony. Perhaps more than either of those, she resembled one of those oracles of ancient Greece, whose pronouncements, though comprehensive with regard to future events, were too cryptic for any mere mortal to decipher. Thus tragedy and good fortune were equally likely and equally unexpected. Which meant that in my still unenlightened state I was at least in good company. In any case, it no longer seemed to matter whether I could depend on her utterances for guidance or not. They were all I had to go on. On my own I would never feel capable of anything more than survival on the most rudimentary level. I would certainly never consider myself worthy of anyone's love. I couldn't talk myself into or out of anything. But it was time to take some definite action, if only to be able to figuratively look Grannie Ingebrittsen in the face. It was time to rise, to emerge from this willful suspension of animation. To leave the cocoon, whether in the form of butterfly or moth, and take wing.

It was time for nothing less than a leap of faith.

I had been in San Francisco nearly six months. In all that time nothing had happened either to dissuade me from or encourage me toward the objective Violetta had described. I had the same questions I'd brought with me when I arrived. I knew no more nor less about who I was or what I wanted. All those days since might have been one day. All those nights might have been one night.

It had either been a waste, I thought, or a penance.

I was not in love. That was the one thing I was certain of. I had been in love before, and this was nothing like any of those times. This was completely different. This was—I had no idea what it was. I couldn't begin to describe it except in the most existential of terms. And until this conundrum was solved, I considered myself incapable of setting a course for the rest of my life. I couldn't imagine what lay on the other side of that night's visit. I was like a tribesman wondering what lay on the other side of the huge body of water he'd found obstructing his path. There was only one way to discover it.

I knew what would happen when I got to his house. Stefano would invite me inside. I'd give him the letters. We'd down a couple of beers, reminisce, promise to stay in touch, and I'd leave. That's what would happen. That's all that would happen. It would take an hour. Perhaps an hour and a half, depending on his mood and whatever else he might have planned for his evening. I knew it would be no more significant than that, so why was I dreading it so much? Why did it seem so daunting?

What was there about the prospect of an anticlimax that was so paralyzing?

I wrapped Stefano Fabiani's letters from Violetta della Torre safely in plastic against the damp. I had shaved that morning, but I shaved again. That morning a barber in Chinatown had trimmed my hair with the care of a diamond cutter. I greased it into place more securely than usual, against that same damp. I wore my best jeans. My boots were immaculate. My crewneck was brand new and freshly laundered. It fitted me like skin. My black leather motorcycle jacket was spotless. I slipped the bundle of letters inside it, snugged against my chest. It was almost as if my heart was beating directly against those letters. How I had agonized over them. The hours of frustration. The sleepless nights obsessed by the secrets they contained. And finally my astonishment the moment Violetta introduced herself. It had never occurred to me that those letters could have been written by anyone but a lover. The possibility that the most spectacular man I had ever encountered might have no one to receive love letters from had never occurred to me. Since that night in Brooklyn I had been back through them. I still had no idea what they said, but I was sure of one thing. The word for "aunt", one of the few Italian words I recognized, never once appeared on those flimsy pages. She had signed each and every letter with her initial only. My misunderstanding had been more profound than ridiculous.

"Listen, Mr. Bentley," she said that night as I was leaving the feast she had organized in my honor. The next day I would get on a bus for San Francisco. I had already decided that much. "It is all written beyond the stars in the great book of life. Everything must be as has been ordained. Simple as the stars themselves. And as unmoving. You must never forget that. Promise me."

"Sure," I said, more dubious by the moment. What could an utterance like that possibly mean?

"Truly," she insisted. "The only proof you need is in your names. Stefano, the disciple whose devotion to Our Lord remained steadfast even as the stones rained down on him. And Tristan, the sad knight who died for love. Devotion until death. Both of you, you see? You must."

The glint in her eyes was otherworldly. I didn't know who I should be more frightened for, her or myself.

I took a succession of increasingly deserted buses from the Tenderloin to the foot of his block in Eureka Valley. I had seen that name on the map and taken note of it. Perhaps that Eureka would prove as momentous as Archimedes' had. On the other hand, sometimes a coincidence was just that.

"'Give me a lever long enough'," I muttered, "'and a place to stand. And I shall move the Earth'."

Old Archy had said it without irony, but I couldn't manage that.

As I trudged up the hill the mist collected on my jacket. It shone metallically as I moved through the glow of streetlights. Finally I stood in front of the place, that Tudor cottage behind its wall of red brick and inky black wrought iron. To swing open the gate, go up the flagstone walk meandering among bare rosebushes, ring the bell. Or to walk on by. Really, it wasn't a choice any more than breathing was. But I waited for a while in case of a belated sign.

Which, just as I had expected, failed to materialize. All I knew was I was not in love. Violetta had never once said the word, and even if I couldn't trust my own instincts there was the possibility, slim certainly but undeniable, that in that solitary respect she had known what she was talking about.

Meanwhile, I was getting soaked. It wasn't love. I didn't know what it was. Or yes, I did. A leap of faith. I rang the bell.

Stefano opened the door almost immediately, as if he'd been waiting there. As if he'd been expecting someone, though not necessarily me. He was wearing only a pair of sweatpants. Familiar as that body had once been, its immensity stunned me. And it wasn't just his magnitude. I had never seen his body in that condition. When had he started shaving his chest?

Idiot. When he got back stateside and got out of the army. The same time he went back to the gym, where he was obviously a regular these days. Before, he had been remarkable. Now he was indescribable.

In the boonies he'd kept the hair of his head a quarter inch long. Hell, I'd wielded the clippers myself, many times, because our base had been too small to boast its own barber and too remote from anywhere that did. Now he was professionally styled in a kind of modified Prince Valiant, raven, glossy and luxuriant. The eyes were as I remembered, glinting pale silvery blue, the color of an iceberg viewed by moonlight.

"Bentley."

He growled just my name as he pulled me through the door. Speechless, I reached inside my jacket and brought out the letters. I handed them to him, unable to meet his gaze and hardly connected to the earth. He glanced at them, nodded, and set them on the small hall table. His huge arms closed around me. He buried his nose in my hair and inhaled.

"Exactly the way I imagined it," he grunted, tightening his grasp on me. He seemed to grow larger as we stood there. He was a giant.

"Exactly," he repeated. His voice was like distant thunder.

"Perfect," he said a moment or several years later.

In all my life my heartbeat had never been so rapid or my head so light.

Until that embrace I had doubted everything. Violetta's testimony had been so metaphorical, allusive, esoteric, and clotted with inference and insinuation that its meaning was more or less completely indecipherable. Listening to her had been like reading a passage from one of those verbose, overheated Victorian novels which to modern sensibilities seemed inexcusably coy in their treatment of sex but actually devoted themselves to rhapsodizing on the wonders of passionate but nevertheless chaste friendship. And anyway, what could an Italian beauty parlor owner, a woman in late middle age, possibly know of certain arcane dealings between men? And Stefano's auntie, to boot? Nothing about her made her credible as an authority on what she had implied was to ensue.

But the episode in her kitchen hadn't been the genesis of my doubt. Rather, it ratified and compounded my pre-existing emotional state. I had gone to her expecting to encounter the love of Stefano's life. Until Violetta identified herself, I had no doubt whatever that such a woman existed and that Stefano had dedicated his entire existence to her worship. The woman who had written those letters could be nothing less than the object of all the desires his extravagant masculinity could conceive, and I had to see her with my own eyes. I had to know what kind of creature could inspire that sort of passion in a man like Stefano. Such comprehension was the only power that might enable me to lay my rampaging fantasies to rest.

I required that sort of deliverance because I had been transfixed from the first instant. Arriving in the boonies that afternoon I had felt the heat of his initial glance. That same heat had raged unabated in every succeeding glance, no matter how apparently innocuous. I had felt the fervent weight of his hands on me, casual and non-committal as he had invariably made those touches appear. Directing my movements on patrol, calming and encouraging me as I ministered to the wounded, gruffly comforting me in my own moments of fear and pain, those massive hands, ever businesslike—a surgeon's hands, a mechanic's—had nevertheless spoken volumes. But they could not possibly have said what my heart insisted it heard. Every moment spent in his presence brought a clear impression of the unseen forces raging between us. And unable to credit those impressions, I had exiled myself into perpetual doubt. That doubt was my only defense. It meant the difference between sanity and madness. Not in such a place. Not at such a time. The war and its horrors; the illness, bad climate, terrible food, and unfamiliar surroundings; the long line of missed opportunities and searing disappointments that had led me there left me incapable of dealing with the shocks and terrors I was forced moment by moment to face. And this imponderable and intangible unnamed thing in addition to everything else I couldn't comprehend: it couldn't be real. I was imagining it. I was projecting. I had lost my reason. I no longer had the power to recognize the truth. I was so overwhelmed by him, so enthralled, so enslaved, that I couldn't discern where my desires left off and reality began. Such a thing was impossible. And with a man like that?

No.

But that embrace, hot, fragrant, and most of all relentless, told me that I hadn't been imagining anything. That Violetta had understood far more than I'd been willing to give her credit for. The shock of this realization was almost intolerable, yet the embrace made everything possible. It recreated the world.

He led me by the hand up the stairs to his bedroom. The rest happened without another word passing between us.

I was nearly asleep when he got out of the bed. It was a long time before he came back upstairs.

"Who was that at the door?"

"Some guy."

"Oh?"

"He thought we had a date."

"Did you?"

"Until you showed up. Come on. Get up."

A third time. In the shower. Afterward he toweled me dry, very thoroughly, with firm, precise movements like a man drying a child. Like generations of fathers, uncles, older brothers over centuries. On all continents.

I could hardly stand.

"Get dressed," he said, leading me back into the bedroom.

I pulled on my clothes. I was apparently leaving, but somehow it didn't feel like being banished.

"Don't worry about your hair," he said. "Hair like that, you don't have to do anything to it."

In the garage two Maseratis slumbered like predators in a nighttime zoo, a fire engine red roadster with a black canvas top and a midnight blue sedan. Violetta had spent twenty years investing Stefano's army pay. Here's how he had spent a good sized chunk of it. He unlocked the sedan, and I sank into its wood and leather opulence. It reminded me of Uncle Gunnar's Jaguar, but when Stefano started the engine it growled with an Italian accent.

"Where are we going?"

"Get some dinner. You must be starving."

"Yes."

"Then over to your place. You do have a place, don't you?"

"Yes."

"We'll get your stuff. You're not spending another night under any roof but mine."

No. That's right. He wouldn't ask my opinion.

It didn't feel like love. If anything, it felt bigger. What could you call a thing like that? Was there any human utterance that could adequately label or describe it? Violetta had spoken of destiny and I'd tried my best to ignore her. When she'd said it she'd sounded like a charlatan and I'd refused to be taken in. She'd sounded like a madwoman and I'd pitied her. She'd sounded like an immigrant woman with a faulty command of English, and I'd been certain she meant something else. Anything but what "you are each others' destinies" meant in plain English. Was it possible she'd understood?

We pulled out of the driveway. It was raining. Halos glimmered, hovering ecto-plasmically around the streetlights. The windshield wipers couldn't keep up. Just like Uncle Gunnar's Jaguar.

"You hear me?"

"Roger, sir."

He had spoken to me that way before. My first glimpse of him, that transcendent, vertiginous first glance from which I had never recovered, at that camp deep in the boonies, had given the unmistakable impression of a man in control of everything. He was gargantuan, taller and with more confrontational musculature even than my uncles, who, until that moment, had been the men I measured all others against. This prodigy was wearing nothing but a pair of briefs that afternoon, peering into a small mirror hanging from the branch of a tree and shaving with a straight razor.

"You the new medic?" he growled. There was nothing to indicate his rank. But his authority was unmistakable in his physique, voice, and, most of all, in his eyes.

"Sir," I said. "Bentley, Sir."

"Bentley, huh?"

Everything started with that look.

"Sir."

"Right," he said and went back to shaving. "Stick with me, Bentley. Stay right with me unless ordered otherwise. Do whatever I tell you the minute you hear my voice. Do that and I just may get you through your hitch."

The words were conditional but I heard them as a promise. One that he had kept. At her kitchen table, Violetta della Torre had insisted that I was an angelic presence sent by providence to be Stefano's protector. Listening to her I knew that she had everything backward. Her nephew had only required my protection once, and any competent medic could have performed the service I performed. I had needed protection every hour of every day, protection only he could provide.

Each day since our paths parted I had sensed the absence of that protection and felt keenly my need of it. The placidity of home was an illusion. There were boonies stateside just as impenetrable as those in 'Nam. There was danger and uncertainty everywhere. You could hardly move for all the land mines and booby traps.

Stefano had made a promise that afternoon in camp and now he was renewing it. Now that I had found my way to him there was nothing left to do but let it happen.

"Tomorrow," Stefano said, shifting gears like he had made love earlier, "tomorrow we're going to put up a Christmas tree. It's not that long until Violetta gets here for the holidays. Wait 'til you taste her panettone."

Hadn't I already?

No. She had served biscotti that afternoon. She had served biscotti and tea and she had woven a spell with her cryptic words. They had brought me to that moment uncomprehending but ready. Stefano had done the rest, just as she had known he would.

"Boy is she going to be happy to see you," Stefano said. "She's been waiting for this for a long time."

He shifted gears again. The engine growled into the darkness.

"She's very patient," Stefano said.

www.ingramcontent.com/pod-product-compliance
Lightning Source LLC
Chambersburg PA
CBHW071634260626
47170CB00001B/98

* 9 7 8 0 6 1 5 8 1 8 9 9 3 *